"Excellent. A psychological thriller about the compromised soul of the secret agent... The character of John Darcy is as convincing as any I have encountered in espionage fiction… Hands builds and holds a palpable sense of tension that has all the drama and intimacy of good theatre. The achingly tantalizing crawl towards the climax is a masterpiece of suspense."

—Peter Millar, *The Times*

"Hands creates a real depth of feeling between the central figures in one of the year's best espionage novels."

—Michael Hartland, *Daily Telegraph*

"This book is not merely a thriller. It is a novel of great profundity... One of the best novels I have read for a very long time. It deserves not only to become a best seller on its own merits, but also because it will promote greater understanding of the best and worst of humanity."

—Jonathan Kemp, *Catholic Herald*

"John Hands's *Brutal Fantasies* prophetically deals with an IRA bomb which shatters the peace process… As in Hands's two previous novels, the research is careful and perceptive, the characters complex and three-dimensional, the action punchy."

—*The Sunday Times*

"Suspenseful and informative."

—*Sunday Independent*

"A chilling suspense yarn that is almost too close to the truth for comfort."

—*Manchester Evening News*

Praise for *DARKNESS AT DAWN*

"Hums with the realism of tomorrow's headlines and the suspense is as sharp as a scalpel."

—Michael Hartland, *The Daily Telegraph*

"Well researched, compellingly plausible… The climax is explosive."

—Askold Kruschelnycky, *The European*

"The suspense is sustained to the very last page."

—Mary Dejevsky, *The Independent*

"The author's artistry means that the book succeeds not only at the adventure tale level – gripping as the plot line is – but more profoundly… A moving, remarkable book."

—Vera Rich, *The Tablet*

"A plot to destabilize the newly independent Ukraine is realistic thanks to the slick writing of John Hands… It all comes together in a stirring climax which exposes the heart of post-Soviet society."

—David Hall, *Oxford Times*

"A tale of growing nationalism in the nuclear-armed former Soviet republics [that] has the true whiff of danger and drama."

—*Manchester Evening News*

Praise for *PERESTROIKA CHRISTI*

"The collapse of communism is of course the great theme of this year, but we are probably too close to it as yet for real history to emerge. There have been two distinguished British books just the same… John Hands's *Perestroika Christi* is a wonderful thriller and I could not put it down. It is set in the crisscross world of the KGB and the Vatican, with scenes (extraordinarily prescient, it turns out) of Ukrainian nationalism: an elaborately crafted plot leads to a surprise outcome."

—Professor Norman Stone, *Guardian Books Of The Year*

"Unerringly, unerringly perceptive… A splendidly thoughtful novel of perestroika."

—Professor Peter Frank, co-author, *The Soviet Communist Party*

"A most impressive political thriller... I cannot think of another which is both so accurate and in many ways so prophetic."

—Sir Rodric Braithwaite, British Ambassador in Moscow

"Thriller writing is in deep trouble. The collapse of the Cold War leaves one of the main platforms bare... One novelist who has overcome the problem is John Hands, in his first novel... Genuinely scary, exciting, well plotted and nicely written."

—Harriet Waugh, *Sunday Telegraph*

Advance Reviews of *THE SERPENT'S EMBRACE*

"Gripping, intelligent and utterly convincing... I was held from the first page to the last."

—Maggie Hamand, author of *The Resurrection of the Body*

"The gripping narrative leads to a horrifying outcome that is inevitable but not foreseeable."

—Frances Hill, author of *A Delusion of Satan*

"A clever and gripping scientific thriller that raises important questions about the ethics of genetic research."

—Charles Palliser, author of *The Quincunx*

"An outstanding, deftly-constructed psychological thriller that is both haunting and entertaining and hard to put down. With master story-telling, John Hands has delivered a rich novel filled with complex, vivid characters faced with the toughest moral choices of our times."

—Humphrey Hawksley, author of *Man on Ice*

"[T]he novel takes the reader on an emotional and intellectual journey of enormous power. John Hands travels with rare ease between the cultures of science and the humanities, and *The Serpent's Embrace* raises urgent questions about the ethics and implications of genetic engineering. Tense, vivid and visceral, this is a terrific book that will make you think hard about science and the future of humanity."

—Leo Kanaris, author of *Codename Xenophon*

Praise for *BRUTAL FANTASIES*

"Why are John Hands's beautifully crafted thrillers (*Darkness at Dawn, Perestroika Christi*), which are published in hardcover in England to much critical acclaim, issued only as paperbacks in the United States? Whatever the reason, this has to be the best reading bargain in the business. In his latest, Hands manages to find an immense amount of vitality in the overworked territory of Irish Republican Army terrorism. A top CIA agent, John Darcy, quickly brought to life with the kind of details that only an artist would include, is forced to take independent action when a ghost from his own past combines with an act of horrific destruction."

—Editorial Review, *Amazon.com*

"John Hands's fast moving first novel explores the penultimate battle, fought with dastardly and Machiavellian brio… Read this clever and vivid book."

—George Bull, *Sunday Times*

"Devilish cunning… Ambitions which aspire to the level of Brian Moore rather than Morris West."

—Chris Petit, *The Times*

"John Hands weaves an ambitious tale of intrigue… Suspense so well built up."

—Michael Dove, *Sunday Express*

"A first novel and a remarkable one. Remarkable for its insight into the behind-the-scenes goings-on in both Russia and the Vatican. Remarkable for the quality of the writing. Remarkable for the creation of a believable set of highly intelligent characters. Remarkable for a plot that is very complex but which is presented cogently and clearly at every stage… A formidable achievement."

—Graham Jones, *Wales On Sunday*

"John Hands has his finger on the pulse in his gripping first novel, Perestroika Christi. "

—*Today*

"A sound piece of plotting that captures a whiff of *Gorky Park* but leaves an aftertaste of *The Omen*."

—Peter Millar, *The European*

"A riveting first novel."

—*Publishing News*

"Compelling interest as it reaches its awesome climax."

—*Western Telegraph*

THE SERPENT'S EMBRACE

John Hands

Published by

Audiobook Publishing Services

633 West Fifth Street, 26th and 28th Floors,

Los Angeles, CA 90071

+1 213-871-1303, +1 210-888-0079

info@audiobookpublishingservices.com

Print book ISBN 978 1 80558 517 6

eBook ISBN 978 1 80558 516 9

Audiobook ISBN 978 1 0685694 1 8

"The immortal gods alone have neither age nor death! All other things almighty Time disquiets."

—Sophocles, *Oedipus at Colonus*, 5th Century BC

"We are about to not only cure and prevent age-related diseases, but reset the aging process itself."

—Michael Fossel PhD MD, *The Telomerase Revolution*, 2015

Prologue

Maria Snowe stares at the bronze crucifix above the bed and thinks of all the hours she has spent on her knees praying for her father's recovery. What kind of God ignores her prayers and lets him suffer like this?

Maria lowers her eyes from the crucifix to the figure she scarcely recognizes from eighteen months before. Her father barely makes a dent in the white pillows plumped against the raised backrest of the hospital bed. His once chubby features are sunken into a hollow-cheeked gauntness, his skin has turned a sickly yellow, the auburn hair he wore in a ponytail has fallen out to leave a shiny skull, and his twinkling eyes are dulled by pain. Head lolling back and hands sprawled on the bed with palms facing upwards, he is slumped like a discarded marionette trailing its strings. A thin black cable meanders from a gray finger sock on his left hand to one of several machines stacked on a trolley by the bed. Three red cables emerge from the top of his pajama jacket and connect his shrunken chest to an ECG on the trolley. From a pendulous vinyl bag hooked to a stand on the other side of the bed, saline drips through a transparent plastic tube into a pale arm that lies indifferently on the starched white hospital bedspread. Morphine trickles through another tube into the cannula taped to the inside of his other arm.

Outwardly Maria tries to maintain the image of the cool, calm, commanding young woman who has masterminded the business side of her father's company. Inside she is wracked by his pain. She would have ended her life rather than suffer what he has borne.

His eyes stray to the red roses that fill half the suite and perfume the air with their musky scent. His lips pull back in a smile showing healthy white, even teeth that appear out of place in his haggard face. "Enough for a mobster's funeral."

This glimpse of his trenchant humor brings a lump to her throat. "Everyone wants you fit and well again, Daddy," she encourages.

The smile twists to a grimace, the crow's feet at the outer corners of his eyes deepen, and a hand reaches out for her. "I want to die at home," he whispers.

She can't bear the thought of losing him: not only the father who always indulged her but also her best friend, her business partner, and the only man she has ever respected. Grasping his hand she gazes into his eyes, as if she can reinforce his failing willpower with her iron resolve. "You're not going to die, Daddy," she insists.

His eyes stare past her into infinity as he struggles with his breath, but his fingers respond to her grip with a gentle squeeze. When the words finally come he sounds at peace. "Take care of your mother, my little goddess."

Tears roll down her cheeks at the name he's called her since she first remembers him, a hippie with shoulder length hair who was always smiling as he lounged in the shade of palm trees that bordered a white beach. "I promise," she vows.

He sighs slowly and deeply, as though each protracted breath is an even greater effort than the one before. His pupils are strangely shrunken. "I'm cold," he murmurs. "Ask them to close the window."

Maria looks over her shoulder at the duty nurse. "Please close the window."

Sister Brigid, who wears a nun's wimple with her white uniform, looks pointedly at the closed window and glances at the ECG. "I'll go and get Father Byrne."

"No," she says.

"Now, now, Maria," Sister Bridget chides gently, "Father will want to hear his confession and give him the last sacrament."

Maria rises from her chair and stands so close that the nun can see only her unblinking black eyes. She speaks in a voice that is low and deliberate and filled with the resentment burning inside her. "You are paid to control my father's pain. Do it. And don't you dare bring a priest in here."

Sister Bridget opens her mouth to protest, but Maria's gaze reduces her to silence.

While the nurse adjusts the flow of morphine Maria stalks out of the suite. Heedless of a gaggle of white-coated interns, a dour attendant wheeling an empty bed, and a respectful Latino family dressed as though for their daughter's first holy communion, she strides down the long antiseptic corridor to the elevator.

Exiting the elevator at the top floor she brushes past two doctors and heads straight for one of the suites of offices that line the corridor. Dr. Marcus Cremer's secretary frowns. "Excuse me, Ms Snowe. Do you have an appointment?"

By the time Maria turns to answer she has crossed the office and placed her hand firmly on the handle of the inner door. "I don't need one."

In the inner office the patrician figure behind the desk overlooked by a large picture window glances up from a medical journal and instinctively straightens his bow tie at the sight of this desirable and formidable young woman.

Maria rests her knuckles on the polished oak of the desk and leans forward. "Do something, Marcus."

"Of course, Maria. I shall instruct the duty nurse—"

"Save him," she half begs, half demands.

"Please sit down, Maria," he says in the voice he uses to convey bad news.

She remains standing, legs astride, knuckles resting on his desk, and body leaning forward to pinion him with her gaze. "You said you could cure him."

"I said there was a good chance that surgery would remove the cancer," he corrects her.

"But it didn't, did it?"

"Unfortunately, the cancer spread from the colon to the liver and then to the spine," he concedes.

"*His* colon, *his* liver, and *his* spine."

The stresses hit Cremer like perfectly calibrated rangefinders. He winces. "I used the latest chemotherapy. Believe me, Maria, your father's had the very best treatment available."

"And now?"

He sighs. "Sadly there's nothing more we can do."

"So, my million dollars bought Daddy eighteen months of a colostomy bag, constant fatigue, jaundice, nausea, vomiting, and acute pain. This is the very best treatment available?"

To divert her attack he stands up and goes to the window. The sweep of the Golden Gate Bridge spans the sun-sparkling waters of the Bay on which a tiny tanker and a host of smaller craft ply their trade; tomorrow the bridge's two art deco towers peaking through a carpet of fog might be the only evidence of human life on the Bay. He turns. "We can never defeat nature, Maria, however hard we try."

Like a cruise missile she pursues him to the window. "What did Daddy do to deserve this? He's the kindest, the best, the most generous person I know."

"Nature is no respecter of people, however good they are."

"But Daddy doesn't smoke. He kept fit. I made sure he had a healthy diet."

"Try to understand, Maria," Cremer says, "that it's something many of us have to face as we grow older, whatever precautions we take. The aging process corrupts our genes, frequently causing a cancerous mutation of cells in organs like the colon."

"It's so unjust." Her eyes flash with anger. "First he gets cancer, then he's told about my mother."

"The diagnosis for your mother was a great blow to him," Cremer sympathizes.

"How can Georgiou be certain?" Maria challenges. "Alzheimer's is an old person's disease. She's only forty-five."

Cremer returns to his desk and opens a file. "Dr. Georgiou sent a copy of the test results," he says. "They show that your mother has a mutant gene that causes the disease to develop in middle age rather than old age."

The implication strikes Maria with the force of a death sentence. Her voice is suddenly subdued. "And me?"

Cremer looks uncomfortable. "There's nothing to be gained by genetic testing for someone who doesn't show the symptoms."

"Why not?"

He hesitates before saying, "I'm afraid there's no known cure for the condition. I advise you to continue your life as normal. After all—"

"What are my chances?" Maria demands.

Cremer looks at one of the most unusual and compelling women he's ever met, a woman in the prime of life who might normally expect to live for another fifty years or more. He holds out his palms

in a gesture of helplessness. "There's one chance in two that you've
inherited the gene."

Part One

LIFE

"O Sacred, wise, and wisdom-giving Plant,
Mother of Science! now I feel thy Power"
—Milton, *Paradise Lost, Book IX*

1

Richard Trent stares out of the window of his small office on the ninth floor of the Human Genetics Building as he waits, nerves as taut as violin strings, for the result of his experiment. His tall, spare frame dressed in T-shirt and jeans, his lock of chestnut hair that tumbles carelessly over a pale forehead, and his blue far-away eyes suggest a poet or philosopher rather than a scientist, but rarely is a poet or philosopher charged with Richard's focused energy.

The sun has set long since, but on this Labor Day few windows are lit in the nearby four-story redbrick buildings of the Los Angeles campus of the University of California. Beyond their shadowy flat roofs rises the dense mass of the Bel Air foothills from which windows shine like a sparse sprinkling of diamonds on crushed black velvet. However paltry his university salary, he wouldn't swap places with anyone living in those mansions nestling in protective foliage. No fortune can buy what he hopes the result will show.

He turns round in the cramped office that is effectively his second home and lowers himself onto his chair. A document lies opened but abandoned on the desk in front of him. He hasn't been able to concentrate on anything else while his assistant is carrying out the experiment that is the culmination of all he has dreamed of and worked for ever since the discovery he made in his postgraduate research at Harvard ten years before.

In the eerie silence of this holiday evening footsteps approach. His shoulders tense as the door is pushed ajar. Dressed in T-shirt and shorts, with her flaxen hair swept back untidily in a ponytail, Lucy Jonnsen looks more like a sixteen-year-old high school student than a twenty-six-year-old postdoctoral fellow. Usually she breezes in with an instinctive lop-sided grin. Now she pauses on the threshold, holding her hardback laboratory notebook as a tray for several tissue culture dishes. Richard looks up anxiously. She avoids his eyes and places the lab notebook and the dishes in the space between books and a microscope on the white Formica-topped work surface that runs along the opposite wall. She turns and hesitates. Her lips part, but she knows no words can console him. She bites her bottom lip and hurries from the room.

Richard places his head in his hands and slumps forward with his elbows on the desk.

Eventually his eyes open and his fingers part to reveal the opened document, his application for tenure at the university. It should have included a major paper credited to him, but the company owned by his department chair used his data and their greater resources to beat him to publication on the isolation of the gene he's been searching for since his postgraduate research. Outrage at this injustice has fueled his single-minded determination to demonstrate how the gene can be manipulated to cure cancer. But now his experiment has failed.

He can't blame Straker and his company for this blow, nor does he blame Lucy. No assistant has proved more enthusiastic, more diligent, or more skilled at bench work. No. This failure is unequivocally down to him. Perhaps the brilliance shown in his postgraduate research had exploded in one brief effulgent burst like a Roman candle, leaving a spent force to splutter impotently for the rest of his career while he suffers the sympathies and minor successes of his contemporaries. Now even the spluttering candle is about to be snuffed out.

He doesn't know why the experiment has failed. There could be hundreds of reasons and he should be able to figure out an alternative approach, but he has run out of time. There is no possibility he can now get the major publication he needs to secure tenure, and when the university refuses his application this time around he will be out on the street. His life as a medical science researcher is over and he will never achieve the breakthrough in curing cancer for which, he still believes, his gene holds the secret.

Wearily he rises to his feet to confirm the verdict. He takes a shallow, transparent plastic tissue culture dish the diameter of a whiskey tumbler and places it below the lens of the phase-contrast microscope that stands on the work surface. Hunched over the microscope, he looks down its binocular eyepiece into the straw-colored liquid in the dish. The view removes any lingering hope: the experiment has failed to kill these cancerous skin cells.

He goes through the motions of checking the cells used as experimental controls. The final three dishes contain aging non-cancerous cells that Lucy has used as toxicity controls. Apart from the pink culturing solution they appear empty, as expected.

He picks up the first of these dishes. It tilts a little in his grasp and, in the glancing light from the desk lamp, he glimpses what only an experienced eye would see. Later he wonders whether his subconscious had attracted his attention to the tiny, pale gray, translucent plaques that are dotted almost invisibly on the bottom of the dish. He scrutinizes the other two dishes of toxicity controls and sees nothing.

After checking the chinagraph writing on the side of the dish, he carefully places the dish on the microscope stand. He peers down the eyepiece and twirls the focusing knob of the microscope with one hand. The knuckles of the other hand that grip the microscope base plate turn white.

With trembling fingers he reaches for Lucy's hardback lab notebook and frantically turns the pages of small, neat handwriting until he finds what he is looking for. He estimates the number of divisions the cells has undergone in the previous six weeks and then he peers once more down the binocular eyepiece.

Richard Trent's greatest thrill as a researcher is to see something that nobody else in the world has ever seen before. And in that instant he sees more than human skin cells through his microscope. He sees the key piece of the puzzle he's been struggling to solve for years: the gene on which he has been working all his professional life is not what he and everybody else assumed it was. Apparently unconnected pieces of data suddenly fit around this aberrant result to produce an insight that both astonishes and explains everything. Once their beauty has been revealed, disclosing their power to unlock seemingly diverse and intractable problems, such insights are recognized by later generations to be self-evident truths, but only one person among the billions on the planet experiences the unprecedented flash of understanding. Its tingling charge electrifies every nerve fiber of his being, fusing mind and body in one ecstatic climax. It is followed by a wave of panic that this is too good to be true, which subsides to leave a warm glow of certainty that nothing so beautiful could be false.

All thoughts of the tenure application vanish in the intensity of his vision. He hurries from his office and lopes down the empty neon-lit corridor with deceptive speed.

He opens the door to the open-plan laboratory used by two other research teams. It is as unremarkable as any other lab. Plastic-capped bottles containing liquids the color of vodka, rosé wine or mature Chardonnay fill shelves above rows of white benches crowded with more bottles, micropipettes, and cartons of Kwim wipes and disposable latex gloves. An aromatic whiff of organic solvents hangs in the air. On this Labor Day evening it is almost deserted. One of Straker's Vietnamese postgraduates sits by a household microwave oven that is defrosting frozen DNA solution in an Eppendorf, a bullet-like polypropylene container, while another pipettes tiny volumes of liquid into a rack of uncapped Eppendorfs. His assistant is about to leave by the far door.

"Lucy," he calls out.

She turns, her face a picture of misery.

Richard suppresses his euphoria and tries to sound casual, so as not to arouse the curiosity of Straker's postgrads. "Have you got a moment?"

In trepidation she trails him out of the lab, but once he is out of sight of the postgrads she has to hurry to keep pace with his bounding strides. He ushers her into the cramped office, closes the door behind her, and indicates the microscope stand. It still holds the tissue culture dish containing pink liquid. "Did you examine the toxicity controls?"

"Why?" she asks. "The experiment didn't work."

"Take a look at the control you zapped with my gene."

She looks down the binocular eyepiece. The phase-contrast microscope shows her a monochrome image. Magnified a hundred and twenty-five times, each tiny gray plaque appears as a single layer of long, spindly cells that resemble dark gray, emaciated sardines edged in white and carefully packed with no overlap on the gray bottom of the dish. Lucy frowns. "This is the wrong dish, Richard. These aren't the aging fibroblasts I used; they're young ones."

"Wrong!" His euphoria bursts out in a huge grin. "Check the label on the dish. And estimate the number of divisions they've undergone."

She puts on her wire-framed spectacles and carefully examines her neat writing on the side of the dish, then checks her lab book. Her brow creases in puzzlement. "Impossible. If they haven't stopped dividing and become senescent, they should have been transformed into cancer cells." Then it dawns on her. She looks again down the microscope so that her eyes can convince her unbelieving mind.

When she looks up the misery on her face has been replaced by incredulity. "How?"

"It's so simple! So elegant!" His words race out in an attempt to keep pace with his mind. "Cancer cells are like Dorian Gray, corrupt on the inside but blessed with eternal youth. Our little baby isn't just another gene that corrupts the cells, it's the one that gives them eternal youth. Just as it gives eternal youth to healthy germline cells and certain blood-producing stem cells in the human body." His eyes sparkle. "Now we've used it to give eternal youth to aging human fibroblasts in culture *without turning them cancerous*."

Richard's eyes focus on his assistant. "You see how we can use this?"

"Yes," Lucy says. "I mean, I think so." She half sits for support, resting her buttocks on the edge of his desk and looking out of the window. "To do it with cells in a dish is amazing enough, but what you're proposing is…" She runs out of words.

He moves round with his back to the window in order to face her. "Is what?"

"I mean, it's *awesome*."

"Right!" he enthuses.

She shakes her head as if to clear it, and the strands of flaxen hair that escaped her ponytail curl across her cheek. Large brown eyes look up at him. "Richard, are you sure you're right about this? I mean, this wouldn't be just pushing the envelope, it'd be bursting right through it."

"Exactly!"

"Wow," she says half to herself.

"Not only can we block the activity of the gene in cancer cells and age them to death, we can switch on the gene in senescent tissue."

His eyes gleam. "We can halt the progress of Alzheimer's, heart disease, strokes, and all the other diseases of aging."

She rolls her eyes. "I'll leave the vision stuff to you, Richard. I'm just thinking of the practicalities. I mean, it's going to take years, resources we haven't got, and… and I mean, who knows what nature will throw at us?"

"But do you believe we can do it?"

The lop-sided grin returns to her face. "Richard Trent, if anyone can, you can."

"*We* can," he said. "My ideas, your bench skills. We're a team."

To hide the rush of blood to her cheeks she gives a flippant shrug. "Hey, ho, I guess we'd better take the first step and get this stuff published."

"No."

His abrupt change of voice startles her.

"We tell no one," he states.

She looks at his grim expression. This isn't the idealist she knows and admires, who argued that progress in medical research depended on the open exchange of scientific data.

"In order to get published," Richard says, "we need corroborating evidence to support my insight."

She nods uncertainly. "Right."

"But if Straker finds out before we can get published, his company will extend its patent on the gene before you can say 'profit'." He stares hard at her. "Promise me you won't breathe a word of this experiment to anyone."

2

Bursting with the urge to tell the world about Richard's discovery, Lucy Jonnsen rushes back to the house in which she lives with three other women postdocs. As soon as she opens the front door she hears Dorothy's booming voice. "Luce, is that you?"

In the large room that serves as kitchen and dining room she finds the ample Dorothy seated like an earth mother at the head of the old pine dining table. "There's plenty more on the stove," she says. "Help yourself." In front of her is a huge mound of rice overflowing with vegetables in a brown sauce that smells strongly of curry. Ada from Holland and Yun from Korea are eating normal-sized portions. Dorothy rented the house and collects stray postdocs like she collects stray cats.

"What's the good news?" Dorothy asks when she sees Lucy's expression.

Lucy longs to share the joy that makes her grin like a madwoman, but Dorothy works for Straker. "Hey, life's just good," she replies with the breezy facade she employs to hide her innermost feelings.

"When do we get to meet him?" Ada asks. Yun giggles.

Dorothy scrutinizes Lucy's face and gives a knowing smile. "You already have."

Lucy's cheeks burn.

"We're going to The Dungeon at nine," Ada says. "They've got a terrific band playing tonight."

"Do come, Lucy," Yun says. "A break will do you good."

"Sorry, you guys," Lucy replies. "I've some notes to write up from the experiment." With a cheery wave she turns and dashes upstairs.

"It's a holiday, for heaven's sake," Ada says to Dorothy after Lucy has left. "Lucy needs to get a life."

"I think you'll find," Dorothy replies, "that Lucy's got the life she wants."

In the privacy of her room Lucy goes to her desk, unlocks the bottom drawer, and takes out her collection of red leather-bound diaries. She allows no one, but no one, to read these books in which she confides her most intimate thoughts. She puts on her spectacles but, before writing up today's entry, she turns to the diary that records the turning point in her life.

Towards the end of her second year at UCLA, when she'd written to thank her teachers and tell them that she was quitting, only Dr. Trent asked to see her. Her neat writing vividly recalls the day she entered his office.

"Take a seat, Lucy," he said. "Coffee?"

She sat down in front of his desk and shook her head.

Richard fingered her letter. "May I ask why you're quitting college?"

"My mom died of a heart attack."

"I'm so sorry." Richard rose from behind his desk, swiveled the other chair next to hers so that it faced her, and sat down. "But why quit?"

She avoided his eyes. "At the funeral my father asked me to come back and take Mom's place on the farm."

He paused before saying, "Is that what you really want to do?"

Lucy looked down at her hands clasped in her lap; her knuckles were white. She despaired of the mentality of the close-knit homesteading community in their part of South Dakota, with its long traditions, narrow horizons, male chauvinism, and casual slaughter of harmless animals, and she was horrified by the prospect of working on the farm until she married a suitable younger son of folks who also farmed locally, which was what her father had planned for her. Mom, however, had been thrilled by her top grades in science at high school and had persuaded her father to relent and let Lucy take up the place she'd been offered at UCLA to study genetics, which had become her passion. "I can't let my father down now," she said. "I'm his only child."

"Do you enjoy the course?" Richard asked.

Shyness restrained her from telling him how she'd arrived in Los Angeles and had been unnerved by the cacophony of car horns and the disorienting babble of one-way conversations, the smell of gas fumes and smog, the heat, the automatic superficial friendliness, the laid-back sophistication, even from waitresses, the confident beautiful women and handsome men, and the sheer oppressive scale of the city in which people walked no further than the nearest parking lot. She wondered if she'd been wrong to rebel against her father, but when she heard Richard's introductory lecture all doubts disappeared. Here was someone who not only shared her passion but also inspired her with his conviction and his vision. "I think you know I do," she said.

Richard stood up and stared out of the window. Then he turned to face her. "Lucy, you've got your whole life ahead of you. You're one of the best students I've had. You've got a real talent for genetic engineering. You can't waste that talent and spend the next forty years hating what you're doing. That's not going to make your father happy."

She blushed.

"I'll write your father if you want. If it's a question of money, I'll find grants from somewhere. I'll hire you as a part-time technician."

He sat down again facing her. "Lucy, I believe you're capable of going on to research cures for diseases, like the heart disease from which your mother died. Wouldn't your father be proud of you for that?"

She closes the diary and sits back. Thanks to Richard she now has the most fulfilling life imaginable, at the cutting edge of medical research. And now…! She opens this year's diary, turns to today's page, and begins to write up the momentous discovery Richard had made.

The creak of the door opening makes her stop. Covering the diary with her arm, she looks round. It is only one of Dorothy's strays, a part Siamese with large blue eyes and a bitten-off ear, which has nosed into her room for a cuddle. The cat jumps up onto her lap and begins to purr. She puts her finger to her lips and instructs it not to tell anybody what she is writing. She finishes off the entry with the words:

"And when Richard said that we were going to be a team pioneering a treatment for aging diseases, like the heart disease from which Mom died, I was almost orgasmic. I owe him everything and I won't let him down."

3

For Richard, science is a drug to which he has been addicted since he sensed its heady possibilities in his high school lab. Now he mainlines in his own lab. No chemical concoction can match the euphoric high of discovery or the erotic charge of confidence it brings. On the evening he made the discovery he drives home from the lab flushed with the conviction that his insight will radically transform medical science, just like Röntgen's discovery of X-rays, Fleming's discovery of the antibiotic properties of penicillin, and Watson and Crick's discovery of the double helix structure of DNA and its genetic implications. Such insights not only solved current problems, they also opened up a new era in science. That paradoxical congruence was the breath of genius, and Richard feels its stimulating caress.

He turns off Santa Monica Boulevard and heads south on Twentieth. Instead of taking his usual route he makes a diversion to the shops at Ocean Park and Seventeenth. He would figure out a solution to the Straker problem tomorrow. This evening is one he is going to remember for the rest of his life.

After collecting a bunch of red roses from Flowers Forever, Richard goes to Marty's Gourmet Wines. A man of indeterminate age who looks as though he bears the troubles of the world on his unshaven face reluctantly turns his eyes from a portable television set.

"Champagne," Richard announces.

The man sniffs. "I got Mumm Cuvée Napa at sixteen dollars and Korbel Extra Dry at eleven."

Richard shakes his head. "The real thing."

"French?"

"That's what I said."

He nods to Richard's left, towards the sliding glass door of a tall refrigerated cabinet that is filled with bottles. "There's a bottle of Moët & Chandon at the back of the third shelf, but that's gonna set you back thirty-nine."

"Believe me, it'll be worth every cent."

Jackie loved champagne. It still gives him a thrill to recall the way she looked at him when they first met, at the champagne party the fraternity house threw to celebrate his Dean's Award for most outstanding sophomore. That gaze made him feel ten feet tall. He was on a roll in those days and the champagne never stopped. Full membership of Sigma Xi while still a junior, Columbia's record for the mile at the Baker Field athletic track in front of ten thousand people, graduation as the top science student, a publication in *Cell* while still a grad student at Harvard Medical School. And Jackie loving every minute of the good times they shared.

There have been precious few causes for celebration since then and, while the successes give him an erotic charge, the downsides are the depressions when his research hits the roadblocks. Those he can't help: they come with the job. If he is honest, though, he can help the time he spends at the lab, driven by the desire to make the big breakthrough. He feels guilty at neglecting Jackie but, now that his dedication has finally paid off, he is going to make it all up to her.

Stripes of television glow escape through the Venetian blinds on the bay windows of their bungalow on Ashland Avenue. His assistant professor's salary could never have paid the mortgage on a place like this, less than five minutes drive from Santa Monica beach. But it was the house that Jackie had craved and he'd swallowed his pride and let her property shark of a father pay for it.

He decides to spring a surprise on her, just like he used to in the old days. Leaving the car on the road he sneaks up the drive by the front lawn. Soundlessly he opens the side door and creeps into the kitchen. The euphoric high sharpens all his senses. The kitchen cabinets radiate whiteness. Bottles and packets and jars rainbow most of the work surfaces. Tomato and basil waft from the debris on the plate and the Angel Hair Pasta cardboard box in the sink. The unctuous questions of a television game show host seep through the wall.

They will go to one of those tony restaurants on Ocean Avenue that Jackie talked of. But first the champagne. He can't find the flutes Larry had given them for a wedding present; they aren't in the wall cabinets or in the dishwasher piled with unwashed glasses, plates and cutlery. He locates the only two clean matching tumblers in the kitchen and puts them next to the champagne.

Holding the roses behind his back, he tiptoes through to the darkened front room. Jackie is lying on the sofa, bathed in the etiolating light of a TV that sucks out her colors and displays them intensified on its screen. In this light it is easy to see why the guys at the fraternity house had wanted her to be Miss July for their calendar. She still dresses as though she were twenty and almost gets away with it.

"Sorry I'm late again, honey," he announces as he reveals the roses and presents them to her. He goes back to the kitchen and returns with the tumblers and the champagne. "It's celebration time!"

She looks up. "They gave you tenure?"

"I've got something that's going to blow everyone away."

"They didn't give you tenure." Her gaze returns to the screen. "Winston Churchill, you dumb asshole!" she shouts at the puzzled face of the contestant as she drops the roses on the floor.

He winces at the fallen flowers. "Honey, I'm serious. This is so big I'm almost afraid to think about it."

"Oh yeah. Another of your breakthroughs?"

He puts down the champagne and the tumblers, picks up the TV controller, and turns off the sound. "This is different, I promise you."

"Like identifying your gene?"

The barb cuts deep. He says in as calm a voice as he can manage, "You know that Straker hosed me."

"Why don't you face it? Those 'mercenaries' you look down on at Don's company beat you to it."

Don! The word is a Judas kiss. He squeezes a button on the controller and kills the TV. "Don't you care about what I've discovered?"

"Shit!" says her voice from the dark. "I won't know if she's won the walk-in freezer." She switches on the table lamp by the sofa and leans down to pick up a tonic and a half-empty bottle of vodka from a cooler.

"Jackie, listen to me—"

"Don't talk to me about caring," she says as she refills her glass. "The only thing you care about is your precious science."

"That's not true."

"No?" She staggers to her feet. "What the fuck do you care about me? If you'd gone into private practice after Harvard Medical School you'd be earning half a million a year right now."

The same old complaint, churned out like a telephone answering machine. Well, tonight he can promise her something that will make a half-million-dollar income unimportant. "You knew that all I ever wanted to do was research—"

"'All I ever wanted to do was research'," she mimics. "Why turn down all those research offers from drug companies? You have some kind of allergy to money?"

"How many times do we have to go through this, Jackie?" he groans. "Commercial research is a whole different ball game. It's about only doing work that's going to make a profit for your company. A university gives you the freedom to tackle the big unknowns in science."

She holds up an unsteady glass to toast him. "So speaks the great academic." Then she splutters into the glass. "You haven't made much of a success of that, have you?"

He stares at the woman he'd vowed to love and cherish till death us do part, the woman for whom he'd sacrificed full-time research and taken a job with a heavy teaching load at UCLA because she wanted to move to the West Coast. "Look at Larry," she taunts. "A full professor, a big shot in the university, and a house with a pool and a hot tub in the back yard. To think he looked up to you at Columbia."

Richard's words come through clenched teeth. "My research isn't about getting a pool and a hot tub in the back yard."

"Right. It's about having delusions of genius."

"It's about understanding the causes of disease. And tonight—"

"At least drug companies do something useful," she interrupts. "How many people have you cured in the last ten years? God, I don't know what you do all that time in your lab. Screw that postdoc of yours, I guess. Well, get your dick in there while you can because she's going to give you the big kiss-off when they turn you down for tenure and you're out on the street. Time's nearly run out on your precious academic freedom."

"Jackie," he says in a desperate effort to stem the venomous outpouring, "you don't know what you're saying."

She grins. "Why not?"

"Because you're drunk."

"Right. And you're a failure. But tomorrow I'll be sober."

4

The curves of the fifteen-foot-high bronze double helix gleam in the sunlight streaming through the large dormer window of the Grace Auditorium lobby. Knapsacks, canvas bags and aircraft carry-on luggage lie strewn at the foot of one of the lobby walls. Babbles of conversation—studiously laid-back, with occasional eager or anxious undertones breaking through—emanate from the informally dressed individuals who congregate around the registration desk in front of the bronze sculpture presented to James D. Watson by his colleagues, friends and students.

Richard waits in line to register for the meeting on The Genetics of Aging. It is the perfect forum to present his data and announce his theory before Straker can extend his patent. The fact that he doesn't know anyone in aging research adds to his excitement: it feels like the very first meeting he had participated in at Cold Spring Harbor Laboratory, the "university of DNA" on Long Island.

The majority of registrants are in their twenties and wear T-shirts, jeans or shorts, sneakers or deck shoes. As soon as these graduate students, postdocs and junior faculty are handed their package of documents, they squat on the nearest available floor space and study the program and abstracts of papers to see whether they have been selected to give an oral presentation to the whole meeting or else allocated a poster display with its much more limited chance to impress.

The other, older registrants, with open-necked shirts or blouses, chain store lightweight suits or jackets and skirts, moccasins or sandals, are established authorities in the field. They exude the confidence of knowing that their oral presentations are assured, but they too thumb through the book of abstracts in order to spot the rising talent, just as Richard had been spotted at his first meeting.

It all brought back the thrill he'd experienced when the laconic Keith Harris, attired in a green T-shirt that proclaimed in gold letters "Your Future is in your Genes", had ambled up and asked if he would consider having coffee and discussing his future with Jim Watson. Would he consider! Harris made it sound as though the legendary

Nobel laureate would be honored to meet Richard. Later, Jim Watson took Jackie and him to a white shingled, whaling era house. It stood among glossy dark green laurels, paler green pines, and goldening oaks and sycamores by the shore of the inlet that formed a natural harbor sheltered by the thickly wooded hills of Long Island's North Shore. From its back porch the three of them watched gulls shriek with alarm as a flock of honking geese in V-formation braked on the mirrored surface of the water at the end of the back lawn. Jim turned and asked casually if he and Jackie would like one of the apartments in the renovated house. Jackie had been proud of him then.

His three years here as a postdoctoral fellow had been the most stimulating of his career. Home to some of the best scientists in their fields, the Cold Spring Harbor Laboratory relieved him and his colleagues from the distractions of teaching, administration, or anything else. It was geared to producing winners in the highly competitive world of scientific research, and its list of Nobel laureates testified to its success. Richard loved the place. He lived, breathed and talked science, whether at his own lab, the Blackford dining hall, or a beach barbecue after swimming in the harbor. For him it was a monastery of genetics in which he had the time and the freedom to pursue his vocation to cure cancer, taking inspiration from the prophets who had gone before and guidance from the priests who now presided.

"Do you expect me to talk genes with your friends?" Jackie asked after a year, "or diapers with their wives? What the hell do I do in this Godforsaken place two hours' drive from civilization?" By which she meant Manhattan.

To preserve his marriage he sacrificed the staff position that Jim offered at the end of his postdoc fellowship and moved, at Jackie's insistence, to the West Coast, where the job Larry recommended him for at UCLA involved a heavy teaching load. And now he is neither a thrusting young postdoc nor an established authority. He wants the line to move more quickly, so that he can find out what other papers are being offered. Surely none would be as significant as his?

"Don't worry, yours is the last paper before lunch on Saturday."

Richard turns to see Keith Harris, still attired in T-shirt, Bermuda shorts and sandals, but now director of the Cold Spring Harbor Laboratory with its six hundred employees. Yet he still runs his own lab and does good science. He is barely ten years older than Richard.

Thanks, Keith," says Richard with relief. Harris had clearly recognized the significance of his paper to have given him a key slot.

5

Richard's hands rest lightly on the sides of the lectern as he surveys the expectant congregation. They pack the Grace Auditorium. They fill the rows of seats banked up to the glass window of the control room from which his slides will be projected; they even sit on the green-carpeted steps that form center and side aisles. The light oak sound baffles below the ceiling are poised to direct his words to their ears. The dark green, double helical border running along the top of the Eau de Nil walls serves as an icon for the message he is about to deliver. He may have felt like a Christian among the lions on the other side of the harbor, but he is at home here in this cathedral of DNA.

This morning, however, he is experiencing more than comfort. Second only to that very private eureka moment is the moment of glory when you first tell the scientific community of your discovery.

As the final mutterings of conversations following the previous speaker draw to a hushed silence, Richard has to remind himself not to get carried away by euphoria. For a scientific meeting he must restrict himself to the facts and merely suggest the consequences, as in that classic understatement Watson and Crick used to preface their seminal paper on the DNA double helix: "This structure has novel features which are of considerable biological interest." That's the way to sock it to a scientific audience.

He waits anxiously to see whether the session chair, Carol Ryder, as permanent a fixture at the Cold Spring Harbor Laboratory as the bronze double helix statue, has really understood the significance of his discovery. "Since Dr. Trent's impressive debut at a Cold Spring Harbor meeting," says Ryder, "we've heard little from him. It seems our wait has been rewarded, though, because he now has something rather dramatic to reveal."

Fired up by the introduction, Richard launches into his presentation. "Ten years ago I identified signs of a protein I named 'immortalin' in every type of immortal cancer cell, but not in corresponding non-cancer cells nor in localized tumors. Since then its physiological role has been shrouded in mystery, but very recent and unpublished data from my laboratory," he continues, sliding over the fact that his laboratory has been reduced to himself and one assistant, "suggest an entirely new and unpredicted role in normal cells."

He doesn't need to look at the audience. A delicious sensation tells him that he has them all intrigued.

"Once a cell acquires those genetic mutations which allow it to replicate out of control so that its daughter cells pile up to form a tumor, lose their shape, invade neighboring tissue, and spill into the bloodstream and the lymphatic system to spread through the body, we call it cancerous. But many people are coming to the view that in most cases these tumor cells prove clinically fatal when, and only when, they become immortal and are thereby enabled to proliferate indefinitely. While investigating the mechanism by which tumor cells become immortalized, I discovered the normal function of the gene that codes for immortalin."

He pauses. "Many of us were surprised earlier this year when researchers at Universal Genes, a commercial company that hitherto had published nothing on this topic, cloned the gene that codes for immortalin and then applied for a patent on the gene." That, in the polite language of science, was tantamount to putting in the knife.

Now he twists it. "I shall demonstrate that their paper in *Science* was fundamentally mistaken in classifying it as another gene that causes tumors."

No shuffling of paper breaks the silence that follows. Tension grips the Grace Auditorium. None among the four hundred scientists present has the slightest doubt that Richard Trent would only launch such a withering attack on the reputation of his own department chair, the renowned media scientist Don Straker, if he had something sensational to support it.

"Drummond," he continues, "has found immortalin in sperm and other human germline cells that carry our genes, undamaged and immortalized, from generation to generation. Crosland has detected immortalin in certain blood-forming stem cells that are, in effect, immortal. I have shown that immortalin has the characteristics of a regulatory protein."

Richard feels the confidence of a master angler, playing his audience like a fish. He hasn't jerked the line with his flash of insight; rather he has fed them the bait and reeled them in slowly, presenting his intuitive conclusion as though it resulted from a process of logical deduction. Now is the key moment that would decide whether he will land them. "The immortalin gene does not cause tumors. It immortalizes cells that are already tumorous." He pauses to let the statement sink in and then he pulls hard. "But clearly that is not its normal function. All the evidence is consistent with it being a master regulatory gene. It regulates a series of genes that control each cell's repair and maintenance mechanisms that prevent the cell from aging. It is, in effect, the anti-aging gene and I propose to call it such."

A buzz of anticipation ripples through the assembled scientists. They are hooked.

"The data led to the hypothesis that the anti-aging gene is active in the development of the embryo, but is normally switched off before birth except in those germline and stem cells that continue to be immortal in the human body. A mutation switches it on in tumorous cells already proliferating out of control and makes them clinically fatal."

Bypassing the fact that his insight was prompted by an unintended by-product of a different experiment, he continues authoritatively, "To test this hypothesis we transfected aging human fibroblasts in culture with the anti-aging gene driven by the beta actin promoter."

The house lights dim. A large white rectangle shines brightly on the screen behind him. He picks up the remote controller for the slide carousel, presses a button, and the rectangle is filled by a slide showing what appears to be an empty circular tissue culture dish viewed from above. "This first slide shows an example of the aging fibroblasts transfected with everything except the anti-aging gene," says Richard. "Over the course of six weeks the rate of cell division slowed, until eventually nearly all the cells stopped dividing. The resulting blue-stained cell colonies are too small to be visible to the naked eye."

He presses a button and the slide is replaced by one showing a black and white image of a few isolated shapes, like scattered pieces of a gray jigsaw puzzle on a gray background. "Viewed in the phase-contrast microscope at a magnification of a hundred and twenty-five times, live cells from the same sample are visible on the bottom of the dish. They exhibit the classical signs of senescence: they have reached the end of their replicative lifespan and appear isolated and flattened."

After more slides showing tumor cells, Richard says, "Finally, compare both these controls with aging fibroblasts transfected with the anti-aging gene." He clicks the button again and the screen shows the bottom of a tissue culture dish dotted by tiny blue plaques, followed by the phase-contrast monochrome image of what had electrified him that Labor Day evening: the magnification showing a single layer of long spindly cells, like dark gray, emaciated sardines edged in white and carefully packed with no overlap. "Not only do these cells have the appearance of young fibroblasts," Richard announces, "they are dividing in a controlled manner at a rate typical of young fibroblasts."

The auditorium lights power up, firstly onto the platform to bathe Richard in a golden glow, and then onto the ranks of his peers discussing among themselves the implications of what they have just witnessed.

Richard's voice stills them with his climax, which spells out his own conclusion in a deliberately implicit and understated way, and suggests he is further advanced than he is in order to dissuade anyone else from trying to beat him to the proof. "We are testing this hypothesis by a series of confirmatory experiments."

The satisfaction he experiences recalls the occasion ten years ago when he had delivered his first, impact-making presentation at Cold Spring Harbor. He had felt like an Olympic gold medalist standing on the winner's podium while the national anthem played and the eyes of the stadium focused on him and him alone.

"What do you hope to prove?"

"Excuse me?" Richard asks.

The questioner, standing in the front row, is tall, with a lean, angular face framed by steel-gray swept-back hair and sideburns that merge into a mustacheless Abe Lincoln beard, giving the impression of a Puritan who has come over with the *Mayflower*. Nathan Hill is professor of gerontology at the University of Southern California. His reputation rests not on the quality of his own research, but on an encyclopedic tome, *The Biology of Aging* compiled five years before, in which he had documented all known aging factors in an extensive list of insects, fish, birds and animals.

"I asked, what do you hope to prove by your confirmatory experiments?" Hill repeats.

Richard thinks it is obvious, but perhaps his conclusion has been too understated even for a scientific audience. "That the gene prevents aging," he replies.

"Is that so?" asks Hill. "You appear to have immortalized some dividing skin cells in a dish. You seem to think that tells us something about aging. It doesn't. It tells us about dividing skin cells in a dish. It tells us nothing about the aging of cells that don't divide, like brain cells. It tells us nothing about aging in a living organism, like a human being that consists of a hundred trillion intercommunicating cells."

Richard is eager that the gerontologists should see what is so clear to him. "Aging of our body is caused by aging of the cells that make up our body. If we can stop our cells from aging, we can stop our bodies from aging."

Hill thrusts out his beard and fixes Richard with gray eyes that carry the conviction of a witch hunter. "How very simple. Are you aware, Dr. Trent, that a number of distinguished colleagues and I have spent our whole professional lives on aging research? If you had given even a cursory glance at the literature, you would have seen that there are many different causes of aging."

Hill has dispensed with the gloves and is into bare knuckles already, but Richard is in no mood to be knocked down so easily by a scientific backwoodsman in front of four hundred of his peers. He deflects the attack with humor. "I'm aware that there are as many causes of aging as there are grants available to study it."

The expected laughter does not come; he has misjudged the response of Hill's fellow gerontologists. Their silence forces him to justify himself. "I accept the validity of all the published causes of aging, but I argue that these destructive forces are *secondary* causes of aging." Now he sets up Hill for the knockout blow. "But, as your own book makes clear, these are countered by cellular repair and defense mechanisms."

"I don't hear a primary cause here," Hill hits back as though he were still top dog.

Hill can't see it coming. "If you permit me to continue," Richard parries, "my point is that in the embryo, and in immortal germline and stem cells after birth, these cellular repair and defense mechanisms operate at full capacity and defeat the destructive forces, giving these cells eternal youth." Richard then unleashes his blow. "I believe the *primary* cause of aging is the switching off of the anti-aging gene in all other cells. This produces a cascade effect on its dependent genes, down-regulating them so that cellular repair and defense mechanisms gradually slow down."

Hill is still on his feet. He turns round so that those behind can see his exaggerated expression of disbelief.

He would need to be battered into submission. "For the first few years of life this slowing down isn't so noticeable," Richard spells out. "But once we're past our reproductive phase and into middle age, the destructive forces begin to get topside. They inflict damage at every level in our bodies. When enough damage occurs, we get the diseases of old age: DNA mutations build up in a cell to turn it cancerous; plaques grow to block vessels to the heart, producing heart attacks, or block vessels to the brain, producing strokes; and cells in our brain age, atrophy and die, producing Alzheimer's and Parkinson's diseases. Eventually, enough damage accumulates in a vital part of our system to produce a fatal effect: we die of an aging disease."

Richard is acutely aware that he has gone much further than he'd intended: much, much further than his data justified. But this is what his insight told him. This is what he believes he can prove, given time and resources.

"I think you should be congratulated on a very persuasive account of the physiology of aging," Hill concedes. "The relationship between this account and your gene, however, reminds me of the relationship between Donald Trump and the truth. I put it to you, Dr. Trent, that you're too far down the pike on this gene of yours to admit failure. It hasn't fixed cancer for you, so you think it'll fix aging. A lifetime's research in this field tells me not to buy your magic bullet theory. I suggest you return to cancer research and reacquaint yourself with scientific methodology."

6

Richard used to love the mile-long walk down Bungtown Road from the Grace Auditorium to the director's residence. Nestling among the trees between the road and the harbor shore are laboratories resonant with memories of geneticists who had worked at Cold Spring Harbor and won Nobel Prizes. The ghosts of Hershey, McClintock and Delbrück, however, fail to raise his spirits now.

The mask of self-assurance he maintained in front of others in the auditorium disintegrates on this lonely walk. He is devastated by the response to his paper. The fact that he has brought it on himself by directly challenging the conventional wisdom in gerontology is no comfort. An inner voice persists in asking if Hill is right. Richard is convinced that all paradigm-changing breakthroughs in science are achieved not by patient toiling through mathematical equations or laborious and repetitive experiments to arrive ineluctably at the answer; rather it is by an inspired vision—a great imaginative leap from what is known to what might be—a vision so compelling in its beauty, so breathtaking in its boldness, so powerful in its synergy that you know intuitively it must be right. But if his insight has led him to a fundamentally flawed conclusion, then his confidence in his own judgment—that fragile tool every outstanding researcher needs—would suffer irreparable damage. He can't imagine worse circumstances in which to have lunch with one of the few scientists whose opinion he values.

Keith Harris had left immediately after Richard's presentation in order to prepare lunch.

As Richard approaches the grand Federal-style house that overlooks the sandspit protecting the inner harbor from the outer harbor and Long Island Sound, a woman gazes at him from a seat on the front porch. She is in her early thirties, with high cheekbones, aquiline nose, golden tan, and straight, lustrous black hair falling to her shoulders and fringed across her brow like a Pharaonic goddess. On another woman her sensuous lips, slightly parted to reveal a glimpse of even, white teeth, would have suggested availability, but what sets her apart, unfathomable and unreachable, are her large luminous black eyes that produce a gaze of formidable strength. It is a gaze that, once experienced, is impossible to forget.

Harris comes out to the porch as Richard walks up the steps.

"Richard," says Harris, "allow me to introduce you to Maria Snowe, a potential investor in gerontology.

She smiles and stretches out a hand in greeting. Coiled round her elegant wrist is a sinuous silver filigree serpent with its head forming the clasp.

Keith Harris's wife, Ellie, who writes on scientific ethics, brings a tray containing a pasta dish and a salad through to a spacious dining room decorated in soft mauves and greens and furnished in traditional country style. The dining table is positioned in a large bay, trapping Richard by the window next to Maria Snowe. Not many of the Lab's potential investors came to a scientific meeting before going to the director's home for lunch.

Maria fixes her gaze on Harris. "What do you think of Richard's paper and the response to it?"

Is she always so direct? Richard stares out of the window at the magnolia, horse chestnut, and cork trees at the end of the long back lawn and wishes he were far away.

"On the record or off?" Harris replies.

"Inside these four walls."

"There aren't many really good people in aging research," Harris says, "compared with, say, cancer and AIDS."

"Meaning?"

Harris's perpetual smile widens. "Many gerontology researchers are not only narrow minded and dull, but also dumb."

Richard's eyes turn back from the window. He's never known Keith to be so indiscreet. He wondered if Maria Snowe always had this uncanny ability to draw out from people what they really think.

"And Richard?" she asks Harris.

"He's no diplomat. As an outsider he should have shown more humility before announcing that he's solved the problem they've been struggling with all their professional lives."

Jesus, thinks Richard, they are talking about him as though he weren't there. Even Keith has been trapped by her all-consuming gaze.

"You have to recognize," Harris continues, "that we're talking big science here."

"For big science read big egos?" asks Maria.

Harris laughs. "You catch on quick. Creative thinkers like Richard are always going to alienate the more conservative members of the scientific community."

"But is Richard right?"

Richard stabs down at the penne with his fork. He wishes Ellie hadn't made the arrabbiata sauce so hot; beads of sweat are forming above his eyebrows and he fears they'll roll down his cheeks and nose.

"I simply don't know," Harris replies. "At Cold Spring Harbor we have a long tradition of supporting untested ideas and radical new approaches. Without this, science would never break new ground." He warms to the theme. "You have to take risks. You have to back the brightest minds. Give people like Richard the chance to succeed—and the chance to screw up."

"But the risks are worth taking?"

"You bet they are," Harris says. "If Richard's theory is right, it could lead to a cure for all the diseases of aging." He grins. "We're in exciting times here. Genetic engineering stands today where physics stood at the dawn of the atomic age."

"With the same potential for good and evil," says Ellie pointedly.

Harris looks down into his glass of wine. "Greater," he says soberly. "Genetic engineering is going to have a far greater impact on civilization than nuclear power." He drains his glass and refills Maria's, Richard's, and his own. Ellie's is untouched.

"Precisely how?" Maria asks.

Richard can stand his exclusion no longer. "Curing the diseases of aging is just the start," he intervenes. "After three and a half billion years of evolution by nature, DNA technology now provides the tools to intervene in that process. It gives us the potential to cure the cause of *all* diseases, extend our lives, raise our intelligence, normalize the insane, and pacify the violent. Genetic engineering gives us the power to take control of human evolution."

"Keith, will you be so kind as to make the coffee?" Ellie asks coolly, "or shall I ask Richard to help me?"

Richard looks across the table. Ellie is distinctly displeased that her husband has given all his attention to Maria.

Harris looks at his watch. "Darn! The afternoon session starts in less than ten minutes." He stands up. "Maria, so sorry to rush you, but there's no time for coffee. We'll have to leave now."

"You go ahead, Keith," says Maria. "I'll skip the afternoon session, unless Richard has to be there."

"No," Richard says. He has no intention of entering the lions' den for another savaging.

"That's settled," says Maria. "I'll help Ellie with the coffee, and afterwards Richard will walk me back to the parking lot."

The day hasn't turned out so badly after all, Richard thinks to himself. Keith Harris hadn't sided with the gerontologists. On the contrary, Keith had called him one of the brightest minds in science, with an exciting theory worth testing. And now he is strolling by the blue waters of Cold Spring Harbor accompanied by the most intriguing woman he has ever met.

"Why did you come to the meeting? He asks.

"I'm interested in aging diseases. My mother was diagnosed with Alzheimer's when she was only forty-five."

"I'm so sorry," he said. Disconcerted by her change of tone, he attempts to change the subject. "What do you do?"

"I make dreams come true."

"How?"

"Long ago my dad saw that the future lay in the Internet, but the corporation he worked for didn't appreciate his vision. He never fitted into the corporate culture; he was a maverick who'd only taken the job to pay me through college. So when I graduated from business school, I set up a company for him and patented his software to raise the finance we needed." Her eyes now sparkle. "He was as happy as a clam, doing what he'd always dreamed of: revolutionizing the way the Net could be used, with nobody telling him what he could and couldn't do."

"Was?"

She hesitates. "He died of cancer. Nobody should have to die like he did."

They walk on in silence, past a wooden bridge that leads to the second story of the white two-story Delbrück laboratory, built on the grassy slope up from the water to the gently rising Bungtown Road. This is what research should be about, Richard thinks, curing painful and fatal diseases, not scoring points in a battle of egos.

"Do you still run the company?" he asks eventually to break the silence.

She shrugs. "I employ programmers to update our software and I count the royalties we earn from the licenses I sold to Microsoft, Apple and the rest. Without Dad it's not fun any more." She turns to face him. "About the time he died I was forced to take stock. What's the point of being wealthy if you still suffer a death like that?" A shadow crosses her face. "Or one even worse."

The road continues rising in a straight line. The waterside curves away from them and becomes hidden by the cascading foliage of willows and chestnuts, interspersed with white-shingled whaling warehouses, Colonial residences, and modern concrete structures: an eclectic village of laboratories united by the desire to understand and manipulate the molecular basis of life.

The sweeps of roofline and large dormer window that give the modern brick-clad Grace Auditorium a Scandinavian appearance looms to their right as they turn off Bungtown Road into the parking lot by the auditorium, where she heads for an open-topped Corvette Stingray convertible, a gleaming lethal missile that stands out from the sedans, four-wheel drives and vans. Banishing her somber mood with a smile, she says, "Put it this way, Richard, I've reached the age I have to take major decisions about my life: which career to pursue, whether or not to have children, whether or not to change men." She made changing men sound like changing trains. "If I wait until my forties it'll be too late."

As she climbs into the car the side slit in her dress parts to show a flash of curved thigh.

"What have you decided?" he asks.

She looks up to him from the black leather seat and her lips part to reveal a glimpse of white teeth, but all Richard sees are those enormous eyes fixing him with an unwavering gaze. "That I'd like to make your dreams come true."

Richard grips the top of the driver's door, as though he can physically prevent the Corvette from leaving.

She nods over her shoulder in the direction of the auditorium. "Most of these are just turn-the-handle researchers. They do safe science that doesn't threaten anybody, so they get their work approved, funded and published. If they're lucky they end up a footnote in scientific history." Her gaze returns to him. "Not many have vision. My dad had it. You have it. And people with vision have a problem. Because others don't see what you see, they're afraid of you, or they're jealous of you. Either way you get marginalized and frozen out." Her gaze intensifies. "I can raise enough money by selling off my company to set us up in partnership and fund your research." She hands him a business card. "Call me."

7

Richard's spirits drop as he reads the thick brochure entitled *Application for Public Health Service Grant.*

"There must be no more than six lines of text within a vertical inch... Applications not meeting these requirements will be returned without review..."

He'd returned from Cold Spring Harbor renewed in his resolve to show how his gene can be used to treat aging diseases, but bureaucratic minutiae bore him. By page 18 he faces:

"Itemize by category and unit cost such other expenses as publication costs, page charges, books, computer charges, rentals and leases, equipment maintenance, minor fee-for-service contracts etc."

This is as much as he can take. He leaves his office, pokes his head round the door of the lab, and beckons Lucy. "I've drafted out the basic stuff," he tells her back in his office, "twenty-five pages of research plan, plus personnel and consultants. Will you do the rest?"

"Consider it done," she says brightly.

"It'll be good practice for when you're running your own lab," he adds to relieve his conscience.

While Lucy studies the documents with her usual conscientiousness, Richard leans back in his chair and reflects on his good fortune. When he'd lacked the funds to accept Lucy's request to study for a PhD in his lab, he fixed her up with Steve Drummond at the Rockefeller and said she could come back and teach him a few things. He'd forgotten that remark three years later when his National Cancer Institute program project grant wasn't renewed and he'd had to relinquish his sole remaining assistant, but Lucy had remembered and offered to bring the NCI postdoctoral fellowship she'd won to his lab. He would have accepted anyone with his or her own funding, but Lucy was the answer to his prayers. She shared his passion to discover and correct the genetic cause of diseases, she had an excellent grasp of the theory while her laboratory skills were outstanding, she was happy to put in the same long hours that he did, and her cheerful personality made her fun to have around. Beneath that unsophisticated exterior lay a very capable and determined young woman: one day she certainly would have a lab of her own. "I already have an offer of funding for the project," he says.

Lucy looks up from the grants brochure. "From the director of the National Institutes of Health who heard your presentation?"

"Sure."

"That's terrific."

There is one problem with Lucy. Irony isn't big in Deuel County, South Dakota, and she takes everything he tells her at face value. "Would it were so easy," he says. "No, actually it was from a..."—he decides not to say "fascinating woman" to Lucy—"...an entrepreneur who wants to set me up in a private company."

A frown crosses Lucy's face. "Have you accepted?"

It had been one of the toughest decisions of his life. Like most of his colleagues he spent more time trying to obtain grants than actually doing the research that motivates him. As the years passed and he didn't deliver the hoped-for breakthrough, interest in his research waned and his grants dried up. The temptation of getting hassle-free finance from Maria Snowe—*and* working closely with such a fascinating woman—was almost irresistible. "In the past, Lucy," he says, "academic researchers dreamed of a Nobel Prize. Now, if you make an important discovery, first you hire a patent attorney, then you call a venture capitalist and start a company, just like Straker did." He sighs. "But monopolizing the use of a gene that everyone is born with in order to make money just can't be right."

He stands up and stares out of the window, over the roof of the Life Sciences Building below. "Thank God we've got public funding for genetic research. The medical benefits from the work you and I do will be available to everyone." He turns and waves his hand dismissively at the grant forms and the wad of instructions on his desk. "All this is a pain in the ass, but at least I've got the director of Cold Spring Harbor supporting the application, so the we'll get a grant eventually."

That evening in the privacy of her room Lucy takes out her diary and writes:

"For a moment my heart dropped when I thought Richard was going to raise finance by patenting his proposed use of the anti-aging gene."

She cuddles the one-eared cat she called Darwin before concluding:

"How dumb can I get to think that Richard, of all people, would sell out?"

The next day Richard arrives at his office and begins watering the plants that Lucy had put there. Shortly afterwards Lucy calls in. "Morning, Richard," she says brightly. "Got a minute?"

"Sure," he says, looking at the grant application she is carrying. "Problems?"

"No problems," she replies cheerfully. "Just one thing I need from you. What do I put for the date of Human Subject Protection Committee approval for use of fetal brain cells?"

"Write 'Pending'," he says breezily. "Approval is a formality. And while you're using the Xerox, copy the grant and my Cold Spring Harbor abstract, and send them to Straker for inclusion in the dossier on my tenure." That, he assumes, is a formality now.

8

The confidence Richard gained by Keith Harris supporting his grant application to the National Institutes of Health begins to ebb.

Following his return from Cold Spring Harbor, he's answered email and voice messages, mainly from people asking for a more detailed version of the abstract he'd submitted to the Cold Spring Harbor meeting, plus all the bureaucratic paperwork. Now he's nothing to do but sit in his office and fret while he waits for a decision from the Human Subject Protection Committee on his application to test the anti-aging gene on fetal human brain cells.

His discovery is now out in the open. Nathan Hill may have been too myopic to see its significance, but Steve Drummond would understand, as would Judith Crosland at Cambridge. Richard is all in favor of the open exchange of research data, provided there is a level playing field. Being robbed of the credit for his years of work that led to identifying the gene, however, almost cost him his career; it has left a deep scar. What he announced at Cold Spring Harbor was an inconclusive experiment and an insight. No more than that. Recognition for the biggest breakthrough in medical science for decades would be awarded to whomever provided experimental proof that the gene really did prevent cells from aging. He is becoming anxious that Steve or Judith or even somebody who hasn't worked on his gene before might be using his insight to race ahead and beat him to the proof while he is kicking his heels waiting to begin.

Worrying though that is, an even greater fear gnaws at him. Exactly what are Straker and his researchers at Universal Genes doing now they know the real function of the gene? Straker is a member of the Human Subject Protection Committee. Is he deliberately delaying approval for Richard's experimental protocol?

"Do you think I'm paranoid?" Richard asks Larry Myers over lunch in the Faculty Center near Murphy Hall, where Myers has been attending one of the many university committees on which he serves.

"Sure you are," replies Myers, chewing a mouthful of food. "It comes with the job."

"What can I do?"

Myers pours Richard a glass of wine. "Get a life outside the lab. Stops you from going over the edge."

"Is there any way to get a quicker response from the committee?" Richard persists.

Myers lounges back in his chair, savors his wine, and looks thoughtful. Finally he says, "I suppose you could always break Straker's legs and then hold a loaded gun to the head of the HSPC chair until he signs an approval."

"Thanks, Larry. You're a friend."

Richard doesn't want a life outside the lab. All he wants is to begin the experiment that will prove whether or not he is right about the gene. But as the days turn into weeks he becomes more and more convinced that no news is bad news.

When Lucy comes into his office and puts on his desk a white envelope marked "Office for Protection of Research Subjects", Richard looks at it with trepidation. Supposing Straker has successfully argued on ethical grounds against the university approving use of fetal human tissue for his experiment? It would be hypocrisy, of course, in view of the work on fetal tissue that Straker's company carries out. But if the committee withholds approval what would he do then? Lucy looks at him. "I'll get coffee."

When she returns, Richard glances up and then punches the air. "We got it! Provisional approval to go ahead!"

"Provisional?"

"Ethical safeguards. We have to obtain the tissue from a source that certifies it has the mother's consent without identifying her. It'll take a few days, but the main thing is that we got the go-ahead."

A huge smile of relief lights up her face. "At last."

"It couldn't have come at a better time," he says, waving the letter as though it were a winning lottery ticket on the day the bank is due to repossess his house.

"Why?" Lucy asks as she puts down the coffee cups on his desk.

"It's my birthday."

"How old?"

"Old enough."

"Then you and Mrs. Trent will have a double celebration tonight."

"Somehow I don't think so," he says wryly. "Jackie never remembers. And anyway, Friday is her bridge evening."

"Then I'll make you a meal."

He studies a face that might almost be flushed with regret at the boldness of the words she's spoken. "I'd like that, Lucy," he says.

Avoiding his eyes, she scribbles her address on her notepad, tears off the page, and gives it. "See you around eight."

Richard found her rooming house in a street off Palms Boulevard, not far from the Santa Monica freeway, and parked behind a Yamaha V Star 950 that stood outside the three-story house. He climbs out of his car and examines the bike, wondering how its performance compares with the Harley-Davidson he owned when a college student. The approval from the HSPC has banished his anxiety and rejuvenated him; he doesn't feel like he's reached middle age with his fortieth birthday, and he imagines burning the freeway with that bike.

He presses the bell and is still thinking about his student days when the door opens. At first he barely recognizes her. This isn't the effervescent, tomboyish Lucy who reminds him of his kid sister.

Released from a ponytail, her flaxen hair falls to her shoulders; a slim, blue button-through dress that ends just above the knee gives an unexpected impression of style; toenails the color of pearl peep through high-heeled sandals; and, for the first time that he can remember, she is wearing lipstick.

"You look, er… lovely," he says in surprise.

She blushes and averts her eyes.

"Who rides the two-wheeled beast outside?" he asks to distract from her embarrassment.

"It's mine," she says, looking up with a flash of her usual lop-sided grin and then, as though regretting an unladylike remark, she turns quickly and retreats into the house.

He stares at her back with a mixture of respect and curiosity. Perhaps the Lucy he knew from the lab might have ridden a bike like that, but not the elegant young woman who opened the door.

She leads him to the large room that serves as kitchen and dining room. Its hardwood floor, well-used but serviceable cupboards, and posters on the wall take him back to the house on 120th Street he'd shared with Larry in their senior year at Columbia. The old pine table with a candle in a wine bottle might have been the one around which they sat when he helped Larry with his assignments. And the kitchen section, with its stained stove and refrigerator plastered with stickers, reminds him of where Jackie cooked meals for Larry and him, and then only for him.

With a diffidence he's never seen in Lucy before, she turns and says, "Take a seat, Richard, while I lay the table and finish the supper."

"I brought some wine," he says holding out a bottle of Chardonnay. "Hope it's OK."

"Thanks. Put it in the refrigerator."

"Can I help?" he asks after placing the wine next to bottles of Budweiser and a carton of semi-skimmed milk in the bottle rack.

"Certainly not. It's all under control." She bites her lip. "I hope."

He sits down on a stuffed leather sofa with splitting seams and watches this new Lucy with fascination as she metamorphoses the old pine table with the aid of lacquered mats, a matching lacquered candlestick, ceramic dishes and cups, wooden chopsticks, and two delicately arranged pots of chrysanthemums. She looks up. "Please sit at the table. It won't be long."

He has anticipated none of this. As he takes his place at the table he feels guilty that he hadn't gone home, showered, and changed out of the jeans and sweatshirt he wore at the lab.

Lucy stretches up to take a pan from a cupboard, and Richard finds the tantalizing hint of young curves beneath her dress far more alluring than Jackie's brazen sexiness.

With the attention to detail that she displayed in the lab, Lucy carefully pours oil in the pan, puts it on the stove, and slices squid, aubergines, and mushrooms into mouthful-sized portions while the oil heats. When she judges the oil to be the correct temperature, she dips the pieces into a bowl of batter and deep fries them in the sizzling oil before transferring them to a tray lined with white paper on which sits a ceramic bowl of brown sauce. After tipping grated ginger and radish into the bowl she presents the tempura to him along with wooden trays of sushi and sashimi that she'd prepared earlier.

"How come you learned to cook like this?" he asks.

"My Uncle Henry married a Japanese lady. Aunt Chisako taught me."

Like the Japanese lacquered mats on the table, Lucy reveals surprising and attractive features the more he looks beneath the surface.

She lights the candle, dims the lights, and brings a slim clay flask from a pan of water on the stove. After pouring warm sake from the flask into small ceramic cups, she holds up one and says with a shy smile, "Happy birthday, Richard."

He touches his cup against hers. "Thank you, Lucy," he replies, moved by all the care she's taken to compensate for Jackie's indifference. "This is the best birthday surprise I've had in years."

Her smile widens with pleasure until it becomes infectious and he finds himself smiling back. The mellowness of the lighting transfigures her face from the pale porcelain it appeared under the neon of the lab into a rich ivory framed by tumbling deep-golden locks. Her flawless complexion provides a perfect setting for eyes that shine like brown onyx and a mouth made sensuous by crimson lipstick. He doesn't know whether he is stimulated by the sake, elated by his research getting the green light, or aroused by the way she made him feel so special, but Lucy seems very desirable.

"Hi you guys! Hope I'm not interrupting anything." Dorothy ambles into the room with a knowing smile. The extra-large T-shirt draped across her ample bosom proclaims "Genetic Engineers Know How To Reproduce."

"Oh no," says Lucy, fiddling demurely with one of the buttons of her dress. "Please join us. We're celebrating Richard's birthday." Then she adds quickly, "And HSPC approval for Richard to show the effect of his gene on brain cells."

Dorothy picks a bottle of beer out of the refrigerator and opens it. "Don't let those brain cells go to your head, you two." She drinks from the bottle. "More important, don't let that shit Straker stitch you up this time."

"No danger," says Richard flushed with confidence. Paranoia? He's been there, done that, and come out the other side. Now he and Lucy have something to prove.

9

Richard collects the mail from his box in the lobby of the Human Genetics Building. He flicks through the envelopes as he rides the elevator up to the ninth floor and finds the one he is hoping for. He lopes into his office, opening the envelope en route, and backheels the door shut behind him. After dumping the other mail on his desk, he pulls out the letter. Anticipation tingles up his spine as he reads that a certified sample of eight-week-old fetal brain tissue will be delivered in a week's time.

Relieved, he goes through the rest of the mail and comes to a manila envelope marked "National Institutes of Health." He guesses it is another reminder that he hasn't yet supplied details of the Human Subject Protection Committee approval in his grant application.

He takes the envelope with him when he goes to find Lucy and share the good news about the tissue delivery. Although nothing more than glances passed between them at the dinner she'd made for his birthday, their relationship has undergone a subtle change. That night he saw a different Lucy, but does she care for him just as a colleague and a friend with a shared passion for discovering genetic cures for disease? He wonders what might have developed if Dorothy hadn't interrupted them. That thought, he concludes reluctantly, has to remain a thought. His priority is to prove that the gene really does prevent cells from senescing without turning cancerous and then to demonstrate how it could be used to treat the diseases of aging. Lucy and he had established a highly productive professional partnership that he can't risk ruining by unwelcome advances. Nevertheless he finds himself wanting to see her face light up with a smile, which it did whenever she saw him. He quickens his steps in anticipation as he approaches the lab and opens the door.

Glassware gleams on the shelves racked above cluttered white benches, a brewery-like smell mingles with the aroma of coffee and organic solvents, and rock music pumps out from a transistor radio perched precariously on a crowded windowsill. But no Lucy. In fact, nobody. Electronic numbers change on the small screens of PCR machines, which resemble supermarket electronic cash registers with a black box stuck on top, as tiny lengths of DNA replicate ten thousand times a minute. Differently sized bits of DNA creep invisibly at different speeds through electrophoresis gel beds—unappetizing candy-box slabs of white jelly—under the influence of an electric field that is separating DNA samples by size. And on the floor a large gyratory water bath judders as DNA is being cloned in shaken flasks of warmed bacterial broth. Experiments on the molecule of human life are pursuing their objectives without human help. Then he remembers. It is the monthly department meeting, which he's disdained ever since Straker's company scientists had published their cloning of his gene.

When Fred Holdsworth was chair, the department meeting had been a stimulating exchange of information and ideas, but Straker had turned it into a circus in which he was ringmaster. When he wasn't probing for findings or insights that his company might use, Straker took every opportunity to demonstrate that he was the alpha male of the pack. Richard had absolutely no intention of feeding Straker's company or his ego.

Lucy and members of the two other labs who share the open plan arrangement drift back from the meeting.

"The certified tissue samples arrive next week," Richard says as Lucy leaves Dorothy to greet him.

She rubs her hands together. "Can't wait to get started." She glances at the manila envelope Richard is holding. "Those are the details?"

Richard shakes his head. "More paperwork from NIH to fill in. Do you mind?"

Lucy slits open the envelope and removes three sheets of paper. Her face turns white. "What is it?" Richard asks.

She glances up at him and then at Dorothy and the others. "Later."

"Tell me now," he orders.

A hush descends around them as, slowly and reluctantly, she reads aloud the covering letter. "Dear Dr. Trent, We regret that your application was not placed in the top fifteen per cent of proposals for which we were able to award a Program Project Grant. Appended is a copy of the two reviews of your proposal, which you may find helpful should you wish to re-apply."

Stunned, Richard says, "Let me see."

Lucy hands him the documents and his eyes race down the first review.

"Although Dr. Keith Harris has agreed to act as consultant for the proposed project, neither he nor the applicant has specialized in aging research. In support of the proposal the applicant has submitted a preliminary study showing that human diploid fibroblasts in laboratory culture have been immortalized without morphological transformation. Such a result is consistent with the immortalin gene being an oncogene. The applicant claims that immortalin has the characteristics of a regulatory protein. He assumes the gene that codes for it is a master regulatory gene controlling repair and maintenance genes. Such an assumption is unsubstantiated."

He grimaces and reads aloud. "The preliminary study tells us nothing about the aging of non-replicating cells, like neurons. It tells us nothing about aging in a living organism..." He breaks off. "These are Nathan Hill's words."

"Where was the application assigned to?" Dorothy asks.

Richard turns to the covering letter as though it were a declaration of war. "The National Institute on Aging."

"That figures," Dorothy says. "Nathan Hill is the chief honcho in their grant review section." She grimaces. "You've got a problem there, Richard. Hill's not a man to cross swords with."

Lucy puts out her hand and touches his arm. "We'll re-apply when we've got the results of the neuron experiment."

"There's an automatic minimum of ten months before NIH will consider a revised application," Richard fumes. "But with Hill making the recommendations it might as well be ten years."

It is an angry Lucy Jonnsen who rides swiftly back to Palms that evening. After parking her bike outside the house, removing her helmet, and unlocking the street door, she makes straight for the stairs to her room, followed by the part-Siamese stray with one ear.

She is about to close her room door and shut out the rest of the world when she sees Darwin look up plaintively. Picking up the cat, she closes the door behind them and cuddles it. She is livid at the way Richard has been treated, she longs to support him, and she is distraught that she doesn't know how. No touch on the arm could bring back that smile in his eyes, the smile that produced a tremor of excitement deep inside her when he looked at her across the dinner she'd made for his birthday.

She puts the cat on the floor, goes to her desk, and opens her diary. Darwin jumps up onto the desk and sits there patiently, tail curled round its front paws, while it watches her write.

"It's outrageous that the National Institutes of Health didn't even wait for the result of our experiment on neurons before turning down a grant for the next three years of our work. What have we got to do to get the funding that will show whether or not Richard's insight will lead to a pioneering treatment for aging diseases? Balanced against all the suffering a successful treatment could relieve in the long term, the cost of this three-year grant is peanuts.

I don't know what Richard will do now. I only know that there are two more years of my NCI fellowship left and I will do whatever I can to develop our project."

He had to tell Jackie sometime.

It is seven in the evening and Jackie is lounging on the sofa in her bathrobe. "No big deal," she mimics. I've lined up a three-year NIH grant." She lifts up one knee and the robe falls back to reveal a well-toned calf and thigh. "That's your trouble. All foreplay and no fuck."

"If Nathan Hill—" he begins.

"There, there," she simpers. "Let's blame naughty Professor Hill, let's blame anybody but himself."

"Hill wouldn't recognize an innovative idea—"

Her voice hardens. "Don't give me that crap again. Face it, Richard. You've lost it." She resumes painting her fingernails. "If you ever had it."

He walks out, changes, and goes for a run to burn off his anger. When he returns he showers, dresses, strides to his study, and closes the door behind him. For a while he sits thinking. In science, he concludes, the same people, in a few powerful positions, control the input and the output. The same people get asked to review your grant and then get asked to review the paper you want to publish. It is more a way of controlling science than doing science. He contemplates a future in which a dinosaur like Nathan Hill and his fellow gerontologists effectively control aging research. It is not a future he is prepared to accept.

10

"Dr Trent?" The deep melodic voice comes from a short, powerfully built Central American Indian in a gray suit who stands just outside the domestic arrivals gate at San Francisco Airport and holds up a card bearing Richard's name. He looks straight at Richard with black oriental eyes set in a broad brown face marked by high cheekbones, aquiline nose, and thick lips. His large, round head is topped by a fringe of short straight black hair and appears to fit on his shoulders without benefit of a neck.

"That's me," says Richard.

The man extends his hand. "My name is Alvaro. I work for Ms Snowe. Please follow me." His greeting is polite, but Richard wouldn't want to get on the wrong side of him in a dark alley.

Alvaro leads him to a large car and opens the rear passenger door for Richard to climb in. On the flight from LA Richard agonized about his position. He disapproved of the commercialization of any research: he'd seen too many good scientists succumb to the subtle pressures only to publish results consistent with the interests of their masters. Commercializing medical research in genetics raised even greater ethical problems. But he has been refused a public sector grant and he desperately needs to finance the work that will prove to those mental myopics at NIH just how his insight could revolutionize the treatment of aging-induced diseases. As the car leaves the 101 North at Van Ness Avenue and appears to be heading for the Victorian opulence of Nob Hill, Richard's unease grows.

Alvaro turns away from Nob Hill onto California Street, which points undeviatingly west, up and down steep hills like some roller coaster. Maria Snowe was astute enough to appreciate the significance of what he's discovered. She has made one fortune from commercially exploiting her father's innovative software. Does she see his discovery as the way to make another fortune? What did she mean by saying that she wants to make his dreams come true? More importantly, what price will she ask for funding his research? Alvaro makes a right. This is foreign territory for Richard.

The car swings left onto an avenue bordered on one side by large, detached houses and on the other by a narrow stretch of parkland above the ocean. Alvaro stops outside a three-story house with large bay windows. "Welcome to Seacliff, Dr. Trent."

Maria Snowe is even more compelling in the flesh than in his fantasies, for he has thought of her many times since their first meeting: what man wouldn't? But now the unwavering gaze that invested her with an imperial quality relaxes into an inviting smile. Her outfit of designer T-shirt, cargo pants and sandals suggests an informality he hasn't anticipated. It increases the discomfort he feels in his best suit, his only suit, the suit he'd got married in, the suit he wore for weddings, funerals, and meetings to ask for money.

She holds out her hand and silver gleams from the same filigree serpent bracelet that he remembers from Cold Spring Harbor. "Richard, welcome," she says huskily as she greets him in her third floor study. "And do take off your jacket and necktie if you're uncomfortable."

"Thanks," he says, feeling the strength of her small hand. "I wasn't sure what to wear for lunch."

Her eyes glint with amusement. "When you're with me, Richard, you wear and do whatever you want. The only rule is that there are no rules."

The knowledge that this formidable woman isn't a spoiled heiress, but has run a successful business while caring for her cancer-stricken father, adds apprehension to the moral turmoil churning inside him. He stares out of the windows. The left bay frames a row of tall weather-beaten Scotch pines that protect the end of a gently sloping golf course from a plunge down a bush-strewn rock face to the ocean. Out to sea, waves spume around the base of a blinking lighthouse built on a rocky islet. The center window looks directly across the restless waters of the bay mouth to cliffs rising starkly to green headlands speckled by early spring flowers. To his right the edge of the forested Presidio parkland launches the Golden Gate Bridge across the neck of San Francisco Bay. "Some people would kill for a view like this."

"Some people probably have," she says softly.

He turns. She is on the far side of the study. It is a room of stark contrasts. Black furniture and black carpet against white walls, white door and white ceiling. The only splashes of color are some Indian masks and prints on the walls. The most striking is a silk print of a mythical beast: the profile of a stylized blue snake adorned with red jewels, a green-feathered headdress, and a bronze human face with an aquiline nose. "What's that?" he asks.

"The Mayan god Kukulkán. The Plumed Serpent."

She leads him downstairs to the dining room on the floor below. It is decorated in a minimalist style, with a polished, light oak floor and white walls, rather like a modern art gallery focusing attention on the triptych of views in the bay window. In the center of the room, pointing towards the central panel of the Marin Headlands, stands a plain, rectangular dining table of light oak identical to the floor. Ten high-backed, white leather dining chairs line the table, one at either end and four on either side. A handsome woman with Alvaro's features and hair swept tightly back in a bun is picking up the silver Scandinavian-designed cutlery that had been laid for lunch.

Maria goes over to the woman, puts an arm round her shoulder, and gives her an affectionate squeeze. "We haven't had lunch yet."

The woman stares back blankly.

"Let's put these back, shall we?" Maria says. The woman looks at the knife in her hand and her brow creases in puzzlement. Maria gently removes it and re-lays the place settings. "Didn't I say that I was having a lunch guest today? This is Richard Trent. He's a medical researcher from Los Angeles."

The woman wanders over to Richard and squints at him. Her brown face creases in a smile of recognition. "Jonathan!" She wags a finger in admonishment. "Patrick will be cross that you've been away so long."

"No," Maria says, "it's Richard. You haven't met before." She turns to Richard. "Carmen's confusing you with my uncle. She has Alzheimer's disease. The early onset kind."

"I'm sorry," says Richard, touched by the kindness Maria is showing one of her maids. "It's very good of you to look after her."

"Why shouldn't I?" Maria says. "She's my mother."

Alvaro serves lunch to the three of them. Richard silently curses himself for being so focused on his own problem that he'd failed to see the obvious. Maria had said at Cold Spring Harbor that she had an interest in aging diseases. Her exotic looks and the Mayan artifacts on the walls should have told him who Carmen was. While Richard toys uncomfortably with his grilled sole, Maria smiles at him between giving spoonfuls of fish to her distracted mother. "There's no need to feel embarrassed, Richard. You'd have understood why my dad fell in love with Carmen if you'd seen her before she developed Alzheimer's."

Richard nods and casts a glance at Carmen. He tries to imagine her with Maria's vitality, perspicacity and drive, before premature aging of neurons in cortical regions of her brain had deprived her of her memory and ability to reason. Now he understands why Maria had wanted to check out the latest developments at the Genetics of Aging conference at Cold Spring Harbor, and why she had seized on his discovery.

"You can talk freely," Maria says. "I'm afraid Carmen doesn't understand much these days." She looks at him and asks, "Well?"

He begins with his planned opening, a frank admission. "I was turned down for a National Institutes of Health grant. Nathan Hill heads the grant review panel. As far as aging research is concerned, Hill thinks I'm a heretic."

"'It is the customary fate of new truths to begin as heresies and to end as superstitions',", she says.

Richard frowns.

"T H Huxley. The English biologist who defended Darwin's theory against the Church."

"You seem to have been researching the subject."

She looks at him. "I don't invest blindly."

"What does your research tell you?"

"That Nathan Hill is bright, very bright," she says. "In fact I'd go so far as to say he possesses the kind of IQ that enables him to tie his own shoelaces." She smiles. "What do you want, Richard?"

This is his big moment; he can't blow it. Launching into the proposal he's prepared, he begins, "To continue my research at UCLA." Then he hesitates. Knowing now what he does about Maria's mother, he feels even more ashamed that he is exploiting her personal tragedy, but he can think of no other way to persuade Maria to make a donation rather than finance a commercial venture. "I propose you establish a research fellowship in aging-induced diseases in memory of your father."

He studies her face to gauge her response, but he might well be trying to decipher the hieroglyphs on the prints in her study above.

"Forget universities, Richard," she says. "They're now the backwater. All important discoveries have come out of commercial labs: the transistor, laser, microchip, hologram, personal computer… You name it."

"A university lab is where I feel comfortable." He wriggles under her gaze. "I'm not inventing some machine for sale in the marketplace or devising innovative software. I'm discovering how nature works and then using that discovery to prevent and cure diseases." He fears that she will think him pompous. "What I'm trying to say, Maria, is that no one has the right to patent nature. Discoveries about our genes should be made freely available to society, not monopolized and exploited for profit."

Her gaze is unchanged. "Richard, you've got four strikes against you for anti-aging research in academia: you've got a radical idea, it works, you're way ahead of the competition, and you're an outsider in gerontology."

He can't argue with that. "What do you suggest?" he asks cautiously.

Her gaze is penetrating. It draws Richard like a rabbit to a snake. "Here's the deal. I will help you develop a gene therapy for aging diseases through a private company in which I will hold fifty-one per cent of the stock; you will have forty-nine per cent of the stock, absolute control over the research, and all the funding you need."

"Absolute control over the research?"

She nods.

"*All* the funding?"

"That's what I said."

"And my part of the bargain?"

"You will surrender all proprietary rights in perpetuity to the company, and you will not publish without the company's agreement."

His heart sinks. "Not publish?" This is one thing he hasn't anticipated.

She shakes her head. "Absolutely no details of your work to be made public."

He gets up from his chair and stares out of the window. The vista sweeps from the Golden Gate Bridge past the Marin Headlands and out to an ocean whose limit lies an unseeable five and a half thousand miles away in Japan. His stare seems to last an eternity. Finally he says, "I can't accept those terms."

"What is it that you can't accept, Richard? Is it not making your discovery freely available to society," she asks perceptively, "or is it not receiving from society the recognition that would rank you alongside Watson and Crick in the pantheon of scientific immortals?"

11

Gossamer-thin white latex sheathes the slender finger and thumb that gently squeeze narrow tweezers holding the tiny butterfly-shaped fetal human brain section kept alive by pink nutrient solution in a tissue culture dish. Lucy's other sterile gloved hand strokes a fine scalpel blade between the waxy white tissue and the rudimentary cartilage and bone.

Richard needs Lucy's keen eyesight and sensitive fingers if he is to succeed, and this time he cannot fail. He has staked his whole future on this one experiment. Having turned down Maria Snowe's offer, this is his last shot at proving his insight really is the breakthrough he believes it to be.

With nerves on edge, Richard watches as Lucy carefully cuts a rectangular piece from the midbrain and takes it to the hood, a glass-fronted biological safety cabinet that looks like the latest in salad bar technology. Richard raises the vertical sliding sash and Lucy places the tissue culture dish inside the hood. A curtain of air flows down the front of the cabinet and into a grille at the forward edge of the hood's interior work surface to protect specimens in the cabinet from outside airborne contaminants.

Lucy sits down in front of the hood, reaches inside, and uses a series of micropipettes to dissociate the brain tissue into its constituent cells, which continue to be nourished by the pink liquid. She pipettes a measured part of the resultant solution onto each section of a triple-chambered tissue culture plate—three square, clear plastic chambers aligned over a common culture plate at their base—and a second sample onto an identical plate.

Next she pipettes into each of the three chambers of the first plate a precise volume of a milky suspension. It contains the anti-aging gene plus promoter sequence within a DNA construct that adheres to white particles of calcium phosphate. To the chambers of the second plate she adds a suspension consisting of everything except the anti-aging gene to act as a control for the experiment. After putting a lid on each plate and gently swirling to mix the contents, she takes them from the hood and puts them in an incubator to allow the DNA constructs to worm their way into the cells overnight.

It is a crude, ineffective method of inserting DNA into cells, but it is quick. Richard believes it will produce enough cells containing a switched-on copy of the anti-aging gene to test his hypothesis.

One of the main causes of aging of nerve cells in the brain—one of the main *secondary* causes, according to Richard's theory—is oxidative damage caused by free radicals. These unstable fragments of molecules or atoms lack one or more electrons and are generated during the normal activity of the brain. But they have the side effect of damaging DNA, proteins and cell membranes. Richard's idea is to use a solution of hydrogen peroxide of just enough strength to subject these growing fetal brain cells to the equivalent of a lifetime's natural free radical damage over a period of a week. If the anti-aging gene resisted this damage, it would prove him right. If it didn't, Nathan Hill would claim victory, and Richard would be consigned to oblivion, if not ridicule.

The following morning Lucy renews the pink nutrient medium in which the cells grew and then pipettes in the hydrogen peroxide solution to attack the cells. With the apprehension of an expectant father, Richard watches as Lucy takes the two triple-chambered plates and puts them back in the incubator. There is nothing more that he can do but wait.

Richard's voice mail shows three messages. The first is from Larry Myers saying they need to meet, soon. He ignores the others and dials Myers's number.

Myers suggests a discreet lunch away from campus since he is a member of the Council on Academic Personnel and doesn't want to be seen talking to someone whose tenure application is about to be decided.

L'Incontro Trattoria is one of those tony restaurants on Ocean Avenue that Jackie talked about. It stands on a bluff overlooking the ribbon of grass and palm trees known as Palisades Park that borders Santa Monica beach. Its windows show to the left the old pier that staggers on wooden stilts out into the sun-speckled ocean, and to the right the golden curve of Malibu beach at the foot of blue-green hills.

"Buon giorno, Larry," effuses the maître d'. "No bella donna today?"

Myers shrugs and orders without consulting the menu.

"I'm not sure I'm supposed to tell you this," Myers says as he watches the waiter pour the wine and place the bottle in a cooler, "but I've just received a copy of the CAP ad hoc committee report on your tenure."

"And?" Richard asks tersely.

"It's not good."

Richard has no appetite for the red snapper that the waiter places in front of him. "Spit it out."

Myers sticks his fork into a whole sardine, winds round spaghetti and fennel, and places the forkful into his mouth. "Your department voted in your favor." When he finished chewing he adds, "But the vote was split."

"Straker wants me out."

"That's strike one against." Myers sips appreciatively from his wineglass. "Try it. Colli Albani is like Frascati, only better."

"Strike two?" Richard asks, ignoring his wine.

"Your record of committee service, publications and research." Myers waves an empty fork in Richard's direction. "Remember what I told you a year back when your tenure application was deferred?"

Richard grimaces.

"Volunteer for committees," repeats Myers, between mouthfuls of his pasta con le sarde, "and get some publications under your belt: forget quality, go for quantity."

"But—"

"So it's all down to your research record," says Myers as he continues eating. "And that, for our purposes, means grants."

Richard breaks the snapper's back with his fork. "NIH turned me down."

Myers savors the last forkful of spaghetti. "That's strike two against." He holds out his glass.

Richard refills Myers's glass. His own is untouched.

"So it's all down to the third criterion, your work in progress."

"But you know about that, Larry," Richard insists.

The waiter hovers, uncertain whether to collect Myers's empty plate when Richard has barely touched the fish that lies mutilated in front of him.

"Delizioso, grazie," Myers says.

"The snapper?" asks the waiter. "It's not good?"

"Terrific," says Richard, pushing his plate away.

The waiter collects the plates. "The menu?"

"Fior di mandorla," Myers says.

The waiter looks at Richard.

Myers shakes his head. "He's in training."

"Larry, you know that this is going to be one of the biggest things this university's ever had."

"Sure I do," says Myers as though humoring a crazy with a knife. "But you'll need more than your Cold Spring Harbor abstract to convince my fellow members on CAP, especially after the roasting Hill gave it."

"When do you decide my tenure?"

"Once the Academic Personnel Office has received the dean's recommendation, it'll put your tenure on the agenda of the next meeting of CAP."

"How soon?"

Myers smiles acknowledgment as the waiter serves him with an almond pastry, and then he turns to Richard with a shrug. "Could be next week. Who knows?"

"I've already begun testing the anti-aging gene on brain cells," Richard pleads. "Surely there's something you can do, Larry?"

Myers takes a large forkful of pastry, places it in his mouth, and chews contentedly.

"Larry—"

"Food helps me think." Myers finishes his dessert before saying, "As a member of CAP I could ask if the candidate has any work in progress that isn't included in the ad hoc committee report. When can you deliver?"

Richard looks at the calendar on his wristwatch. He decides to foreshorten the experiment. "I'll complete this weekend."

"That should give us time." Myers finishes his wine and signals for the check. Richard tries to pay, but Myers waves him aside.

"How's Jackie?" Myers asks as they leave the restaurant.

Richard shrugs. "The same, you know."

"Sure."

They emerge from the restaurant into the brightness of a mild, smog-free day. A pair of club runners making good pace along Palisades Park reminds Richard of his training runs in Central Park with Larry. Beyond, a group of noisy youngsters play volleyball on a golden beach that curves round and out beyond Malibu to Point Dume on one side and the Palos Verdes Peninsula on the other. The sparkling blue water of the bay opens into a Pacific that stretches out to the sky.

Myers climbs into his flame red Mustang and lowers the window. Richard leans across. "Larry, I owe you."

"Don't even think about it."

Late Saturday afternoon Lucy removes the two triple-chambered plates from the incubator. She looks at Richard. "Are you sure we've given them long enough?

"Do it."

She pours off the nutrient medium and pipettes in formalin to kill and fix whatever living cells adhered to the base plates.

Richard takes one final look at the two triple-chambered plates that contain his reputation before Lucy puts them back in the hood to let the formalin preserve the evidence.

That night Richard is glad Jackie is away at some bridge competition. He doesn't sleep at all.

On Sunday morning Richard arrives at the lab. Four of Straker's postgrads are busily engaged in their research. Lucy is at her bench, standing over a cell-staining bath. She looks up anxiously when he approaches. "Richard. Are you OK?"

"I'm fine," he says, trying to control his nerves.

Lucy has already poured off the formalin and removed each triple chamber from its base plate, washed the two plates, and immersed them in the bath. The solution in the bath stained only dopaminergic neurons, which would be cultured a fluorescent red when excited by green-yellow light and viewed through a microscope.

Now she removes the plates from the bath, covers each with a glass cover slip, and gives them to Richard. With his heart pounding in his ribcage he takes the two plates to the fluorescence microscope.

He peers down the microscope and moves the first plate backwards and forwards and from side to examine the three stained squares where the three chambers had been. All he sees is an occasional fluorescent red shriveled tadpole with one filament sprouting from its tail and three to five short branching filaments from its head. These few dopaminergic neurons that hadn't died and detached from the plate are atrophied: just what he expects if the neurons had succumbed to the free radical attack. He re-checks the chinagraph label. They are the control cells that haven't been given the activated anti-aging gene.

He takes a deep breath, replaces this first slide with the second, and examines it under the microscope.

All the tension that has stretched him to breaking point over the past week leaves him with the suddenness of an uncoiling spring. He sinks limply onto a chair.

"Richard, what's wrong?" Lucy asks apprehensively.

"Take a look for yourself." He nods towards the fluorescence microscope.

She peers down and moves the slide around. In every field of vision she sees five or six bright red, plump tadpole-shaped dopaminergic neurons amid a robust tangle of filaments. These cells have not only survived the free radical attack, their axons and dendrites—the single long filament and the shorter branching filaments that respectively send and receive signals from other nerve cells—have grown healthily. When she looks up, her brown eyes are wider and brighter than ever. "How?"

He brushes aside the lock of hair that has fallen across his brow. "The anti-aging gene went into battle," he says as his confidence flows back. He gets to his feet, his face one large grin. "Our little baby upregulated the cells' own antioxidant genes—superoxide dismutase, catalase, glutathione peroxidase, you name it—to fight off the free radicals." He punches the air exultantly above the microscope. "And our beautiful little baby won."

Lucy's irresistible grin transmits enough energy to light up the whole building. She high-fives Richard in excitement.

"Didn't I say we were a winning team?" he high-fives back.

She shakes her head. "Wow! This'll show old Nathan Hill."

12

Richard stands in front of the window in his office, hands in jeans pockets, lock of chestnut hair falling across his forehead, and eyes focused on infinity. He is unable to stop smiling. Euphoric moments like this justify everything: the sacrifices of social life when experiments on living cells can't stop because the clock says six or the calendar says Sunday; the setbacks when experiments obstinately decline to support hypotheses; the commiserations of some fellow scientists and the pleasure of some competitors at these setbacks; and the shafts of self-doubt that undermine the confidence to persevere across uncharted terrain with no end in sight. All this, Richard reflects, is the price that nature demands of a penetrating mind before she will reveal her secrets.

Many, like Larry, either lack the vision or find the price too high and are content to meander among familiar foothills, unearthing small increments of knowledge. But if he pays the greater price and experiences the greater depths, he also scales the greater heights and sees a new world on the other side. Confronted by the established wisdom of Hill and the rest that his anti-aging gene is simply another gene that turns replicating skin cells cancerous without changing their shape, he's demonstrated that the gene prevents non-replicating brain cells from aging. Proof that he has discovered a master regulatory gene controlling cell repair and maintenance would open up a whole new era in medical science.

"What now?" Lucy asks.

"First, a phone call." He has to get the good news to Larry so that he can inform the Council on Academic Personnel. With a result like this the university would not only give him tenure, it would also ensure that the next stages of his research are funded.

Larry's cell phone doesn't answer and so Richard calls his home landline. Larry's wife, Sandy, answers. "Afraid that Larry's not around right now, Richard. I'm expecting him this evening."

"Please can you have him ring me as soon as he gets back, Sandy, it's important."

Richard's mind races ahead to the next stage. He'll need to expand his lab. So much work to do. But first, after the emotional wringer they've been put through to get this result ahead of the CAP decision on his tenure, something special is called for. "Celebration time, Lucy. We deserve a good dinner."

"I'm not dressed," she demurs.

She is wearing T-shirt and shorts as usual. "You look terrific to me," he insists.

She blushes. "After I take photographs and record the data."

Dear Lucy. What would he do without her? "Right," he concedes. "But no mention to any of Straker's group, not even Dorothy, until we've published."

While Lucy sets up the camera, Richard sits down at his desk and plans the paper he'll write. The smile that hasn't left his face since he saw those healthy neurons now broadens as he imagines Nathan Hill's expression when presented with evidence like this. He wanted this in *Cell*. He could see it as the cover item. But then a thought strikes him and the broad smile turns into a mischievous grin. Quickly he drafts a paragraph:

"This result contradicts an earlier report in this journal (Jerriman et al) which claimed that the gene was an oncogene. Several explanations for this difference can be put forward. One is that the Jerriman study was limited to cells that were already cancerous and took no account of previous reports of the activity of the gene in germline cells (Drummond et al) and in certain stem cells (Crosland et al), nor of the earlier studies of this gene that we carried out (Trent et al)."

The editor of *Science*—and its readers—would seize on the obvious explanation: that Jerriman and the other scientists at Straker's company were, at best, incompetent, and he should never have published a paper on Richard's gene without having Richard review it first. Publishing in *Science* would be poetic justice, Richard concludes with satisfaction.

By the time Lucy has taken photographs of the slides through the fluorescence microscope and written up all the data, and Richard has prepared a first draft of his paper, the light is fading. "*Now* will you celebrate?"

"Are you drinking?" she asks.

"Try to stop me."

"Then you can't drive."

"But—"

"I've a spare helmet in my locker."

They stand outside the multistory parking lot on Westwood Plaza, separated by her black Yamaha 950. "Where are we going?" Lucy asks.

Richard tries to think of a suitable restaurant. He doesn't want one of the student hangouts further down the plaza, but he hardly ever eats out. Then he remembers the place Larry had taken him. "L'Incontro," he says, "a quiet little place I know on Ocean Avenue, Santa Monica."

"Evil," she says with widening eyes. "How far?"

"Twenty minutes, I guess." He gives her the directions.

"Ever been on a bike?" Lucy asks as she puts on her helmet.

Richard suppresses a grin. "Once or twice." One day he'll tell her how Larry, despairing of ever beating him on the athletics track, challenged him to a bike race. Larry proposed the route: start at the lights before George Washington Bridge, cross the Hudson on green, burn up Palisades Parkway for 17 miles, then peel off at the exit for Spring Valley and head for the main post office where Jackie would be waiting to flag the winner. Larry had been born and raised in Spring Valley and it was a route he knew like the back of his hand. Richard beat him by four minutes. Being given a ride by Lucy was hardly in the same league. Still, it would be good to feel a bike between his legs again.

He watches her mount the machine and then climbs on behind. Putting his arms round her waist, he feels firm but yielding flesh beneath her T-shirt. She kick-starts the bike and leans forward. With a roar from the engine they set off down the plaza. Richard tightens his hold and leans with her, so their bodies fit together like two spoons as Lucy accelerates down Wilshire Boulevard. They reach L'Incontro in ten minutes, leaving several white-faced drivers in their wake and Richard exhilarated.

Richard's feet never touch the ground that evening. When he enters L'Incontro, the maître d' recognizes him with a beam. "Buona sera, signor. To any friend of Larry I give good table." He looks at Lucy, who has released her hair from its ponytail, "But to one who brings such a bella donna, for him I give my best."

Lucy giggles, and follows Richard and the plump maître d' to a table set for two in the window bay.

"Is table Larry have. Is my most romantic table. Here you see moon. Soon you hear romantic music that carry you to paradise."

Lucy sits down opposite Richard. He is sure her smile will infect the whole restaurant.

"For to drink, signor?"

He thinks with a pang of regret of the name of the champagne that he bought for Jackie the night he realized the real function of his gene. If only Jackie hadn't lost faith in him.

"What's wrong?" Lucy asks solicitously.

"Nothing." Jackie isn't going to ruin this celebration. "Taittinger Brut," he announces.

"Perfetto!" The maître d' smiles knowingly. "But a man with such exquisite taste in women, naturally he will have exquisite taste in wine."

With Un Bel Di from *Madame Butterfly* playing softly in the background, he returns holding the champagne in an ice bucket and two flutes.

"No thanks," says Lucy as he uncorks the bottle and holds it over her glass. "I'm riding a motorbike."

"Surely one glass is permitted," Richard says.

"No! No!" The maître d' puts down the bottle and throws his hands in the air. "One glass is not permitted!" He looks at Richard. "One glass is essential." He turns to Lucy. "Brings blush to palest of cheeks."

After he poured the champagne and departed, Lucy leans across the table. "Oh, Richard, you're wicked. I should wear a dress in a restaurant like this."

"The guy's right." Richard raises his glass. "Here's to my bella donna assistant."

A full moon hangs in the black sky and dapples the ocean silver. The strains of Puccini's love song float hauntingly in the distance. A rich bouquet sizzles from the skillet of strips of veal, black olives, lemon halves and garlic cloves that the waiter brings to their table. The heady, biscuity flavor of the champagne celebrates their triumph. It is all that he hoped for when he wanted Jackie to share his discovery that Labor Day evening, but what exceeds his expectations are the eyes gazing at him from across the table. Lucy recognizes what he has done, and what he will go on to do. The secret of the experiment and its implications, which they alone share this evening, draw them together in an intimacy far more arousing than any romantic view, music, food, or wine.

The bike ride to Ashland Avenue is slower, but no less stimulating for Richard. It is gone ten when Lucy pulls up outside his house. He dismounts and she climbs off after him.

They stand facing each other and their eyes meet. He feels the bond between them deeper is than ever he experienced between Jackie and himself. He glances towards the darkened living room. "I think Jackie's already gone to bed."

The mention of his wife breaks the spell. Lucy's smile vanishes. She turns away quickly. "See you tomorrow."

Richard watches her slender bare legs straddle the machine. Without glancing back, she presses her small foot down on the pedal, twists the clutch, and the bike roars off down the avenue.

Richard switches on the hall light and tiptoes through to the living room. He needn't have taken the trouble: the house is empty. He pours himself a bourbon and sits down in an armchair, wondering if Lucy misinterpreted what he meant. Did she think he'd been eager to join Jackie in bed? He sighs. Science he understands; women are far more complex. His head is too full for him to go to sleep, and so he sits back and lets his mind replay the events of the day and the evening.

He is still there when Jackie comes in past midnight. "You still up?"

He looks down at his sweatshirt and jeans. "Looks like it." He doesn't mention the successful outcome of his experiment; he no longer feels the need to show her how wrong she's been about him.

"I decided to stay over in Santa Barbara after the bridge competition and do some shopping," she says by way of explanation. "Now I just want to sleep."

"Sure," he says.

It is late Monday morning before Larry returns his call.

"That's terrific, Richard," he says after Richard has summarized his findings, "but there's no way *Science* is going to be able to publish before CAP meets."

"Meaning?"

"I'm no expert in this field. When I ask for your work in progress, CAP is going to want the opinion of your department chair."

"No."

"Yes. Unless you show your draft paper to Straker, he won't be able to comment on it."

"Larry, you know what happened—"

"Cool it, Richard. You announced at Cold Spring Harbor what you thought your gene is, and you submitted your experimental protocol to the Human Subject Protection Committee, right? You're covered up to your eyeballs. If Straker's company tries it on a second time they're going to get lynched."

"I still don't trust Straker with my data before I see it in print."

"What can he do?"

Richard pauses. "I don't know, but I don't trust him."

"Richard, do you want tenure or do you want tenure? With your record, you're going to have to kiss ass. See Straker and say you'd appreciate his opinion on your draft paper. If it's as sensational as you say it is, there's no way he can fail to recommend it to CAP and to the Senate research funding committee without losing all credibility as a scientist."

"But—"

"Once you've gotten tenure and a grant you can stick a potato up his exhaust pipe, or whatever other orifice you prefer."

13

Herminda, the department secretary, says, "I'm sure Professor Straker will be along soon. Do you want to wait here or in the seminar room?"

"Here, thanks." Richard lowers himself onto an uncomfortable plastic stacking chair that faces the rear of Herminda's computer and monitor. She returns her attention to the front of the monitor, which sits on a small desk with a peeling veneered surface in a windowless office. Dark gray metal filing cabinets, battered gray metal stationery cupboards, and another veneered table cluttered with overflowing filing trays fill the rest of the office. Richard checks his watch with the clock above the sheets containing rows of passport-sized photographs of faculty and students. Both say 10:30 am.

Straker's unavailability to department faculty and students is legendary. Don Straker has other priorities. These are all designed to maintain his visibility: giving speeches at conferences, serving on committees, publishing pop books on genetics, writing for newspapers, and appearing on TV and radio. Richard had wondered why he bothered to take up a university position when he'd already set up his own research company, but Larry had put him right on that score.

"Prestige. The *LA Times* isn't going to give a weekly column to the chief scientific officer of Universal Genes Inc. But the chair of UCLA's Human Genetics Department, a member of the National Bioethics Advisory Commission, and God knows how many other committees, that's a whole different ball game. The *LA Times* can syndicate his column, and the column gives Straker marketability with publishers and TV producers."

"So why did the university hire him if he's never here?"

"Don't be so innocent, Richard," Larry sighed. "Because of his visibility Straker attracts the brightest grads and postdocs. They do good research, he puts his name as senior author on their papers, the papers get published in the best journals, that attracts big grants for the university, which attracts even more bright postdocs, and so it snowballs. The university gets a well-funded prestigious department and Straker gets even more visibility." Larry grinned. "The relationship between Straker and the university is a match made in the marketplace."

Richard grips the draft paper and steels himself to be civilized to a man he despises.

It is ten past eleven before Straker pops his head round the door. If people came to resemble their dogs, Richard wonders, then how much more does Straker resemble the animals he works on. The beady eyes and the pointed nose protruding from sunken cheeks, together with the large ears, evoke a distinctly rat-like image. "Traffic was a bitch," Straker says by way of apology.

Richard follows the small, wiry Straker as he goes through to his office while taking off his cream linen jacket. "Long time no see, Richard. What can I do for you?" he asks as he hangs up his jacket and hunches into a swivel chair by a wall-length work station below a wall-length window from which you can see Santa Monica Bay.

He shows absolutely no recognition, still less guilt, that he used his company to appropriate and patent Richard's data and, Richard is convinced, has voted against giving him tenure after Richard attacked his company at Cold Spring Harbor. "I'd appreciate your opinion on this paper I've written," Richard says through gritted teeth.

"Sure," says Straker and swivels round towards his workstation in order to stab his finger on the telephone message playback button. While the electronic voice announces the time of the first message, Straker picks up the gold-plated paperknife presented to him by his publishers to mark 100,000 hardback sales of his book, *GENES: THE GOOD, THE BAD, & THE UGLY The Ethical Guide to Genetic Engineering*. He slits open the first of the stack of letters in his in-tray.

"It involves the gene I was working on that your company people cloned," Richard says to Straker's back.

"Is that right?"

"Don," says the first message, *"it's Ralph Harlsden. You agreed to send the full sequence of the gene we think may be involved in colon cancer. It hasn't arrived. We've got stuff here on three generations of a Utah family with the disease. Your data could help corroborate or disprove some ideas we have."*

Straker swivels back to face Richard. "Harlsden wants the full gene sequence to get the edge on work that my people are doing. If he believes I'm going to send it to him he must be even dumber than I think he is."

"It shows that the gene isn't what people think it is," says Richard.

Straker waves an opened letter to Richard. "This high school wants me to give up half a day to talk to their senior students on genetic engineering as a career."

"It's not an oncogene," says Richard.

"Professor Straker", says a woman's voice, *"this is Sally Tyler at KCET. Pat would love for you to guest on Life and Times this Friday. Do phone me on 666 6500."*

"That," says Straker with a wink to Richard, "is more like it. So what is it if it isn't an oncogene?" He punches the dial buttons on his phone.

"It's a master regulator—"

"Is that Sally? Hi, this is Don Straker, Professor Don Straker. You're new at the station, right?" Straker speaks with the deep voice he uses to impress female graduate students. "Right. I'll be happy to schedule Pat's show Friday." He smirks to himself. "Terrific. I look forward to the studio car at seven and, even more, to meeting the owner of that sexy voice. Ciao."

"—that prevents neurons from aging," Richard persists.

Straker's eyes dart up from the next letter he's opened and fix on Richard for the first time. He holds out his hand.

Richard passes him the paper. In an attempt at diplomacy he has temporarily removed the paragraph that discredited the *Science* paper by Jerriman and other researchers at Straker's company.

Straker reads the abstract. He presses his intercom. "Two coffees, Herminda, and no phone calls. Not even the Pope."

Richard pretends to sip his coffee while he watches Straker read the complete paper and compare the color slides of the atrophied neurons with those of the healthy ones.

"You don't comment on Jerriman's paper," Straker says eventually.

"It's a first draft."

"Has anyone else seen it?"

"Only Lucy."

"Who?"

"My postdoc."

Straker nods. "My advice to you, Richard, is not to mention this to anyone in the university and delay submitting your paper."

Richard tenses even more.

"This is just between the two of us, you understand. I'm thinking of your best interests, Richard."

Larry was wrong. He should never have shown his paper to Straker until it had been sealed in print.

"Arcadia Pharmaceuticals," says Straker, "are one of the major players in Parkinson's disease. They're investing heavily in Alzheimer's. Take this to them and you name your own salary."

Richard takes a deep breath.

"I know a few people there," Straker says. "I'll introduce you."

What would the university Office of Technology Transfer say if it heard this? But he can't afford to alienate Straker before he gets tenure. "That's very considerate," Richard says carefully, "but I want to stay here."

Straker gives him a quizzical look.

"It's where I feel at home."

"C'mon, Richard." Straker waves his hand at his overflowing in-tray and the stacks of dissertations spread on the floor. "Do you really feel at home with all this administrative crap? At Arcadia you wouldn't have any of this, or," he smiles, "waste your time teaching pain-in-the-ass medical students who only want to become surgeons anyway. You'd have the freedom to do what you want."

"I want to be free to publish."

"I understand. I'm sure that could be arranged once Arcadia's lawyers have got all the patents tied up."

This puzzles Richard. If Straker were interested in making money for himself, surely he would have suggested his own company rather than Arcadia? "I'd prefer to develop this discovery into a treatment that is freely available to benefit the maximum number of people."

Straker pauses. "You've got to look to your own long term interests, Richard."

Could it be that Straker assumes he shared his own mercenary values and is actually trying to help him? Richard says nothing.

"What size is your lab here?"

Richard hates admitting that his failure to secure NIH grants has reduced his lab to virtually nothing. "One postdoc."

"Think what you could do with as many assistants as you need. With all the latest equipment, instead of the garbage you have to use here."

Straker is certainly doing his utmost to present a tempting prospect at Arcadia, but he doesn't seem to understand what motivates Richard.

"What else do you want, Richard? Stock options? A cut of the patent income? You tell me and I'll see what I can fix."

"I want to be known for pioneering a revolution in the treatment of aging diseases, not for patenting a discovery to make a fortune."

Straker sits back in his chair. His beady eyes examine Richard and see the unshakable determination. Then he says, "Richard, I really admire those sentiments. It's too easy to get tempted by all the big bucks offered to guys like us by the pharmaceutical corporations. I need someone like you around to remind me what medical science is really about."

He fishes out the letter from the high school. "I'll tell them that you'll give the talk to their senior students. They couldn't have a better scientist to do it." He punches his intercom. "Two more coffees, Herminda."

Richard waits for the next move, no longer sure what Straker is after.

When Herminda has left, Straker says, "Tell me what I can do to help, Richard."

Richard seizes the opportunity to test Straker's sincerity. "I'd like for you to recommend my tenure to CAP and support a grant application to the Senate Committee on Research."

"No problem. Anything else I can do for you, Richard?"

Richard hesitates. He couldn't have asked for a better response. "I *was* thinking of submitting this paper to *Science*, but—"

"Quite right. That's where it should go. The editor's a friend of mine. I'll give him a ring." He stands up and leads Richard to the door. "If you think of any other way I can help, Richard, just let me know."

Richard doesn't stop at the ninth floor, but rides the elevator down to the first. He needs to clear his head.

He wanders through the modern, brutalist Court of Sciences. His walk brings him to the Main Quad, framed by the original buildings of a UCLA campus designed to evoke the academic ideals of the Renaissance. On his left is the elegantly simple facade of the Powell Library, decorated with blind arcades and Lombardy bands. Ahead, two solid square bell towers flank the airy double-tiered portico of Royce Hall, modeled on the basilica of San Ambrogio in Milan, while to his right the Physics library is housed in Kinsey Hall, with its Romanesque arched doorways.

The people who founded this campus, Richard reflects, knew how to name buildings. They didn't call them after some crooked tycoon who made a donation in his dying years to ease his conscience; they immortalized their academic stars, from Lawrence Clark Powell the librarian, Josiah Royce the philosopher, to Edgar Lee Kinsey the physicist. That golden age of physics is now drawing to a close. The future is the age of genetic engineering, which would be trailblazed by its own stars. Richard George Trent sits down on the steps of Royce Hall to contemplate his future.

He still disapproves Straker blurring the line between basic and commercial research, but he's been wrong to suspect that Straker would try and appropriate his discovery for his own company. He wonders if he's also been wrong about Straker's company appropriating his protein sequences. Had he succumbed to occupational paranoia? Is it possible that Hal Jerriman really had been working on the same gene and Straker's quizzing him about his research disclosed that the Universal Genes scientists were ahead of him?

Whatever the truth of the matter, all that is in the past. He, not Universal Genes, had understood and demonstrated the real function of the gene. With tenure and a Senate grant, he could devote all his energies to trailblazing the genetic treatment of aging diseases, with the recognition of his peers, not big bucks, as his reward.

14

Richard drives into a bay and brings his car to a halt facing the concrete wall of the multistory parking lot. He stares at the gray surface, pitted like a lunar landscape viewed from afar, and wonders anxiously what he'll find in his voicemail or his email. Sometimes months elapsed before a journal completed its peer review process for papers submitted for publication, but he had heard that the editor of *Science* phoned one researcher on receipt of a paper he considered hot and published the following week.

He walks through the concrete wasteland and takes the elevator to the Court of Sciences. His hands are buried in the pockets of his jeans and his head is bowed, as though he were studying the cracks in the paving. He's been immersed in this mood of edgy expectancy ever since he'd sent his paper to *Science*. Don Straker's response would ensure the paper was seen straight away. This time he'd taken the utmost care to restrict himself to the facts; he just had to hope that others would appreciate the implied consequences. He can do nothing now but wait for the response that would signal whether the journal recognized the epoch-making nature of his discovery.

"Dr. Trent?"

Richard looks over his shoulder and is startled by a photographer clicking away with his camera.

"Terrific, thanks," says the shaven-headed man who has two other cameras slung over the shoulder of his multipocketed sleeveless jacket.

Could he be from *Science*? Richard wonders of the departing photographer's back. Could they be making it their cover story? Maybe he'd have to get used to this kind of treatment.

When he reaches his office he finds a message from an *LA Times* reporter asking him to return her call. For items they considered really hot, *Science* often ran trailers in major newspapers. What he *mustn't* do, he tells himself, is succumb to the temptation to tell people what he really thought the gene could do. That had nearly got him unstuck at Cold Spring Harbor. Everything was running along smoothly. He must say nothing controversial, at least not until his tenure and his grant had been confirmed.

He telephones the reporter, who asks him to summarize the key findings of his brain cell experiment and explain in simple language what benefits the general public might expect. Richard isn't going to be caught out like this only to find some sensationalist headline in the following day's newspaper; he's seen how experienced people avoided such traps. "I'm afraid I've no comment to make," he says politely.

Don Straker uses his personal cell phone rather than his office phone to speak to the chief executive of Arcadia Pharmaceuticals. "Lionel, I wanted to warn you that one of my untenured faculty has submitted a paper to *Science* claiming he's done an experiment that proves a master regulatory gene can stop brain cells from aging."

"Are you serious?" is the reply. "Get him on board and let's patent the stuff before it's in the public domain."

"I tried that, Lionel. Told him he could name his own salary at Arcadia, have whatever staff and equipment he needs, even stock options and a slice of the patent income like the deal you made with my company."

"Well done, Don."

"There's a complication, Lionel. He's not interested. He wants to make it freely available."

"What!" Lionel Upton explodes. "That would wipe millions off Arcadia's share price. You've got to stop the fucker."

"It's all under control. I've warned the editor of *Science* that it's a very flaky paper and suggested he gets an established gerontologist like Nathan Hill to review it for publication. Hill will kill it. I've also alerted an ethics prof here about what this guy really wants to do, tipped off the *LA Times*, and I'll ensure he doesn't get tenure. He'll be out on his ass with no funding to develop his work. Then you and I will have the time to see if there really is any potential in his plan to halt brain aging rather than just control symptoms of Alzheimer's, Parkinson's, et cetera."

"Don, I always knew I could rely on you."

15

Richard drives to the lab with a growing unease at *Science*'s delay in contacting him. While he is checking his voicemail Lucy comes into his office and closes the door behind her. Her face is as white as a sheet. She holds out the *LA Times* Science section. "Dorothy showed me."

On the opened page is an article headlined "Immortality Boffin Attacked by UCLA Colleague." Beneath the headline are two photographs. The first shows Professor Angela Williams, with her extra-large white-framed spectacles against her ebony skin enhancing a studious expression that is reinforced by the bookshelves behind her. The second shows Richard's startled glance over his shoulder in the Court of Sciences, as though he has been caught in some nefarious act.

"This is the woman who voted against me at the Human Subject Protection Committee," Richard says. His indignation grows as he reads the article, which cites his experiment with fetal human brain cells as an example of all that is unethical in genetics research. The article ends: "Dr. Trent declined to comment".

Richard is still fuming when his speakerphone rings. He stabs the On button.

"Dr. Trent?" says a woman's voice.

"Yes?"

"This is *The NewsHour with Jim Lehrer*. You've seen the *LA Times*?

"Yes," he says tersely.

"Would you like the chance to explain your experiment and answer Professor Williams's criticisms?"

"You bet. When?"

"Today. Jim will interview you through a link at KCET. I take it you know their studios on Sunset Boulevard?"

"No."

"Don't worry. We'll have a car collect you at, let's see, two thirty your time. OK?"

On the way to the studio Richard tries to collect himself. He needs to maintain his cool in the face of this attack and put his case calmly, restricting himself to the facts and refusing to be drawn into controversy.

After Richard signs in at KCET reception he is directed to the brightly lit cavern of Studio 2, where he is met by Penelope, an overweight young woman in jeans who wears earphones clamped over bubbly blonde hair. "Hi, I'm the floor manager. You've done this before?"

Richard shakes his head.

"Nothing to worry about. Pick your seat." She indicates a table and two chairs. We'll be using these two cameras, right? The live one will have a red light on top, right? The mics are here, out of shot." She goes to talk to one of the camera operators, and then turns round. "Oh, I nearly forgot. We have no visual link this end, right?"

Richard frowns. He hasn't a clue what she means.

"Jim and three million other people can see you, right, but you can't see him, right?"

"But—"

"His voice will come through the speakers, right? Look into whichever camera is live and pretend it's Jim. I'll do this"—she makes a series of circles with her right index finger—"if you're going on too long, and this"—she stabs the air repeatedly with the same finger—"if we need more from you, right?"

Richard sits down in this unfamiliar world. He guesses the second chair is used when the interviewer is in the same studio.

"Hi Angie!" Penelope shrieks. "Just made it!"

In bounces Angela Williams. "Hi, sugar." Today her extra-large spectacles are bright pink to match a set of extra-large pink earrings. Her beaded dreadlocks glisten under the studio lights like a Gorgon's snakes. She grins at Richard and takes the second chair.

The woman who had phoned Richard never said that anyone else would be participating in the program. He turns to the floor manager, "Excuse me—" he begins.

Penelope points towards the large wall clock with its second finger ticking inexorably towards the top of the hour. "Ten seconds and we're on air."

The red light above the door glows. The speakers to his left, like black slabs against the azure walls and ceiling, breathe Jim Lehrer's tones. "The desire to cheat death and achieve immortality is as old as the human race. It has spawned myths in every civilization, from the quest of the Sumerian king Gilgamesh to gain eternal life, through the belief of the ancient Egyptians and, later, Christians and Muslims, that they would live on through their immortal souls, to the east European folklore of the vampire, and even Oscar Wilde's neat variation in Dorian Gray.

"But now, according to one scientist, that myth can be turned into reality through genetic engineering. Dr. Richard Trent of the Department of Human Genetics at the University of California, Los Angeles claims to have discovered the gene that will give us immortality."

Richard is outraged by this exaggeration of his claim that emanates from the speakers. He tried to suppress his anger by focusing on the speakers' tightly meshed black fabric and mouthing the words "Keep calm." Out of the corner of his eye he notices a red light shining over the camera that points towards him from the other side. He turns to the camera in time to see the light go out, while Lehrer's voice continues, "Before we move on to a discussion of the ethical and social implications of this Brave New World technology, we'll get an explanation from the scientist involved. Dr. Trent, can you summarize in a couple of sentences how your work will lead to the genetic elixir of eternal youth."

He looks round to find which camera is showing a red light and sees Penelope furiously stabbing her right index finger at him.

"First of all," says Richard as his eyes swivel to find the live camera, "my work is not designed to produce the genetic elixir of eternal youth. It's designed to treat diseases."

"OK", says Lehrer's voice from the opposite side of the studio, "then help us understand what you have discovered and what diseases it will treat."

"I've discovered a gene that regulates a cell's repair and maintenance systems," Richard says. He notices the other camera moving up close. "When the gene is switched on, the cell's repair and maintenance systems operate optimally and the cell is protected from the destructive forces that tend to age it."

"Let's back up there a minute," Lehrer's disembodied voice says. "Explain how this discovery can lead to a treatment of diseases."

"In the long term," Richard says cautiously, "I hope to switch on the gene in degenerating tissue and stop further aging damage to the cells that make up that tissue."

"Can you give me a for instance, a specific disease?"

"If we can switch on the gene in aging blood vessels, I believe we can halt the build up of plaques in the vessels and so prevent further heart attacks and strokes."

"This sounds like an exciting development," Lehrer says. "Can you apply this technique to the treatment of any other diseases?"

"I believe so," says Richard, reassured by Lehrer's positive response. "If we can switch on the gene in certain regions of the brain of an Alzheimer's patient, for example, we could halt aging of the brain cells in those regions and so prevent further deterioration in the patient's condition."

"In a sentence," Lehrer's smoothly authoritative voice says, "would you say that your discovery could lead to a treatment that prevents the degenerative effects of aging in any part of the body?"

"That's what I hope."

The siren voice summons him from the depths of the dark speakers. "Including death through aging?"

"In principle, yes," Richard concedes, "but—"

"That sounds very much like the genetic elixir of eternal youth to me," Lehrer concludes.

Richard has been drawn onto the rocks by his own honesty. He just hopes that scientists are busy in their labs and not watching this program.

"We have in the studio," says Lehrer, "Dr. Leonard Morris, director of the National Institutes of Health. NIH is a major biomedical research center and also dispenses the bulk of federal funds to American scientists everywhere. Dr. Morris, just how significant a scientific breakthrough is this?"

Richard groans inside when he hears the measured tones of Morris. "Let me say straight away that we are talking about one scientist's theory, a very controversial theory. Other scientists have challenged it."

"But as I understand it," Lehrer says, "Dr. Trent has conducted experiments that support his theory. He has manipulated that gene to stop human skin cells from aging, and now human brain cells. Is that right, Dr. Trent?"

"Yes," Richard concedes again.

"So far," says Morris, "the scientific community has only been given an oral presentation of an experiment with skin cells in laboratory culture, not in the body, and nothing at all on the experiment with brain cells. I would want to study the experimental data first before commenting on this any further."

"OK," says Lehrer. "But let's assume, just assume, that these experiments do support Dr. Trent's theory. I want to explore how this development impacts society. The Reverend Luther Arbutnott is pastor of the Southern Baptist church in Birmingham, Alabama and a leading member of the Christian Coalition for Responsibility in Science. Reverend Arbutnott, how significant is this?"

The voice, with each vowel drawn out to last a week, sounds as though it were addressing all three million viewers without benefit of a microphone. "I believe this whole issue of genetic engineering is going to dwarf the abortion debate. Genetic engineers are altering God-given life forms and now, you tell me, even immortalizing human life. This as a revolt against God's sovereignty, an attempt by mankind to usurp God by taking over his creative role."

"Dr. Trent," says Lehrer, "you have something to say on this?"

"Too right," Richard replies. "We've been down this road before, from a pope condemning Galileo for saying that the earth went round the sun to biblical fundamentalists insisting that the human species didn't evolve from primates but was created by God in the Garden of Eden six thousand years ago. If religion squares up for a fight with science on this issue, science will win like it always has done."

"This is a view, Dr. Morris," says Lehrer, "that I imagine you agree with?"

At least this bible banger has forced Morris to support him, Richard thinks with relief.

"Not at all," Morris replies. "I find no conflict between my beliefs as a Christian and my beliefs as a scientist. If Dr. Trent is right about this gene, and I have to say that I'm extremely skeptical about his claims, he is assuming that switching on the gene will be beneficial. But God works through nature, and nature must have a reason for switching off this gene in most kinds of cell in the human body so that aging and death become part of the natural process."

"Can you give me a scientific reason, rather than a religious one, for this?" Lehrer inquires.

"Certainly," says Morris. "There is a strongly held scientific view that says nature's job is to keep us fit enough to produce and nurture offspring, and then send us packing so that succeeding generations can carry forward a human gene pool capable of evolutionary adaptation."

And there is an even more strongly held scientific view, Richard fumes to himself, that if you don't challenge existing assumptions and systematically test out new ideas you'll never make progress in unlocking the mysteries of life.

"If that's the scientific view," says Lehrer, "I want to turn to the ethical implications. Dr. Trent, do you consider that your work is ethical?"

"Of course it is," Richard asserts. "I can think of nothing more ethical than curing diseases."

"Angela Williams," says Lehrer, "is a professor of philosophy specializing in bioethics at UCLA, the same university where Dr. Trent works. Professor Williams, will you tell us why you came out publicly and attacked Dr. Trent's research as unethical?"

Richard braces himself for the Gorgon's claws.

The knowing grin disappears from Williams's face before the camera moves towards her and goes live. She interlocks her fingers and puts her hands on the table as she leans forward towards the camera in the manner of a family doctor dispensing advice to a well-loved patient. "Who would argue that curing diseases is unethical? Nobody. But many of us have grave reservations about what is going on secretly in genetic engineering laboratories. Many of us are worried that genetic modification of human cells interferes with what it is to be human."

She turns to face Richard. "I fear that Dr. Trent is being less than frank with us. Under questioning from Jim Lehrer, Dr. Trent was forced to admit that his research will lead to the creation of a human being who will never age or die."

"This is not—" Richard begins.

"Let's hear out Professor Williams," Lehrer says. "You'll have an opportunity to reply."

"This is not curing diseases," Williams continues smoothly to the camera. "This is not even introducing some minor genetic change. It is creating a new kind of human species, an immortal *Homo superior*. Nobody has thought through the ethical implications. Have we got the right to do this? What will these immortals do in the world with an indefinite lifespan ahead of them? What will be the relationship between this new species of *Homo superior* and us plain old *Homo sapiens*? What will—"

"I think we get the point, Professor Williams," Lehrer intervenes. "Dr. Trent?"

"This is ludicrous," Richard retorts. "It's not my aim to create a new species of immortal human, but to cure human diseases."

"Dr. Morris," Lehrer asks, "is this the type of work the National Institutes of Health should be funding?"

"Until Dr. Trent can prove that there are no adverse consequences from the genetic intervention he is proposing," Morris replies, "then it would be irresponsible for NIH to support trials with human subjects, still less approve this genetic modification getting passed on to future generations."

Richard feels betrayed, as though the high priest of medical research has sacrificed him to the barbarians in order to appease the civic elders who fund his temple. "The only way to get answers to the questions that Dr. Morris quite rightly asks is to carry out controlled scientific research, which is exactly what I'm doing."

"I say the government should bar this work of Satan right now," Arbutnott declares.

"Dr. Trent?" Lehrer asks.

Richard makes a great effort to appear conciliatory. "I appreciate that people get frightened by what is new and what they don't understand. It happens every time, whether it's artificial insemination, or in vitro fertilization, or transplants, or whatever. But we now have people walking around who wouldn't be alive today if they didn't have pig valves inside them. Whatever is new is scary, but that doesn't mean it's ethically wrong and that progress should be halted."

"Dr. Trent," says Lehrer, "given that the scientific community appears to be extremely skeptical about your claims, don't you think you should call a halt to your work until the ethical issues it raises have been explored?"

Richard feels has though he is navigating between Scylla and Charybdis: his attempts to avoid controversy and to avoid dishonesty make him appear defensive. He decides to steer a bold course. "Established medicine has no cure for the diseases of aging. The idea of not doing this research is unthinkable. It has the potential to prevent the suffering experienced by a majority of old people these days. It would be unethical to delay."

"Who is to regulate the use to which your work will be put, Dr. Trent?" Williams challenges.

"I'm content for my work to be judged by whatever body society appoints," Richard retorts. "Right now it has appointed the Human Subject Protection Committee at UCLA. That's why I submitted my experimental protocol to gain their approval before I went ahead with my research.”

Williams turns back to face the camera. “Dr. Trent has just proved my point. I was the only non-scientist on that committee, and the only woman. I was also the only member who voted against giving Dr. Trent approval. The time has come to stop scientists from regulating their own work.”

“Has the train already left the station?” Lehrer asks.

“No,” says Williams. “It’s still there. Just. But we’ve got to stop it leaving before it’s too late.”

“Thank you all very much,” Lehrer concludes.

The red light over the door goes out. “Cool, Angie,” says Penelope as she kills the spotlights. “Coming for a drink?”

“Sure, honey,” says Williams and grins at Richard.

Richard watches them follow the two camera operatives out of the studio. For a while he stays seated in the empty cavern and stares at his distorted reflection in the lens of the nearest camera. His fury that he’s been stitched up by media-savvy opponents only increases his determination to develop a safe, effective treatment for aging

diseases.

16

Richard holds the single sheet of paper between his fingers and stares at it in disbelief. This can't be happening to him. He feels strangely distant, almost as though he were watching someone else sitting at his desk in his office trying to make sense of a letter from the University of California, Los Angeles. The printed words, couched in bureaucrat-speak, advise him that, on the recommendation of the Council on Academic Personnel, with which the chancellor concurs, he is not to be offered promotion to associate professor (regular series) with tenure and, in accordance with university policy, his contract will terminate upon completion of his eighth year of service on June 30.

Larry was a member of CAP and knew he had demonstrated that his gene prevented brain cells in laboratory culture from aging when subjected to free radical attack. Straker had seen the data, had even seen the photographs of the shriveled neurons in the control sample compared with the healthy neurons containing switched-on copies of the anti-aging gene, and he had promised to support his application.

The feeling of unreality overwhelms him. Surely it is impossible that the university has fired him now, when he is on the brink of one of the greatest breakthroughs in medical science, simply because his work has been distorted on a television program?

The response to that program had been worse than he'd expected. Following the broadcast, reporters from television channels, radio stations and newspapers had besieged his office and his home. Messages filled his landline and his cell phone, emails poured into his computer every time he switched on, and his university mailbox couldn't cope with the flood of letters that arrived by the sackful. Roughly half the people who tried to communicate with him wanted a treatment that would stop them from aging and half demanded that his work be barred. Many colleagues, with the exceptions of Lucy and Dorothy, were careful to keep their distance, as though he had contracted a contagious disease. Don Straker hadn't returned his calls, and even Larry apologized that he had a heavy workload and wasn't able to meet right now.

He stares again at the letter. The only thing that he believes right now is that the tenets which had underpinned his life were false:

ability, insight, and dedication are not qualities to be valued; government funding for science research is not allocated disinterestedly in order to advance our understanding of nature and how it operates; a university is not committed to defend academic freedom. He feels like a Trappist monk who has lost his faith and is cast adrift from the support of his brethren and the guidance of his God. All he can see ahead is a forty-year void that overwhelms him with its pointlessness. For the first time he understands the feelings of those who climb to the top of high buildings or reach for a bottle full of barbiturates.

The letter slips from his fingers. Word would get out soon, it always did: gossip from members of the Council, the department chair, the secretarial staff, whoever. He can't allow Jackie to find out from somebody else, to get a telephone call of condolence that catches her by surprise; he must spare her that humiliation, at least. He doesn't expect any understanding, but he needs to tell her himself, and as soon as possible.

Still in a daze, Richard drives home along a familiar route but at an unfamiliar time of day. The traffic is different: less of it, but noisier and more aggressive. The light is strange: brighter and harsher than the misty early mornings or the softness of dusk. Even Ashland Avenue is disorienting: deathly quiet and almost deserted, apart from the flame red '69 Mustang parked outside the bungalow.

Richard pulls in behind the car and stares at the smooth, raking lines of the fastback and the simulated air scoop just ahead of the wide rear wheels. Slowly it occurs to him. As a member of the Council on Academic Personnel, Larry has avoided him because he couldn't disclose CAP's confidential decision until the chancellor had approved it. Larry must have known that the contract letters from the Academic Personnel Office went out today and he'd taken the first opportunity to come round and explain just what the devil had happened at CAP.

If Richard doesn't exactly bound into the house, he moves less reluctantly now he knows Larry is here. At least Jackie will have to be civilized in front of Larry.

The front door opens into the hardwood-floored living room with a stone chimney and fireplace to his right and, next to that, a bookcase. On the top shelf is the wedding photograph taken on the steps of St. Patrick's Cathedral: Jackie, in white designer bridal dress paid for by her doting father, is on his left, while on his right stands his best man Larry, who'd threatened to wear a yarmulke during the nuptial mass. The room is in its usual untidy state, with magazines and glasses strewn everywhere, but it is deserted, as is the dining room through the wide arch in the far wall. On a sunny day like this, Richard guesses, they are outside.

From the dining room he goes into the kitchen and out through the old scullery, which he'd converted into a laundry room, and from there to the backyard. For a moment he is dazzled by the sun shining directly in his eyes. A warm breeze wafts the scent of roses from the bushes at the borders of the short stretch of lawn, and the fluting song of a thrush comes from the juniper that shades part of the patio. Two sun loungers on the patio wear padded covers of the currently fashionable design that Jackie seemed to replace every three months.

On the table between them, near the brick barbecue that he'd built, stand two glasses. The ice cubes haven't yet melted away.

Puzzled, he returns to the kitchen and then he hears it. A grunt followed by a moan, followed by a grunt followed by a moan, followed by—. This latest betrayal strikes him with the force of a sudden blow to the solar plexus. He grabs at the kitchen table for support and sends a bottle of vodka crashing on the floor.

"What the hell!" Jackie's voice shrieks.

Richard leans heavily on the table, dazed and trying to suppress waves of nausea like a drunk on the rolling deck of a liner going nowhere in a heavy swell.

Tying her robe around her, Jackie stalks into the kitchen. She looks from Richard to the shards of shattered glass scattered amid a spreading pool of vodka on the floor tiles. "Clear up that fucking mess."

Richard stares at her contemptuous eyes, her smudged lipstick, her disheveled hair, and then over her shoulder, across the corridor and through the opened door of the master bedroom. Larry climbs into a pair of combat pants and sits down on the rumpled sheets on Richard's side of the bed to put on his boots.

Richard stands up straight. The nausea abates. Hurt, outrage, humiliation, bewilderment, anger and guilt flood through him in a chaotic dizzying confusion. How could they? Why? In his bed? Today, of all days? Had they been laughing about him? Celebrating the end of his career?

Larry pulls on a Gap T-shirt and comes through to the kitchen. Richard doesn't know how to deal with the conflicting emotions or how to handle a situation like this. He seeks Larry's eyes for answers to questions he can't articulate.

"You're never back this early Fridays," Larry says.

Richard shakes his head. "You. Of all people…"

"Look, Richard, there's no need to mention this to Sandy, right?"

As Larry begins to turn towards the door and the waiting Mustang, Richard's fist smashes into the side of his jaw.

Larry staggers back. His legs buckle as his head hits the row of saucepans hanging from a line of hooks. He slides down the wall, bringing a clatter of pans with him. Blood trickles from his bottom lip.

Jackie rushes to Larry and crouches to peer into his dazed eyes. She turns to look up to Richard. When she speaks the contempt is gone from her voice and her eyes gleam as though with pride that two men should be fighting for her. "Richard," she breathes. "What's come over you?"

He stares at her. "The realization of what I should have done long ago." He turns on his heel and storms out.

"Richard, they said you'd gone home." Lucy hovers in the doorway to his office.

Richard is seated in his swivel chair facing away from her, towards the year planner on the wall behind his desk. He's returned to the one place where he feels at home. In this cramped room he is surrounded by the comfort of his books and journals, his computer and its Internet connection that gives him access to nearly all the published research in his field, his whiteboard for playing around with ideas, his lab just down the corridor for testing out those ideas, his microscope for examining the results, and the coffee from the room next to the lab for sustaining him through the hours that slip by without his noticing. Here he has been cocooned against the world outside, free to pursue the goal that matters most to him. He stares at the year planner and counts the days to June 30. "I have no home."

His voice alarms her. It is slow and measured and devoid of all its usual warmth. She closes the door behind her, yet still he doesn't turn round from the chart. "I… I don't understand," she says.

"Jackie and I have split."

"I… I'm sorry," Lucy says, horribly conscious of the insincerity of her words, but inhibited from saying that he is well rid of the selfish bitch.

He thinks of what Jackie said that night he'd brought champagne to tell her of his breakthrough. *That postdoc of yours is going to give you the big kiss-off when they turn you down for tenure and you're out on the street.* Little did he realize that he would be literally out on the street. Was the first part of her barb going to prove equally prophetic? He can't face another betrayal. Without looking at her he says, "There's a letter on my desk you should see."

Lucy picks up the dismissal notice from the desk that separates them and the color drains from her cheeks. "Oh, my God," she breathes. "Was this the reason?"

Richard shakes his head slowly. His marriage has been dead in all but name for a long time, but he was so focused on his goal that he hadn't seen it, or he hadn't wanted to see it. His conviction that it would all come right when he made the big breakthrough had been exposed as yet another innocent belief that withered in the harsh light of reality.

Lucy steps round three piles of student scripts until she stands in front of the window, within touching distance of him. His shoulders are tensed and his hands grip the armrests of his chair. When he swivels towards her, she sees eyes hardened like chips of ice against further treachery. Lucy desperately wants to comfort him, to hug him and restore his warmth and enthusiasm, but fear of rejection stops her. She channels her frustration and helplessness into anger. "It's outrageous," she declares, waving the letter. "They can't do this."

"They've done it," he says flatly.

She yearns to help, but doesn't know how. "What are you going to do?"

"I'll fix you up with another lab head so you complete your postdoc fellowship."

"That's not what I want!" she explodes "Why do you think I brought my fellowship to your lab? When Steve Drummond and the others at the Rockefeller said it was a bad career move? That you'd become so obsessed with immortalin that you hadn't published anything for years and nobody wanted to fund your work any more?"

He is stunned into silence by Lucy's outburst; he's never seen her so passionate.

Indignation that he should think she was just like the others, deserting him when he no longer served their interests, sweeps away the self-protective barrier and out pours the feelings she'd shared only with her diary. "When I was about to give up my studies because my father wanted me back on the farm, you were the only one who cared. You made me believe I could go on to research a cure for the heart disease that killed Mom. You got grants for me, you hired me as a part-time tech, you even persuaded my father that staying on at college was what my Mom would have wanted. Why do you think I'd let you down now?"

He looks at eyes liquid with hurt and reaches out to take her hand in his. "Forgive me, Lucy. I feel kind of vulnerable right now."

She flushes at the pressure of his hand round hers and her voice softens. "There's nothing to forgive. I'm sorry I blew my top. I can't imagine what you must be going through. But we'll find another university to work on the gene," she says with all the encouragement she can convey as she squeezes his hand.

"No," Richard says with the finality of one who has already made up his mind.

"Richard, you can't give up now." She puts her hands on the armrests of his chair and crouches down so that her eyes are level with his. "Remember what you said on Labor Day in this very room? We'll be able to switch on the gene in senescent tissue and halt aging diseases in their tracks. You and I, you said. We're a team in this." She looks into his eyes and tries to transmit all the belief she has in his ability. "We can still do it," she insists.

"After the neuron experiment I'm convinced of it."

"Then why not try for another university?"

The chips of ice in his eyes haven't melted. "Because I'm going to find a cure for aging diseases and I'm not going to be stopped by a scientific establishment that resents outsiders, by pharmaceutical corporations with vested interests, or by universities that betray their principles for the sake of public relations."

Part Two

EDEN

"[Satan] with inspection deep

Considered every Creature, which of all

Most opportune might serve his wiles; and found

The Serpent subtlest beast of all the field."

—Milton, *Paradise Lost*, Book IX

18

Richard can't even see the edge of the cliff. Like the Golden Gate Bridge, it has been devoured by the chilling leviathan of fog that rolled in at dusk from the ocean, consuming everything in its path. Nothing is visible but the spectral gray mass that blankets all sound save for the occasional foghorn moaning like a tormented soul. Richard, however, is insulated from its clammy touch and bitter taste, secure in the warmth of Maria Snowe's third floor study. The ink on his signature glistens at the end of the thirteen-page agreement lying on the table between them.

Maria turns her head from the triptych of windows and a curtain of jet-black hair brushes her cheeks before falling straight to frame her imperial features and compelling eyes: each is like the shining surface water of a well that draws him down into its bottomless black depths. "I knew you'd come back."

It had gone against the grain to make those irrevocable commitments, especially the undertaking not to publish or otherwise disclose his work without the company's agreement, but he willingly set aside his scruples for the opportunity to fulfill his dream unhindered by the bureaucrats, the dinosaurs, the jealous, the ignorant, the cowards, and the cheats. Having secured the finance he needed, he is light-headed with relief. "I wasn't sure you'd still want to go ahead after the publicity from that TV debate."

"Now do you understand why I said no publication when you came to ask me to fund you?" Maria says. "I knew how the establishment would respond to your work."

"So what do we do now?"

She pours champagne into the two flutes standing on the table next to the agreement. "Not only must we not disclose the results of your work, we must hide the fact that you're doing it."

He guesses that means moving to someplace where he isn't known and questions won't be asked. He hates the idea of leaving the States, but better to carry out his research abroad than have it blocked at home. "Where to? Central America or further afield?"

"A laboratory in the Bay Area."

He almost chokes on his champagne. "Here?"

"Of course. Moving to some Third World country would simply draw attention to you. The best way to hide your work is to appear not to hide it."

"How?"

"First thing tomorrow morning you email the editor of *Science* with a letter for publication. You withdraw your paper because you've discovered an error that negates the results."

"I can't do that."

She gazes at him.

"There is no error." It was one thing not to publish his work, it was quite another to falsify scientific data. "I can't lie about the results."

"Don't think of it as lying about these early results," Maria says "Think of it as withdrawing them from the public domain in order to develop them into a treatment that will benefit society."

"To say that I've found an error when I haven't is more than withdrawing data," he protests.

She leans across the table and puts one hand over his. "Richard, I trust your judgment on science. You must learn to trust mine on how to deal with the world."

"But—"

"You have to make some big decisions. Do you want your research barred by people who don't yet understand it? Or do you want other companies with much greater resources to leap ahead and exploit your insight for their own profit, just like Straker did?" She looks into his eyes. "Or do you want to give yourself the time to do your research quietly and thoroughly, and then present the world with irrefutable proof of its benefits?"

He is acutely conscious of her hand on his. It is cool and reassuring. There is sense in what Maria says. He doesn't want his research barred, but if it isn't barred then it is open season. He can't bear the thought that Straker's company would do a deal with one of the giant pharmaceutical corporations and beat him to producing a treatment for aging diseases that they would then patent. But no researchers are going to waste several years and their reputations on a project whose champion has admitted that he was wrong and his ideas didn't work. Nor would anyone finance such a project. "I suppose I could imply there'd been a labeling error," he concludes, "and when the experiment was repeated a negative result was obtained."

"Good," she encourages. "Nathan Hill, Don Straker, and the rest will all have a laugh now at your expense. But you and I will know that you're right. And you and I will have the last laugh." She refills his glass. "That's the only laugh that matters."

He sips his champagne pensively. "How are we going to hide the fact that I'll be doing this work, right here under everybody's nose?"

"Can you devise a research project that involves similar work?" she asks. "The company can say publicly that it is undertaking this project while working on the anti-aging gene."

His prophet-blue eyes focus on infinity, not in a nebulous way, but as if he were figuring out how to get there. "I can go better than that," he says eventually. "The company will actually be doing work that I need for the anti-aging gene therapy."

"Go on," she coaxes.

He turns to her. "With brain cells in laboratory culturing solution, I inserted extra copies of the anti-aging gene activated by a bit of DNA called a general promoter. These activated copies of the gene got into enough cells to show that my idea works, but it's a crude method."

"I think I follow."

"For human gene therapy," he continues, "I need to switch on each cell's own, dormant anti-aging gene in the tissue affected by an aging disease." He warms to the plan. "The beauty of it is that most of the research needed to discover how to switch on the anti-aging in the body is identical to the research needed to switch *off* the anti-aging gene in cancer cells." He smiles at the elegance of his stratagem. "Everyone will think I've gone back to what I was doing for most of my career."

"Problem solved?"

He leans back in his chair with an air of satisfaction. "Problem solved. The public mission of the company is to research and develop a cancer therapy by switching off, or blocking the activity of, the anti-aging gene in cancer cells. Only we need know that the ultimate purpose of the research is to enable me to switch *on* the gene in normal aging cells."

"Brilliant," she says. "Richard, you're a genius." She smiles. "But then I knew that when I first saw you." She holds up her glass in a toast. "To our partnership. May it flourish and show just who is right."

He holds up his own glass. "I'll drink to that."

"Tomorrow, after you've emailed *Science* and Congressman Wilby, I want you to draw up a wish list of everything you need: people, equipment, resources, anything." Her eyes look into his, her lips are parted and wet with champagne. "My part of our bargain is to make your dreams come true."

He feels the blood pumping through his veins. What had she said at Cold Spring Harbor about having decided to change men?

She sits back, picks up her pen, and writes a note on the pad next to her. Her bottom lip toys with the barrel of the pen. "You'll stay here, with me," she muses, "until I've organized things to your satisfaction."

"I need to go back to LA first. There are some matters, personal matters, that I need to deal with."

Her unblinking eyes meet his. "Are you married?"

He found her directness slightly shocking, but exciting. "Not any more."

A hint of a smile flickers on her lips. "Children?"

"No," he says, sadly.

"Then why go back?"

"For one, I need to start divorce proceedings."

"Richard, are you a research scientist or a divorce attorney?"

Maria is right. It would be much easier to handle the divorce through lawyers, but he doesn't want to go back just to formalize the end of his marriage. He is also thinking of Lucy: Lucy, who shares his dream; Lucy, who has never let him down; Lucy, whose technical skills are matched only by her enthusiasm and dedication. She is waiting for him, longing to know if he has found a way to finance their research, and he wants to go back and celebrate the good news with her before he does anything else. "There's my assistant..." he begins.

"Assistant?" Maria raises her eyebrows. Then she focuses her gaze on him. "Richard, how important is this project to you?"

He frowns. "It's everything."

"If I enter into a partnership I commit myself fully from Day One. I expect no less of you."

He hesitates. He can't risk starting this partnership on the wrong footing. "I suppose I could deal with the matters by phone."

"Good," she says. "That's settled." She stretches dreamily and her body presses against the silk of her dress in a way that Richard finds almost unbearably erotic. "It's late." She rises and looks over her shoulder as she walks to the door. "Come."

He drains his glass. The sealing of the contract that would enable him to fulfill his life's dream flushes him with euphoria, the formidably desirable Maria Snowe makes him feel that he is the most important person on the planet, and the champagne removes his inhibitions. This heady cocktail proves a powerful aphrodisiac: the temptation to commit himself fully to this partnership is one that he would not be able to resist.

He follows the gently sinuous movement of her hips down the corridor. Imagine, he thinks, that once he had considered her unfathomable and unreachable.

She opens the door and beyond her body he sees a large double bed.

She turns and her eyes soften into an inviting smile. "I hope you find everything to your satisfaction." Beckoning him past her into the room, she glances towards the side of the bed. "If there's anything you want in the night, use the bell pull and the maid will provide."

She pauses by the door. "Happy dreams."

He watches her leave and close the door behind her.

19

Richard has no complaints about Maria's commitment to her part of the bargain. No sooner has she polished and transmitted the email he drafted for *Science* than she helps him organize his wish list. He's always regarded drawing up an inventory of personnel, equipment, and materials for grants as a chore that distracts him from what he is good at, but she sets about the task with an intensity that is palpable and a skill that is impressive. He finds that he's no time to think of anything, or anybody, else. Maria is all-consuming, but also exhilarating.

"Where to today?" he asks as he lounges in the passenger seat of her convertible, admiring the way she deftly maneuvers the car through the traffic and onto the five-lane double-decked Bay Bridge to the East Bay. He also enjoys the envious looks he gets, from truck drivers to chauffeured executives.

"A surprise," Maria says.

The bridge dips towards Oakland, passing over docks and train yards. Maria expertly threads the convertible through the stock car race for position, accelerating out of trouble rather than braking, as the bridge road merges into one of the biggest and busiest freeway intersections in the country. Instead of heading north for the science facilities at Berkeley, as he anticipates, she peels off south on Interstate 880. Soon the car exits the freeway, drops down a narrow white-tiled tunnel, and emerges onto Alameda, a long flat island separated from Oakland by a quarter-mile-wide channel. Two lefts take them down a parkway into the Marina Village Business Park, a modern development of almost identical single-story white shed-like buildings set back from the parkway or subsidiary service roads by tarmacadam forecourts. Less than forty-five minutes after leaving Seacliff, Maria pulls into one forecourt and parks by an ash tree in front of one of the redbrick columns separating large windows that form the building's facade.

She hands Richard a magnetized plastic security card for the door lock. "This week's code is 606060. Try it."

The card gives Richard access to a high security Aladdin's cave. Gleaming pale green corridors with non-slip floors lead from the empty reception area past electronically coded and locked doors that open into offices, a conference room, and two eerily spotless and silent laboratories. The large and the small lab each boast a Class 2 biological safety cabinet, incubator, and other major appliances, while subsidiary rooms hold an autoclave, a large freezer, an oligonucleotide synthesizer, a transilluminator, an autoradiograph, a flow cytometer, and all the equipment he'll need, including a totally enclosed Class 3 biological safety cabinet for handling hazardous materials. And all state-of-the-art, far superior to anything he had at UCLA.

It gets better. One security door opens into a Magnetic Resonance Imaging room, while another opens into the clothing change room and thence into an animal facility. The individual monkey cages are fairly basic, but the shining steel downdraft table and apparatus of the necropsy room would be the envy of most hospital autopsy labs, while the surgery suite might have come from one of the best pediatric hospitals.

"How?" he asks.

She shrugs. "Just another over-ambitious biotech company that went belly up."

She leads him back into one of the offices and motions him to take the executive chair behind the workstation while she sits on one of the guest chairs.

He leans back and a gas spring tilts the backrest to a relaxing position. "It's perfect. We could have the vector team, the team screening for small molecules to block expression of the anti-aging gene, and the team screening for small molecules to inactivate immortalin all working in the large, open plan lab. My assistant and I could use the small lab."

Maria smiles approvingly. "Minimizing any chance the other teams will find out precisely what you're doing."

"If only we could rent this place and manage to lay our hands on some of this equipment," he muses, "I could be up and cooking within a month."

"Start your countdown from yesterday."

He leans forward and the backrest comes with him. "Say again."

"I didn't want to risk losing it, so I took over the lease."

"The equipment?"

"The biotech company had a cash flow problem. I saved them a garage sale."

He shakes his head. "What can I say?"

"You can say, 'Maria, I'm going to use this place to kick shit in the face of Straker, Hill, and the rest'."

He rests his arms on the leather armrests and leans back. "Maria, I'm going to enjoy using this place to kick shit in the face of Straker, Hill, and the rest."

She laughs. "Let's grab lunch."

They leave the lab and walk a short way along Eden Avenue before crossing the Marina Village Parkway. "I like the name," says Maria, putting on a pair of sunglasses. "We should use it for the company."

"Marina Village?" Richard asks.

She shakes her head. "Eden."

"Eden Biotechnics?"

"Too hard edged and technical."

"Eden Genetics?"

"Too Brave New World."

"Eden Therapy?"

She turns her head to face him. "Now that I like." She laughs. "Richard, I think you and I are going to have some fun working together."

They pass by a small shopping mall with a supermarket, drugstore, bakery and greengrocer, and walk on down a grass-verged tree-lined road past buildings similar to Richard's new lab. The business park merges into a small marina. Maria leads him along a boardwalk to a waterfront deli.

They take their lunch to one of the tables by the boardwalk railing. The sun shines from a cloudless sky to transform the water of the basin into a blue-tinged rippling mirror that reflects the white hulls of the sailing yachts and motor yachts berthed along narrow piers radiating from the quay a few steps below. A gentle breeze lazily slaps the water against the quay and flutters the plastic red, white and blue pennants strung along the shrouds of many of the yachts like patriotic shark's teeth. Richard looks through the idly bobbing grove of white masts across the channel to the dozen or so unbudging skyscrapers of downtown Oakland. To the right, beyond the waterfront, rise the wooded Oakland Hills to form a skyline that meanders as far as he can see. The ambiance here is not American, more Mediterranean. The marina reminds him of that remodeled fishing village—Port Grimaud, was it called?—they had visited on their honeymoon to the French Riviera paid for by Jackie's father. Lunching with him now, however, is no eager bride but a woman with the looks and cool of a movie star.

"This place OK?" Maria asks between licking traces of low-fat Greek yogurt from her spoon.

"I think I can manage to adapt," says Richard like a stray cat that has found a new mistress who serves cream with every meal.

"Good. I'll have a press release issued by a not very competent PR firm in town. It'll say that you've left UCLA to become research vice president of Eden Therapy, a new company investigating cancer treatments. It'll be there for the record if anyone follows up on the TV program, but it won't make any waves. We'll be lost among all the other biotech startups in the Bay Area."

"Sounds good to me."

"As far as possible we want to be indistinguishable from the rest. We'll start with a lean machine." She opens a carton of lemon grass and walnut salad. "I'll operate as president, chief executive officer, and chief financial officer. Three admin staff from Snowe Software will join us. OK?"

"How will that affect Snowe Software?"

"What Snowe Software?" She sips from a glass of mineral water. "I sold the company to Apple to pay for this."

This lady, thinks Richard, is a ball of fire.

"You hire the scientists," she says.

"Right."

"We don't want to go to the wall like the previous tenants of our building, so we need a policy on salaries."

"Right," he agrees.

"I propose you pay whatever it takes to buy the people you want."

When would this woman cease to amaze him? She is relaxed, confident, witty, commanding with other people, and she makes things happen. He finishes off his salad and blesses his good fortune in securing her as his partner.

"Richard," she says, holding an apple poised in front of her mouth, "what's the first thing a regular biotech startup does?"

"It applies for a patent on all its inventions." It's not what he wants, but it is this or put himself at the mercy of Nathan Hill and the rest. "I guess," he says regretfully, "that we need a patent attorney to file for uses of the anti-aging gene not covered by Universal Genes' patent. We'll have to figure out a way to cover switching on the anti-aging gene as well as switching it off without giving away our real work."

"Uh, uh." Maria shakes her head. "No patents."

"Good," he says with relief.

"Why do you think Coca-Cola never applied for a patent?" she asks.

"I've no idea."

"A patent protects you for twenty years, always assuming some place like China doesn't simply ignore it. Coca-Cola thinks long term. So must we."

"Right," he says uncertainly.

"We bind every employee and consultant in a non-disclosure agreement that covers every conceivable piece of information owned by the company, from the color of the carpet upwards." She bites into her apple. "And that lasts for all time."

"I'll stick to getting the coffee."

When he returns he says, "Biotech startups also apply for NIH funding for their research. I guess it would look odd if we didn't."

"Good thinking." She sips her coffee. "Have the anti-cancer research teams draft NIH grant applications for you, but make sure they stand no chance of success. We don't want any transparency, still less accountability, to outside bodies."

"Right." He finishes his coffee.

"Anything more?"

"Can't think of anything right now."

"OK," says Maria, "that wraps up the first board meeting of Eden Therapy Incorporated."

Richard shakes his head. "And I always thought a committee meeting was one dumbo taking minutes and everyone else wasting hours."

Maria stands up and tosses the empty cartons and polystyrene cups into a trash bin. "Stick around for the ride."

"I intend to."

20

Beneath the cheerful exterior she maintains to hide her feelings, Lucy is in turmoil as she stands just beyond the Domestic Arrivals barrier at San Francisco airport after her flight from Los Angeles.

Apart from a brief, cryptic phone call to say that he'd obtained funding for his research, she's heard nothing from Richard until an envelope arrived with a United Airlines ticket and a scribbled note saying that he wanted her to join him at his new company. At first she'd been sustained in her wait by recollections that dominated her waking hours and her dreams: the way that Richard gazed at her over the birthday dinner she made for him; the magical evening at the Italian restaurant when their shared elation over the successful neuron experiment drew them close—until mention of his wife broke the spell; and his holding her hand the day the university fired him and he left that bitch of a wife. She can still feel the warmth and firmness of his grip, hear the unshakable determination in his voice, and see the frightening intensity in his eyes when he resolved to find a cure for aging diseases. That recollection caused a thrill mingled with apprehension that touched the essence of her womanhood. As the days following his telephone call passed, however, and she heard nothing from him, the flush of his memory had to fight fears that eroded her confidence.

She'd agonized over the possible reasons he hadn't contacted her or responded to messages she'd left on his cell phone. Was he ashamed that he'd joined a company after all he had said about the commercialization of genetics research? What kind of company was it? Who was financing it? And why? Had the funding fallen through and he was too depressed to call her? Had he already begun the next phase of his research and was so engrossed that he'd forgotten about her? Had he found an assistant more skillful?

When the letter came she rushed out and spent most of that month's salary on a linen suit, a blouse, and a pair of shoes. Now she wonders if she looks ridiculously overdressed as she stands by the barrier while the world bustles by in denims, shorts, tracksuits, and sweat pants. She'd studied the note carefully and found no signs of endearment, not even an affectionate cross after the word "Richard".

Had she read more into his holding her hand than she should? She knew his marriage was over. She knew he treasured her support when the entire world seemed to have betrayed him. But were his feelings no more than appreciation of a loyal assistant?

And what of her own feelings? Her longing to be with him, her fears at his absence, her inability to concentrate on anything else… Was it love, or had she let gratitude to him for enabling her to pursue a career in science, recognition of his brilliant mind, admiration for his principles, and the closeness of their working relationship inflate in her own imagination like some adolescent fantasy?

She glimpses his untidy thatch of chestnut hair among the crowd, and the anxious suspense of not seeing him turns into an anxious joy at his presence. This isn't fantasy on her part. But what does he feel?

He eases his way past a Chinese family, neat and disciplined compared with the waving and noisy Californians who spot arriving relatives. She dare not risk rejection by overfamiliarity. As the panic inside grows she composes her features into a cheerful smile and waits for him to give the lead.

As he approaches, his craggy features crease into a grin and his eyes gleam. He holds out his arms and she is flooded with relief that her emotions are reciprocated.

He grasps her by the shoulders and kisses her briefly on each cheek. "Great to see you, Lucy." He bends down to pick up her briefcase. "Wait till you see what I've got to show you," he says before turning towards the exit for the parking garage.

Lucy stares at the silver BMW 4 Series convertible and hopes her demeanor doesn't betray the dismay that has driven the hope from her like air from a deflating balloon. He hasn't even noticed the suit she is wearing or her new hairstyle.

She sinks into the passenger seat while he says with boyish enthusiasm, "Strap yourself in tight. The gas pedal's more like a fast forward button on a video recorder."

"This is what you want to show me?"

Her voice clearly has betrayed her feelings because he twists round to face her. "Of course not." He tries to read her expression, but it is partly hidden by hair whipped by the wind. "It's not what you think. There's no danger of me turning into a Straker." He grins. "This is just a toy, but it shows how much Maria values our work."

Lucy stares straight ahead. Who is Maria?

He parks outside the single-story red-brick-and-glass facade of his lab in the Marina Village Business Park. "This is what I want to show you."

She climbs out of the BMW and looks at the new signboard. Against a black background, gold letters proclaim "Eden Therapy Inc", and above that is a stylized gold caduceus.

"Maria's idea," he says as he joins her. "Don't you think it's brilliant?" In Maria's version of the oldest symbol of medicine in the country, the two serpents intertwined round a winged staff take the form of the DNA double helix coiled round the tree of knowledge.

Lucy follows Richard inside where he proudly shows her round the laboratories before leaving her in the light-oak conference room to read a folder of documents. She watches him disappear through a door marked President and Chief Executive Officer.

Engrossed in thought, Maria is reclining in her executive chair when Richard enters her office. She presses a lever on the armrest to tilt the chair upright and her eyes focus on him. "I'm still convinced you should hire a new assistant, Richard," she says. "Someone who doesn't know the ultimate purpose of your research."

He frowns. "We agreed I would choose the science staff."

"Right," she concedes. "But I do think it'll be safer if you choose someone who doesn't pose a threat, someone who couldn't disclose your real work and get it barred."

Richard doesn't want to argue with Maria, but he is determined to honor his promise to Lucy and repay her faith in him. "Lucy will never betray me."

Maria raises her eyebrows. "Let's have her in and find out."

When Richard opens the door and says, "Lucy, come on through," Lucy Jonnsen carefully collects the documents she's been studying and prepares to meet the woman called Maria.

What strikes her first are the woman's eyes: large, black, unblinking, and gazing directly at her. Lucy's dismay increases when she sees how young and attractive Maria is. Relaxed in her executive chair, slender bronze arms laid confidently on the armrests, Maria doesn't have the open, cheerleader good looks of Jackie Trent, but she possesses a strange, almost mysterious, beauty that Lucy finds daunting. It makes her conscious of how unattractive and unsophisticated she feels; she has never been less at ease since she first arrived in Los Angeles from Deuel County, South Dakota.

"Maria," Richard says, "this is Lucy. I couldn't manage without her."

Lucy's heart leaps at his introduction.

"Lucy," Richard says, "Maria Snowe is president of Eden Therapy."

Maria rises from behind her workstation to offer Lucy a cool, firm handshake. Not once do her eyes leave Lucy.

Lucy glances down, but can't see whether or not Maria Snowe is wearing a wedding ring. "Pleased to meet you, Mrs Snowe," she blurts out cheerily, hoping to hide her nervousness.

"It's not 'Mrs Snowe'," says Maria. For an instant she appraises Lucy like the number one wife examining the latest addition to the harem and then she warms into a smile. "It's Maria. Pleased to meet you, Lucy. Take a seat."

It isn't the tone of Maria Snowe's voice, or what she says, but something disturbs Lucy: an intuition that this woman has her own agenda. Lucy sits down on the chair facing the workstation while Richard joins Maria on the opposite side.

"Do you have any questions, Lucy?" Maria asks.

A whole raft of questions occurred to Lucy when she'd studied the documents Richard had given her, but one troubles her most of all. She turns towards her mentor. "Richard, this here." She indicates a clause that occupies a full page of the contract. It accepted unlimited liability for reparation in the sum of all future loss of company earnings estimated by the president of Eden Therapy Incorporated that may result from violation of the employee's undertaking not to disclose any information whatsoever about the company or its activities.

"Standard non-disclosure clause," Maria says airily.

"Does this mean we don't publish papers in scientific journals?"

"Bright girl."

This confirms Lucy's intuition. Even a company like Straker's permitted its scientists to publish. Her nervousness is overtaken by a compulsion to find out just why Maria Snowe is financing Richard's research. "Is Eden Therapy planning to monopolize a secret treatment for aging diseases in order to make a fortune?"

"Lucy." Richard's eyes show surprise and hurt. "How on earth can you think that?"

"Because you always say that publication of experimental data is essential for progress in science."

"Richard was hosed when he was at UCLA," says Maria. "I do not intend to let that happen here."

Lucy turns back to Richard. "But this clause says that I may not disclose anything about my work, even to other employees, without permission from the president of the company."

"Lucy," Richard reasons, "you saw how people reacted to that television program. They want to bar our research." He shuffles in his seat. "To prevent that I've implied to *Science* there was a flaw in the research that nullified the results."

Lucy's brow creases in puzzlement. "That's not true. There's no flaw."

"I know, but..."

"But a little inaccuracy can save a lot of hassle," Maria says.

"The point is," Richard amplifies, "that it's essential our work isn't barred just because people don't understand it yet. So, as far as everyone here is concerned, we're researching a cancer therapy. If nobody knows what we're doing, then nobody can leak out information that'll have people like Angela Williams and the preacher demanding we're closed down."

This is worse than she'd feared. What is Richard asking her to do? She composes herself and looks into his eyes. "I can't lie about the work I'm doing."

Maria glances at Richard and then turns her attention to Lucy. "No need," she states. "Say nothing." Her smile has the warmth of winter sunshine glinting on a coffin lid. "Just like it says in the contract."

Lucy avoids her gaze. "How long do you plan to keep the research secret, Richard?"

"Once we've got incontrovertible proof that we can halt aging-induced diseases, then we can publish the results and society can make an informed decision whether or not it wants to use the treatment."

Lucy remains silent while she weighs up all the arguments. Then she looks at him. "Richard, are you really sure about this?"

"Trust me, Lucy."

In the end it is her heart that sways her decision. "OK," she concedes.

"We shall double your present salary," Maria says.

"Salary is irrelevant," Lucy retorts. "Richard and I aren't interested in making money. We want to continue our partnership to develop treatments for diseases."

"I see." Maria gazes at Lucy and then at Richard. "Is this purely a professional relationship we have here? If it goes further than that, I fear the conflicts of interest would render Lucy's employment untenable."

The inner calm that descended after Lucy made her decision to accept the non-disclosure clause is engulfed by a turbulence greater than before. For a moment Richard hesitates and then, with an apologetic glance towards her, he turns to Maria. "It's purely a professional relationship."

Maria looked at Lucy and raises her eyebrows quizzically.

Lucy fears that this woman can hear her rapid heartbeats and see the tell tale flush of her cheeks. Lucy understands obsession. And she recognizes that Richard's obsession is to develop his discovery into a pioneering treatment that could relieve suffering for millions of people. He needs her practical skills, and she mustn't allow her feelings for him to get in the way of the dream they share. She stares at Maria. "Of course it is."

Good," Maria smiles. "I think it's important that we establish our ethical parameters."

21

The drive back to the airport is charged with unspoken thoughts. When Richard tries to explain his reply about their relationship, Lucy changes the subject and talks about the practicalities of winding up her work at UCLA so that she can begin at Eden Therapy as soon as possible. For the rest of the journey she stares straight ahead and, apart from single-word responses to his attempts at bridge-building, she remains silent. At the curb in front of the departures level she takes her briefcase, bids him goodbye, and walks through the automatically opening glass door without a backward glance.

Richard drives slowly through the evening gloom straight to Seacliff. He pulls into the garage by Maria's house and sits in the car. Maria's ultimatum had caught him by surprise. He feels guilty about saying that his relationship with Lucy is purely a professional one. Certainly he's never had a better assistant: her dedication matched his own and her practical skills complemented his theoretical approach, but this symbiosis had developed into something much more. Lucy shared his dream and his values, his triumphs and his setbacks, and she cared for him in a way that Jackie never had. He fondly recalls the evening she made dinner for his birthday, and how close they'd been when celebrating the success of the neuron experiment. At his bleakest hour, when he'd been derided by the scientific establishment, pilloried in the media, and sacked from his job, she had stood by him. It is far more than gratitude that he feels for her. He wanted her to understand that he'd denied all this because he needed Maria's funding but didn't want to lose Lucy as his assistant. Yet Lucy hadn't wanted to talk about it; on the contrary, she'd brushed it aside as of no consequence. His penetrating insight, he concludes ruefully, doesn't extend from science into the minds of women.

He leaves the garage and enters the house by the front door. Alvaro appears. "Would you like a drink before dinner, Dr. Trent?"

"Too right," Richard replies. "A large bourbon, please. No water." He goes through to the first-floor reception room. The sound of his entrance must have alerted Maria's mother, for she scurries into the room with an excited whimper and asks, "Now?"

"Now?" is a question that Carmen repeated often. It meant everything and nothing. Now could she be given food? Now could she watch television? Now would Maria give her a cuddle? Richard looks from the expectant face to the shoe in one hand and the spanner in the other, and tries to figure out which Now? is intended. Alvaro comes in with a drinks tray and puts it down on a side table. He gently removes the shoe and the spanner from Carmen's grasp and gives her a glass of lemonade. "La Madre will be home soon," he says encouragingly, as though to a child. She smiles. It is the tone of voice she responds to, not the words. Alvaro serves Richard his bourbon and departs.

Richard watches as Carmen carefully pours a portion of her lemonade onto each of the potted plants by the window. Maria was right: he must be thoroughly professional in his work. Any man could indulge in the vagaries of personal relationships, but only one man could develop an effective treatment for the diseases of aging like Alzheimer's. Nothing must distract him from his goal.

After resigning her position at UCLA, Lucy returns to San Francisco on her motorbike, with all her possessions in panniers either side of the rear wheel. Maria's secretary offers her a one-bedroom company apartment ten minutes' drive from the Marina Village Business Park, but she refuses to be beholden to that woman. She opts instead for the small apartment at the top of her Uncle Henry and Aunt Chisako's house in Nihonmachi, the Japanese neighborhood on the slopes of San Francisco's Pacific Heights. Simply furnished with a pine wardrobe, a desk, an office chair, and a folded futon that serves as floor-level sofa, the main room is all white. Apart from the vase that Chisako fills with a fresh flower arrangement every day, the only decorations are a hanging scroll with a single vertical line of Japanese characters on one wall and on the opposite wall a picture of a *karesansui* rock and gravel garden designed for Zen meditation.

Once Lucy closes the window and cuts out the sing-song of Japanese chatter plus the smoky barbecue smell that drifts up from the *yakitori* stall on the narrow street three stories below, it becomes a haven of tranquility. And tranquility is what she needs to try and make sense of her conflicting emotions. Sitting down at her desk after her first week at Eden Therapy, she takes out her red leather-bound diary, picks up her pen, and chews the end of it while she struggles to put her thoughts into words. Finally she writes:

"At times I find it almost unbearable to treat Richard as though he's simply a professional colleague. The drive back to the airport was a nightmare. I just hope Richard didn't see how upset I was. How long can I keep up the pretense? I did think that Richard felt the same way, but now I'm not so sure. For the most part he's totally focused on his work, but sometimes he seems bewitched by Maria Snowe. Why does he always have to fall for beautiful, selfish women? I don't want him to get hurt like he did with his wife.

I don't trust this woman. Despite appearing ever so friendly, I'm sure she didn't want me to take this job. Is it because I argued for the open publication of experimental data? Because I asked if the company intended to monopolize use of the anti-aging gene for profit? Why did she make it a condition that my relationship with Richard is purely a professional one? I don't buy the ethical argument. Obviously I can't compete with her in the boobs and sophistication stakes, so what is she afraid of? She's not dumb. Does she sense that the bond between Richard and me is much deeper than physical attraction?

I don't know. I'm still confused. Richard must hate working in a commercial environment as much as I do, and hate the secrecy even more. But if he feels this is the best way to develop a treatment for aging diseases then I accept his judgment.

I guess all I can do is devote myself to finding a way to switch on the body's own anti-aging genes in diseased tissue. If we succeed in preventing further degeneration, we can make our work public and then we'll no longer be dependent on her funding."

She chews some more on her pen and then completes her entry:

"I'm prepared to come second to Richard's commitment to pioneering a cure for aging diseases, but not second to her."

Having disparaged commercial research all his professional life, Richard comes to appreciate its advantages. He takes a breakfast tray of juice, toast, and coffee through to the rear terrace of the newly remodeled white clapboarded house that Maria acquired for him. An early morning swim in the twenty-five-yard pool between the back lawn and the fruit trees of the two-acre plot has refreshed him. The surrounding Oakland Hills insulate him from the bustle of San Francisco and gives him a sense of tranquility.

He eats his breakfast and reflects on how Eden Therapy is taking shape. At academic laboratories in which he'd worked he had to tolerate overcrowded chaos presided over by people who were good scientists but incompetent managers. Pop music blared from transistor radios in the labs. Researchers complained of outdated equipment. Cooperation between research teams frequently degenerated into disputes about allocating credits in published papers, while the intended cross-fertilization of research teams sharing the same laboratory foundered on complaints of hogging limited incubator space by tissue culture dishes of dubious importance. Coherence of research programs remained a fiction in the pages of university prospectuses when autonomous lab heads veered off in the direction prompted by the new idea they'd had that Monday morning. Teaching, grading papers, and evaluating dissertations always seemed to intervene at crucial times. Targets and schedules were alien concepts proposed in vain by university bureaucrats who didn't understand the creative mind.

Richard believes in the power of the creative mind, but he also believes in focusing that power to achieve a specific goal. At Eden the quiet, spacious laboratories are designed for one purpose only: to help him develop a gene therapy for aging diseases that would rewrite the textbooks. Guided by Maria's management expertise, he has set clear objectives for each of the staff he hired. They accepted the objectives because they presented an intellectual challenge, because the company provided every facility they needed to meet that challenge, because no distractions intruded, and because they were well rewarded. They also knew there was no safety net. In a small commercial startup there was no teaching or administrative work to fall back on if the research wasn't going well: if they failed, the company failed, taking their research, their salaries, their company cars, and their company houses with it.

Maria had created a stimulating and productive environment for him that is outstripping his expectations. Two things, however, blight his satisfaction. The first is Lucy's attitude towards Maria. True, Maria had suggested he employ a new assistant, but once he'd made it clear he was going to appoint Lucy, Maria couldn't have been more friendly towards her. Lucy, however, didn't reciprocate; she didn't seem to appreciate just how much help Maria was providing for them.

The second thing is that, in the privacy of her office, Maria hinted at an impatience that she never showed in her public face at the monthly staff progress meetings. Richard found himself repeatedly explaining that Lucy was engaged in a lengthy and laborious process of elimination: first to identify the precise sequences of DNA upstream and downstream of the anti-aging gene that regulated the gene, and then use that data to track down the protein that is repressing the gene in human cells. There was no way to predict how long this process would take, and only when it was complete could they construct a DNA sequence that would block the protein and so switch on the gene. But Maria wasn't interested in technical explanations, only the bottom line.

It was after one such meeting with Maria that Richard returned to the lab wondering just how long Maria would be prepared to pump in the money that sustained his research. He found Lucy waiting for him with a lopsided grin on her face.

"You haven't…?" Richard hardly dares complete the question.

"See what you think."

Richard checks the data and examines cells through the microscope. Lucy's dedication and painstaking skills have at last paid off. He gives her a huge hug of relief.

Lucy's face lights up: although their personal feelings had to be put on hold until Richard completed his work at Eden Therapy, the warmth of his hug tells her that their bond is unbreakable.

Immediately Richard phones Maria and asks her to come to the lab.

When Maria pushes open the lab's swing doors, she sees Richard and Lucy standing next to each other, positively radiating joy. For an instant the look she gives them might have been that of an abbess catching one of her nuns *in flagrante delicto* with her chaplain, and then she smiles. "Well?"

"Lucy's cracked it!" Richard announces. He guides Maria to the microscope.

Maria peers down the phase contrast microscope and sees just what had prompted Richard's insight on that Labor Day evening: healthy fibroblasts like dark gray emaciated sardines edged in white and carefully packed with no overlap to form a single layer on the bottom of the tissue culture dish.

"Instead of inserting extra copies of the anti-aging gene with a crude activator like I did before," Richard explains, "Lucy's succeeded in switching on each cell's own repressed anti-aging gene so that it's under the control of its own regulator. That means it produces just the right amount of immortalin to respond to the cell's repair and maintenance needs." He puts an arm proudly round Lucy. "It's the breakthrough that's essential for using the gene in humans."

"Well done, Lucy. The three of us will have a celebratory meal this evening. I'll go and make the arrangements." When Maria reaches the lab door she stops and turns. Looking at Lucy she says, "You remember, of course, that under the terms of your contract you may not mention this to anyone else."

The joy leaves Lucy's face. She looks up at Richard. "What do I say at the monthly staff progress meeting, Richard? You promised me that I wouldn't have to tell any lies."

"You don't have to lie, Lucy," he says encouragingly. "You just say nothing."

Maria smiles.

22

The brass nameplate shines in the September sun before falling into shadow as the casket is eased into the mausoleum. The sweet smell of burning copal resin rises in blue-gray swirls from one of three brightly painted gourds standing on the black marble structure. Alvaro's deep drumbeat chant of strange-sounding words fill the air. The powerfully-built Maya, transformed from factotum to priest dressed in white high-collared shirt and pantaloons, picks up a gourd containing a pile of thin, round, unleavened corn breads, holds it aloft with both hands, and then kneels to place it inside the gaping rectangular hole of the opened mausoleum. He repeats this ritual next with a gourd containing a colorless drink made from the bark of a balce tree fermented with honey, and finally with a smoking gourd of incense.

He stands, turns towards the sun, and raises his arms, with fingers stretched as if to touch the golden disc. Three times, each on a higher note than before, his barrel-chested voice intones the same rhythmical phrase, first imploring, then stating and, in the crescendo, commanding the heavens. His voice resonates round the hillside cemetery of white stone crosses and granite angels before silence falls, as though the birds had stopped their singing to listen for a reply. Alvaro lowers his arms, bows his head, and turns to the two mourners. The mortician's assistants who had borne the casket watch uncomfortably from a distance while they wait to seal the mausoleum.

During the last months Maria had stopped coming into Eden so that she could care full-time for Carmen: washing her, dressing her, taking her to the toilet, and seeing to all her needs as a mother would for a helpless baby, which in many ways Carmen was. Every Friday lunchtime Richard went to brief Maria. He found the visits increasingly stressful. Carmen shuffled towards him and seemed to fix him with her eyes, and then she shuffled on past, as though the signal from eye to brain no longer worked. As Carmen's condition deteriorated, Maria's questions about the progress Richard was making became ever more pressing. His repeated reminders about the pace of medical research offered little comfort as he watched Carmen bump into doors and chairs and whimper with terror at this loss of spatial awareness. On one visit Richard saw a flash of lucidity, when Carmen suddenly cried "What's happening to me?" Sometimes frustration took over and she hit out savagely at Maria. Alzheimer's was a disease that robbed Carmen not only of her dignity but also of her personality: the essence that was Carmen had died, but her body was taking longer to die. Richard tried to imagine what Maria must be feeling. For the most part she maintained the composure and control that the outside world saw, but occasionally he noticed the mask slip, as when Carmen slumped to the floor, eyes closed and immobile as though shutting out the strange and terrifying world she no longer understood, and wailed. A look of horror crossed Maria's face; she turned and looked at the mirror on the wall.

Now that the disease has finally triumphed, Maria stares at the casket inside the mausoleum. She stands motionless, her aura of confidence replaced by such desolation that Richard feels powerless to comfort her. But behind the grief he senses something else that he can't identify.

Alvaro's hands clasp hers with gentle reassurance. "Have no fear, Madre. Carmen rests in the bosom of Hunab-Kú. She will be reborn again, bright of eye, fleet of foot, and quick of mind. Just as she was before."

Maria nods. Alvaro releases her hand and goes to the car.

Excluded from this pagan sodality, Richard waits uneasily on the gravel path between the graves. He is at a complete loss to understand how such an intelligent and educated woman can find consolation in a primitive rite like this, but when he turns to her, groping for the right words, he sees no comfort in her eyes.

"Carmen is Maya," she says. "Do you think I'd let the Catholic priests claim her for their Church?"

"I…I never thought about it."

"Was your Christian God that Carmen prayed to every day able to spare my father from cancer and her from Alzheimer's?" she demands. He is taken aback by the bitterness in her voice, but before he can answer that he had long since abandoned belief in God, she spins on her heel and strides towards the car.

The bright early morning sun slants through Maria's office window and lusters the black hair that frames her features. She sits at her workstation, below a photograph of a Mayan pyramid formed by a stack of ever smaller square stone terraces; from between two monumental serpent heads at its base, a stone stairway climbs one face to the uppermost terrace on which was built a temple to the reborn god Kukulkán, the Plumed Serpent.

"The vector team have delivered," says Richard triumphantly. "They've constructed a retroviral vector that will enable Lucy and I to deliver the anti-aging gene to any kind of cell."

Maria leans forward. "When do we start human trials?"

Richard pauses, thinking how best to reply. After the death of her mother, Maria continued to stay at home. Richard feared that she had lost faith in him and in Eden Therapy. His telephone call to say they had made a breakthrough in vector production had brought her back, and he is anxious to maintain her interest and her funding, but he hadn't planned to go straight to testing the gene therapy on humans.

"We haven't run safety tests," Lucy says without hesitation.

Richard casts a warning look in her direction. Maria had proposed a meeting between the two of them to discuss future plans, but Richard had brought along Lucy. She would have to incorporate the gene switch in the vector in order to switch on the anti-aging gene.

"My question was addressed to Richard," Maria says.

"Lucy's right," he says.

The smile that Lucy gives Maria lacks the spontaneity and warmth that Richard found infectious; it was a smile of satisfaction.

Maria looks at Richard. "How come?"

"We've only tested the gene inducer and the vector in the lab. We don't know if there'll be any side effects in humans."

"Isn't that the point of human trials?" Maria asks.

The realization of why Maria is so anxious to begin human trials strikes him like a bolt of lightning. Her eyes betray what he had failed to identify at the cemetery; no longer masked by grief and anger, they show fear: a premonition of her own fate. Everything falls into place: her remark at Cold Spring Harbor about being forced to take stock of her life, her querying the point of being wealthy if you suffer from a horrible fatal disease, and her throwaway remark about forty being too late to make major decisions. He was blind not to have seen it before: beneath that self-assured exterior Maria must be afraid that she had inherited the dominant gene for early-onset Alzheimer's disease. His first instinct is to offer genetic screening. But what could he offer if the screening proved positive? Would she withdraw her funding if he didn't proceed to human trials?

"Richard, we can't do it," Lucy insists. "It's not ethical."

He and Lucy had developed an almost telepathic understanding about their work. He knows what is in her mind right now: it is one thing to hide the truth about what he is doing, it is a different matter entirely to subject patients to unapproved and possibly fatal risks. "We need to test on monkeys first in order to see if there are unanticipated side effects, he says."

From the look that Maria gives her, Lucy is left in little doubt what Maria thinks of her ethical stance.

23

The van from the Regional Primate Research Center at the University of California, Davis delivers six monkey transfer boxes, each about twenty inches by twenty inches by two feet, with ventilation holes in the longer sides and a carrying handle on top. Richard signs for them and feels no guilt at falsifying the purpose of his research. Elderly monkeys that were no longer useful for breeding were often sold by the Center for Cancer Research; the experiment he planned would subject them to less stress.

The animal house manager they had hired, a swarthy Mexican called Miguel, carries the boxes through to the monkey room in Eden's animal facility where two steel-barred single cages, not much larger than the transfer boxes, stand on each of three tiers in a rack.

"Shall I sedate it?" Richard asks as Miguel puts a lab mask over his pockmarked face and picks up one of the transfer boxes.

Miguel peers through the ventilation holes at the monkey, which fills most of the box. "Is no need. Young males give plenty trouble, sure. But these? No problem."

After opening the door of one of the cages on the top tier, he undoes the bolts on the door of the transfer box, lifts up the box with one hand to the opened cage door, slides up the transfer box door, and tips the monkey into the cage. "Adelante!"

The old female rhesus macaque stumbles into the cage and grabs onto the bars of the far wall for support. She lowers her haunches to sit on the floor, but keeps hold of the rear bars with her human-like hands. Miguel slams the cage door shut. Slowly the monkey turns her head and looks over her shoulder. Two large sad eyes stare out from a long pink face with a flat nose above a large upper jaw and a mournful mouth. Graying brown fur surrounds her face, from her low brow ridge round to cover half her pouch cheeks and the underside of her jaw.

Miguel fills the other cages with equal ease. Two of the old macaques tentatively explore their small cages while the others squat down, resigned to whatever fate awaits them.

Three people remain in the conference room after Eden Therapy's monthly progress meeting ends, the only people who know that the monkeys are not going to be used for testing a gene switch designed to kill cancer cells as Richard announced at the meeting.

Richard looks across the table to his left, at the beautiful and dynamic Maria; since their strategy meeting he'd tried to imagine her fear of being reduced by early-onset Alzheimer's to padding round her house in bewildered anxiety, unable to communicate or to grasp the concepts of bathing, dressing, and using the toilet.

He turns to his right. "Lucy, I want us to start on the monkeys this afternoon."

Lucy's brow creases. "Richard, you know how I feel about experimenting on animals."

"I understand," he says. "I hate animal research myself, but there are times when it's the only option, just like we had no choice but to test the gene on fetal brain tissue."

Maria watches this interchange carefully.

Lucy's expression doesn't alter. "The fetus was already dead. I want to help, and I'll do the benchwork, but I can't work on a living creature."

"You argued that it was unethical to move straight to human trials," he reasons. "If we don't test it on humans, what's the alternative to testing on animals?"

"I don't know," Lucy says unhappily, "but I do know that I can't do it."

"Well, Lucy," Maria says, "I'm sure we all understand how you feel. I guess that just about wraps up this research strategy meeting. If you'll excuse us, Richard and I do have to deal with some company matters."

With a sideways glance at Richard, Lucy gets up and leaves.

"What company matters?" Richard asks.

"Why is your assistant unwilling to assist you?"

He shrugs. "Many scientists won't experiment on animals. In Lucy's case I guess it's because she had a particularly traumatic experience as a child: her father made her strangle chickens she'd been keeping as pets."

"That's unfortunate," Maria says, "but I guess Lucy's served her purpose by helping you develop the gene inducer. Now we need to get you a new assistant who doesn't have a hang-up about working on animals."

"No," Richard retorts immediately.

"Why not replace her with someone who *is* willing to experiment on monkeys?"

"I need Lucy for the analyses after I've treated the monkeys," Richard replies. No sooner has he uttered the words than he feels guilty at hiding the fact that Lucy is much more to him than simply a skilled colleague.

Maria gives him a quizzical look. "Is that the only reason you need her?" She taps the bottom row of her teeth with a pen while she thinks. Then she says, "Richard, what's involved in assisting you?"

"I need an extra pair of hands to pass me instruments and reagents when I ask for them, and to record data in a lab book."

"You tell your assistant what to write down?"

"Right."

"Then *I'll* assist you."

"You?"

"The fewer people who know what you're doing the better."

The wide white door to the MRI room is decorated with two black-edged yellow triangles containing black symbols that warn of magnetic fields and radio frequency emissions, plus half a dozen red rings enclosing black symbols slashed by red diameters that prohibit metallic objects, pacemakers, jewelry, and credit cards: ferromagnetic objects would be sucked into the strong magnetic field that, combined with low-energy radio waves, produce images of any cross-section of a body, including tissue hidden behind bone.

After he and Maria have changed into surgical greens, Richard opens his medical case in the MRI anteroom and fills a hypodermic syringe from a vial of ketamine. He tilts the first transfer box so that the monkey is thrown against one side. Looking through the dime-sized ventilation holes to identify a leg, he jabs the needle of the hypodermic and injects.

Inside the MRI room Richard opens the transfer box. The monkey is conscious, with its eyes open, but rigid. He lays it on a platform that points into a circular tunnel running through a white metal cube seven feet high.

Richard shaves the inside of the monkey's left thigh, inserts a catheter into a vein, tapes it in place, and connects the catheter to a line from the dispenser of gadolinium, an image-enhancing dye, in the control room. "Make sure the line doesn't get snarled," he says to Maria as he turns the monkey on its back and places its head in a stereotaxic frame at the end of the platform. Gently he screws horizontal white plastic bars from this cubic plexiglass frame into the monkey's ear canals, and then maneuvers a small platform running at right angles to these bars so that a white plastic bar moves into the roof of the monkey's mouth and the points of a V-shaped fitting rest on the lower orbital ridge of each eye. "It doesn't feel a thing," he assures Maria.

She shrugs.

He makes some fine adjustments, reading out the calibrations for Maria to note so that this particular monkey can be placed in precisely the same position the next time it is scanned, and then covers the monkey's body with a plastic insulating blanket to keep it warm.

After closing the MRI room behind them, Richard and Maria go to the control room where Richard switches on the machine. They watch through the large radio frequency-screened window as the MRI machine hums and the platform edges forward into the circular tunnel. The calm is shattered by a noise like the continuous burst of machine gun fire, followed by a respite of metronomic swishes that suddenly give way to an ear-splitting pneumatic drill, and then another deceptive lull of metronomic swishes that is broken by more machine gun fire as the machine makes magnetic resonance images of preprogramed cross-sections of the monkey's head and body. These show up on the computer monitor as X-ray-type images of the monkey's brain, liver, lungs, kidneys, spleen and, finally, a whole body image.

Half an hour later the noise stops and the platform comes to rest. Richard switches on the intravenous flow of gadolinium and begins another scan.

After Richard scans all six monkeys he monitors their activity patterns, which Maria records. He then infuses them with a vector solution.

A week later Richard extracts blood samples from the monkeys and takes the samples from the animal house to his lab.

Lucy doesn't greet him with her usual smile. Her eyes flash with anger. "What was she doing in the animal house?"

"Assisting me," he replies.

"She's not a scientist," Lucy asserts.

"But she is prepared to help with the animal experiments."

Lucy gives an exasperated sigh. "Richard, just how much do you know about this woman?"

"Not a great deal," he concedes. "She's very discreet."

"She's probably got a lot to be discreet about."

"Why are you so hostile to Maria?" Richard asks. "Hasn't she provided us with all the resources we need?"

"I don't care if she owns everything including the coffee we drink," Lucy retorts, "I'm not having her in *this* lab until she's got a PhD in genetic engineering."

Richard grins and hands her the blood sample tubes. "Go ahead, ace."

It takes two days for Lucy to separate out all the proteins from each blood sample and transfer them to a nitrocellulose sheet, which she then incubates for a further twelve hours with a radioactive probe that binds only to immortalin. After washing each nitrocellulose sheet, she covers it with a sheet of undeveloped film and leaves it overnight. If no immortalin is present in the blood sample, there would be no radioactivity to expose the film and it would show nothing when it was developed.

The following morning she takes the undeveloped films to the autorad room, which resembles a small photographic dark room. Richard switches on the dull red light and switches off the neon light. Lucy carefully removes the first sheet of undeveloped film and feeds it into the automatic developer.

The film emerges blank, as do the films derived from the blood of the other two control monkeys. Then Lucy feeds in the film from the first of the three monkeys whose vector incorporated the anti-aging gene inducer.

The next five minutes last an eternity. The more confident Richard is about the outcome of an experiment, the greater the blow to his scientific judgment if he were wrong. Waiting for this result, he is gripped by the dread that some unanticipated factor has crept in to undermine him. As each minute ticks by, Richard's fears tighten and constrict his blood supply, causing his heart to pound feverishly against his ribcage. He is sure Lucy can hear it.

The film emerges slowly from the top of the machine. Richard snatches it out and holds it up to the light that glows like the red votive lamp in the dark Catholic chapel of his schooldays to signify the Real Presence. A strong black band crosses the film: the vector has inserted the inducer into the chromosomes of the monkey's blood cells, the inducer has switched on the monkey's own anti-aging genes, and the blood cells are manufacturing immortalin. Just as he'd forecast. "Hallelujah," he breathes with relief.

It is the same with the autoradiographs of the other two experimental monkeys. In the intimacy of this small room flushed by a roseate half-light Lucy can't resist the urge to put her arms round him and give him an excited squeeze. "Awesome!"

He returns her hug and she grins from ear to ear. Then he lets her go and says, "I need to tell Maria." Lucy's grin vanishes.

Maria listens calmly while Richard enthusiastically relays the good news. "How long before we know the monkeys have stopped aging?" she asks.

The strong black band on the films has banished Richard's fears. "Six months," he replies confidently.

But Richard doesn't have to wait six months.

24

After the confidence booster of successfully switching on the monkeys' anti-aging genes, Richard subsides to a state of edgy tension while he counts the days until he can run another set of MRI scans. Six months, he reckons, should be enough to show a statistically significant aging shrinkage of the brain, liver, lungs, kidneys and spleen, plus a growth in fat, of the three control monkeys whose vector contained everything except the anti-aging gene inducer. If the three elderly monkeys who had been given the inducer show no such aging degeneration, it would vindicate his claim about the benefits of switching on the gene in a nonhuman primate.

At the sound of a car he glances out of his office window. Alvaro parks and opens the passenger door. As Maria climbs out her skirt rides up her thighs. Richard's fascination with her has grown, and yet Lucy was right: how much does he really know about her? When he tried to elicit clues about her private life and her other interests from Alvaro, he found the Maya factotum's devotion to Maria was matched only by his discretion. The one thing that Richard gleaned was that her absences from Eden in recent weeks were due to visits she was making to the land of her mother's people.

Richard hears a knock at his office door. "Come in and sit down," Richard says, surprised to see the animal house manager.

Miguel shakes his head. "I think you better come."

Richard frowns. "What's wrong?"

"I think one of monkeys is not so good. I think she have problem."

"What kind of problem?"

"She don't look no good. She picks her neck."

Richard had wanted someone better qualified than Miguel as Eden's animal facility manager, but Maria had persuaded him that Miguel was ideal: he had worked in commercial animal facilities, he was competent enough to feed and look after the animals, but he wasn't bright enough to figure out that Richard wasn't using them to test a cancer therapy.

A better qualified manager, Richard thinks, would know that a monkey picking itself was part of its grooming, and that an elderly monkey, like the controls who hadn't had their anti-aging genes switched on, was going to look increasingly pathetic. Richard follows the stocky Mexican down the corridor. Miguel unlocks the door to the animal facility clothing change room, where they each put on a green lab coat and bouffant cap, sterile plastic shoe covers, a linen face mask, and disposable latex gloves.

The steel bars of the six cages gleam dully in the halogen light from the ceiling panel of the windowless monkey room, which has a strong musky smell. Richard bends to read the label on the cage Miguel indicates. His heart begins to beat faster. It is a female who'd been given the anti-aging gene inducer. And she isn't just grooming herself, she is picking at a lump below her ear.

Richard hurries to the surgical suite for his medical bag, telling himself that it could be nothing at all: maybe a fleabite that had become infected. But that doesn't stop the pounding in his breast.

Back in the monkey room, he opens the cage door cautiously, jabs the monkey in a leg with the needle of a hypodermic, and injects ketamine. After the anesthetic takes effect he removes the monkey from her cage, places her on a trolley, and wheels her to the surgical suite where he cuts a slice from the lump, puts the slice in a sterile transparent plastic tube, and fills the tube with ten per cent formalin solution to fix it. After returning the monkey to her cage, he disrobes and takes the specimen to his lab so that Lucy can prepare tissue slides for examination.

Stunned by what he's seen through the microscope, Richard takes Lucy's report to Maria's office.

"Hi," she says, getting up from behind her desk. "I was just about to leave." Then she sees his expression. "There's a problem?"

He closes the door behind him. "One of the monkeys. One that's had its anti-aging genes switched on."

"You'd better sit down," she says as she resumes her seat.

From across her workstation Richard looks at the woman who has shown such faith in him and his abilities, and he fears how she will respond to the news.

"Well?" she queries.

He retreats behind the dispassionate words of the report's summary. "Histopathological study of the tissue revealed a diffuse, high grade lymphoid neoplasm consistent with lymphoblastic lymphoma."

"In plain English?"

"It looks like cancer of the lymph gland," he says grimly.

For a moment she stares at him, and then she says, "What now?"

"I need to run an MRI scan."

Richard takes the X-ray-type films of the scan and puts them in light boxes.

Maria looks at his face. "Bad?"

Richard is so devastated that it takes a while for him to speak. "The thymus is enlarged." Then he points to black spots. "Tumors in the lymph nodes below the ear and under the armpit. See those little black tumor nodules in the lungs, kidneys, and liver? This cancer's spread like wildfire."

Richard steels himself for what he has to do next. This is the part of animal work that he hates most of all, but he has no choice.

Dressed in surgical greens, he anesthetizes the monkey and wheels her down to the necropsy room, where he lays her on the stainless steel downdraft table, adjusts the position of the bright, overhead halogen lamp, and switches on the downdraft. Next he opens a large plastic container of colorless liquid, screws an electric pump to the opening, inverts it, and fixes it to a stand next to the table. To the other end of the pump he secures a translucent plastic tube that ends in a large-bore needle.

Richard puts on a plastic apron over his greens. "The next part is gory. You're sure you want to stay and help?"

"I've never found blood a problem," Maria says, slipping a plastic apron over her greens. He is relieved at the way Maria has taken the news, accepting his judgment that he couldn't draw any conclusions until he's ascertained the cause of the cancer. Coolly she'd asked what could she do to help.

He rolls the monkey on her back. She stares straight up. When he touches her eyeballs, the monkey's eyes move but don't blink. He opens her mouth; she doesn't resist. Satisfied by the depth of anesthesia, Richard takes a large scalpel from the surgical tray, draws three sides of a large square on the monkey's chest, and peels back the skin to expose her left ribs. "Saw," he says.

Maria hands him the saw and he cuts away ribs to expose the monkey's heart beating among glistening red muscle and tissue. He picks up the large-bore needle and inserts it through the thin wall of the monkey's heart into the left ventricle. Once the needle is secure in this pulsating lower chamber that pumps blood into the monkey's arteries, he asks Maria for surgical scissors and snips a hole in the right atrium, the upper chamber that receives blood from the veins. He switches on the electric pump, and colorless phosphate-buffered saline solution in the plastic bottle flows down the translucent tube, through the needle into the bottom of the monkey's heart, and out into her arteries. Blood spurts out from the hole in the top of her heart. Some splashes onto his apron, but most pours onto the downdraft table, where it drains via a pipe into a removable plastic container beneath the table.

When all the monkey's blood had been flushed out of her system and only a pale pinkish liquid spurts out of the hole in the heart, Richard turns off the electric pump. He replaces the large plastic container above the pump by another containing a liter of sharp-smelling formalin. He switches on the pump again and the colorless liquid empties into the monkey, fixing her like a board.

Richard cuts and saws his way through the body cavity in order to take slices from the tumors in the stiffened monkey's lymph nodes, lungs, kidneys and liver, carefully placing each sample in a labeled sterile plastic container. For comparison he removes samples of healthy tissue and then he puts the monkey's corpse into a black plastic bag. While Maria takes the bag to the incinerator, Richard disposes of his face mask, bloodied apron, surgical greens, shoe covers, cap, and gloves in the change room, scrubs his hands with antibacterial soap, and takes the samples to his lab.

With a sense of foreboding he hands them to Lucy and says, "You know what to look for?"

Lucy nods.

He thinks of what would have happened if he'd skipped safety tests on animals, as Maria had wanted, and his dread about what Lucy might find in the samples is mitigated by gratitude. "Thanks," he says.

She looks up. "I said I'd do the benchwork."

"I mean thanks for reminding me that it would be unethical to go straight to human trials."

She reaches out to give his arm a consoling touch.

The full moon casts a ghostly light on the Eden Therapy signboard outside Richard's office window. He turns from the intertwined serpents at the sound of the door opening.

Lucy stands there. She bites her lip and places her written analysis on his desk. For a while he stares blankly at the sheet of neat handwriting. He doesn't want to believe what it spells out, but the scientist in him is forced to accept the report: the anti-aging gene switch had got into between seventy and eighty per cent of normal cells, but *every* tumor cell in the samples contained the gene switch.

He slumps in his chair. All the evidence pointed to the cancer being caused by switching on the monkey's own anti-aging genes. Straker, Hill, and the rest were right: the gene is a tumor-inducer.

He covers his face with his hands. Lucy puts her arm round his shoulder, but she can't lift his depression. All the work he'd done on this gene since he began his PhD nearly fifteen years before had come to nothing. The dumbest gene was smarter than the smartest genetic

engineer.

25

As a cardinal article of faith Richard believed in the power of the mind. More particularly, he believed that if he set his mind to a science problem he would eventually discover the answer.

It was these discoveries that Richard lived for: the euphoric highs of seeing a truth before anyone else, of advancing an hypothesis that others in their blindness scorned, and then demonstrating the validity of that hypothesis in a manner so compelling that it peeled the scales from the eyes of the blind. But the price of the highs was the lows: the insidious downers of self-doubt that threatened to paralyze his mind. He wouldn't swap his life on the high wire for a seat in the stalls, but the older he became, the more he looked down, the more the fear of failure threatened to undermine the brash self-confidence that had carried him ever higher when he was young.

The monkey's cancer forced him to look down. He saw a bottomless pit surrounded by a sea of faces willing him to trip over his ambition and plunge into the depths of failure. For the first time he didn't know how to move forward without losing his balance.

"You're sure we need your assistant?" Maria asks.

He looks up, unshaven and tired from the sleepless night of pondering the result Lucy had given him. Neither Maria's voice nor her expression betrays her feelings. She sits, stately and impassive, behind her workstation. Surely she must be regretting her decision to gamble on his ability, he thinks, for that was what her investment amounted to. "Lucy might help me figure out what we should do now."

Maria raises her eyebrows, but then presses the intercom buzzer on her workstation. "Roger, please ask Lucy to join us."

Lucy looks at Richard's haggard face and her brow creases in concern. She hurries towards him and stretches out a hand to touch his arm, but is stopped by Maria's glance. She sits down and turns her chair so that she faces Richard rather than Maria. "What do we do now?" she asks.

Richard shakes his head. "I just don't know. It looks like the end of the road."

"No, Richard," Lucy protests. "You've achieved so much. You've discovered the anti-aging gene, you've designed an inducer to switch on the gene, and you and I have made a powerful new vector to deliver the inducer to any kind of human cell. You've so much to offer sufferers from aging diseases."

"What can I offer them now?" Richard asks dejectedly. "A quick way to get cancer?"

"What is your scientific solution, Lucy?" Maria asks.

Lucy ignores Maria and addresses her answer to Richard. "Take your data to the National Institutes of Health," she urges. "With their experience they'll see where we went wrong. Hopefully they'll be able to develop your discovery into a gene therapy that's safe."

Maybe Lucy is right again. Maybe that is the only way to avoid the bottomless pit. Working in isolation from other researchers in the field has its disadvantages. Maybe a fresh approach could throw light on the problem and help him see the way ahead.

Maria's tongue is soft, but her eyes are like weapons. "Are you seriously suggesting the second-rate minds at the National Institutes of Health?" she says to Lucy. "The same people who turned down

Richard's grant for this work because they failed to recognize its genius? The same people who mocked him at Cold Spring Harbor?"

"But—" begins Lucy.

"If Richard crawls back now with his tail between his legs, Nathan Hill and the rest will make him a laughing stock."

"If we want Richard's achievements developed to cure diseases, we must show the results to other experts," Lucy insists. "We've got to find out what went wrong."

"The scientific establishment have shown neither the capability nor the will to develop a radical therapy like Richard's. Your report will simply confirm their prejudice."

But it would be far worse than that, Richard realizes. "If I go back to the National Institutes of Health, I'll have to admit that I lied in my letter to *Science* about the results of my successful brain cell experiments at UCLA and that I've been secretly working on the anti-aging gene in a private lab. That would finish my career." Worse still, the more enterprising types, like Straker, would repeat and confirm his experiment with cells in laboratory culture and go on to exploit his unfinished work. If they manage to eliminate the side effects, they would gain the glory for developing a safe gene therapy, while he would be a footnote in history for lying about his results.

Maria's large luminous black eyes focus on him, transmitting their strength to fan the fading embers of his self-confidence. She speaks to him as though Lucy were not in the room. "You are the only scientist capable of solving this problem, Richard. You've been overworked, that's all. Take a few days off. Relax. Use the flotation tank. You'll come up with the answer."

A chilling fog hangs heavily and inhospitably over San Francisco, reducing the traffic to a crawl. Its spectral tentacles swirl in the breeze from the ocean, caressing the steel hanger cables of the Bay Bridge. It covers the whole city, even Pacific Heights, where it blankets the wooden drum tower and Peace Pagoda, the Zen and Konko missions, and the colorful markets and restaurants of the Nihonmachi district, muffling the sounds from the *yakitori* stall below Lucy's window. It makes her feel more isolated than ever as she struggles with her conscience.

She has no one to turn to for advice. Henry is her favorite uncle. Unlike all other members of her family, he empathized with Lucy's aversion to slaughtering animals or experimenting on them. The pretty, petite Chisako treated her as the daughter she'd never had. But, true to her word, Lucy has never told them of the covert research that Richard and she are conducting and so she can't share with them her fears about the influence Snowe is exerting on Richard to compromise his principles. The discussion in that woman's office weighed on her like an oppressive burden as she confides to her diary:

"It was bad enough that Richard falsified the successful outcome of the brain cell experiment in his letter to *Science* and is misleading everyone at Eden about the purpose of our research. But will he really withhold information about the monkey tests?"

She bites the end of her pen and agonizes about her own position. Finally she writes:

"I know I've given a legal undertaking not to disclose our work, and I've vowed never to let Richard down, but do I have a greater obligation to inform the scientific community about the cancerous effects of the gene if Richard refuses to do so?"

Richard focuses on the white gatepost as soon as his run takes him round the final bend in the lane leading to his house. The gatepost becomes the finishing line of the Olympic ten thousand meters final, the world record is within his grasp, but the world champion is breathing down his neck. Richard digs deep and forces his leaden legs into a sprint. A hundred thousand spectators are on their feet roaring his name. His legs protest, but his mind drives him on. He lunges for the line and stops his watch.

He holds onto the gatepost to regain his breath while he looks at the watch. It is his best time for this five-mile course since he'd moved to Alamo. Not exactly a world record, but not bad for a forty-one year-old.

He jogs round by the side of the house to the back porch where he sits down to take off his running shoes. Sweat streams off his face onto his damp T-shirt. The company house Maria had acquired for him meets his needs perfectly. Out here in Alamo the country lanes and traffic-free roads are ideal for running. No fog reaches this side of the Oakland Hills; most days there is a clear blue sky, while warm air from the Central Valley keeps the temperature a good ten to fifteen degrees higher than in San Francisco.

This morning the unpolluted air smells of damp fresh grass. The bright spring sun shines on dew bespangling the lawn, and a gentle breeze rustles the leaves of apple trees in pink bud on the far side of the swimming pool. Daisies, buttercups and clover speckle the field that slopes upwards from the end of the orchard, transforming it into a pointillist landscape. From the wooded green hills beyond come the faint, raucous cries of scrub jays seeking mates.

His isolation at Eden from all distractions helped focus his thinking, but at times it felt like a pressure cooker. Maria was right. He needed a few days away and some hard physical exercise to keep his conscious, logical mind off the problem while his subconscious worked away intuitively. His best ideas always came in a flash, after he'd stopped wrestling with the problem and was either thinking about nothing or about something else.

He swims a few lazy lengths of the pool, showers, puts wax plugs into his ears, and walks naked to the flotation tank Maria had installed in the second bathroom. He opens the end hatch of the plastic sarcophagus, lowers himself into the ten-inch-deep concentrated solution of Epsom salts warmed to skin temperature, closes the hatch of this light-, sound-, and vibration-proofed capsule, and turns off the internal lamp.

He relaxes and floats effortlessly, feeling nothing, seeing nothing, hearing nothing, tasting nothing, and smelling nothing. He visualizes dark waters lapping the stern of a dive boat. He imagines stepping off into the water and looking up to see the bottom of the hull become smaller and smaller, and the dark water close around him, as he descends slowly and weightlessly, down and down and down. When he looks up again he sees only blackness. He no longer knows if he is looking up or down. There is no sense of panic, just the deep relaxation of a body deprived of all sensations. His mind floats free and wanders at will through the black void.

After what could have been seconds or hours a part of the void metamorphoses into a cell's molecular soup in which swims a double helix. He zooms in and the double helix magnifies into the anti-aging gene inducer sequence of DNA. He follows it through the translucent membrane of the cell's nucleus. It swims around until it collides randomly with the DNA in one of the twenty-one pairs of a monkey's floating thread-like chromosomes into which it embeds itself. It switches on and sends out a stream of messages to jam the messages of the gene that is repressing the anti-aging gene. The anti-aging gene springs into action.

Shoal upon shoal of double helices fill the void, each one entering a cell's nucleus and inserting itself randomly into one of the cell's chromosomes. Randomly.

The void glows with the golden realization that he has not failed; rather he has succeeded too well.

26

"I worried that the vector wouldn't deliver the anti-aging gene inducer to enough of a monkey's cells." Richard's eyes gleam as he sits opposite Maria over the low coffee table by the window in her office.

"In fact it's been *too* successful." He is back on a high. "It got the inducer into between seventy and eighty per cent of the monkey's ten trillion cells and inserted it into one of the chromosomes in each cell's nucleus." He leans forward and lowers his voice to draw her closer. "But it needs to find only one cell whose DNA has already been corrupted into a potentially cancerous state. If it inserts the inducer near a dormant tumor-promoting gene in that cell, then disaster! When it inserts and switches on, it also switches on the tumor-promoting gene and turns the cell cancerous. With upwards of ten trillion hits the odds of that happening in one cell are significant."

"But if that is only one cell in all those many?" Maria queries.

He raises his index finger. "All it takes for a cancer to begin is the corruption of *one* cell. Replication takes care of the rest."

Confidence exudes from him. "It all fits in with the monkey's lymphoma. T-lymphocytes are the cells that replicate the most. You turn one of those cells cancerous and it proliferates out of control, spreads through the lymphatic system, *and* is now immortalized by our gene."

"If that's the problem, what's the solution?"

Richard had done a forward somersault on the high wire and landed back on his feet even higher up the wire. "Once you understand the problem," he says, "the solution is simple. We need to engineer the vector so that it doesn't insert the inducer randomly, but inserts it in a safe region of a chromosome, far away from any potential tumor-promoting gene."

"Well done, Richard," she says with relief. "That monkey's cancer really had me worried."

He recalls the cool way in which she'd received the news when he feared that he'd failed. "You could have fooled me."

She leans across and puts a hand on his arm. "I don't pretend to understand all the science, but I did know that if the problem could be solved, there was only one person capable of solving it."

A warm glow of gratitude permeates Richard. Maria had kept faith in him even when he'd been on the point of despair.

"How long will it take to engineer the vector?" Maria asks.

"If we start from scratch it could take Lucy and me years." He sees the dismay on Maria's face. "But one scientist set up a company to develop such a vector targeting technique. The word is that he's succeeded."

"Who?"

Richard grimaces. "Randy Bew."

"You know him?"

"He was in my class at Harvard Med School. He was bright, I'll give him that."

Maria is intrigued by Richard's obvious disdain. "So tell me why you love him so much."

Richard shrugs. "He came from a privileged background and thought that wealth and social connections were the only things that mattered."

"I guess they didn't help much in your field."

"On the contrary, his father got him off a coke rap and stopped him being thrown out of Med School."

Maria purses her lips. "OK. No need to ask for favors. Ask him for a license. When it comes to a question of money, get a feel of how much he'll charge, and then come back to me."

Richard returns to his office to find Lucy waiting for him.

"Richard," Lucy says, "while you've been away I've been thinking."

"And?" he asks.

Her normally cheerful voice is solemn and determined. "We have a responsibility to tell the scientific community that the anti-aging gene causes cancer."

It is clear from her troubled expression that she's been worrying about this for the whole week he spent at home solving the vector problem. "Why?" he asks.

"Isn't it obvious? If anyone didn't read your letter in *Science* and tries to use the gene to treat aging diseases..." She breaks off when she sees his expression. "Richard, why can't you see it? At best it will produce cancer in whatever animals are tested with the gene. At worst, if it's used in clinical trials …" She shudders at the idea. "I insist that we publish, whatever *She* says."

Buoyed by the prospect of the new experiment that would vindicate him, Richard decides to have a little fun. Adopting a thoughtful pose, he pauses and says, "I've considered your advice, Lucy, and I've come to the conclusion that it would be wrong to mislead anyone about the gene."

"Thank goodness for that."

"Therefore I shan't tell anyone that the gene causes cancer."

Lucy's brow creases in incomprehension. "But… I don't get it. You saw my analysis of the tumor samples."

"From which," he reproves gently, "you drew the wrong conclusion, as I'm about to demonstrate."

Richard's ebullience had vanished when he goes to see Maria.

"Randy Bew won't license his gene targeting technology."

Maria is used to getting her own way and doesn't take kindly to being denied. "He doesn't know what we're prepared to offer. Everyone has his price."

"He's made a patent application, and his company is going for an IPO on the strength of it. The sale of stock to the public will raise the finance to develop his targetable vector to FDA marketing approval stage. He's not going to do anything that might conceivably lower the price he'll get."

"OK," she says, unruffled. "You've delivered on the science. It's my turn to deliver on the rest."

"He was adamant, Maria."

"Richard, you must learn to trust my ability."

27

Maria Snowe studies the document lying on her workstation. This is going to be a challenge. The type of challenge she enjoys.

The red herring prospectus for the initial public offering of two million shares of common stock by Bew's company didn't include the share price: that would be negotiated by the company with the underwriters after the latter had gauged the response of institutional investors. The word from the underwriters was that they were going for twelve dollars a share, raising $24 million from the IPO and valuing Arrow Vectors at $106 million.

She rolls the barrel of her pen abstractedly along her bottom teeth, and then she focuses on the key players. Two directors call the shots at Arrow. The first is Nat Aransky, one of two general partners of Clay Biomedical Ventures, which had led in the first two rounds of Arrow's venture capital financing. The second is the director who would still hold the largest single block of shares after the IPO: the founder of Arrow and vice president of research and development, Randolph Lafayette Bew MD.

She sits back and a smile plays across her lips. Bernard Harvey, the investment analyst who had written the prospectus, had done a good job.

The first call Maria places is to Daniel Goldberg, who headed the New York investment bank Goldberg Farber, the lead underwriter. She doesn't know him, but he would know of her. The price she'd extracted from Apple for Snowe Software, and her use of the proceeds to establish Eden Therapy, had given her visibility in the small world of investment bankers who specialized in emerging high tech companies.

"Mr Goldberg, I'm in town Friday to explore the possibilities of injecting more capital into Eden Therapy, maybe through an IPO. Interested in the ride?"

She is right about the reputation the deal with Apple has given her. Goldberg is *very* interested in any plans she has. "Fine," she says. "I want, of course, to meet with the people on your team I'd be dealing with if I decide to go ahead. I've heard good things about one of your investment analysts, Bernard Harvey."

Harvey is the rising star of biotech investment analysis, Goldberg assures her. She wouldn't find anyone better. "Good," she says. "Let's say you and your head of equity capital markets at two thirty and Harvey at three."

She then makes two appointments in the Bay Area, one for Thursday afternoon and one for the following Thursday morning.

On Thursday afternoon Alvaro drives Maria south down Highway 101 past the airport and takes the exit before Stanford University and Palo Alto. West at the lights leads to the city of Menlo Park. Alvaro turns east, towards reclaimed marshland and salt evaporators that border the Bay. Shortly afterwards he turns down a narrow road that possesses no sidewalks, just grass verges planted with silver birches and weeping willows that fail to soften the stark single-story units constructed from rectangular slabs of pastel concrete and tinted glass: another characterless, high-tech business park that marks the northward march of Silicon Valley.

Ensconced behind a semicircular workstation that faces the green-tinted glass door, the receptionist of Arrow Vectors Incorporated reluctantly looks up from a paperback novel. She informs Maria that Dr. Bew is busy and, without inquiring if she wants any refreshments, asks her to wait. Three quarters of an hour after her scheduled appointment a secretary comes to say, without apologies, that Dr. Bew will see her now.

Perhaps because the only genetic engineers she had met were the scientists at the Cold Spring Harbor meeting and the small staff at Eden, Maria is surprised by Bew's appearance. No T-shirt and shorts for him. Bew is impeccably dressed, with the kind of custom-made business suit worn by bankers, while his silver hair is neatly trimmed and his cherubic face glistens with aftershave lotion that smells of violets.

He gestures for her to sit down on the other side of the desk in his spacious office. Its walls are hung with photographs of himself: posing in a tuxedo with President Donald J Trump, in a white lab coat with a model of DNA, in a suit surrounded by proud staff, and at a lectern with a rapt audience. "I'm not sure what can be served by this meeting, Ms Snowe," he says with an air of confidence that merges into arrogance. "I've already told Trent that I have no intention of licensing my technology to you."

"I understand that, Dr. Bew." Maria smiles and carefully crosses her legs, but Bew pays no heed. "From a strategic point of view," she says, "it seems to me that our two operations are complementary. We develop therapeutic gene constructs for cancer treatment and you develop targeted vectors to deliver them. I'm thinking of forging an alliance by investing in Arrow."

"You've missed the boat." He opens the top drawer of his desk and hands her the Goldberg Farber prospectus. "Didn't Trent tell you? I'm going for an IPO."

She leans forward, revealing her cleavage, and gazes at him. "I don't think it's a good time to go to the market right now. I think we should preempt the IPO and come to a mutually satisfying arrangement."

He sits back in his executive chair and his fingers tap the armrests. "I'm listening."

Maria pauses before saying, "I propose to buy the two million shares you intend to offer to the public, plus two million of the three and a third million that you hold."

His lips curl in amusement. "You propose to take a controlling interest?"

Maria smiles.

"You haven't got that kind of money."

"What kind of money?" She looks down at the red herring prospectus. "There's no price here."

Bew looks at his watch and then at her. "Goldberg Farber is talking twelve dollars a share. And that's for an IPO of just over twenty-five per cent of stock. There's no way I'd sell my shares. And certainly not for anything like twelve dollars."

"I'm not sure that's wise, Dr. Bew, in these market conditions."

"Ms Snowe," he says smugly, "you clearly haven't been in genetic engineering very long. I don't know if Trent's gene is going to fix cancer, but I doubt it. I do know that for any team playing gene therapy, the injected targetable vector is the grand slam home run. It's the smart bomb that delivers its payload to just those cells, just those chromosomes, and just those sites on the chromosomes that the gene therapists want to hit, with no collateral damage. Can you imagine the numbers that Novartis, Merck, Pfizer, BMS, and the rest will pay for a license on that?" He stands up. "May I suggest you spend a few more years in the minor leagues before moving up to play in the majors?"

"That's your last word?"

"My last word is that if you want to make a shrewd investment, I'd contact Goldberg Farber and bid for some of those two million shares." He presses a buzzer on his desk.

Maria sighs. "That's a shame. However, it was instructive meeting with you, Dr. Bew."

"My secretary will show you out."

After leaving Bew's office, Maria says to his secretary, "Is there a bathroom I can use here?"

"Sure. Third door on the left."

"Thanks. There's no need to wait. I know the way out."

After leaving the bathroom, Maria stops by a storeroom, opens her handbag and, with gloved hands, removes a bottle labeled Calcium

Phosphate and leaves it among other bottles of white powder on a shelf.

Like many investment banks, Goldberg Farber had opted out of Wall Street and located in mid-Manhattan. Alvaro pulls up outside a tower of polished green granite and wraparound windows on Madison Avenue. "What time shall I call for you, Madre?" he asks.

"I think I'll be an hour, but I'm not absolutely certain so I'll phone you."

Daniel Goldberg's secretary welcomes Maria with an offer of coffee, mineral water, or fruit juice. She escorts Maria to the conference room in the company's twenty-ninth-floor office suite. The curve of the casket-lid-shaped light oak conference table is echoed by the curve of the stainless steel rods that run from top to bottom of the opaque glass doors and serve as stylish door handles.

Maria charms Goldberg by being impressed with the Barnett Newman on one of the Eau de Nil walls as much as she is with the row of framed notices offering stock in biotech and software companies on the opposite wall. She charms Gloria, the head of equity markets, by complimenting her astute observations quoted in the *Wall Street Journal*. But she reserves her most lethal charm for Bernard Harvey, an earnest young man with a neat black beard.

"May I see your business plan, Ms Snowe?" he asks after Goldberg has left them alone at the conference table.

She fixes him with her most formidable gaze. "You may, Bernard, if I decide to give it to you." Her lips part in a smile that show perfect, white incisors. "And that depends upon whether you satisfy me that Goldberg Farber is good enough."

"You've talked with Daniel and Gloria. You know the strength of the relationships they have with institutional investors in this field. Look at how many successful IPOs and equity private placements we've arranged for companies like yours."

"Their relationship with investors depends ultimately on the quality of your analyses, Bernard." She turns round to look at the framed certificates on the wall. "The last biotech IPO was over a year ago. What's your current track record?"

"We're about to place two million shares in Arrow Vectors," he boasts, "a company that's set to dominate vector technology in the long term."

"You're teasing me, Bernard," Maria says with a wicked grin. "Randy Bew's company?"

"Straight up, Ms Snowe. Dr. Bew and his advisors have chosen us to lead with the offering."

Maria shakes her head. "Bernard, I do believe you're serious about this."

"Too right I am."

Maria looks thoughtful for a moment and then says, "Well, Bernard, I can see you're a very busy man, and so I won't detain you any longer. It was pleasant meeting with you."

Harvey's face hits the floor before rebounding. "Have you decided against an IPO, Ms Snowe?"

"I've decided that if I go for an IPO I need an investment bank with a biotech analyst whose recommendations carry respect." She stands up.

"Just hold it right there, Ms Snowe," he blurts "Are you implying—"

She stares at him. "I'm implying nothing, Bernard."

"What are you trying to say?" he demands.

She shrugs. "I'm simply saying that I was interested in investing in Bew's company until I ran my own check. And if Goldberg Farber's the kind of bank that's prepared to underwrite a man with the problems Bew has, then it's not the bank for me. I'll drop Daniel a line and thank him for the coffee."

Harvey attempts to recover. "I didn't mean to be rude, Ms Snowe. If it seemed that way, then I apologize." He swallows. "What problems?"

Maria pauses by the door and decides to take pity on him. "I assume you're familiar with Public Law 100-690, Title V, Subtitle D?"

Harvey stares back blankly.

"Otherwise known as the Drug-Free Workplace Act of 1988?"

"You're not telling me—"

"And Bew's arrest when an intern at Harvard Medical School for possession of cocaine?"

Harvey tries to beat the count. "If so, then that was decades ago."

Maria shakes her head sadly. "Once a cokehead, always a cokehead. Does your biotech analysis stretch to analyzing the white powder that Bew snorts from a bottle labeled Calcium Phosphate in the store room when he wants his next bright idea?"

For Maria Snowe's morning appointment the following Thursday, Alvaro drives along the straight-line roller coaster of California Street until he is slowed by the bustle of Chinatown. He makes a left and then a right to join the honking congested mass of steel and humanity inching through the fumes in a canyon between the soaring skyscrapers of San Francisco's Financial District. Only the swarms of tribally cultured messengers on mountain bikes slaloming past automobiles and pedestrians seemed to make any progress along Clay Street. Eventually Alvaro pulls up near the junction with Montgomery, by a speckled-brown-marble-clad thirty-story tower that is dwarfed by the white obelisk of the nearby Transamerica Pyramid.

"What time shall I call for you, Madre?" Alvaro asks.

She consults her watch. "In forty-five minutes, Alvaro."

Offices on the fifteenth floor have neither the prestige of those on the top floors and the courtyard level nor, judging by the number of companies squeezed onto that floor, their size. Still, Maria reflects, Clay Biomedical Ventures had moved out of Sand Hill Road to establish a toehold in downtown San Francisco. Did this venture capital firm have aspirations to respectability? Or was it a bunch of short-term speculators who invested in an academic's promising idea on the gamble they could turn it into a sufficiently credible company to be floated for a big pay-off? Maria pushes open the door bearing a plastic company name tag and sees an olive-skinned young man wearing earphones who is seated behind a small switchboard.

"Dr. Spencer's private office," the young man says into the telephone operator's microphone cradled in front of his mouth. "I'm afraid that Dr. Spencer is in a meeting right now, may I take a message?"

He nods to Maria before flicking a switch on his console to answer another call. "Clay Biomedical Ventures," he says this time. "I'll have Dr. Spencer or Mr Aransky return your call as soon as possible."

He scribbles something on a yellow post-it note while saying, "May I help you?"

"Maria Snowe. I have an appointment with Mr. Aransky at ten thirty."

He presses a button on his console. "Nat, a Professor Williams from Stanford University phoned. He didn't ask for anyone by name so I said that you or Ed would return his call. And your ten thirty appointment has arrived."

Maria is still standing.

The receptionist says, "Mr. Aransky will be with you shortly." The telephone rings on his console. He looked at the LCD display and replies, "Mr. Aransky's private office." Then, "I'll put you through straight away." He presses a button, "Nat, it's Jack from Sand Hill Biotech Investments, I'm putting him through."

Ten minutes elapse before an overweight man in his fifties, wearing a loosened red necktie and red suspenders over a white shirt, emerges from behind a door. He has the nose of an unsuccessful boxer, but the self-satisfied look on his face and ostentatious rings on his fingers of one who'd successfully turned to promoting mugs who'd make his fortune for him. "So, you're Maria Snowe?" The rasping consonants and bent vowels come out of Manhattan's Lower East Side. The probing eyes might have been those of an Arab inspecting a thoroughbred racehorse and approving what he sees. "How was it with Tim Cook?"

Maria glances at her watch. "He's a professional."

Aransky grins and waves towards the opened door of the conference room that leads off from the small reception area. "Enter my den."

It lacks two-thirds the size of Goldberg Farber's conference room and any of its style. Maria takes the center seat on a long side of the conference table. Aransky sits next to her and swivels round to study her more closely. She smells stale cigar smoke on his breath and notices the damp patches under the armpits of his shirt.

"So," Aransky says, "either you didn't screw Cook for as much as the rumors said, or else Eden Therapy's running through your cash quicker than Ivana Trump on a bad day. Maybe, just maybe, I can help find you some more capital."

"That's very considerate of you, Mr Aransky. But I'm here as a potential investor."

"Even better. We're setting up a new fund.

Aransky takes a pack from his pants pocket and removes a cigar. "I take it you don't object."

"Yes," she said.

He puts the cigar in his mouth and reaches in his other pants pocket for his lighter.

"Yes I do object." She smiles sweetly.

He shrugs, puts the cigar and lighter away, and nods towards the draft prospectus. "This is going to net a bigger return than the '48 gold rush."

"I was thinking of investing in Arrow Vectors."

"This may be your lucky day, Maria," he says with no flicker of reaction at the mention of Arrow. "Maybe, just maybe, I can bring you into the game on this one."

Her eyes examine him, but his self-assurance doesn't waver. "You seem to be a little out of touch, Mr Aransky. Goldberg Farber have packed up their cards and gone home. There is no game."

His face shows the reaction of a poker player. "A minor hiccup."

"Goldberg Farber didn't think Bew's drug problem was a minor hiccup." She leans back and crosses her legs. "Let's face it, Nat. Valuing an unproven biotech company is all about confidence. The market doesn't have confidence in a cokehead who could get arrested any day *and* lose all his government grants."

His eyes stray to the shapely legs encased in sheer silk before he looks up with a lascivious grin. "We kiss off Bew, restructure, and go ahead with an IPO later in the year."

"Without Bew Arrow is nothing."

His eyes glint in amusement; Maria might have suggested that the A's were doomed without their recently retired fourth pitcher. "No way."

"Really?" She places a forearm vertically on the table, leaned forward to rest her chin on her fist, and gazes at him. "Then why is Bew the only staff member with a key person life insurance policy worth ten million dollars?" She smiles sweetly. "Which is five times more than the net tangible book value of the company."

Aransky appears unperturbed. "Novartis have the hots for the patent on Bew's vector."

Maria sits back in her chair. "The most Novartis can cuddle up to is a patent application, and that is going to burn their balls when it's challenged."

His face maintains its mask of self-assurance, but the damp patches beneath his armpits are spreading. "Challenged?" he repeats, as though querying a subway inspector who asked to see his ticket.

"Seems like you need a hearing aid, Nat. "

His bulk leans forward. The wry grin is more intimidating than a snarl. "Suppose you tell me what interest you have in this company, little lady."

"Would you mind sitting back a yard, Nat? Your air conditioning isn't working too well."

His eyes lose their glint of amusement. "Cards on the table time."

"One of our staff members can prove prior art for Bew's targeting technology."

"Bullshit. Our inquiry agent reported no one else with a competing claim to the invention."

"Seems like you need a new dick as well." She smiles again. "Now that Goldberg Farber has pulled the plug on the IPO, Arrow doesn't have the funds to defend the patent challenge we plan to bring worldwide. To avoid both of us making legal fat cats even fatter, the best cut would be for you to sell out to me."

Denied a cigar to brandish, Aransky's right hand fingers the rings on his left hand. "I don't buy your four flush. After all we've put into Arrow we're not about to walk away from a big upside."

"What makes Arrow so different from Cassidy Biotech and Wondergene? You took big losses when you pulled out of them."

"They were burning too much."

"Arrow's burn rate is ten million dollars a year."

He tries to avoid her gaze, but her large eyes seem to draw him into a black hole from which there is no escape. "We organize another round of venture finance, have Bew take us through till the Novartis money kicks in, and then give him a plastic parachute." His voice now has the overconfidence of one who is trying to convince himself.

"Go ahead," she says softly. "But your two and three quarter million is approaching the ten per cent limit for your fund's investment in a single company. How many other VCs can you bring to the plate? And if they don't play ball, Arrow goes down the toilet and your one million share certificates become toilet paper." Her penetrating eyes stare unwaveringly. "This may be your lucky day, Nat. Maybe, just maybe, I can offer you an exit."

"What kind of exit?"

"Fifty cents a share."

"Lady, you must be joking. You seriously expect me to take a haircut on this one?"

"A haircut now or a scalping later."

He sits back and his horse-trader eyes are at work again, but he doesn't know if he is seeing a mare or a centaur. "If that's a formal offer, I'm obliged to put it to my partner." He stands up. "But I warn you, he's gonna want to see chips of a different color before he sits at the table."

"My offer drops ten cents an hour."

"Yeah, yeah," he says as he leaves the conference room.

Five minutes later he returns with Clay's managing general partner, Ed Spencer, a leaner and more polished version of Aransky. His appearance suggests a bridge player rather than a poker player. He sits down at the head of the table, intertwines his fingers, and rests his cuffs on the polished surface. He speaks politely, with the hint of a Midwest accent. "Miss Snowe, we both know that Arrow Vectors is a goose that will grow to lay a whole basketful of golden eggs." He returns her gaze and doesn't blink. "Frankly, I do not believe there is a credible challenge to Bew's patent application."

Maria collects her attaché case and stands up. "In that case, gentlemen, I'll see you in court."

"However," Spencer continues smoothly, "I appreciate that Goldberg Farber's unaccountable loss of nerve means complications. In the interests of our fundholders, I'm prepared to cut a deal."

Maria opens her attaché case, removes a folder, and pushes it across the table to Spencer. "The contracts are already made out. You just need to sign and return two copies to me."

Aransky reaches for the folder and opens it. "You said your offer was fifty cents a share. This says forty."

"I also said my price drops ten cents an hour." She smiles sweetly. "Or part thereof."

Spencer opens the folder, signs the documents, and returns two copies.

Maria takes the signed copies and looks at her watch. "If you gentlemen will excuse me, I'm running three minutes late."

When she'd gone, Aransky turns to Spencer. "Jesus. There's no way I'd play poker with that chick, but as sure as hell I'd love to fuck her."

"That right?" Spencer asks as he stands up and collects his copy of the documents. "She'd take your dick and put it through the mincer."

The other venture capitalists follow Clay Biomedical Ventures like lemmings. By the following Monday Maria Snowe has acquired 83.7 per cent of the shares of Arrow Vectors for an outlay of $2.29 million.

28

"Maria," says her assistant's voice on the intercom, "I have Dr. Randolph Bew on line two."

It is the call she's been waiting for. "Keep him on hold, Roger," she says. "I'll buzz you when I'm free."

She looks at her watch, pulls the backrest tilt lever on her executive chair, and leans back. Closing her eyes, she imagines the man who had been impervious to her feminine charms and smiles. After two minutes she brings the chair back to a sitting position and buzzes Roger. "Put Bew on the line and listen in."

She cradles the phone on her shoulder and says in her huskiest voice, "Dr. Bew, it's so kind of you to call."

"I've been thinking about the strategic alliance you proposed between our two companies," he says smoothly. "On reflection, it seems to make sense."

"Good. I'm so pleased. Perhaps we should discuss it at the next meeting of Arrow's board."

"Fine. That's scheduled for, let me see, 5:30 p.m. on the twenty-fifth."

She pauses before saying, "There seems to be some confusion here, Dr. Bew. My diary has the next meeting of the board of Arrow Vectors scheduled for, let me see…" she looks at her watch, "…three o'clock this afternoon in my office."

"That's absurd!" he retorts.

"Why?" she asks innocently.

"Only the secretary can call board meetings."

"That's what Mr. Durkin has done."

"Who?"

"I believe a majority of the shareholders recently appointed Roger Durkin as company secretary."

The telephone goes silent.

"Are you still there, Dr. Bew?" Maria asks.

"I need to speak to the other directors about this."

"You're speaking to the only other director. I do hope you can make the meeting."

"Dr. Bew," says Maria with a welcoming smile, "or may I call you Randy? Please come in."

Bew hesitates in the open doorway to her office. As on their first encounter, the dapper silver-haired scientist smells of aftershave and is attired in an expensive business suit with button-down shirt and tie, but the amused conceit on his cherubic face is replaced by a mask of suspicion.

"Tea, coffee, fruit juice, mineral water?" she asks.

"A cup of hot water."

Maria looks to the pretty young receptionist who had brought Bew to her office. "Please ask Roger to bring a cup of hot water for Dr. Bew." She waves Bew towards the coffee table by the window. "Do take a seat."

Bew sits down on one of the low chairs by the table, unlocks his Italian-designed executive briefcase, and removes a leather box.

The silence is broken by the entry of Maria's assistant, who places a cup and saucer on the table in front of Bew. Bew takes a bag of chamomile tea from his leather box and places it in the cupful of hot water.

"Dr. Bew, this is Roger Durkin, Arrow's new company secretary," Maria says.

Roger holds out his hand and smiles. Bew takes the hand while his eyes appraise Roger's cropped hair, hazel eyes, mustache, and tight-fitting T-shirt and jeans that reveal a powerfully muscled body.

"I guess we'd better start the board meeting," Maria says.

Roger pulls out a shorthand notebook from his back pocket and sits down between them. Lounging with his right ankle resting on his left knee, he places the notebook on his right thigh and holds a pen poised above it.

"As responsible directors," Maria says, "we have to conclude that Arrow's burn rate is unsustainable, and therefore I propose we accept Eden Therapy's takeover offer."

Bew switches his attention to Maria. "Which is?"

"To acquire all of Arrow's shares, close down the Menlo Park facility, sell off the unexpired lease, and transfer operations here."

Bew shakes his head. "There's no room for all the staff here."

"There's no room for *any* of the staff here, Randy. Staff costs are the biggest part of the burn."

Bew's lips tighten. "How much per share is Eden offering?"

"Their par value," she says casually. "One thousandth of a dollar."

Bew reaches out for the chamomile tea. The cup rattles when his thumb and index finger grip the saucer. "Three thousand dollars for my stake?"

"No," she says. "Three thousand three hundred and thirty-three dollars thirty-three cents."

"You can't do this to me!" The angelic features beneath the silver hair distort into the rage of a spoiled child deprived of his favorite toy. "Two weeks ago you were trying to buy two million of my shares."

"That was then. This is now."

"You and Trent set me up," he accuses. "They cited adverse market conditions for pulling out of the IPO, but a couple of days after I turned down your offer Goldberg Farber sent a private investigator. He found coke on the premises. Trent knew I'd been busted at Harvard."

Maria looks at her assistant. "I'm sure Dr. Bew doesn't want his ill-considered and libelous remarks minuted, Roger." She turns to Bew. "I understand you must feel badly let down if Goldberg Farber discovered that one of your staff has a cocaine habit, but I fail to see how that has anything to do with Dr. Trent or me. Paranoia, I'm afraid, is the occupational hazard of the research scientist. I sensed it was the wrong time for an IPO and told you so when I made you an offer. You mustn't blame me for taking advantage of your banker's withdrawal."

He glowers at her. "Aransky said that you were taking legal action to challenge my patent."

"*Arrow's* patent," she corrects him. "I now control that patent. As for Aransky," Maria sighs, "is he the type of person you'd invite to dinner, Randy? You must learn whom to believe and whom not to believe."

"Dinner? What dinners can I afford?" he pouts. "You tell me that my company is bankrupt, that I'm out of a job, and that if I try selling my own gene targeting technology you'll sue for patent infringement."

"That's the way the ball bounces," she says. "I declare the motion carried and the meeting adjourned."

Tears of resentment glisten in his eyes. "I'll fight this. I'll fight it through the courts, through the scientific societies, through the media, any way I can."

Maria's voice softens. "I sympathize with your plight, Randy, believe me. My role as president of Eden is to protect my scientists from gamblers like Aransky who're only in it for the quick buck. I don't like what's happened to you."

He stares at her. Her attitude had changed. He doesn't know precisely what it is, but he senses he has a weapon she fears.

"I'll tell you what I'll do, Randy," she says. "I'll exchange your worthless share certificates for a contract of employment here at Eden Therapy."

The unknown weapon was potent. Bew scents victory. "The package I had at Arrow was worth $497,000 a year."

I'll match that," Maria says.

29

Richard stares at the year planner on his wall. The need to prove that he can successfully treat aging-induced diseases obsesses him even more after the setback of the monkey's cancer. He is *almost* certain that targeting a safe site for the gene switch to insert in the chromosomes would solve the problem, and the frustration of being denied the technology to confirm that he is right mounts with each passing day.

With the frustration also came a fear. More than two weeks had elapsed since Maria had gone to see Bew, and all she'd said was that Bew repeated what he had told him. The question that insinuated itself in his mind is: what has Maria been doing since her first meeting with Bew? She'd hardly been in the office except for one day last week when Bew had spent the afternoon with her. She hadn't asked Richard to join them. He couldn't develop a safe gene therapy without Bew's technology, but Bew could develop the therapy himself if he had access to Richard's data. Was Maria using her majority shareholding in Eden to strike a deal with Bew behind his back?

At the sound of his door being opened he swivels his chair round. "We need to speak," says Maria. She looks cool and confident and carries a document.

"Sure," he says, attempting to disguise the anxiety that he is about to be cut out of his own project.

"But first, a present," Maria says as she places the document on his workstation.

He picks it up and sees on the cover the initials PCT and, beneath, the legend "International Application Published Under the Patent Cooperation Treaty (PCT)", followed by the title "System for Integration of Foreign DNA at Specific Sites in Chromosomes" and applicant "Arrow Vectors Incorporated, Menlo Park, California 94025, USA".

Richard scans the contents and his anxiety is swept away by a flood of relief: now he'll be able to test whether he is right about developing a revolutionary gene therapy that is safe as well as effective. Like a condemned man who has just read the words of a last-minute pardon, he looks up at his savior.

"You delivered on the science," she says, as though reading his thoughts.

"How on earth did you do it?"

"Didn't I ask you to trust me?" she reproves.

"I shall never doubt you again. Promise." She gazes down at him, lips slightly parted in amusement. He wonders if she'd sensed his fear about being cut out. "I'll have Lucy in," he says, reaching for the phone. "She can start refining the vector straight away."

"That's what we need to talk about," she says as she put her hand over his to prevent him dialing. "There's a complication."

"Like what?"

She sits down on the other side of his workstation so that her eyes are level with his. "Bew was going to fight us."

Richard frowns. "He hasn't sold us a license?"

"He can't. We've taken over Arrow Vectors and own all its assets, including all its intellectual property rights."

"Then the targeting technology is legally ours?"

"Correct."

"So, tell him to take a running jump." It pleases Richard greatly that Bew can't call the shots any more.

The amusement leaves Maria's face. "Not a good idea, I'm afraid, Richard. Bew was going to fight us. He was going to mount a publicity campaign. Can you imagine the line he'd take? Gene therapist calls foul. Medical benefits of new technology threatened by takeover."

"That's hypocritical bullshit. He's not interested in medical benefits, only in making money."

"Of course. But why should he stick to the truth? He's got nothing to lose."

Richard groans. "Science journals, some newspapers, maybe even some TV programs would pick up a story like that."

"It'd bring you right back into the headlines."

"That's the last thing I need right now."

"Precisely. Too many people would ask too many questions about the research you're doing here."

Richard grimaces at the memory of how bad publicity had led to demands that his research be barred. "What on earth do we do?"

"There was a way out."

"Tell me."

"I offered Bew a sufficiently lucrative employment contract to apply his targeting technology to your vector. The non-disclosure clause shuts him up."

30

On the large whiteboard that dominates one long wall of Eden Therapy's conference room Richard scrawls ideograms using red, blue, green, and black markers. Arrows link thin colored rectangles threaded on black lines to similar figures, to circles, and to polyhedrons inside circles that radiate matchsticks. Esoteric labels, like "pol" and the Greek letter psi, invest the figures with arcane symbolism: the genetic engineers' version of ancient hieroglyphs.

He looks down from the whiteboard to face Bew, flanked by his two assistants, Rosina and Carol, seated directly across the conference table. Bew is a ghost from a more distant past. If you replace his neatly trimmed silver hair and business suit with auburn shoulder-length tresses and a custom-made velvet outfit, he would be the Harvard vintage Randy Bew who looked down on Richard's working class background and mocked his dedication to medical science at the expense of the good life. His face had changed little. Richard still finds something disturbing about the way Bew's small eyes and thick lips belie the innocence of his cherubic expression. "Can you target this vector?" Richard asks.

Bew examines the diagrams and gives a self-satisfied smile. "This stuff is good. Once my targeting technology is integrated, we'll clean up in the vector stakes. I trust Eden Therapy has a good patent attorney?"

"Are you able to produce what I want?" Richard repeats.

Bew glances from one assistant to the other, as though inviting them to scorn the imputation that anything lay beyond his ability. He rises and picks up a marker from the ledge below the whiteboard. "You tell me where you want your genetic material integrated," he says, "and Carol and Rosina will make the appropriate RNA sequence"—he scribbles a wiggly line—"to stitch in here"—he draws an arrow directed at part of the vector diagram—"and it will transform your random high-powered missiles into smart high-powered missiles."

"I'll provide you with two DNA constructs," Richard says brusquely. "I want three hundred mil of vector for each construct to integrate here on chromosome 3." An arrow indicates the site that Richard is sure will be safe.

"Two lots of three hundred mil at this concentration?" Bew queries.

"Can you do it?"

"Why so much?"

Richard's irritation grows. "I asked if you can do it."

Bew's lips curl in a smile. "I noticed you've had six monkeys delivered. That's enough vector to infect every cell in three experimental monkeys and three controls, assuming the second DNA construct contains everything except the sequence that's meant to destroy the cancer."

Carol and Rosina gaze admiringly at their mentor. His face is a picture of innocence. "Do these poor monkeys have cancer in every single organ and tissue?"

Bew is sharp. He won't be diverted as easily as the rest of the staff, but Richard is now more adept at the plausible lie. "I want to see if the DNA sequence has side effects on any organs or tissues. The simplest way is to hit every cell in a monkey and see what happens."

Bew returns his stare. "Give me your vector and I'll have it targeted in six weeks time."

As soon as the monkeys' three-day quarantine is over, Richard brings in a vet to examine them, give them a TB test, and certify that they are free of contagious diseases and fit for drugs testing.

Fit is not a word that springs to Richard's mind when he begins his baseline monitoring. Dressed in a lab coat, bouffant lab cap, sterile plastic shoe covers, linen face mask, and disposable sterile latex gloves, he unlocks the door of the left-hand cage on the top rack. It smells of urine. The female macaque remains squatted on the floor of the cage. She turns her head sideways so that the large sad eyes below her low brow ridge look away from him. The eyes show the milky white discs of cataracts.

"Come on, old girl, let's get you dressed," he says kindly as he offers her a primate jacket. She doesn't resist when he fits each arm through the half sleeves of the string vest, gently turns her round, and zips up the back. Into the pocket on the back he places a small black box that will record the duration of movement compared with non-movement. She remains on her haunches, facing the rear of the cage. The personal activity monitor isn't exactly going to go off the scale, he thinks. He closes the cage door and offers her a marshmallow as a reward. Slowly she turns and reached through the bars. The hand that takes the marshmallow is shaking. He makes a note to give this monkey the anti-aging gene inducer rather than an infusion of everything except the inducer.

After fitting out all the monkeys with a primate jacket and a personal activity monitor, Richard hands Maria a video camera and tells her to film each monkey now, and then when he hands it a puzzle ball. From a cupboard in the monkey room he takes a box of hollow green plastic balls; each is about the size of a baseball and is studded with dime-sized holes. He unscrews one into halves, puts in an apple from the bag he'd brought with him, and screws the ball back together again. He looks at Maria. "OK?"

"Right," she says through her face mask and points the camera at the first cage.

Richard opens the cage and drops in the ball. The old monkey reaches out, picks it up with one hand, smells the apple, tries to bite, and then drops the ball when she fails to taste the apple.

"Not exactly the liveliest animals I've ever seen," Maria says after he's given a ball to each of the monkeys. She bends to take a close-up of a male who is examining the stainless steel mirror suspended in his cage. The monkey turns his back on Maria and moves the mirror to keep her reflection in sight as she tries to attract his attention, but he refuses to make direct eye contact with her.

A week later Richard removes the personal activity monitor from each monkey's primate jacket and plugs it into his computer, which gives a statistical readout and graphical display on its screen. To complete the baseline monitoring, he and Maria take MRI scans of the monkeys.

Finally, the day arrives. Brushing aside Bew's offer to help, Richard infuses the monkeys. Two days later he takes blood and skin samples from each monkey and gives them to Lucy.

Richard's absence from the laboratory has tormented her: the more time he spent in the animal facility with that woman, the more

Lucy determined not to lose him. "Relax, Richard," she says when she sees the anxiety on his face. "Let's do the analyses together."

For the rest of the day they work as a team, extracting DNA from each sample, using a PCR machine to amplify the section of DNA he is looking for, and sequencing the product. As evening falls they watch her computer print out a chart showing spiky peaks and troughs in four different colors representing the four bases, A, T, C and G, of the DNA molecule. Together they check the sequence of the bases. It corresponds to the sequence of the anti-aging gene inducer attached to the section of chromosome that he'd targeted for insertion. Richard turns to Lucy with a grim smile of satisfaction. Now all he has to do is wait to see if successfully inserting the inducer far away from all known potential tumor-promoting genes will prevent the monkeys from developing cancer.

31

What had Jim Watson told him at Cold Spring Harbor when Richard wondered whether his determination to find the immortalizing gene was unbalancing him and affecting his marriage? All the best scientists, Watson said, are obsessives. The fight in the laboratory is hard: the science problems, the funding problems, the competition, the tension, the strain, the discoveries of others, the jealousies, the prizes beckoning, and the frustrations. It may be that some scientists enjoy a normal life with their partners, but even normality for the dedicated scientist merges imperceptibly into pathology. Where is the boundary? Mental balance is at best a precarious state.

Never has Richard felt that precariousness more than now. The period between carrying out an experiment and waiting for the result that would either support or disprove a theory of his is agonizing. There is nothing more he can do.

Richard's daily medical checks on the monkeys find no lumps or other indications of cancer in the three experimental monkeys; on the contrary, they appear healthier and livelier than the three control monkeys. The definitive proof of whether or not he has succeeded in halting the aging process would only be detected when he runs the complete set of tests scheduled for December.

His growing optimism is shattered in August when Maria comes into his office and closes the door behind her. "What's wrong with the monkeys, Richard?"

"Why?" he asks, failing to hide the alarm in his voice.

"The new technician has complained that a monkey grabbed his hand and bit him. When they came here, those monkeys weren't capable of biting an apple, much less taking a mouthful of someone's hand."

His heart pounds as tries to figure out what has gone wrong this time. "Let's go see."

After putting on protective clothing, Richard and Maria leave the changing room and open the door of the animal room to be met by the musty odor of the monkeys' bodies mixed with the pungent stench of their urine. The three control monkeys remain hunched on the floor of their cages, oblivious of the plastic puzzle balls containing apples; the jackets they'd been fitted with would have given them a comical appearance were it not for their mournful eyes. The three experimental monkeys, however, respond noisily to Richard's approach. The two females chatter anxiously, back away, and climb to the upper corners of their cages while never taking their eyes from him. Their jackets are ragged with bite holes, while their plastic puzzle balls lie unscrewed on the floor. The experimental male flings himself from one side of his cage to the other, baring his teeth and making barking noises. His plastic puzzle ball is torn to shreds.

"What's wrong with him?" Maria asks.

He shakes his head. "I don't know." The realization of just how aggressive this monkey has become disturbs him deeply. The aggression could be a sign of anxiety or of something much worse; it is certainly abnormal for a monkey of his age. "No point in waiting," he says grimly. "I need to carry out the tests now." The demons of doubt chortle in triumph.

Three weeks later, Richard's pale features loom like a specter in the darkness as he moves to the lectern. Thick black roller blinds cover the windows in Eden Therapy's conference room. Apart from a narrow tungsten beam from the reading lamp focused on the lectern at the head of the conference table, the only other sources of light are a thin wedge of neon escaping from the bottom of the closed door, a rectangle of white projected onto the screen on the wall opposite the door, and three opaque white squares from the three adjacent light boxes on the wall facing the whiteboard. Richard has set the stage to reveal his conclusions to Lucy, who sits on one side of the table, and Maria, who sits on the other side with her back to the light boxes.

"First, the good news," he says. "The three experimental monkeys display no signs of cancer or, indeed, any other disease: no tumors show on their MRI scans, and the autopsy of the sacrificed male revealed only healthy tissue in the lymph nodes, lungs, kidneys, and liver. By contrast, tumors are indicated in the MRI scans of two of the control monkeys and cancer was confirmed in the colon of the sacrificed female."

His hands grip the sides of the lectern. "What worried me, however, was the abnormal behavior of the experimental monkeys. I hoped that the MRI scans might suggest a possible explanation."

Richard leaves the lectern and moves to the light boxes, on which he places a series of MRI films. "The second scans of the control monkeys show the expected age-related shrinkage of major organs compared with those taken three months before." He replaces the films with another set. "The scans of the three monkeys infused with the anti-aging gene inducer surprised me. They show not a stabilization, as I'd anticipated, but an *increase* in the size of liver, lungs, and kidneys. Most remarkable of all are these scans."

He places on the light boxes six MRI films. Each shows a dozen images that resemble white walnut halves with thick gray borders against a black background. "Comparisons of the brain of each monkey before infusion and three months later show an *increase* in white matter." He points to a black comma-shaped region in the right- and left-hand lobes of each brain. "The lateral ventricles have shrunk, consistent with a restoration of atrophied brain cells or a growth of new brain cells." He pauses and turns to the two women. "I didn't dare believe what I was seeing. It was essential to find out exactly what had occurred: hence the need to sacrifice two of the monkeys."

Maria turns round from the light boxes and studies Lucy's reaction. She is still staring at the films; her fists are bunched.

Richard returns to the lectern and picks up the controller of the slide projector that stands next to it. "We stained the brain cells in order to identify dopaminergic neurons, just as we did with fetal human brain cells in laboratory culture." He presses a button and the white rectangle on the screen is replaced by an image of fluorescent red cells: many resemble shriveled tadpoles, with only a short filament sprouting from each tail and three to five short filaments from each head. "These cells are derived from the control monkey; many of its neurons are atrophied, as expected at its age."

The next slide, like that from the laboratory experiment, shows only bright red, plump tadpoles sprouting tangles of long, branching filaments. "These cells are from the monkey infused with the anti-aging gene inducer. There are only healthy neurons and no, repeat no, atrophied neurons."

He pauses to let the observation sink in, and then he spells out his conclusion. "Like all the other tissue samples taken from the experimental monkey, the brain tissue resembles that of a monkey in its prime. It explains the monkey's behavior. That behavior was abnormal for an elderly monkey, but it was perfectly normal for a healthy young male."

Richard is presenting his findings to two people in a small conference room, but in the darkness he sees ranks of scientists in an overcrowded Grace Auditorium at the Cold Spring Harbor Laboratory eager to witness an historic event. "The accumulation of evidence is irrefutable," he declares. "Switching on the anti-aging gene in a monkey with our technique doesn't just prevent further aging degeneration; it repairs existing damage, restoring the body to prime condition. With no adverse side effects."

Lucy breaks into spontaneous applause and then rushes to hug Richard. "This is going to be the biggest medical breakthrough since… since I don't know when!"

For once Maria seems unconcerned at Lucy's display of intimacy with Richard. A smile of satisfaction plays on her lips.

"Well, Richard Trent, it seems to me that you've made the genetic elixir of eternal youth."

Richard is on a high, experiencing a foretaste of the moment he would know that his name was immortalized alongside Pasteur, Fleming, Watson and Crick, and the other pioneers of medical science. What he has accomplished justified the minor deceptions.

Still smiling, Maria presses a button on the speakerphone and says, "Roger, didn't I say that we weren't to be disturbed?"

Her assistant's voice comes through the amplifier. "I told that to Dr. Bew, but he said he guaranteed you'd want to hear what he has to say."

Maria glances at Richard. He shrugs. "Put him through," she says.

Bew's voice is measured and confident. "I think it's about time I joined your little meeting, Maria. I know what that vector is being used for. And it isn't for treating cancer."

32

The dapper Bew, carrying a briefcase, saunters into a conference room exposed to the afternoon sun streaming through hastily unshaded windows. He takes the seat vacated by Lucy and looks round at the slide projector and the screen opposite, and at the switched-on light boxes from which the MRI films have been removed. "Do I get to see the son et lumière?"

"You get the floor for ten minutes, Randy." The very lack of expression in Maria's voice carries a greater menace than any overt challenge. "I trust you'll make good use of it."

Richard fears his own impulsiveness when threatened. He resolves to keep quiet and let Maria handle Bew.

"I think you'll find I make as good a use of this next ten minutes as of the last three months," Bew says smoothly. "I haven't exactly been over-employed since I targeted the vector, and so I did a little fishing."

It is the smile that irritates Richard most: not just self-confident, but too angelic to be true. "I was, I'm sure you understand, mildly curious about the company I'd joined," Bew continues. "I worried that none of its scientists has published anything, received any external funding, or applied for any patents. Nothing remarkable in that for a biotech enterprise struggling to produce something salable to a pharmaceutical corporation before its startup finance runs out. Except, of course, that your new method of making a retroviral vector at that concentration should have been patented and licensed for a small fortune."

He waits for a reaction. Maria remains expressionless. Richard tries to follow her lead.

"As for the chief scientist himself," Bew's oleaginous tone continues, "he declined my offer to help with the monkeys, while I saw lights burning long into the night. But of reports to the rest of us mere mortals in the company, not a word, still less any publications. I wonder why?"

Maria stares at Bew but says nothing.

"If you won't give the answer, I will," says Bew with the assuredness of one who now understood what his secret weapon was when he'd turned the tables on Maria Snowe. "You've avoided drawing attention to the gene you're working on because you've been secretly developing an anti-aging therapy, the project you publicly abandoned when announcing that you were wrong about the gene and its effect on neurons." He smiles. "You've used the powerful vector that I refined to switch on the gene throughout a monkey's body." His smile becomes positively cherubic. "And it worked."

Still Maria remains impassive.

"I understand your need for secrecy. But what intrigues me is what you do next. You need to undertake clinical trials, but you don't stand a snowball's chance in hell of getting approvals."

"Why not?" Richard retorts before he can stop himself.

"Let's all stop playing little innocents, shall we?" Bew retorts. "Here are three reasons for starters. First, until NIH and the World Health Organization change their policies, the FDA is never going to allow you to put a gene inducer like this into human germline cells. Second, this." He removes photocopies of press cuttings from his briefcase and scatters them on the table. They include the original *Los Angeles Times* article headlined "Immortality Boffin Attacked by UCLA Colleague", plus news stories and features following up the debate on The NewsHour With Jim Lehrer. "And third, this," he adds as he places on the table a copy of Richard's letter to *Science*, "is a blatant lie about your original research results. No way will the FDA approve human trials by you. In fact, if the FDA finds out just what you're doing, it will close you down."

Richard looks at Maria. She might have been a sculpture for all the reaction she shows. He tries to restrain himself.

"I suggested we all should stop playing little innocents," Bew says. "Let me be frank. I couldn't give a rat's ass what laws you've broken."

"We've broken no laws," Richard snaps.

Bew shrugs. "You're in a classic dilemma. You can't get approvals to do the trials necessary to prove that your therapy halts human aging diseases. But if you *can* prove that it halts them with no side effects, you'll be unstoppable because nobody will deny you anything."

Maria hasn't spoken a word since giving Bew the floor.

"You must think I'm as dumb as the rest of the people here. But I've been doing some research of my own. Not in the lab, you understand, but in the databases. Shall I share with you what I've found?" he asks innocently.

Maria's glance instructs Richard to say nothing.

"As you're so eager to know, I'll tell you." He removes a sheet of paper from his briefcase and reads from it. "The current value of the US market for cancer drugs is four billion dollars a year." He looks up. "If we assume half of that is for cancers caused by an age-related accumulation of genetic mutations, that gives us two billion dollars a year." He resumes his reading. "The market for drugs to treat skin aging is three billion a year, to treat osteoporosis and osteoarthritis is five billion, to treat vessel aging that produces cardiovascular diseases and strokes is ten billion, and to treat Parkinson's, Alzheimer's, and other neuron-aging diseases is eight billion. That gives us a drugs market for aging-induced diseases in the USA alone of twenty-eight billion a year."

He places the paper on the table. "Throw in Canada, Europe, Japan, and other developed countries and we're talking around ninety billion dollars *every* year. That's right now. But the scientifically advanced countries are graying fast. By 2026 one in every six people in the USA will be over sixty-five years old."

Bew sits back. "As medical technology continues to improve, we're trading in earlier, and usually quicker, deaths from contagious diseases for painful degenerative diseases as we live longer. My calculator ran out of zeros when I tried to project the value in ten years time of the world drugs market for aging diseases."

"But," he leans forward, "current drugs only treat the *symptoms* of these diseases. What, I asked myself, would be the value of a company whose product stopped those diseases in their tracks?" His small eyes glint at Maria and Richard in turn. "Or does it even *cure* them?"

Richard needs no glance from Maria to remain silent: Bew's velvet words had delivered a stun grenade.

Bew turns to Richard. "That's why nobody would deny you anything once you've proved your therapy is safe and works with humans. That size of world market decides what happens, not some bible bangers down in Alabama, or some ethics professors in California, or some science desk jockeys in Maryland. But I don't need to tell you that, do I, my dear Richard? You figured that out long ago."

Richard had never really hated anyone before. Nathan Hill, Don Straker, and the others had provoked his anger, but Bew's assumption that Richard shared his own despicable mercenary motives for doing science evoked utter loathing.

"I confess that I also underestimated you, Maria," Bew says. "There was I, figuring out how much in excess of twelve dollars a share I could sell out to Novartis for. But if your anti-aging gene therapy does work in humans you won't be selling out to Novartis or Merck or Pfizer or BMS, you'll be taking them over."

Maria looks at Bew and speaks for the first time. "We hear you, Randy. What do you want?"

"One third of your shares in Eden Therapy and one third of Richard's. Naturally I will buy them from you." He treats her to his most angelic smile. "At, let us say, their par value of one thousandth of a dollar."

She doesn't blink.

"Then we'll all be one happy family," says Bew smugly, "with Richard and I becoming the wealthiest scientists in history."

This is too much for Richard. If there had been any way of wiping this vermin from the face of the earth, he would have taken it.

"Come, come now," Bew tuts when he sees the hatred in Richard's eyes, "you shouldn't find it too difficult to swallow. After all, the future value of those shares is so far off the scale it hardly matters whether they're split two ways or three."

"I'll have my attorney draw up the appropriate documents," Maria says. "We'll sign in my office Monday lunchtime."

For a moment Richard looks at her in disbelief, and then he storms out of the room.

33

When Maria had agreed so readily to Bew's demands it was as though Salome had dropped all her veils at once, without even the shake of a hip. The tantalizing mystery was gone, the base motive revealed for all to see.

Richard had first assumed that she wanted to finance his research in order to find a treatment for the Alzheimer's disease from which her mother suffered. Her desire to press ahead with human trials after her mother died convinced him that she was afraid she had inherited the gene for early-onset Alzheimer's. Her sole purpose in imposing secrecy, he'd been certain, was to protect him from the Luddites who wanted to bar his work. But Bew had uncovered her real motive: to ensure she had a monopoly on any cure for aging diseases that he developed. To maintain that monopoly she was happy to give Bew an equal partnership in the company and let this blackmailer share the credit for his medical breakthrough. The assurances that she wanted to make his dream come true, the ways she had made him feel that he was the most important person in her life, all these were now exposed as part of a cynical stratagem to use him in order to make her wealthy beyond his comprehension.

Angry and humiliated, Richard went straight from the conference room to his laboratory. "Lucy," he says, "we need to talk. Will you come to supper this Sunday at my place?"

She looks up in surprise; a strand of hair that had escaped her ponytail curls across her cheek. Since the time he'd declared to Snowe that his relationship with her was purely professional, they'd never met outside the lab. For her part she understood that to continue working with him on the project they both passionately believed in she must not cross that professional boundary—at least until Richard no longer depended on Snowe's financial backing. She toys with the strand of hair in order to cover the blush of anticipation that burns her cheeks. "I'd like that."

The lazy drone on a hot, somnolent late Sunday afternoon grows in volume. Richard goes to the front porch and sees Lucy's motorbike head towards him along the narrow, deserted lane between the yellowing fields that separate his house from the distant blacktop. After that meeting with Bew, Richard has stayed away from Eden Therapy and hasn't answered Maria's messages. He needed to calm down, he needed time and space to think, and he needed to share his dilemma with Lucy.

The bike turns off the lane and roars up the gravel driveway by the side of the front lawn. Lucy brakes to a halt and switches off the engine, leaving only the hum of bees among the flowerbeds to disturb the silence. The handlebars gleam in the sunlight as she dismounts, parks the bike, and removes her helmet. He greets her with a hesitant kiss on the cheek, unsure how she will react after nearly a year and a half in which they'd treated each other as no more than professional colleagues. Lucy responds with a smile that recalls the night she had taken him back from L'Incontro after they'd celebrated the success of the neuron experiment. Exhilarated by a shared triumph and a shared dream, they'd faced each other after climbing off her bike; he wondered what might have developed if his clumsy reference to Jackie hadn't broken the spell.

"Where can I freshen up?" she asks.

"Second door on the right."

Removing a knapsack from the pannier by the rear wheel, she slings it over her shoulder and heads for the house. "I'll be out the back," he calls after her.

When she emerges onto the back porch Lucy has let her hair down and changed into the blue button-through dress she'd worn the evening she made dinner for his birthday, transforming herself from the youthful, almost tomboyish, Lucy of the lab into the young woman who had taken such care to compensate for Jackie's indifference. He finds himself repeating what he'd said that evening: "You look lovely."

"What a super house," she says to hide her embarrassment. She gazes from the white clapboarded bungalow to the back lawn, the swimming pool, the fruit trees, and the ragged straw-colored field that rises beyond. In the shimmering light the bottle green of bay trees, the olivine foliage of spreading oaks, and the emerald of tall gum trees daub the distant yellow hills like strokes on a Cezanne canvas.

"What would you like to drink?" he asks.

"Diet coke, please," she says instinctively, undermining her attempt to appear sophisticated.

He goes to the kitchen, removes a can of coke and a bottle of Chardonnay from the refrigerator, puts them on a wooden tray, adds glasses, and takes the tray through to the stone terrace where he has lit a barbecue. He pours the drinks and offers her the coke.

She knows she has been invited for a purpose and seeks his eyes as she takes the glass from his hand, but sees that he isn't ready to unburden himself. "Thanks."

He sips his wine and watches her slender, long-limbed figure wander down the back lawn, sometimes bending to inspect shrubs. Occasionally she glances back at him, half shyly, half questioningly. How many times had Lucy said that Maria was a control freak? How many times had she asked if he was certain that Maria's sole reason for funding their research was to find a cure for Alzheimer's disease? And how many times had he dismissed her questions as paranoia? She understood Maria. She also understood him: his vision and his obsession, his ambition and his insecurity, his self-belief and his self-doubt. And yet there was also something deeper that attracted him:

she possessed an uncorrupted innocence, an innate instinct for what is right.

She walks back from the lawn and sits patiently on the edge of a sun lounger to watch while he grills skewers of monkfish. The aroma of charcoal-broiled fish and wisps of blue smoke from the barbecue drift past her and rise towards the cloudless sky.

He serves the fish kebabs with rice and a green salad on a wooden trestle table. While they eat he recounts the meeting with Bew. She listens without comment until he finishes, puts down his fork, and looks at her.

"Publish our work and put it in the public domain," she says promptly. "Then Bew can't blackmail us."

He sighs. "It's not that simple."

"Why not?"

He stares into his wineglass. "The agreement I signed with Maria includes a non-disclosure clause, just like yours."

"But Bew is prepared to ignore that clause of his contract if you don't give him a one-third stake in the company."

Lucy's readiness to break her contract surprises him.

"What other choice do we have, Richard? Either we go along with her plan to monopolize your discovery about a gene that everyone possesses in order to make a fortune, or else we break our agreement with her and make your discovery freely available."

He vividly recalled that May evening in Maria's study when fog blanketed out the rest of the world. Then, it seemed, the agreement liberated him from a future of constant battles with the scientific establishment and ruthless pharmaceutical corporations, and enabled him to fulfill his dream; now it haunts him with the price it exacts. "It's not my discovery any more."

She pushes aside her plate. "I don't understand."

"That agreement gives Maria ownership of the discovery and all my subsequent work through her majority shareholding in Eden Therapy."

"The discovery doesn't belong to her," Lucy asserts, "or even to you. It belongs to the world."

It might have been him talking, back in those days at the university before betrayal had hardened his heart as well as his resolve. "It's not just the discovery. I want to prove how it can be used to cure aging diseases."

"Then share our research with the National Institutes of Health. Tell them you want their help to secure FDA approval for clinical trials to be carried out at the NIH."

He sees in her an innocence that he has lost, an innocence that part of him wants to reclaim. But a greater part has been seared by bitter experience. "Bew was right. The FDA is not going to sanction the clinical trial we need."

She frowns. "That TV program and your letter in *Science*?"

"It's not just that." He refills his wineglass. "The FDA thinks we don't know enough about the long term consequences of modifying human genes, especially something as radical as switching on a master regulatory gene throughout the whole body. In its view it'd be unethical to allow the anti-aging gene inducer to get into germline cells where it would be passed on to succeeding generations."

"Because any side effects we failed to identify would be inherited?"

"Right." He collects the empty plates and takes them to the kitchen.

When he returns she has taken her glass from the table and is sitting on the edge of one of the sun loungers, immersed in thought. As he approaches she looks up. "Surely we can use the immortalin inducer to treat diseases without letting it get into germline cells?"

He stares into the far distance, beyond the green-dappled yellow hills. It was what he'd originally planned: a localized treatment for a specific diseased organ. But that was before he'd achieved an incomparably greater scientific breakthrough. He sits on the lounger next to hers. "I've shown that with a single infusion I can cure every aging disease in a monkey's body."

"Richard," she says passionately, "do you want to help Snowe and Bew make a fortune or do you want act ethically?" Like a child her candor makes allowances for nobody.

All his life he's gone for the home run. Now that he is sure he can hit the ball out of the stadium, the idea of tapping it and jogging to first base runs against his nature. And he may not even be allowed to reach first base. "Even if I do propose a limited application of the gene inducer, there's still a risk the FDA will refuse approval for a human trial."

"It's a risk we have to take," she declares.

But if he breaks his agreement with the company and discloses his research to the FDA, Eden Therapy would still legally own that research and have the right to patent it. The Maria who happily cuts a deal with someone like Bew doesn't have any scruples. She'd find a way to enable Bew to take forward the research to the next stage, the only stage that history would record: the first successful trial of a gene therapy that cures all aging diseases in a human with a single infusion. Bew being acclaimed for Richard's vision and years of hard work would be far worse than Bew making a fortune from it.

Tenderly she places a hand on his arm. "I know what you're going through."

Does she really understand how vulnerable he feels? How afraid of losing his life's dream of revolutionizing medical science? How humiliated he is by falling for Maria's allure only to discover that she is cynically exploiting him?

"You know I'll do anything to help," she says diffidently.

He looks at Lucy's open, honest face, and in her eyes he sees compassion. She is the only one who has never let him down, the only one who has truly cared for him. Never did he need her more than now. Reaching out a hand he brushes aside her hair and touches her cheek.

She blushes and turns her head to avoid his eyes. Her lips meet the palm of his hand. The kiss is the gentlest and most sensuous he's ever experienced.

He rises to his feet, taking her with him. Wrapping his arms round her, he holds her close, comforted by her warmth and reassurance, and breathing in the fragrance of jasmine. For a while they stay like that, with her head burrowed against his shoulder. "Let's go inside," he whispers into her hair.

Holding his hand tightly she glances round the white-walled bedroom with its blond wooden floor and pine bed. The crumpled white duvet is thrown carelessly back from the white sheet.

He releases her grip, takes her face between his hands, and kisses her on the lips. It is what she's dreamed of, but now that it is happening she is frozen with anxiety that her lack of experience and her slender, almost boyish, figure will disappoint him.

Sensing her nervousness, he tries to contain the urgency rising within him. He runs his hands through her hair and kisses each eyelid and the end of her nose before placing his lips on hers and gently probing inside her mouth with his tongue. As she responds with a quickening of her breath, he strokes her cheek and lets one hand slide slowly down her neck and onto the cotton of her dress. The phone rings. His hand finds and undoes the top button of her dress. The answerphone cuts in followed by Maria's husky voice saying, "Richard, I've been trying to get hold of you. Please phone. You know where to reach me." Lucy pulls away and stands taut and uncertain, like a foal that suddenly finds itself in unfamiliar territory.

"Lucy," he says, holding out his arms.

She lowers her head and bites her lip.

"Look at me, Lucy." He puts a hand under her chin, lifts her head, and gazes into her eyes. "Forget her. It's you I want."

Her eyes glisten and he thinks she might cry. Then she puts her arms round his neck and pulls him to her.

Later he was to remember not her initial timidity but her unrestrained appetite for arousal that excited his own desire as her open-mouthed gasps of pleasure merged into one ecstatic cry of abandonment when he released himself into her.

After they finally separate, she nestles her head on his shoulder, trails one arm protectively across his chest and one leg over his thighs, and drifts off to sleep. Beads of perspiration on her brow glitter like tiny diamonds in the rosy glow of the setting sun, strands of flaxen hair stick damply to her face, and her small breasts rise and fall as she breathes deeply through lips parted in a smile. Gently he pulls the duvet over her gracile young body.

Liberated from the humiliation that threatened to paralyze his mind, he lies awake and begins to figure out a solution to his dilemma.

34

Lucy stretches dreamily and reaches across the bed, but he isn't there. She opens her eyes and sees him standing, fully dressed, in front of the window. The bright light makes her squint.

"Good morning, Lucy." He smiles and placed a cup on the bedside table. "Coffee."

She strokes his arm and says with a newfound boldness, "I can think of something better than coffee."

He kisses her on the forehead. "Me too, but I've got to go in and deal with Maria and Bew."

She gives a resigned sigh. She is always going to come second to his pioneering a cure for aging diseases. "Well," she says, putting on a brave face, "you didn't let Straker, Hill, or UCLA stop you before. You're not going to let *Her* stop you now."

"No way."

Richard imagines that the scent of Lucy's body must still be clinging to him when he enters Maria's office. Her normally captivating smile is replaced by a terse, "Richard, where on earth have you been? I phoned your house but there was no reply."

He is tempted to tell her in graphic detail precisely where he had been shortly after she'd left her last message on his answerphone, but that is not his purpose. "Thinking."

For a moment she is nonplussed by his air of quiet assurance, which contrasts with his angry walkout from the meeting with Bew the previous Wednesday. Regaining her composure, she indicates the chair in front of her workstation. "Do you want to share your thoughts with me?"

He remains standing, places his palms on her workstation, leans forward, and looks her in the eyes. "I'm not going to sign over one third of my shares in Eden Therapy to Bew."

"Let's discuss this sensibly."

"There's nothing to discuss. I'm not prepared to let you and Bew take control of my work and monopolize the world drugs market for aging diseases."

"Richard," she says with a pained expression, "how can you say that?"

He straightens up, incredulity written on his face. This woman deserves an Oscar. "So I totally misheard?" he says with arms spread in exaggerated bafflement. "You haven't scheduled a meeting at twelve thirty to transfer one third of my shares and one third of your shares to Bew?"

"Can't you see that I only agreed the deal because it was in your best interests?" she answers calmly.

"In my best interests!" he erupts. "Since when has it been in my best interests to give a prick like Bew an equal share in my research?"

"Agreeing to his demand was a tactical necessity."

"When will it become a tactical necessity to dispense with me?"

"Never!" she protests. "Richard, look at me."

She rises from behind her workstation and approaches him, appearing so wounded that instinctively he feels it must be she, not he, who is the wronged party. But he can't permit himself to be seduced into her plan. He has come prepared to exert blackmail of his own to ensure that he remains in charge of his research and carries it forward to a successful conclusion; he would figure out a way to get rid of Bew later. "Doesn't the agreement I signed give you a controlling stake in Eden Therapy?" he challenges.

"Yes, but—"

"But it also provides that I direct Eden's research program. If you break that clause," he says with a triumphant gleam in his eyes, "then the agreement becomes null and void and the rights to that research revert to me."

"Oh, Richard," she sighs. "What do I have to do before you trust me?"

She looks so hurt, but he stands his ground and says nothing.

"Haven't you always been in sole charge of the research?"

"Until now," he concedes.

"You still are."

"What about Bew?"

"You poor thing. There's no need to feel threatened by Bew. I know how to handle someone like him." She puts out a hand and touches his arm. "Let's have coffee and talk this through."

He watches her go to the alcove, pick up a tray containing a silver thermos flask and two cups, and take it to the coffee table by the window. She turns to him. Her gaze is hypnotic; it has the disturbing ability to drive thoughts of everything and everybody else from his mind. Her graceful bronze neck is as smooth as silk. Her elegant clothes never reveal but always suggest parts of her body that invite his caress; at times the merest glance or subtle change of body position consume him with a physical yearning. He has to remind himself of how he had lain, reassured, with Lucy in his arms.

She bends to place the tray on the table, sits down on one of the low armchairs, smooths down her skirt, and gestures for him to take the chair facing her.

He lowers himself onto the chair and grips the armrests. He is determined to test her assurance that he controls Eden's research program. "Suppose I say that the FDA are right about not giving a one-shot infusion to cure all aging diseases in a human, like we did with the monkeys."

"If that's what you really believe, Richard, then fine," she replies as she pours out the coffee. "But give me your reasons, not those of some bureaucratic institution. Or," she adds, "of some sweet country girl who wouldn't dare cross a road against a Don't Walk sign."

"It will put the genetic modification into germline cells, where it will get passed on to future generations. That's not ethical."

Maria sips her coffee. "What does 'ethical' mean?"

Richard frowns. Since he no longer believes in God, he can hardly give the explanation promulgated by Father Simon at St Ignatius High School: ethics are those moral laws of God governing human beings that can be deduced by reason. "Ethical is... well, it means morally right."

"Who decides what is morally right?"

She invests the question with a childlike simplicity, as though asking why the sky is blue. Richard drinks his coffee slowly. Human reason decides. But if there is no God as ultimate judge, and no Church to arbitrate when humans reason differently, then who does decide? "Society, I guess," he concludes.

"Tell me, Richard, why should society decide that what you want to do is morally wrong?"

"Because society isn't prepared to take the risks of unknown genetic consequences being passed on to succeeding generations."

"Are automobiles banned as unethical?"

"I don't follow."

She puts down her cup. "Fifty thousand people are killed every year in automobile accidents. Society is willing to accept reasonable risks when the benefits exceed them by far. You are the world expert on this gene. In your opinion, do the benefits to society of eliminating aging diseases outweigh the risks?"

Richard has no doubt that they do.

"It's a fact of life that there's no such thing as zero risk," Maria says. "But haven't you done everything possible to eliminate risk by testing your gene inducer and the vector in monkeys?"

He remains silent.

"A pioneer is, by definition, way ahead of society," she continues. "Bew was right about one thing. Being a pioneer puts you in a Catch-22 situation. Because it runs scared of public opinion that doesn't yet understand what you're doing, the FDA daren't approve you switching on your gene in a human until you can prove that it cures aging diseases with no side effects, but you can't prove that until you switch on the gene in a human."

Mesmerizing black eyes hold him fast. "*That* was why I agreed to do a deal with Bew. Not because I share his greed, but because keeping him quiet to prevent bad publicity is the only way to enable you to proceed with clinical trials."

Those eyes look into his soul. "You, Richard, not I, must decide whether it's your destiny to take medical science into a new era. Or will you allow the bible bangers and the self-appointed guardians of society's ethics to deny progress that will benefit society?"

Richard stands up and stares out of the window. From the time Father Lawrence had inspired him with the story of Watson and Crick's discovery, he'd felt it was his destiny. But which of two paths will enable him to achieve his destiny?

He turns to Maria, who sits waiting for his decision. She hadn't reacted angrily to his impugning her motives, but had given a quietly reasoned response. Has he jumped to the wrong conclusion that she is using him to make a fortune?

The intercom on her desk buzzes to break the silence. Roger's voice says, "Maria, there's a detective here. He wants to interview you and Richard."

35

"I apologize for disturbing you, Ms Snowe," Detective McKenna says as he enters her office and shows his San Francisco Police Department badge.

Maria looks from the badge to the young McKenna. His gray eyes seem lost in thought. Curly black hair reaches the shoulders of the creased linen jacket he wears over a T-shirt, while long, elegant fingers add to the impression that he is an artist or musician rather than a policeman. "Not the local Alameda police?" she asks.

He shrugs a smile. "I guess my enquiries wouldn't interest them. I was kinda hoping you might help me out."

"Anything to assist the law," she says huskily. "Coffee?"

"Don't mind if I do, Ms Snowe," McKenna replies.

"Maria, please." She goes to get another cup from the alcove. "Let me see," she says, scrutinizing him, "for you, black with no sugar?"

"Whichever way it comes, Ms Snowe," McKenna says with a vague smile. He wanders absentmindedly round Maria's office, looking at the examples of Mayan culture that hang on the walls. "I wanted to ask about one of your staff."

"Who?"

"Dr. Randolph Bew."

"Then you're in luck," says Maria as she sits down on one of the low armchairs next to Richard and pours out a third cup. "We have a meeting scheduled for twelve thirty. Dr. Bew will be here shortly."

"I doubt it," says McKenna. He gazes at the photograph of the pyramid hung on the wall above Maria's workstation. "Chichén Itzá. That's Mayan, isn't it?"

"Why won't Dr. Bew be here?" asks Maria as she slides the coffee cup across the table towards the vacant seat opposite.

McKenna turns from the photograph to face her. "He died on Saturday night."

For a moment Richard is stunned, and then a wave of relief washes over him: Bew's demise eliminated the threat to his dream.

"My God!" says Maria in surprise. "I never knew he was ill. What was it?"

"A kind of heart attack," says McKenna as he ignores the coffee and continues his wandering. "Someone stuck a knife in his heart."

The color drains from Richard's face. He glances at Maria. She is wide-eyed with astonishment. "Who on earth…?" she begins.

McKenna's perambulation has taken him round the office and back to where he'd started. He nods towards the door, beyond which is the ante-office occupied by Roger. "Employ many gays?"

"Is that a pertinent question?" Maria asks.

"I guess not in progressive Alameda," McKenna replies, "but in provincial San Francisco we like to ascertain the facts."

"I have no idea of the sexual orientation of my staff. They're hired for their ability to do the job, that's all. Why ask?"

"Bew's car was found abandoned outside a bar in the Castro." He scratches his head abstractedly. "It's known as one where gays can pick up rough trade."

"This is all very distressing." Maria takes a handkerchief from her pocket and sniffs.

"Distressing, maybe," McKenna says, "but rather fortunate for your company."

Richard's relief turns to panic. How does McKenna know about Bew's blackmail?

McKenna takes a notebook from his jacket pocket and opens it. "To the tune of ten million dollars."

"What on earth are you talking about?" Richard demands.

McKenna looks round as if seeing Richard for the first time. "Ah, the quiet man. You're the only other shareholder in this company and you don't know about the key person life insurance policy?"

"Dr. Trent is our vice president of research," says Maria. She puts away her handkerchief. "He's responsible for all the science, I deal with all administrative and financial matters."

"I see," says McKenna pensively. "Then we ought to enlighten him. Do you want to or shall I?"

"It's perfectly simple," Maria says. "Arrow Vectors had a key person life insurance policy on Dr. Bew. When our company took over Arrow we inherited the policy."

McKenna makes a point of studying his notebook. "And you renewed the premium?"

"Standard business practice. I'm afraid I don't see the relevance."

"Oh, just ignore my ramblings," McKenna says, and resumes his wandering round the office. He stops in front of the window and gazes out at the Eden Therapy signboard. "The caduceus. A male serpent copulating with a female serpent round a messenger's staff."

"Does detective training includes mythology," Maria asks coyly, "or is that your recreation?"

McKenna turns and smiles. "Symbol of Mercury, god of merchants and thieves. What does Eden Therapy actually do?"

"And of medicine," Maria says. "Isn't the answer in your notebook?"

"Thanks for reminding me." McKenna opens his notebook, turns back a few pages, and reads out loud, "Eden Therapy's mission is to research, develop, and commercialize proprietary processes for the genetic modification of cells and their use in the treatment of human cancers." He looks up. "Very laudable. What does it mean?"

Maria gives him a coquettish look. "You're teasing me. Doesn't an intellectual like you know all about gene therapy?"

McKenna snaps his fingers. "Gene therapy. Right. That means gene research outfits like yours operating at a loss, right? Taking a gamble your scientists will produce some magic potion that'll win the big jackpot from a multinational drugs giant before you run out of cash?"

"I can't speak for public companies whose shareholders may exert pressure for quick returns. At Eden Therapy we provide the resources for Dr. Trent to develop what I believe will prove to be a big step forward in fighting cancer." She looks at him appealingly. "Have you lost any relatives through cancer?"

"Very altruistic," McKenna says, heedless of her seductive charms. "You have a bottomless purse?"

"You've lost me." Maria appears bewildered and vulnerable in the face of McKenna's insinuations.

"I think you should get to the point," says Richard, whose nerves have been set on edge by McKenna's implications that he knows far more than he reveals.

"You know, I've forgotten what it was," McKenna says. "No, wait a minute. That's it. If you're making big losses, I guess ten million dollars comes in handy."

"Are you suggesting—" Richard begins.

"Just musing out loud," says McKenna. "Apart from mythology, we were taught motives. I'm wondering why anyone would want to murder Dr. Bew. Any suggestions?"

"Did he have any money or valuables on him when he was found?" Maria asks.

"No," McKenna concedes.

"Then isn't it simple? He was attacked and robbed outside the gay bar."

"Of course," says McKenna. "Occam's Razor. But then as someone once said, truth is rarely pure and seldom simple."

"I daresay William of Occam would have made a better detective than Oscar Wilde," Maria replies.

"Ah, there I bow to your greater erudition, Ms Snowe." He consults his notebook. "Dr. Bew was working on vectors, right?"

"What are you implying?" Richard demands.

"Nothing," says McKenna, making a point of studying him. "I just wondered what you've got to hide."

Fear runs through Richard like an electric shock. He is sure McKenna can detect it in the pallor of his face, the tightness of his jaw muscles, and the dryness of his throat.

"Do sit down, Detective McKenna," Maria intervenes, "you're making me dizzy. And do tell me your first name. Detective McKenna is such a mouthful."

"I apologize, Ms Snowe. They make me sit down at the office, so this is the only exercise I get, I hope you don't mind." He continues ambling round the room without giving his first name. "You'll not believe this, but I've never seen as heavy a non-disclosure clause as in the contract we found in Dr. Bew's house. What's the size of the jackpot you're hoping to hit with your vector work here and how close are you to it?"

Maria has clearly decided that McKenna is not going to be won over. She assumes a commanding gaze. "The answers to those questions involve commercial secrets that you cannot expect me to divulge without a court order. Unless you have such an order, or any relevant questions, I'm afraid that we do have a cancer research corporation to run." She stands up.

McKenna reaches down and picks up the cup of coffee that Maria had poured for him earlier. He tastes it, grimaces, and puts it down. "Cold. That always happens to me." He smiles ruefully. "I guess the non-disclosure clause wouldn't be enforceable against information relating to a breach of the law."

"That," Maria states, "is not a relevant question since we've broken no law." She stares at him. "Unless you know something that I don't." McKenna holds out his open palms. "I thought not."

"I do apologize for taking up your time, Ms Snowe. I trust this will be my last visit on this matter." He pauses. "Unless, that is, you think of anything that may assist my investigation." He hands Maria and Richard his card.

"Well," says Maria as she goes to the alcove, "after that I think we could do with something stronger than coffee."

Richard watches as she opens a cupboard and removes a bottle of brandy and two glasses. Could she really have had Bew murdered?

But what motive did she have? If she wanted to exploit his discovery in order to make a fortune, then Bew would have made her ideal science partner. If she only wanted a cure for the early-onset Alzheimer's disease she would develop if she had inherited the gene from her mother, then Bew posed no threat; on the contrary, he had been happy to break any laws in order to move ahead to human trials. If anyone had a motive to get rid of Bew, it was Richard himself.

Maria pours the drinks and passes one to Richard. "A penny for your thoughts."

Richard picks up his glass and stares into the amber liquid. There wasn't a shred of evidence linking Maria to Bew's murder. The clear link was with the robbery. If you go to seedy bars to pick up rough trade, then a mugging like that was something waiting to happen. It was a fortunate coincidence that it had happened now, but that's all it was. There is nothing to be gained by looking beyond the obvious explanation for Bew's death, Richard concludes. "I'm thinking," he says as he raises his glass, "that it's good riddance to bad rubbish."

36

Lucy snuggles back down under the duvet and recalls how she and Richard had made love. It was the most awesome sensation she's ever experienced, but most of all she treasured their intimacy afterwards, lying in his arms, legs entwined, and sinking into a sated sleep with the knowledge that it was her he wanted.

Reluctantly she surfaces from the memory and gets out of bed. No longer concerned that she lacks a voluptuous figure like Snowe's, she wanders naked through to Richard's bathroom. Sumptuously furnished, it is very much a man's room, with few toiletries other than soap, shampoo, shower gel, and antiperspirant spray. She decides to try the whirlpool bath; there probably wouldn't be another opportunity once Richard has told Snowe he intends to develop a government-approved treatment that would be available to everyone and not be monopolized by Eden Therapy.

Luxuriating in the warm, bubbling water she guesses they'd probably move to Maryland to carry out clinical trials at one of the

National Institutes of Health facilities. As her mind drifts she thinks of all the husband and wife research teams. Although professionally she wants to remain Lucy Jonnsen, she finds herself testing the sound of Lucy Trent. Suddenly she brings herself up with a start: this is silly and presumptuous. Richard's priority is always going to be his research; she should just enjoy what has happened between them and see how things develop.

She climbs out of the bath, washes her hair, and dries herself with one of the thick, fluffy towels from the linen cupboard. With a giggle she sprinkles her body with Richard's talcum powder, which smells of sandalwood. In the bedroom she finds her clothes scattered on the floor. She puts on her bra and briefs, packs her dress and shoes in her knapsack, and slips into the T-shirt, shorts, and sneakers she'd worn to ride to the house.

After a breakfast of orange juice, toast, and coffee, she collects the glasses, plates, cutlery, and cooking utensils from the barbecue and puts them in the dishwasher along with her breakfast things, makes the bed, and tidies up before locking the house with the keys Richard had left her.

Such a shame Richard had to leave, she thinks as she looks back at the house: she could get used to living in a place like this. Kick-starting her bike with a grin, she roars off for Eden Therapy, eager to learn how She responded when Richard told her he was disclosing their research results.

Lucy can't find Richard in the lab or his office, and so she goes along the corridor to Snowe's office suite. Roger looks up from his keyboard when she opens the door. "Do you know where Richard is?" she asks.

He turns his head in the direction of the inner door that leads into Maria's room, turns back, and gives her a quizzical look. "Is it urgent?"

"No. When he leaves, tell him I'm in the lab."

Puzzled that the meeting is taking so long, Lucy goes back and waits anxiously, wondering what She and Bew are up to.

It is another half hour before Richard strides into the lab. Lucy hurries towards him, ready to greet him with a kiss, but stops when she sees his face, taut and unsmiling. "Richard, what's wrong?"

All thoughts of their lovemaking have been driven from his mind by the dramatic events of the morning. "Maria's summoning a staff meeting. I wanted to warn you first."

"Warn me?"

"A detective interviewed us this morning. Bew's been found murdered."

At the special staff meeting in the conference room Maria announces simply that Bew had died during the weekend. One of his assistants, the normally effervescent Rosina, bursts in tears; the blonde English Carol stares back disbelievingly. The responses of the other sixteen faces round the table range from shock through curiosity to Richard's tight-lipped brooding. "Those who wish to do so," Maria continues, "may take the rest of the day off as a mark of respect." She turns to Carol and Rosina. "I'm afraid we're going to have to close the vector lab. I'll be away on a business trip for the next few days. Roger will handle all your arrangements."

Maria leaves the room and the others trail out in groups of two or three, engaged in animated low-voiced conversations. "I'll see you back in the lab," Lucy whispers to Richard before she goes to comfort the distraught Rosina. Richard remains seated, staring blankly at the screen on the far side of the room. If he is unwilling to look beyond the obvious explanation for Bew's death, McKenna's questions have, nonetheless, unnerved him. The longer he stares, trying to figure out what McKenna's investigation might throw up, the more probable it seems that McKenna will find the Immortality Boffin press cuttings among Bew's possessions. Is there anything else in Bew's house that suggests he knew what research is really being carried out at Eden? What else would McKenna find? Each question prompts another, increasing his preoccupation until he is oblivious of the passage of time.

"You still here, Richard?"

He focuses on Lucy standing in the doorway.

She comes to sit beside him and places a hand on top of his. "What's the matter?" she asked sympathetically.

"Nothing," he replies.

"Was it that detective?" she said, disturbed at the way he has retreated into himself after their intimacy of the day before.

He looks away to the screen. Could it have been less than a week, he thinks, since that screen had been lit up with a picture of the monkey's rejuvenated neurons? Had Bew confided in Rosina or Carol, or anyone else, who might disclose the results of his covert research now that Bew is dead? Would McKenna find any evidence that Bew was blackmailing them?

"What did he want?" Lucy persists.

"Just a smart-ass from the city fishing around for a motive for Bew's murder," Richard retorts.

"Why here?"

"As Maria said, he's reluctant to accept that Bew was killed and robbed by some rough trade he'd picked up in a Castro bar. It gives the gay scene a bad reputation."

"As Maria said?" Lucy queries.

"What's that supposed to mean?"

Her eyes sought his. "You told me that she'd agreed to give Bew an equal stake in the company in order to maintain a monopoly on our research."

He looks down at the table top. "I was wrong about that."

"So she got rid of him instead?"

"That's absurd." He stares hard at her. "Don't even think like that."

"Why not?"

"There's a lot you don't know about Bew. We've had a lucky escape as far as he's concerned."

At first she makes no reply. Then she says, "Richard, it's this secrecy. It's putting us all under strain."

He gets up and to close the conference room door, but she pushes it open. "We need some fresh air," she says.

As soon as they are out of sight of Eden Therapy, Lucy slips a hand in his as they walk in silence through a Marina Village Business Park dulled by an overcast afternoon sky. Apart from the signboards, there appears little to distinguish the single-story buildings with redbrick-and-glass facades and tarmacadam forecourts. But Richard knows that only one building contains the secret to making aging diseases as rare as tuberculosis. The question is: how many other people know?

They reach the marina and continue until they can go no farther. Richard frees his hand and grips the blue handrail at the end of the deserted boardwalk. In the harbor the forest of white yacht masts sway erratically in a swirling wind that rattles the plastic sharks teeth pennants strung along the shrouds. Last week's calm, reflective blue water is transformed into agitated gray ripples.

Richard turns to her. "Did Bew tell Rosina about our research?"

Lucy frowns. "I don't think so. Why?"

"You left with her after the meeting. I thought she might have said something that indicates she knows what we're actually doing."

"She was upset by Bew's death."

"Are you sure she didn't say anything?" he asks again.

"Only that a police officer wanted to see her."

"What was his name?" Richard demands.

Lucy's brow creases in thought. "As far as I remember it was McKendrick, or something like that."

"McKenna." Trent pales.

"We can't keep this research secret any longer," Lucy persists. "We've got our opportunity when she goes away on her business trip."

Richard turns back to the harbor. Overhead, gulls wheel and shriek, driven inshore by the wind. Out in the channel a lone yacht battles against the headwind in an attempt to reach the ocean. His work is going to have to come out into the open sometime. It is a matter of when and how so as to give him the best chance of leading medical science into a new era.

"Richard, listen to me, we have got to show our work to the FDA."

If he takes his data to the FDA now, behind Maria's back as Lucy wants, he would still need funding to carry the research forward to completion, always assuming that the FDA give approval for a limited use of the inducer and that Maria fails to enforce Eden's exclusive rights to his discovery. The Catch-22 dilemma means there is a strong possibility that the NIH would confirm their previous refusal to provide funding. He tries to figure out who else would provide him with the millions it cost to develop a gene therapy through all the stages of clinical trials. And, critically, on what terms they would provide the funding. Only a large pharmaceutical corporation like Arcadia could produce that kind of money, and they would require exclusive rights before they invested in him.

"Well?" Lucy prompts.

"I'm going to submit our data to the FDA," he concludes.

She puts her arms round his neck and kisses him. "I knew you would."

Rigid and unresponsive, he says "But I'm not going behind Maria's back."

Lucy lets him go and stares at him.

"I'm going to try and persuade her to fund FDA-approved clinical trials."

"She'll never agree," Lucy protests.

Richard looked beyond her, towards the business park. "There's only one way to find out."

"This time I'm coming with you," Lucy declares.

37

The closer Richard approaches Maria's office, the drier his throat becomes. He has never felt as tense as this when presenting a paper to a conference of scientists honed to pick holes in his arguments, but far more is at stake than the opinion of a few hundred of his peers.

Maria is packing her attaché case when Richard enters her room. She looks up and smiles. "Hi, Richard. I'm just about to leave."

"We need to talk," Richard says.

"Can it wait until after my trip?"

"No, it can't," says Lucy, who follows Richard into the office.

Maria raises her eyebrows. "Is this a delegation?"

"The decision you take affects me," Lucy replies.

"I guess we'd better be comfortable, then," Maria says, gesturing to the low chairs round the coffee table by the window. She observes the newfound confidence in Lucy, the way she positions her chair close to Richard's and, most especially, the glances she gives him. "Is there something I should know?" she asks Lucy.

"Maria," Richard intervenes, "I've thought a lot about how we should proceed from here."

"Tell me." She turns to Lucy. "Be a pet and get the coffee."

"I'm employed as a researcher, not a waitress."

"Well, I guess that puts me in my place," Maria says. She rises and goes to the alcove to fetch the coffee flask and cups.

Richard gives Lucy a disapproving look. The last thing he wants is to provoke Maria unnecessarily.

Maria pours out the coffee and sits back to listen attentively while Richard spells out his case. "Testing the full potential of the anti-aging gene inducer on a human isn't just a question of ignoring some ill-informed view of what is ethical or else bypassing a bunch of conservative bureaucrats," he concludes. "If we're caught breaking the law, that will be the end of the project. Better to volunteer our data to the FDA and propose a clinical trial limited to using the gene inducer on a specific diseased organ as a first step."

Maria places both hands on the armrests of her chair, leans back, and looks straight at Lucy. "Who thinks we're breaking the law?"

"It's McKenna," Richard says quickly. "He's still fishing. He's going to interview Rosina and Carol."

Maria turns from Lucy to Richard. "What laws have we broken?"

"None yet, I trust. But we will if we go ahead with a clinical trial without FDA approval."

Maria shakes her head. "The Food and Drug Administration issues guidelines, not laws."

"Those guidelines are mandatory," Richard counters.

"For institutions in receipt of government money," Maria says. "The only penalty for non-compliance with FDA guidelines is withdrawal of federal funding. Since we don't receive federal funding, the guidelines don't apply to us." She picks up her cup of coffee.

"You don't understand," Lucy asserts. "Everyone must comply with the guidelines. Why do you think the big pharmaceutical corporations submit their clinical trials for FDA approval?"

"Because they use research hospitals for their clinical trials, and the hospitals receive federal funds," Maria answers without hesitation. "Besides, public corporations follow the guidelines to protect themselves from an irrational public fear of human genetic engineering."

"But wasn't that Bew's point?" Richard persists. "The FDA is scared of a public backlash against all human genetic engineering. That's why it'd close us down if we tried to go ahead with clinical trials of the full anti-aging gene therapy."

Maria is impassive. "Are you prepared to submit to a body that lets public opinion dictate what progress should be made in science? Let's face it, most people in this country don't even know the difference between astronomy and astrology."

He leans forward in his chair. "Are you saying that the FDA can't close us down?"

"In theory the FDA could ask a federal attorney to try and convince a judge to order a cessation of activity on the grounds of public safety." She sips her coffee. "The legal opinion I've been given is that the case wouldn't have a leg to stand on."

"Then why the secrecy?"

"Because it could lobby Congress to pass a law barring our work." She smiles confidently. "But that will never happen because the FDA is so under-resourced that it won't be aware of what we're doing unless there's a public complaint. Or," she says, putting down her coffee cup and looking at Lucy, "more realistically, a staff member informs them, despite the non-disclosure clause in our contract."

A stab of fear shoots through Richard. He looks sideways at Lucy; her face is flushed. She had never let him down before, but would she inform the FDA if he didn't? And there is still McKenna. Richard doesn't want the world to learn of his work through a police officer exposing the fact that he is secretly testing a treatment for aging diseases: that would seal his fate as an outcast from the scientific community. "*I* want to get FDA approval for clinical trials limited to treating a specific, localized disease, rather than repairing aging damage throughout the whole body," he states.

"And if the FDA refuses to approve a trial of even a limited treatment?"

He hesitates. "We cross that bridge when we come to it."

For a moment she gazes into his eyes, and then she says, "It's your call, Richard. You're in control of the research program."

Lucy stares, not sure whether to believe her ears. "You agree we submit all our data to the FDA and ask approval for a limited trial?" she queries to ensure there is no doubt.

"Haven't I always made it clear that my role is to enable Richard to do whatever he wants?"

Richard breathes a huge sigh of relief.

Lucy puts a hand on Richard's arm and gives it an affectionate squeeze. "I'll begin preparing the data for submission." She looks at Maria with an undisguised smile of victory. "Before I start I'll have an another coffee."

For an instant Maria's eyes flash, and then she fills Lucy's cup from the flask. "I apologize if I was rude earlier," she concedes graciously. "That detective has put us all under a great deal of strain."

"Hey, no problem," Lucy says, secure in her triumph.

Maria turns to Richard. "If we're going to do it your way, Richard, then we're going to do it properly, to give you the maximum chance of success."

"Right," he says, buoyed by her positive response.

"You've been under most strain of all. You'll be much more relaxed and prepared to face hostile questions from the FDA after you've had a vacation to recharge your batteries."

Part Three

PARADISE

"Why then was this forbid? Why, but to awe;

Why, but to keep ye low and ignorant,

His worshippers? He knows that in the day

Ye eat thereof, your eyes that seem so clear,

Yet are but dim, shall perfectly be then

Opened and cleared, and ye shall be as Gods"

—Milton, *Paradise Lost, Book IX*

39

At the sound of the doorbell Richard picks up his suitcase and opens the front door. His bleary eyes squint at Alvaro standing like a statue in front of the morning sun that burns through the haze over the Oakland Hills.

"Where am I going?" Richard asks.

"Didn't La Madre say it was a surprise?"

"I wasn't sure what clothes to pack."

"Didn't La Madre say pack only basics?" With one swift movement Alvaro reaches down, takes the suitcase from Richard, and turns towards the car parked on the lane that borders Richard's front lawn.

Richard settles into the soft black leather of the car's rear bench seat. He feels as though he's been through the wringer: battling to outwit nature, riding the anxiety roller coaster while waiting to see if he really could halt aging diseases in monkeys with no dangerous side effects, risking the ever-present danger of exposure, exulting in a success beyond his hopes, and then facing the loss of everything by Bew's blackmail and what he first assumed was Maria's betrayal, followed by McKenna's probing and the struggle to decide when and how to disclose his work. It has left him drained, physically, mentally, and emotionally.

He tries to remember when he'd last had a vacation. His only breaks from the lab in recent years had been the scientific meetings he attended, but those were work. Vacations were a distant memory of his younger self, when Jackie and he scheduled time to scuba dive off the Massachusetts coast or dive the wrecks off Long Island's South Shore. The older he became the more vacations seemed a waste of productive time, time that was slipping away from him at an ever increasing rate. He feared time would run out before he made the scientific breakthrough that he believed was his destiny. That fear had concentrated all his energies on his research, but Maria was right: now that he had made the breakthrough, he needed to recharge his batteries before presenting his results to a hostile scientific establishment that had already rejected his ideas.

Lucy had begged him not to go on a vacation organized by Maria: after Bew's murder she feared for his safety. But this was paranoia. He'd already told Lucy that it was absurd to link Maria with Bew's death at the hands of a pickup, and hadn't Maria agreed that he could disclose his findings to the FDA? When Lucy saw that he was unmoved by her entreaties she wanted to accompany him.

In truth he is glad to be going on his own. It would give him time and space to think, without the distraction of Lucy's hostility towards Maria. He feels an immense affection for Lucy and greatly values her loyalty and support, but he wonders if it had been a mistake for them to sleep together. Had he been wrong to succumb to an emotional and physical need when he'd been at his lowest ebb? Since they'd made love, Lucy had come out of her shell: she flaunted their relationship and her antagonism to Maria. He didn't want her to give Maria any excuse to dismiss the best research partner he'd ever had or, God forbid, put at risk Maria's funding of the clinical trials, now that he is in sight of his goal. It was all getting too complicated. Perhaps Maria had been right to insist that his relationship with Lucy should be an exclusively professional one. It would have helped, though, to allay Lucy's fears if he'd been able to tell her where he was going.

A silver bullet with sleek finned wings and two power tubes either side of its tail fin waits on the private parking lot at the airport. The first thing Richard notices as he stoops to walk down the Learjet's narrow, low-ceilinged central aisle between the four pairs of seats is that the rear two pairs have been removed; the spaces either side of the aisle are filled with crates. He settles back in one of the front seats where his view won't be obscured by a wing.

Richard glances out of the window at the other passengers leaving or entering planes parked on the lot. Is he the only one who has no idea what lies in store?

The outer door opens and in comes Alvaro followed by Maria. She takes the seat across the aisle from him.

Richard turns to her in surprise. "*You're* coming?"

She smooths down the skirt of her casual, low neck, mid thigh dress. "Did you think you'd get rid of me so easily?" She gives him a quizzical look. "Why the grin?"

At least with Maria on board the plane isn't going to blow up in mid-flight. "Where are we heading?" he asked.

She smiles. "Paradise."

The Learjet hugs the coastline south. After a refueling stop at San Diego the plane turns inland towards a mountain range. Alvaro serves lunch. Richard drinks the greater part of a bottle of Chablis Grand Cru and surrenders to his exhaustion.

When he wakes Richard peers out of the window, curious to know what is Maria's idea of paradise. The plane is flying above blobs of cotton wool cloud that cast Rorschach blot shadows on what appears to be an unremittingly flat carpet of tightly packed broccoli florets.

The jungle ends abruptly with a narrow white strip. The beach shelves into an aquamarine glaze that coarsens into rippled indigo speckled with white spume. The plane begins to descend. The indigo sea smooths to translucent sapphire, revealing mysterious dark shapes beneath. The sapphire shallows to transparent turquoise, disclosing multicolored coral reefs growing from an underwater desert. The turquoise pales to expose a strip of white sand bordering jungle. The plane decelerates and dips towards a gray landing strip that carves a straight line through the jungle. It bumps onto the strip, slows, and swings left to park near other private planes in front of a square, bright yellow column below a control tower.

The aircraft door opens into heat that makes Richard feel he is entering a sauna and brightness that makes him squint. Above the low jungle, on the other side of the airport perimeter fence, an eagle hovers, using air currents to glide with deceptive gentleness in search of prey. A line of dwarf palm trees guard alternating rectangles of glass and bright yellow concrete that supports the blue architrave of a passenger terminal. Richard reads the single word emblazoned on the architrave. He glances over his shoulder to Maria, who is standing behind him. "Cozumel?"

"The island of Ixchel," says Maria. "The Mayan goddess of healing and fertility."

Outside the gaudily pasteled terminal stands a white air-conditioned limousine into which porters load their baggage. Within minutes of leaving the Learjet, Alvaro is driving them down a road bordered on the right by a sapphire sea. An old ferry pier projects into the sea, followed further down the coast by a new international pier dwarfed by a giant multistory cruise ship.

The limousine eventually pulls up outside the flag-bedecked entrance lobby of an hotel. Intrigued, Richard accompanies Maria into the cool red-tiled lobby. A concierge proffers a silver tray with two glasses of champagne. Not exactly the greeting he was used to when registering at a scientific meeting.

"The manager is waiting at your convenience, whenever you care to register," says the concierge.

"Shall I—?" begins Richard.

"No need," Maria says. "I'll register for both of us."

He watches the gently sinuous movement of her hips as she follows the concierge through to the reception desk. Does that mean she'd booked one room for both of them?

"Please, señor," says a bellboy.

Richard follows him down a tiled corridor and into a large, marble-floored suite. A bowl of tropical fruit stands on a circular marble-topped dining table between two dining chairs by the far window. A heavenly scent emanates from the vase of exotic flowers on a low, marble coffee table near an arched opening in the wall. The opening leads into a room with the largest bed he's ever seen. The bedside cabinet on one side is a refrigerator, on top of which stands a tray with two champagne flutes.

Richard lies down on the bed. In the mirror above the long marble shelf opposite that serves as a dressing table he sees a reflection of himself and everything on the bed. His imagination conjures up images of what he might see later in that mirror.

Flushed with anticipation he rises and opens the glass door that leads onto the terrace outside. He steps from the air conditioning into the heat and into the setting for a fashion photo in one of Jackie's glossy magazines. A powdery white beach, planted with a line of well-spaced sun shades made of thatched palm leaves, gently slope into a Caribbean Sea of inviting turquoise that deepens to merge with an azure sky burnished by a low golden sun below wisps of cirrus. Like one of those fashion shots, the beach is deserted, apart from a grackle; with its long black beak, anorexic body and long tail, it squawks and struts on long spindly legs in search of food. All that is needed to complete the picture is a supermodel in a short, clinging dress.

"Do you approve?" a husky voice asks.

Richard spins back towards the bed, but Maria is nowhere to be seen.

He goes onto the beach and looks round the high wall that separates the terraces of adjoining suites. Maria is standing in the doorway to the adjacent suite, hands on hips and legs astride. An amused expression plays on her face, as though she knows exactly what has been in his thoughts.

"Could be worse, I suppose," he says to hide his embarrassment.

She comes down and links his arm for a stroll along the beach. The sun grows and reddens and dips into the sea, sending a river of what looks like glowing molten lava to the shore and scorching the clouds with incandescent ambers, oranges, and scarlets.

"It's been a long day," she says dreamily when they return.

They head towards her suite, but when they reach her door she slips her arm free and turns to him. "Be on the pier at nine tomorrow morning, Richard."

"Why?"

Her eyes laugh. "Didn't I say that I'm taking you to Paradise?"

The sun has already heated the flagstones that lead from the rear of the hotel, round past the swimming pool and terracotta terrace, to the stone pier that separates the hotel's main beach from the secluded stretch in front of the ground-level luxury suites. Walking quickly over the burning flagstones, Richard wishes he wasn't barefoot.

He spots Maria in sundress and sandals talking to someone in a boat moored at the end of the pier. She turns to greet him with a captivating smile and glances down towards the boat. On the deck of the thirty-foot white powerboat stands a rack of yellow air cylinders and scuba equipment. "You haven't forgotten how?" she asks.

Resolving not to be surprised in future by this woman's ability to know what he wants, he jumps down into the boat.

Alvaro, no longer wearing his gray suit but dressed in T-shirt and shorts, is laughing with the skipper, another Maya whose large, round head is topped by a fringe of short straight black hair. As soon as Richard helps Maria climb on board, Alvaro casts off. The boat accelerates out from the pier and curves left to parallel the coastline. From two hundred and fifty yards or so the island seems to consist of low, flat, scrub jungle bordered by a strip of white sand.

Richard grips the handrail, exhilarated by the rise and fall of the surging boat, the wind streaming through his hair, the hot sun on his face, the salty spray when the prow hits a wave from a larger boat, and the prospect of diving in this crystal clear water.

They dived twice that day, the second to Paradise Reef. Forty feet below the surface Maria leads him to queen angelfish, like vertical blue plates with Cadillac fins at the top and bottom, that cruise regally above purple anemone coral, while three-foot-long filefish, with spiny horn and unblinking eyes set well back in fawn bodies decorated with black dots and blue dashes, use their pouting lips to feed on yellow leafy stinging coral, sights that Richard had only dreamed of in the times he'd dived with Jackie.

For dinner that evening Maria chooses a table on a terrace outside the hotel's palm-thatched restaurant. The red sun slips below the

Caribbean, darkness falls suddenly, extinguishing the scarlet afterglow, and myriad stars blaze in a moonless black sky. Underwater searchlights from the pier pick out colorful fish that swim into their beams. Brushwood torches blaze from poles stuck into the shadow-flickering beach. From the restaurant come the sounds of two musicians: a wiry intense mestizo with an acoustic guitar accompanies a Maya whose bamboo flute creates a haunting resonant melody that soars and swoops like a bird. Richard can imagine no setting more romantic, and opposite him is the embodiment of his fantasies who, until now, has remained unfathomable and unreachable. "After working with you I still know very little about you."

She spears a piece of turkey with her fork and swirls it in the black burnt-chili sauce on her plate. "What do you want to know?"

"Everything," he says, stabbing his fork at slices of seasoned suckling pig baked in banana leaves. "Where you come from. How a software expert like your father met your mother. What you want from life."

"It's a long story."

"I have all night."

She laughs and looks at him over the top of her wineglass. She could have asked him to perform a backward somersault off the pier and he would have done so. "If you really want to know, my father was majoring in math at Berkeley when he figured that Aldous Huxley had more to offer than his professors."

"Aldous Huxley?"

"The insights he achieved with psychedelic drugs." She smiles to herself as she douses a slice of hard-boiled egg in the chili sauce. "Dad backpacked to Mexico looking for mescaline and enlightenment, reached the Yucatán, and ended up in a Mayan village near the ruined temples of Tulum." She nods in the direction of the Yucatán peninsula. "Directly across the water from here. That's where he met Carmen and that's where I was born. She gave me my Mayan name, but he called me Maria."

Her fork plays with her Yucatán meal while she looks dreamily across the sea. "For the first seven years of my life I was brought up as a Maya. They were wonderful times. I remember Dad as this happy, laid-back man with long hair who laughingly called me his little goddess." She eats a forkful of ground meat covered in the sauce. "I guess I was spoiled, always the center of attention. I only had to ask for something and I got it.”

“Because you were the only child with an American parent?”

“That wasn’t the main reason.”

“What was?”

“My mother’s people were Catholic, in theory, but they mixed their Christianity with pre-Hispanic beliefs about the gods and about destiny.” She swirls the wine round in her glass. “According to Alvaro, who was a kind of shaman in our village, the time and circumstances of my birth coincided with an event predicted in the Tzolk’in, the sacred calendar of the ancient Maya.” She takes a deep draft from the glass.

He refills their glasses. “What event?”

Her eyes glint with amusement. “The reincarnation of a goddess.”

While he eats he tries to imagine what it must have been like for this lighter-skinned, beautiful child to be treated as divine by the other Maya in the village. “That’s why Alvaro calls you Madre even though you’re young enough to be his daughter?”

"He's addressed me as Mother ever since he named me in a ceremony after I was born."

"What *is* your Mayan name?"

She gazes into his eyes and laughs. "Ixchel."

He smiles ruefully: he should have guessed. "And after you were seven?"

"Mom was very strong-willed. She was very bright, but she'd never been to school and she wanted me to have a proper education, like Dad had." She pushes her empty plate to one side. "So, Dad took us back to San Francisco, where he took a job as a software programmer to pay for my schooling."

A waiter removes their plates and replaces them with dishes of *ciricote*.

"It's good," Richard says as he tries the plum-like fruit soaked in a liqueur that tastes of aniseed and honey. "How did you find the States?"

"I hated it at first. It was a big culture shock. Dad wasn't around all day. The other kids thought I was... well, kind of weird." She shrugs. "But I showed them that I didn't have to rely on Dad or anyone else to get what I want. I sailed through high school and eventually took an MBA. Which," she adds with a smile, "wasn't predicted in the Tzolk'in."

"Then you set up a company for your dad?"

She nods. "We made a good team. He just enjoyed thinking up new ideas and writing the software, while I got a kick out of the business side: running the organization and making the deals to achieve our goals."

"You never married?"

She shakes her head, and shiny black hair brushes her cheeks. She has never looked more entrancing.

A deep, physical yearning overcomes Richard's pang of guilt about Lucy. "Let's take a walk along the beach and then have a nightcap in my suite. I'd like us to get to know each other better." It is clumsy, he knows, but he is out of practice.

She gazes at him with an intensity that makes him feel that no one else exists. "You're a very attractive man, Richard, and I'm very flattered." She reaches across and puts a hand over his. "But let's keep to a professional relationship until you've completed your work, and

then…" She smiles enticingly. "Then we'll see."

40

As Richard reaches the pier the following morning his steps slow. Maria is standing at the far end. She is dressed in an elegant cotton suit and patent leather shoes and she carries an attaché case: every inch the professional woman. Listening to her is a gray-haired Maya in T-shirt and shorts.

If she sees the disappointment on his face she'd doesn't show it. "Good morning, Richard," she says brightly. "I'm afraid I have to go away on business." She introduces the Maya. "This is Vicente, Alvaro's cousin. He knows the reefs better than any man on Cozumel."

"What business?"

She smiles and taps his nose. "I'll be back."

Inside the gently rocking cabin of the powerboat, Vicente's rheumy eyes stare out at Richard from a grizzled leathery face. "Where do you wish to go to, my friend?" He sounds as though his vocal chords are rusted by the local white rum.

Richard shrugs and glances through the window. Maria has already disappeared.

"The coral reefs off Cozumel," Vicente boasts, "are so large that a man could spend his whole life exploring them. My friend, I will take you to some of the best." He turns and speaks to the skipper, who nods and starts the engine.

Despite his appearance, the gnarled Vicente proves a skilled as well as a knowledgeable diver, but for Richard, diving without Maria isn't the same. It hadn't seemed so unusual for her to take days away from Eden Therapy to attend to business matters, but it is a blow to his ego for her to leave him after only one day of their vacation together. It showed what she really thought of his clumsy pass at her.

Vicente acts as if his mission in life is to show Richard the whole of his home island, above as well as below the waves. After the morning dives he offers Richard a guided tour. "You will not be disappointed, my friend," Vicente says as they drive off after lunch in an open-topped VW Beetle. "Today I will take you to one of the three most sacred shrines of the ancient Maya."

The sun shines dully and hotly through a diaphanous gray sky. Richard's T-shirt sticks to his body like a warm wet rag. He is not impressed. Only a few small weathered limestone altars and monuments remain among the broken columns and lintels that litter the field stretching in front of him. "My friend," says Vicente, "more than fifteen hundred years ago pilgrims came here from all over the Yucatán and what is now Honduras and Guatemala to worship the goddess of fertility and healing."

Richard idly examines the larger stone pieces. Many are carved with two long, sinuous lines enclosing geometrical patterns. "The serpent was the first creature on this earth," says Vicente. "It was also the wisest and most powerful."

"The wisest?" Richard queries.

"Of course, my friend." He cups his hands to light a filterless cigarette, lifts up his head, and blows out a stream of gray-blue smoke. "The ancient Maya were skilled in mathematics. They learned this science from studying the circles, squares, and triangles on the skin of the rattlesnake."

"But not the most powerful," Richard argues, irritated by the man's lack of logic. "I thought the jaguar had that reputation in this part of the world."

Vicente's smile shows yellow stumps of teeth. "The jaguar grows old, my friend, but the snake has the power to shed her skin and become young again." He beckons Richard closer and Richard smells the sourness of his breath. Vicente points his first two fingers, which hold his cigarette, towards a sculpture of a serpent possessing a human face with an aquiline nose. "They venerated it as the sign of Ixchel."

In the comfort of the Learjet seat Richard reads through the FDA submission requirements, but the pages of bureaucratic details begin to drain the energy he's accumulated on his vacation. He planned to make considerably understated claims, coupled with a proposal for clinical trials merely to use the anti-aging gene inducer for treating plaques in hardened arteries. Such a modest approach, avoiding germline cells, ought to be acceptable to the scientific establishment.

But another part of him rebels against denying his own achievements and proposing a Band-Aid approach when he possesses the means, with a single infusion, to restore senescent tissue throughout the body and banish aging diseases from the face of the earth. The harder one part of his mind works at scaling down his proposal, the more another part resists belittling his accomplishment.

The conflict is compounded by Maria refusing with a laugh to tell him what business she'd conducted while she'd been away from the island. He doesn't want his submission used as the basis for a patent application, but if Maria has decided that this is her price for funding the clinical trials, then he is left with no choice. Her eagerness to leave the day after she returned only increases his suspicion.

He glances out of the window as the aircraft climbs away from Cozumel and out over an indigo sea that soon turns sapphire and then turquoise before washing onto the strip of white sand that borders most of the Yucatán peninsula. Barely half an hour out of Cozumel the plane begins to lose height. Richard glances across to Maria, but she is looking out of her window.

Beyond the patchwork of fields lies a grid of streets transected by converging wide avenues that stop short of meeting in the center of a city. The plane continues to drop.

"Do we have a problem?" he asks Maria.

The outer grids magnify into squares lined by gray concrete dwellings whose corrugated tin roofs would be sliced off if the plane continues its trajectory.

"No problem."

The plane wheels away from the shanty outskirts and appears to be heading for the emerald green of a baseball diamond before it banks again and descends onto a black runway. It taxis past the main terminal and the control tower before coming to a halt on a tarmac parking lot for private planes.

"There's something I want you to see," she says.

The long straight four-lane avenue with a grassed central reservation takes their Land Cruiser past a zoo and then a complex of hospital and medical school buildings. It meets other main routes at sunbaked plazas across which trundle ancient green buses. Alvaro ignores the signs to the center of Mérida and continues down a wide, tree-lined avenue bordered by grandiose mansions and intersected by other avenues at spacious traffic circles round pedestaled bronze heroes. At one such junction he turns down a busy main road signposted "Progreso". After leaving the Mérida city limits, the road becomes a straight white concrete highway divided by a barrier of flame trees, whose red foliage arches over the paving to form a canopy from which hang long green seedpods. The highway is bordered on either side by a grass verge and limestone walls that mark the boundaries of former colonial henequen plantations.

Richard's curiosity as to what Maria wants to show him has mounted with every change of direction the car has taken, but she laughingly chides him to be patient and all will be revealed.

Alvaro makes a right off the Progreso highway and heads down a single-track potholed concrete road between henequen plantations reclaimed by the jungle before the road expires at a large clearing. Exposed to the pitiless glare of the sun, single-roomed Mayan huts stand along three sides of the grassed square. Some are oval shaped and made from vertical staves bound by rope woven from henequen fiber and thatched with dried palm leaves, some are square and made from breeze blocks, while the most modern boast breeze block walls roofed by corrugated tin sheets.

No adults pay them any attention: neither the Maya women in colorfully embroidered sack-like white dresses who carry boxes on their heads or babies slung on their left hips, nor the men wearing straw Stetsons who squat in the shade outside their homes, smoking and drinking, or who sprawl in hammocks inside the open-doored huts. Only the bare-footed black-eyed children scamper to watch the Land Cruiser. It raises a cloud of yellow dust as Alvaro drives carefully along the rutted track across the clearing towards a golden limestone citadel flanked by perimeter walls that extend as far as Richard can see. A two-story building with barred windows links a rectangular balustraded tower to a missionary church whose rectangular facade is surmounted by a bell-shaped wall containing three empty bell-shaped apertures. Carved into the limestone above the closed church door are human arms embracing a cross, the symbol of the Franciscans.

The Land Cruiser halts at a gateway in the perimeter wall. Next to it stands a new, upright timber with a crosspiece bearing the legend Clinica de Paraíso and the symbol of a single serpent coiled round a staff. Alvaro points an electronic controller at a panel in the new black wrought-iron gate and presses a button. The gate slides sideways behind the wall. He drives into a dirt courtyard and parks next to the tower.

His curiosity at bursting point, Richard follows Maria out of the vehicle. Their footsteps echo down a cool, arched, stone-flagged passageway until they emerge into the brightness of a barrel-vaulted cloister carried by square stone pillars. It forms the ground level of a two-story cloister that surrounds a lush green garth in which tropical trees grow.

Everything is so beautifully restored that Richard half-expects cowled friars to emerge from their cells off the upper level, descend the stone steps, and process silently round the lower level past the doors to workrooms until they reach the arched door into the church that forms the north wing of the cloister.

He turns to see Maria studying his reactions. "The huts round the square outside?" he asks.

"The Franciscan missionaries moved the Maya from their villages to a settlement outside the friary in order to control them better."

Richard feels the rough thickness of the walls. "This place is built like a fortress."

"It had to withstand the attacks of Maya who weren't so easily pacified." She indicates the carved hieroglyphs on the keystone of the nearest arch. "Bishop Diego de Landa ordered the destruction of Mayan culture. Like most missionary centers this was built from the stones of a sacred Mayan pyramid that the good Franciscans forced the Maya to dismantle. But," she looks at Richard, "it's now been put to better use."

She climbs the stone steps next to the passageway and walks along the upper cloister, stopping to open one of the mahogany doors that punctuate the inner wall at regular intervals. Inside is a modern office. "These used to be the rooms of the Franciscan priests. The lay brothers' rooms in the west wing have been converted into accommodation for in-house staff. The infirmary and the visitors' lodgings that surround the outer courtyard where we parked have been remodeled into suites for patients and guests."

"The Franciscan friary has become the Paradise Clinic, with the snake replacing the cross?" Richard inquires.

The look of pride when showing him the conversion gives way to a stare. "The cross is a symbol of death," she says tersely. "Only Christians think the snake is evil." Her unblinking eyes fix him. "The snake was a sacred symbol of regeneration for all ancient civilizations: Babylonian, Egyptian, Greek, Roman, you name them."

"And a symbol of the goddess Ixchel," Richard says.

"Bishop Diego accused the Maya of worshiping the devil." She shrugs. "I suppose he knew no better, but I do. And so I've chosen a single serpent coiled round the staff of Asclepius." Her glance conveys a challenge. "Just like the American Medical Association."

"*This* was the reason for your business trips?"

She nods. "The payout on Bew's life insurance policy will cover part of the loan I took out to build this clinic." She leads him back down the flight of steps and round the cloister to the arched door into the church. After inserting a plastic card in the electronic lock next to the mahogany door, she taps six digits on the keypad. "The original detailing on the outside has been preserved as far as possible, but inside the nave has undergone a slight change." She opens the door and ushers him into the lobby.

A modern drinking fountain with chilled water stands where he imagines the baptismal font had once been, and next to it a coffee machine. He pushes open the white swing door into the nave and stops in his tracks. Bright sunlight from the tall narrow embrasured windows illuminates white workbenches, each divided lengthwise by a central stack of triple-tiered shelving. Filling the shelves and the benches are plastic-capped bottles, reference books, PCR machines, computers, and all the other apparatus of a modern genetic engineering laboratory.

Maria comes to stand next to him. "We're less than half an hour's drive from the airport, which is an hour and half's flight from either Houston or Miami. I can get most equipment the same day."

Richard wanders down the aisle between the benches, passing a biohazard lab, until he comes to the door in the wall built at the end of the nave where the altar rail had been.

Maria unlocks the door. The chancel has been converted into an operating room and the vestry is now a scrub room.

Richard stares at her. "What do you intend to use the clinic for?"

"That, Dr. Trent," she says, "is your decision."

41

In a vain attempt to distract herself from fears for Richard's safety, Lucy began compiling all the raw research data from their laboratory and animal experiments into the format required by the Food and Drug Administration to demonstrate the activity, efficacy, and non-toxicity of the anti-aging gene inducer. But as she prepares this preclinical evidence supporting the key part of the FDA submission, the clinical protocol that Richard said he'd write on his return, she finds it increasingly difficult to concentrate. The failure of Richard to answer his cell phone or return her messages grows more ominous with each passing day.

Finally she can bear it no longer. She decides to confront Snowe and threaten to tell Detective McKenna of her suspicions unless she can speak to Richard on the phone.

With her heart palpitating she walks down the corridor and opens the door marked President and Chief Executive Officer. Roger looks up from his desk in the outer office and gives her a lazy smile.

"I want to see her," Lucy says.

"Didn't you know?" Roger asks. "Maria's on vacation."

"On vacation?"

The smile gives way to a look of amusement. "With Richard."

The color drains from her face as she stands rooted to the spot in shock. Then she turns away and strides out before Roger can see the tears of humiliation that start to stream down her face. Visions of Richard lying pale and lifeless on a mortuary slab or, worse still, buried in a secret grave or weighted down at the bottom of the ocean never to be traced, are replaced by visions of Her making love to him in some luxury hotel bedroom.

Stopping only to collect her motorcycle helmet from her locker, she runs out of Eden Therapy and jumps on her bike. Twice she nearly has an accident on the ride back to Nihonmachi.

After opening the front door, Lucy hangs up her helmet, kicks off her sneakers and places them in the rack for outside shoes, puts on her slippers, and hurries out of the entrance hall. On her way to the stairs to her apartment her aunt intercepts her. "Lucy," says Chisako in surprise, "you're back early." The pretty, petite woman sees Lucy's red-rimmed eyes and takes her in her arms. "There, there, child, tell me what's wrong."

Lucy bursts out sobbing, and Chisako guides her into a living room, on one wall of which hangs a Japanese scroll and on another a picture of Himeji Castle in spring, its white pagoda-like structure rising from a sea of white cherry blossom into a cloudless blue sky.

Seated on the sofa, Lucy burrows her head on her aunt's shoulder and pours out what hitherto she has confided only to her diary: her love for Richard, the position Snowe put them in over the ethics of their professional relationship, the suspicions she harbored about that woman's own intentions towards Richard, her jealousy of Snowe's attractiveness, and her joy when Richard invited her to his house and they'd made love.

"I've always known you were in love with Dr. Trent," Chisako says.

Lucy sits up and looks at her aunt. "You did?"

"Of course. Just because you hide your feelings behind that carefree exterior doesn't mean that I can't sense them." She dabs

Lucy's tear-stained face with a silk handkerchief. "But I thought things had gone badly when you stayed the night with him. You've been tense ever since."

Lucy shakes her head. "No. It was… it was wonderful, better than I'd ever imagined." She sniffs. "I've been almost out of my mind because Richard went on a vacation arranged by Her. I don't know where he is and he hasn't answered his cell phone for over two weeks."

"But why are you so upset today?"

Lucy feels hot tears welling up once more. "I thought he was on his own." The tears spill over. "But I just found out that She is with him."

Chisako holds her close and strokes her back. "You mustn't assume that her plan has succeeded," she says comfortingly.

"But she's so… so glamorous," Lucy says into Chisako's shoulder.

"Are you attracted to Richard just because of his physical appearance?"

"Of course not!" Lucy protests. "He's been so kind to me, he's got a brilliant mind, and he's dedicated to curing diseases, not making money from his work…"

"Exactly," Chisako soothes. "Love is about much more than good looks. It's an attraction to what lies beneath the surface, the essence of the person. You must listen to what your heart tells you."

"It tells me She is evil."

"Then all the more reason for Richard not to fall for her."

"He's too focused on his work to see what she's really like. He only sees that she looks like a film star and she's funding his research."

"Is she in love with him?"

"No!" Lucy declares vehemently.

"Then what does she want from him?"

Lucy is sure that Snowe wants to control the revolutionary gene therapy that Richard and she have developed. But has that woman taken him away to eliminate him, like she'd gotten rid of Bew, because Richard insisted on making the treatment available to everyone? Or has she seduced him into supporting a plan to make her the Elon Musk of gene therapy? She no longer knows what to think. Love has consumed her. It brooks no half measures, raising her to the heights of ecstasy and plunging her into the depths of misery, multiplying her joys and magnifying her fears. Of rationality and balance, it leaves no trace. "To make a fortune from our research," she says.

"That's not what the man you've described would want," Chisako says.

Lucy nods.

"You've shown Richard that you love him," Chisako counsels. "When he returns, look him in the eyes. Then you will know if he is still the man for you."

An atmosphere of foreboding takes hold of Eden Therapy. Members of the two remaining research teams continue their work, but with one eye scanning the horizon for portents, as though they have been abandoned to the stillness before an approaching storm. Bew is dead and his two assistants laid off. As far as they know, chief executive Maria Snowe is away on business for an unspecified period and research director Richard Trent has taken an unannounced vacation. Two of the senior staff begin looking for other jobs.

Lucy stays at home: she can't concentrate on her work at Eden and she is too embarrassed to explain to the other researchers that she doesn't know where Richard is or when he will return.

One evening, when Lucy is confiding her misery to her diary, her cell phone rings.

"Lucy," says Richard's voice, "forgive me for not answering your messages. I switched off my phone because I wanted a complete break, to give myself the space and time to think."

"And?" Lucy asks with her heart palpitating.

"I've begun preparing the clinical protocol. I want you to join me in Mexico to assist me."

With a tingle of anticipation running through her body, Lucy writes in her diary

"Richard was right to say that I'm paranoid about Maria Snowe. My fears for his safety were totally out of line. A vacation in Mexico has restored him."

Early the following day Lucy rides into Eden Therapy to collect the lab notebooks, videos, MRI films, optical disks, and all the data on the laboratory and the monkey experiments that Richard has asked her to bring. When she arrives in the lab, she finds a yellow post-it note stuck on the frame of her computer monitor: Roger has details of the flight he's booked for her.

She hurries from the lab and along the corridor to the Snowe's office. As Roger hands her the tickets, the inner door opens and out walks Maria Snowe herself. Lucy almost drops the tickets in surprise. "I… I thought you were on vacation," she says.

Maria shrugs. "My vacation's over." She strides off towards the animal facility.

Lucy feels like flinging her arms round Roger. With all her glamour and money, She has failed to seduce Richard. She would be alone with him in Mexico!

42

Some silences are impossible to describe, so fraught with expectations shattered, memories betrayed, hopes crushed, and questions too painful to ask. For several moments after Richard told Lucy that the clinical protocol was to give a total infusion at the Paradise Clinic, such a silence drowned the hum of the air conditioning unit.

Dressed in her best linen suit and blouse, with her hair tumbling loose and free as he liked it, Lucy sits on the other side of the mahogany desk in Richard's spacious second-floor office, created from three of the friars' rooms. The silence threatens to choke her. Taking a deep breath she says in as controlled a voice as she can manage, "Before you left you promised to apply for FDA approval to conduct a limited trial. When you phoned you never said that you'd changed your mind." Although her voice is measured, her eyes reveal anger at his deception; her gaze falls on the lab books, MRIs, videos and optical disks that lie on his desk like a dowry that he's taken with no intention of honoring his part of the agreement.

"I wanted to explain things to you, here at the clinic, so you understand," he replies.

Recalling Chisako's advice, she looks him in the eyes to see if he is still the man she loved.

He stands up to escape her stare. "While I've been away I've had the time and space to think." He begins to pace the room. "The Food and Drug Administration would never approve a clinical trial for even a limited use of the anti-aging gene inducer without the agreement of the National Institutes of Health. NIH would refer it to the Office of Recombinant DNA Advisory Committee, and they lack the imagination, the objectivity, and the guts to back a radical therapy like this." Her eyes follow his restless pacing. "Whenever has a committee been responsible for a great leap forward in science?" he challenges.

He stops by one of the windows, which overlooks the rear of the friary buildings. Beyond the dark green limonaria hedge surrounding the tropical garden and swimming pool that Maria had built, a Maya in white vest and baggy cotton pants is watering pea plants that cling to neat rows of twiggy jabin branches in the restored friary vegetable garden. It must have been in a garden such as this, he reflects, that the Augustinian monk Gregor Mendel carried out his experiments of crossbreeding the peas that proved his seminal insight into genetic inheritance. And in such a garden that he spent his declining years, frustrated by the inability of his scientific colleagues to understand what was so clear to him and which later generations would recognize as the basis of modern genetics.

"But the scientific community—" Lucy begins.

"There's no such thing." He turns to face her. "It's just a collection of individual egos competing with each other."

Part of Lucy wants to understand him, to see the justification for his action, but it battles with a greater part that stares back in accusation.

"Who has the vision and the impartiality to judge my work?" Richard asks.

"People need time to adjust to new ideas."

How young she looks. She doesn't know what it is like to wake up in the early hours with the fear that all your best years are behind you. She's never felt creativity slipping away like sand through an hourglass. "It was twelve years after Fleming discovered the antibiotic properties of penicillin before the medical establishment were prepared to test it in a human. Do you want me to wait that long? And we're only talking about a limited clinical trial, using the anti-aging gene as a Band-Aid to restore blood vessels after a heart attack. What do I do if they refuse approval?" He resumes his restless pacing. "Even if they eventually sanction a limited trial, how many more years do I spend waiting for approval to go ahead with what we both know I can really do: cure *all* aging diseases with a single infusion?"

"But that means putting the anti-aging gene inducer into germline cells and passing it on to succeeding generations."

"So?" he says from the end of the room.

"But Richard," she protests, "when we talked about this, you said that it's one thing to change the genes of a patient who gives consent, it's another thing to change the genes of someone yet to be born without her permission."

"You're beginning to sound like Angela Williams," he retorts. "Which is the greater abuse of the rights of an unborn child? Giving it a gene therapy to cure diseases without its permission, or else doing nothing and allowing that child to develop heart disease, cancer, Alzheimer's, and the rest as it grows old?"

Maria had wanted to make Lucy redundant along with the rest of the staff when she closed down Eden Therapy, saying that they could hire a Mexican postdoc to assist him. He refused, arguing that only Lucy was familiar with the particular DNA sequences and their functions, and he could rely on her totally. At least he'd thought so. "Don't you want to help me?" he demands when he reaches her chair.

"Have you forgotten the Sunday you invited me to dinner at your house?" she flares.

The angry words cut him to the quick. "Of course not," he apologizes. "You know how much you mean to me." It was because of everything that had passed between them that he feels a compulsion to justify himself to her. "If we're to develop a treatment for aging diseases we must prove that the anti-aging gene works safely in a human like it does in monkeys."

Her eyes blaze. "After I'd collected all the data you asked me to bring, she told Miguel to kill the monkeys."

"We couldn't take them with us," he reasons. "The poor things had spent all their lives in cramped cages. Euthanasia was the most humane solution."

"Don't you remember telling me about Martin Cline doing the first gene therapy outside the United States without permission from US authorities?" she demands. "They barred him from research. You said it would never happen to us."

Why did she hark back to the past? Couldn't she see that time didn't stand still, that things moved on? "Cline was way ahead of the scientific establishment. They took their revenge on him because his treatment didn't work. But mine will." He looks down to her hands clasped in her lap. Her knuckles are white.

"You said we'd never break the law," she asserts.

"But we won't. In Mexico we break no laws and no regulations, provided we have the patient's consent."

"This is her idea."

"No!" he protests, "you're wrong about Maria." He lowers his voice back to normal. "It's my idea. She simply provided the facilities."

Lucy stands up. "In that case, count me out."

"Lucy, wait!" he says as he intercepts her at the door.

Gone from her eyes is the compassion when she'd said at his house that she would do anything to help.

"Lucy," he pleads, "we've come so far together. Let's see this through."

"Who is the patient?" she retorts. "Some Mexican she bought cheap?"

He shakes his head. "*I've* chosen the patient. At least wait till you see him."

43

A carved mahogany eagle with outstretched wings had once supported the bible on its back. Relieved of its burden, it perched by the side of a white screen and eyed a friars' meeting room that had been converted to provide technological aids while retaining the best features of the original. Richard, in a white clinician's coat, and Lucy, taut with apprehension, sit either side of a new mahogany conference table designed to blend with the seventeenth century doors and window sills.

The paneled door opens and in walks Maria. She is followed by Vince Lambert, a balding former policeman whose paunch is partly hidden by a Hawaiian shirt hanging over the waist of his Bermuda shorts, together with his wife Martha, a plump woman dressed in a floral sun frock. They are accompanied by a Mexican nurse who pushes Tim Lambert in a wheelchair. Except for his nose, Tim resembles the typical alien described by claimed abductees. Less than three feet six in height, his body supports a normal-sized bald head that appears grotesquely large compared with his shrunken frame. Button eyes gleam either side of a long, beaked nose that projects from a face lacking eyebrows and eyelashes. His thin, wrinkled skin is like that of an eighty-year-old. Tim Lambert is fourteen and suffers from progeria, a disease of premature and rapid aging. Maria moves two chairs aside to make room for the wheelchair, but Tim struggles out of it and says in a croaking voice that sounds like early computer speech simulation, "I'll take a proper chair. Think I'm some kind of invalid?"

Maria smiles, but her eyes have already betrayed a momentary glimpse of the horror she feels whenever she sees him.

Lucy looks at him as though she wants to hold him in her arms and breathe life into him. "Here, Tim, sit next to me."

Tim's button eyes examine her. "Pretty girls I like." He clambers onto the chair she's pulled out for him, wheezing with the effort. Lucy pushes the chair nearer the table and sits down. "Thanks," he croaks. He nods towards the head of the table where Maria is now seated. "What's it like working for the big enchilada?"

Lucy puts her hand over her mouth to hide a smile. Maria gives the Lambert family her most dazzling smile. "Tim, Martha, and Vince, I'd like to introduce our senior medical staff, Dr. Richard Trent, and his assistant, Dr. Lucy Jonnsen. Dr. Trent is a pioneer in the treatment of aging-induced diseases—"

"Is this the guy who was attacked on that TV program?" Tim's rasping voice interrupts. He turns to Richard. "What you been up to since then, Doc?"

"This is a set-up," Vince accuses. "When you came to Boston you invited us for a vacation in Mexico so Tim could be spared the winter."

"You're very welcome to treat the Paradise Clinic as your vacation home for the winter, just as I said," an unruffled Maria replies. "But I thought it only fair to give you the opportunity to hear about a pioneering treatment for Tim's condition."

"Pioneering or experimenting?" Vince challenges.

"In a manner of speaking, both," Maria replies.

"Has this treatment been approved by the US authorities?" Vince demands.

"Not yet," Maria replies.

"I thought not." Vince stands up. "Come on, you guys," he says to Martha and Tim, "let's move."

"Before you go," Maria says calmly, "at least give Dr. Trent the opportunity to answer Tim's question about what he's been doing."

Vince remains standing. Martha hesitates. Tim says "Nothing to lose."

Richard feels Tim's beady eyes on him as he goes to the eagle lectern next to the screen. "You'll appreciate that before we begin human trials of any new treatment, we test it first in the laboratory and then in animals," he says.

He presses several buttons. Blinds roll down the windows and a rectangle of light appears on the white screen. Richard summarizes his initial work, showing slides of the magnified senescent and rejuvenated skin cells in tissue culture dishes. Tim's eyes dart to his mother when Richard mentions monkeys. Even Vince becomes absorbed when he sees the magnetic resonance images of the monkeys' organs before and after anti-aging gene therapy, the restoration of atrophied brain cells, and the date-imprinted videos of the old, lethargic monkeys on arrival compared with the active monkeys three months later.

"That's... that's wonderful," Martha says when the blinds go up.

"What I want to know," Vince says, "is why you aren't making this treatment available back home? Why come to Mexico?"

"How many people with Tim's condition are there in the United States?" Maria asks.

Vince shrugs. "The Sunshine Foundation thinks there's no more than thirty worldwide."

"You've answered your own question, Vince. Dr. Trent failed to obtain funding for his work in the States because it wasn't considered a high enough priority. At every stage he met a bureaucracy that wasn't interested in supporting him. To put it bluntly, if Dr. Trent had wanted to research a cure for coronary artery disease, money would have been thrown at him and accelerated approvals given almost by return of post. But securing FDA approval for his gene therapy for progeria would mean years of bureaucratic delay, years which people like Tim haven't got."

"So, you got approvals to go ahead with trials in Mexico?" Vince asks.

"In Mexico Dr. Trent has the funding to develop his treatment. Consent to proceed with clinical trials is the only consent that matters in a free country: the consent of the patient."

Tim turns to Lucy. "Can this guy do it?" he croaks.

Lucy appeals to "Richard. "Can you cure Tim?"

Richard's compulsion to strike out for the home run, to take on a challenge so enormous that its successful completion would prove conclusively that he is the best, is assailed by self-doubt when he looks at the shriveled figure with a bald head who has lived a year longer than the average lifespan of a progeric. With a confidence he no longer feels, he says, "All the laboratory work and all the animal work point to a high probability of success."

44

Lucy stares out at the rectangles of light cast by the other windows on her side of the upper cloister. Of the other staff who are her neighbors, only the two Mexican nurses speak English. Beyond the stone balustrade, on the other side of the cloister, is Richard's office, but no lights shine from his windows; he lives off-site, in some restored hacienda that Maria Snowe has acquired for him. Never has Lucy felt so isolated.

Snowe lives at the end of the cloister in the Guardian's Tower, the lodging of the former Franciscan superior that overlooks all the rooms in the cloister. Lucy imagines her watching from her window on high. She closes the louvered wooden shutter.

In the security of her small room, Lucy bends down and removes her red leather-bound diary from the bottom drawer of the compact chest of drawers. The drawers have no locks and all that she can do to hide her diaries is to bury them beneath her clothes. She takes the current diary to the table by the shuttered window and sits down on the upright wooden chair. A narrow bed, a single wardrobe, and a hand basin comprise the only other furniture in this room that once had been a Franciscan lay brother's cell.

Opening her diary, she tries to make sense of her confused emotions.

"She is controlling our lives. By providing Richard with accommodation away from the clinic she's made it impossible for us to meet outside working hours without her knowing about it. I'd hoped that Richard would be as unhappy as I am about the arrangement, but he shows no sign of it. I can't help getting this terrible thought: is she manipulating Richard or doing what Richard wants? I used to think it was her, but now I'm not so sure. Richard seems to be taking all the decisions."

Lucy bites on the end of her pen and agonizes about the decision she has to make.

"Shall I stay here and help Richard bypass the FDA in order to treat Tim?"

She puts down her pen and recalls the hope in Tim's eyes. Then she writes:

"My heart tells me that Richard is right not to risk the delays and even outright refusal from the FDA that would result in Tim's death within the year. However much I dislike working here, I should devote all my energies to helping cure Tim. Richard is totally focused on this task and thinks of nothing else."

Including, she thinks with a resigned sigh, that Sunday at his house.

Richard turns over and looks yet again at the luminous digits on the bedside clock. 04:58. After more than a week of subjecting Tim to medical checks, baseline MRI scans, and blood and skin cell tests, he has finally taken the decision to begin the treatment at eleven o'clock this morning. Adrenalin has kept him awake all night. The time is now infusion minus six hours: six hours before the operation that will either catapult him to the ranks of Fleming and of Watson and Crick in the pantheon of scientific immortals or else provide the ammunition his critics sought to consign him to ignominy. There is no point any more in trying to sleep.

He gets up, showers, and dresses. His stomach muscles are too knotted to take food, and so he just has coffee before leaving the hacienda. He climbs into his Jeep Cherokee, which stands beneath a thatched shelter in the former corral, and sets off for Paradise Clinic where he double checks all the equipment he will use later that morning.

Dressed in pajamas decorated with South Park cartoon characters, Tim is sitting up in his cot when Richard and Lucy enter his room in the friars' infirmary across the dirt courtyard. Inside it has been transformed: only the arched windows recessed into the thick stone outer walls distinguish it from a private suite in one of the best

American hospitals. Vince and Martha hover protectively round the cot. Maria is already there, sitting in an easy chair. Lucy gives Tim one of her infectious smiles. He grins back and holds up his thumb from a bunched right fist.

"All systems go, Doc?" Vince asks anxiously.

Richard forces a smile. "All systems go. I'm requesting formal clearance for gene launch." He sits down at the table by the window and reads aloud from the statement he's modeled on FDA-approved patient consent forms. "Although we have discussed the proposed treatment with you on several occasions, we want to ensure that you understand its potential risks and benefits. Undertaking this treatment is entirely voluntary and you may withdraw Tim at any time before the treatment commences." Richard looks up.

Vince nods.

Richard continues reading. "There is no known effective treatment for aging and the diseases of accelerated aging, like the progeria from which Tim suffers. Therefore I have developed an experimental approach that involves inserting new genetic material into the maximum number of cells in Tim's body. This new genetic material will be transported into the nucleus of the cells by a vehicle we call a vector. The vector is a highly infectious retrovirus that has been inactivated so that it cannot cause disease and cannot reproduce itself. The new genetic material it delivers to a chromosome inside the cell nucleus is called a gene inducer. It is designed to switch on a specific gene, called the anti-aging gene which, I believe, regulates other genes that control cell repair and maintenance. By this method I hope to boost cell repair and maintenance, and so prevent further aging damage and even repair existing aging damage to some organs and tissues."

He looks at the glazed faces of the Lambert family and formally asks a series of questions based on those used by the FDA to confirm that terminally ill patients understand the possible consequences of an experimental treatment.

"We do," Vince and Martha respond to each question, as though renewing their profession of faith at the Easter mass.

Richard keeps his eyes lowered while he reads out the last question, which Maria has inserted. "Do you agree to keep confidential and not to disclose to anyone whomsoever any matter whatsoever relating to the treatment?"

Vince frowns. "Is this really necessary?"

Lucy stares at Richard. Maria says, "You're aware of the opposition to Dr. Trent's research. Whether the treatment works or not with Tim, Dr. Trent must be allowed to present his findings at the right time to the right people. Premature news of the treatment might provoke a hostile climate that could prevent others from benefiting from Dr. Trent's work."

"We agree," Martha says.

Richard slides the document towards them and holds out a pen. "Before I proceed, I must ask you to sign the consent."

Vince looks towards Martha. She is looking at Tim, who knows full well that he is living on borrowed time. He decided a week ago to put his trust in Richard. "Let's cut this crap, Dad," his voice croaks, "and get the show on the road."

Lucy maneuvers Tim's wheelchair along the cloister and through the door that the Franciscan friars had used to enter the chancel. Sunlight streams through the chancel window onto the east wall. It illuminates a huge fresco of the Mother of God, whose head is surrounded by a halo of stars and whose feet crush the head of a serpent coiled round the world. The canopy above the altar has been supplanted by a bank of bright halogen lights. They shine down on an operating table, one end of which has been raised and plumped with pillows so that Tim can sit up. Lucy helps him clamber onto the table. His pajamas have been exchanged for a white hospital gown, loosely secured at the back to allow quick access to his body in case of emergency.

Tim peers at the instruments on the trolleys either side of the operating table. Cables connect them and color-coded tubes to an overhead horizontal beam through which are routed electricity, oxygen, air, and nitrous oxide. The trolley on his left carries resuscitation equipment, while the one on his right hums with gray steel boxes linked to a large computer monitor.

He lets Lucy make him comfortable on the clump of pillows while Vince and Martha watch from a respectful distance. Lucy steps aside to make room for the Mexican nurse, who wraps a black pressure cuff round Tim's skinny upper arm. His button eyes take in every detail while she sticks three red electrodes to his chest. "What's that?" he asks Lucy as the nurse places a small black box next to him.

"Put your index finger in this, Tim," the nurse says, indicating a finger sock that projects from the black box.

"It's for measuring the percentage of oxygen in your blood," Lucy explains and goes to the computer monitor. Rows of differently cultured wavy lines move across the screen, and a number flickers next to each row. She points to the blue line. "It's this one. The others show the electrical activity of your heart, your pulse, your blood pressure, your temperature, and your breathing rate."

"If the blue number drops below ninety," the nurse says, "I'll put this mask over your face and feed you oxygen." She showed him the transparent mask. "Would you like to try it now?"

"Don't need it."

The door to the former nave opens. Richard, dressed in surgical greens, carries in a translucent vinyl bag that holds a rosé liquid in which is suspended enough microscopic particles of an infectious viral envelope to deliver the anti-aging gene inducer to all hundred trillion cells in Tim's body. With Richard aiming to insert this DNA construct at a precise spot in the three billion chemical units comprising the chromosomes in each of these cells, and switch on a gene that will produce a self-regulating amount of immortalin in every cell, the chances that something will go wrong somewhere in this horrendously complex and massive project make a NASA moon shot look simple.

Richard suspends the pendulous bag from a hook projecting from the arm of a stand and connects a transparent plastic tube from a valve at the bottom of the bag to an IVAC pump that controls the rate of infusion. The theoretical warnings that he'd read aloud to Tim's parents assume a terrifying reality with each step he takes. It is not even as though Tim is in a physical shape to withstand the stresses of the infusion. His arteries are clogged with atherosclerotic plaques and he'd had a heart attack the previous year. Tiny beads of sweat form on Richard's hairline. The trauma of a massive infusion like this could prompt another heart attack: Tim might die right here on the operating table.

"Need a hand, Doc?" Tim croaks.

Richard swallows.

Tim holds out his left hand as he's been briefed. With his skin so thin it isn't difficult for Richard to pick out the blue cephalic vein in Tim's arm, but Richard's first attempt to sink the needle of the intravenous catheter fails.

"Wanna borrow Mom's glasses?" Tim asks.

Tim barely winces as the needle slides in at Richard's second attempt. This time the needle stays put in the vein that leads to Tim's heart. Tim's beady eyes watch as Richard connects the catheter to the tube from the IVAC pump.

The moment of truth is seconds away. In the history of medicine it will be seen as a transforming moment—one way or the other.

Tension stifles all sound except for the hum of the instruments. The nurse stands ready with a syringe filled with adrenaline in case Tim needs resuscitating.

The digital wall clock identifies the moment as 11:02 a.m. when Richard turns on the IVAC pump. Pink fluid begins to travel through the transparent plastic tube at a predetermined 125 milliliters an hour. It disappears into Tim's arm while Tim rhythmically squeezes a black sponge ball. Richard stands, transfixed, as a hundred trillion virus particles began to drip into the vein, where they are drawn down into Tim's heart and pumped out into his body.

His power over Tim ceased when he turned on the pump. Control over life and death now resides in the gene inducer he has designed. It is protected by a knobby envelope of proteins that drift through Tim's bloodstream until its pattern of protuberances and cavities locate a receptor in the outer membrane of a cell, much as a space vehicle finds a docking port in a giant space station.

Richard looks at the digital clock. Launch plus one minute.

If the mission profile is being followed, two trillion infectious viral vehicles are now docking with two trillion cells in Tim's body and injecting their gene payload, encased in an inner protein capsule, through the membrane and into the cell's interior. Each capsule's trajectory takes it past proteins, enzymes, and other orbiting molecules in its search for the cell's nucleus. On contact with the nuclear membrane it signals its access code and thrusts its cargo of double-stranded DNA into the nucleus. Bew's sequence of bases takes over, scanning the three billion bases on the stringy threads of twenty-three pairs of chromosomes to lock onto the complementary sequence and insert the gene inducer at the target site on chromosome 3.

If the mission profile is being followed.

Vince and Martha try unsuccessfully to hide their anxiety. Martha fingers her rosary beads, silently mouthing invocations to the Mother of God who watches impotently from on high. Vince grips his wife's arm, trying to give her the strength he does not possess.

Another ten minutes go by. Tim's puckered face grimaces. His croaky voice breaks the silence. "I guess I haven't turned into a monkey yet."

Tears of pride and apprehension roll down Martha's cheeks.

"Keep squeezing the ball," Richard instructs.

Tim gives an impish grin. "Make it worth my while."

"Whatever you want, son," says Vince.

Tim screws up his face. "A Big Mac."

At 11:55 a.m. the dregs of the retroviral vector run into the pump, out through the tube, and into Tim's arm. The vinyl bag is empty. It seems that Tim is surviving the ordeal.

"How are you feeling, Tim?" Richard asks as he removed the catheter.

"Not good," Tim croaks.

Panic edges Vince's voice. "What's wrong, son?"

"I'm still waiting for my Big Mac."

Vince hugs him. "You got it, son. All the Big Macs you can eat." He turns to Richard. "Can he...?"

"Sure," says Richard. "It's all over. There's a McDonald's on the Paseo de Montego. We'll send a car down."

But it isn't all over.

While Alvaro goes to buy half a dozen Big Macs, the nurse withdraws blood from a vein on Tim's right arm. Lucy immediately takes the sample to the lab for analysis.

Late that evening Richard anxiously examines the computer printout of spiky peaks and troughs in the four colors corresponding to A, T, C and G, the four bases of the DNA molecule. So far, A-OK. The retroviral vector has done its job as programmed and landed the gene inducer precisely at the target site on chromosome 3 in the nucleus of Tim's cells. Richard breathes a sigh of relief. One small step for a gene, one giant leap for gene therapy.

But would it send out its signal to switch on the anti-aging gene? And if so, would the activated anti-aging gene boost a cascade of cellular repair and maintenance mechanisms, which have been running down rapidly since Tim's birth, without overloading the fine balance of chemicals that keep him alive?

45

Maria slides back the floor-to-ceiling glass panels that form the long north wall separating the living room from the terrace. The room's dark green marble-tiled floor continues through to the edge of the terrace, where four stone pillars support the ceiling that slopes down from the back of the house. Sliding back the panels extends the living room onto the terrace and exposes it to the elements. Twenty-five yards beyond the terrace, small waves break onto white sand. Gulls wheel and cry above as a file of pelicans skims silently over the pearly green sea like a flock of prehistoric predators. The midday sun blazes down, but a cooling northerly breeze from the Gulf of Mexico wafts into the opened living room like air conditioning with a faint salty tang.

Vince walks through to the terrace and gapes. "Is this your house, Miss Snowe?"

She shakes her head. "It belongs to a business acquaintance in Mérida. He only uses it during July and August."

"What do you think of *this*, son?" Vince asks.

Dwarfed in a Red Sox shirt and baseball cap, Tim glances round. "With business acquaintances like this," says the croaky voice, "who needs friends?"

"Tim!" Martha scolds. "Where are your manners?"

"They managed to escape from the clinic."

Lucy tries to suppress a giggle.

"I do apologize Miss Snowe," says a flustered Martha. "We really appreciate you bringing us here."

"It's my pleasure, Martha," says Maria regally. "Just make yourself at home."

Richard joins them. The December sun shines on deserted, unfenced private beaches, some with planted coconut palms and others with wild vegetation, that fringe the shallow coastal waters as far as the resort town of Progreso. The town's four-mile-long commercial pier projects into the Gulf like an angry black line dividing the milky blue sky from the milky green sea.

"*This* is how to spend Christmas," Vince enthuses to Martha. "It'll be snowing in Boston!"

Ernesto, the Maya gardener and general factotum, brings a tray of drinks. "Do help yourselves," Maria gestures. Vince grabs a beer, Martha takes a glass of wine, Lucy a Diet coke, but Richard declines. "I think I'll go for a swim before lunch."

Tim's wizened old face looked up plaintively. "I want to swim too."

"I don't think that's wise, Tim," Maria says, "in your condition."

Tim screws up his face. "Want to swim! Want to swim!" he insists like a child demanding a candy.

"You do what Miss Snowe tells you," says Vince.

"Tim's been in a paddling pool," Martha says, "but never in the sea. What do you think, Doctor?"

Richard wants to take no unnecessary risks. "Let's wait until we see how Tim's strength increases in the coming months. In the meantime Tim must be covered in maximum sunblock cream if he goes outside."

Richard wades through the shallow water until he reaches swimming depth. Then he strikes out like a man possessed, trying to exorcise the fear of failure.

Half an hour later he emerges from the water, squinting at the brightness of the white sand. Tim is sitting in the shade of the pale green finger-sized leaves and tiny white flowers of a large clump of sikimay that grows wild on the beach. His skinny legs are splayed in front of him and his frail body is supported by a backrest and armrests of sand that Lucy has made for him. He looks like a diminutive potentate surveying his kingdom from a desert throne. "When I'm strong enough," his croaking voice declares, "Lucy's going to teach me to swim just like you."

From the terrace Ernesto summons them for lunch.

Tim looks up to Richard. "What's the hidden agenda, Doc?"

"What hidden agenda?"

"What does she get out of it?"

He senses Lucy watching him as he says, "She wants to develop treatments for diseases that conventional medicine can't cure."

"How wrong can you get," Tim says. "There I was, assuming she wants to see if it's safe to take a shot herself so she'll never get old and wrinkly like me."

46

Maria Snowe stares out of one of the four windows of her office, which occupies the top floor of the Guardian's Tower. Its commanding views differ in only one respect from those that the Franciscan superior had enjoyed. The window facing south looks down on the dirt courtyard enclosed by the limestone perimeter wall and entrance gate, the visitors' lodgings, and the friars' infirmary; the window facing west lets her see every one of the Mayan huts surrounding the grassy square outside the friary; the window facing north overlooks the rooms in the cloister; the window facing east, however, at which she now stands, shows the recently constructed stone-flagged patio leading to the blue rectangle of the swimming pool glinting in the midday sun and, beyond, an expanse of lawn between tropical bushes and trees all enclosed by a dark green hedge of limonaria. Her attention is focused on Tim, who has stopped part way across the lawn to hold Lucy's hand while he wheezes for breath.

Maria recalls with a shudder the way her father had struggled for breath in the last weeks of his life.

At the sound of her door opening Maria banishes the memory and turns to greet Richard with a smile. "How's it going?"

"Lucy completed some antibody staining this morning." Richard lowers himself into one of the two chairs in front of her desk.

"And?"

"The anti-aging gene's still producing immortalin in Tim's blood cells and skin cells twenty days after the infusion."

"Good," she says with satisfaction as she resumes her seat behind the carved, seventeenth century mahogany desk that she'd found in the room after she bought the abandoned friary.

"It's far too soon to put out the flags," he warns. "We reached this stage with the first lot of monkeys and then it all went horribly wrong." Richard has sunk into his pessimistic phase, dwelling on all the ways in which his experiment might fail while he waits, with little else to do, for the result.

"But you used Bew's targeting technology with the second batch of monkeys to overcome that problem," Maria encourages.

"Humans aren't just big monkeys," he replies edgily. "Especially a human like Tim."

"You're worried that his progeria is already too far advanced?"

There is no point in trying to hide anything from Maria; her eyes can read his mind like an open book. "Back at Eden we were treating normal monkeys. Old, but normal. Tim's progeria makes him abnormal. I'm worried that his condition will turn fatal before the anti-aging gene's had time to do its job."

Richard's daily medical checks on Tim show no indication of any impending crisis. The days turn into weeks and Richard's mood swings to optimism as Tim grows in strength. Tim becomes intensely curious about the tests being carried out on him and the science behind them. He asks so many questions that Richard relents and lets him into the laboratory.

The tiny figure, baseball cap on back to front, looks up in wonder at the rows of gleaming bottles shelved above bench tops crowded with scientific apparatus.

Lucy lifts him up and puts him on a swivel chair by the bench on which Eppendorf tubes, plastic dispenser bottles, micropipettes, and a water bath are waiting to help extract cells from his tissue. "Richard needs to take another sample of skin."

"Is the guy a cannibal?" asks the croaky voice. "At this rate I'll have no skin left."

Richard pinches part of Tim's arm and uses a scalpel to scrape off a small section of skin that he places in a sterilized container and gives it to Lucy.

"So, how do I compare with the monkeys?" Tim asks.

"The monkeys never asked questions," Richard replies.

Tim looks to Lucy. "Is the guy a genius or is he a comedian?"

"As far as the blood cells and the skins cells are concerned," Richard says, "the results are very similar. The gene inducer got into between eighty-five and ninety-five per cent of the cells, but switched on the anti-aging gene in all cells. That's a phenomenon known as the bystander effect. For the monkeys this pattern was the same in other kinds of cell as well."

"What about other cells in me?"

"To find out if the anti-aging gene is working in your key organs," Richard says, "I'm going to have to do to you what I did to the monkeys: remove your brain, slice it up, and give the pieces to Lucy for testing. Then we'll know if you're being cured."

Tim turns to Lucy, "Is the guy a comedian or is he a maniac?"

"A genius," Lucy says. "And don't worry. Progeria doesn't affect your brain."

Richard smiles. "I've lost far more brain cells through aging than you have."

"If he's a genius," Tim says to Lucy, "and I've got more brain cells than he has, what does that make me?"

"A budding genius."

For the first time Richard sees Tim put aside his protective carapace of humor. The button eyes in his wizened face burn with determination. "If this treatment really does work, Doc, and I don't die, then I'm going to study to become a genetic engineer like you."

As the weeks turn into months the temperature rises, the long pods hanging from the flame trees on the Progreso road blacken, the ceiba tree in the center of the garth became covered with balls of cotton, like snowballs, and Tim's strength grows. With that strength comes a restlessness.

The lessons with a tutor that Maria arranged at Martha's request keep him busy from eight thirty to twelve thirty every morning. For the rest of the day he and Lucy are inseparable, but even Lucy finds there is a limit to which the genetics lab, the swimming pool, and the gardens at Paradise Clinic keep him occupied.

"The tutor warned me that Tim has been talking more and more about going to high school in Boston," Maria says to Richard as they stand at her office window watching him study a textbook with Lucy beneath a parasol.

"Not yet," Richard says in alarm. "It'll take another month at the very least before the tests show statistically significant data."

"We're keeping him too tightly caged. Why not take him out of the clinic on sightseeing trips to distract him from thoughts of home?"

Richard seizes on the suggestion. "Will you show us round?"

She gives him an enigmatic look. Sensing the impenetrability of the barrier that Tim and Lucy have drawn up against her, she avoids direct contact with either whenever possible. "Alvaro will drive you. He knows all the places to visit."

The excursions prove a welcome relief for Richard too, distracting him from the tension of waiting to see if his therapy proves successful. Lucy is thrilled to spend most afternoons with Richard and Tim, the two people she cares most for in life. At first Tim, who has rarely been out of Boston, relishes the opportunity of exploring the nearby Spanish colonial city of Mérida with its grandiose European-style buildings, its plazas and pavement restaurants, its noisy, slow-moving traffic, and its shops, markets, and street vendors selling everything from tacos through straw hats to silver jewelry. The chateau-like private mansions that border the tree-lined boulevard of the Paseo de Montejo on their way into the center, and the ostentatious public buildings facing the large, main plaza, Alvaro points out, were erected by landowners whose wealth had been generated from the labor of dispossessed Maya peons. Tim is fascinated by the richly carved facade of the sixteenth century palace of the city's founder, which depicts Conquistadors trampling savages underfoot, and intrigued by the gunnery slits that served as windows in the huge, stark twin-towered cathedral built on the site of the sacred pyramid of the demolished Mayan city of T'ho. But after the parks, shops, markets, museums, art galleries and churches have been exhausted, his restlessness returns. Driving back from the coast one day with a bored Tim, Alvaro takes a diversion to the Mayan ruins at Dzibilchaltún.

"It's got to be taller than the upper deck at Fenway Park," Tim says in awe.

Towering above them is the east face of a vast limestone monument the color of gold. The Pyramid of the Magician rises from an oval base to a lofty platform on which is built a second, smaller oval pyramid, whose flat top supports a rectangular construction forming the base for the topmost temple. A stairway about one third as broad as the eastern face climbs at a terrifyingly steep angle up to the temple.

They had set off early in the morning, but the drive to Uxmal has taken an hour and a half and the sun now beats down from a cloudless sky. Martha finds the heat overpowering and stays with

Vince in the shelter of a restaurant near the site, but Tim, grasping a bottle of mineral water and shaded by his Red Sox baseball cap, seems unaffected. "How long did this pile take to build?" he asks.

"One night," Alvaro states solemnly.

"Oh yeah," Tim says. "Superman built it."

"A dwarf," Alvaro replies.

"A *dwarf* built this?"

Alvaro's slow, deep voice seems to resonate in his barrel chest. "As a reward the people proclaimed him Magician and Supreme Ruler of all he could see from the pyramid."

Tim scampers to the west side of the pyramid to view the partial reconstruction of one of the largest and most beautiful cities of the Maya. Long, low symmetrical buildings embellished with intricately carved friezes rise from clearings in a flat jungle that stretches to the horizon.

"What do you think, Tim?" Lucy asks when they catch up with him.

"I think it's bullshit that a little guy like me ruled over all this."

Alvaro stares at Tim; his gaze carries the weight of stones.

Tim glances nervously towards Lucy.

Alvaro takes a step towards Tim, seizes him beneath the armpits, and hoists him onto his shoulders. He strides to a rectangular group of four long single-story buildings that are punctuated by a row of open doorways into cell-like chambers. The buildings enclose a grassed square just as a convent's cells enclose a garth. Alvaro stops before the center of the west building, which faces the Pyramid of the Magician. Here the elaborate frieze above the line of doorways shows a throne, but instead of a ruler sitting on the throne a dwarf stands on it.

Tim turns to Lucy and Richard. "Hey, this could be me!" he cries. "And look, Doc, there's the DNA double helix!" The intertwined bodies of two snakes undulate along the length of the frieze.

"No, my small friend," says Alvaro, putting him down. "The two serpents represent the two sides of a goddess."

"Two sides?" Tim queries.

"The Christians have a God and a devil. Other religions have good gods and evil gods. But the ancient Maya had true wisdom. They knew that, like us, a god can be both good and evil."

"Which goddess?"

Alvaro points to the end of the frieze where the rattlesnake tail of one serpent hangs over the opened jaws of the other, from which a human head emerges. "Ixchel, the goddess of life. From her mouth mankind is born."

"She's also evil?" Lucy queries.

"As goddess of the moon, Ixchel controlled the tides that flooded the world in ancient times. Ixchel is both creator and destroyer."

Richard examines the carving. It reminds him of the silk print of the Mayan god Kukulkán that he'd noticed on his first visit to Maria's house at Seacliff. "This isn't like the other serpent effigies on these buildings. Why does it have a feathered headdress and a feathered body?"

"This frieze was added later," Alvaro replies, "after Ixchel was reborn as the Plumed Serpent Kukulkán, the god-king who wore a headdress of long green quetzal feathers."

Richard recalls Maria's laughing disclosure over dinner at Cozumel that Alvaro believed the time and circumstances of her birth coincided with the predicted reincarnation of Ixchel. "What's with Ixchel and this reincarnation myth?" he probes.

"The ancient Maya knew that the cycles of life repeat themselves, even for the gods," declares Alvaro in a sonorous tone that brooks no doubt. "When Ixchel was reborn as Kukulkán, a new cycle of life began for the Maya. He led them into an era of glory. Their lands became fertile. Their trade prospered. They built great cities to honor the gods. Their priests were blessed with knowledge of mathematics and astronomy. Their armies ruled the known world and dispensed the justice of the gods."

"So how come you see them begging in the plazas?" Tim asks.

Lucy looks at him aghast, afraid that he's insulted Alvaro, but the Maya takes no offense. "After the cycle of life comes the cycle of death," he says as though stating the obvious. "The white man came with his Christian god. They drove out our gods and oppressed our people." A smile forms on Alvaro's lips. "But the cycle has turned once more. The Christian god grows weak. No longer do the people obey his teaching. His priests become fewer. The people desert his churches. Many, like the friary that La Madre bought, are abandoned." His black eyes focus on something that nobody else can see. "Ixchel has been reborn once more. The time approaches when she will be made known. She will give birth to a new era."

"How do you know?" Tim challenges.

"The priests carved this knowledge in the Tzolk'in, the sacred calendar that can be read by those with eyes to see."

"What do you make of all this stuff, Doc?" Tim asks.

"People create myths to explain what they don't understand or to fulfill a deep need," Richard replies. "Most religions have a similar myth, like the Messiah prophesied to lead God's chosen people from bondage to a new kingdom, or Jesus the Son of God coming again in glory to take the just into heaven."

"You don't believe in God?" Tim queries.

As far as Richard is concerned, there is little to choose between the Mayan belief in the Tzolk'in and the Judeo-Christian belief that the bible is the word of God. There is only one god, Nature, who wrote the entire code of life in the four letters A, T, C, and G, the language of DNA. He looks down at the inquisitive, bright-eyed Tim, transformed from the wheezing invalid who had found it difficult to walk unaided across the Chicxulub beach at Christmas. And that transformation gives him hope that, with the tools of genetic engineering, our destinies are no more determined by what Nature has written than by what the Mayan gods or the Judeo-Christian God are claimed to have written. "I believe in the power of man to write his own destiny."

As the harsh afternoon light softens, anticipation grows like a mounting electrostatic charge inside the laboratory. Few words are exchanged between Richard and Lucy. He has planned in detail how he would test the effects of the anti-aging gene inducer on Tim, and Lucy knows precisely what she must do.

From the incubator below the center of the three recessed, arched windows on the nave's northern wall, she removes a test tube containing a sample of Tim's white blood cells that she had incubated with an antibody to new CD4 T-lymphocytes coupled to a fluorescent dye. She places the test tube into a slot at the bottom of an electronic fluorescence-activated cell sorter, a black box that counts the number of fluorescent cells and consequently the number of new CD4 T-lymphocytes. Lucy taps the keyboard of a computer linked to the cell sorter, and the computer monitor shows a spiky bell curve of the original count of these cells, which form an essential part of Tim's immune system. When he'd arrived at Paradise, Tim's body was producing only a fifth of the CD4 T-lymphocytes needed by a normal healthy adult.

She looks over her shoulder.

Richard nods. She takes a deep breath and taps the keyboard to superimpose the new count on this display.

Richard and Lucy stare at the screen. A new spiky curve starts to form. It peaks at more than five times the height of the original curve. They look at each other and grin like children who've hit the jackpot in a computer game.

A further test shows that Tim's skin cells have been restored to a youthful vigor.

"Well?" asks Lucy expectantly when she sees the satisfaction on his face.

"We wait," Richard says prudently. The results of one test remain: the MRI scans that would tell him whether he is curing just some of Tim's symptoms or whether he has indeed succeeded in defying the gods.

The skeleton mask, a molded white plastic face mask with holes for eyes, nose and mouth, grips Tim's head below his bald skull; it makes his prone figure look even more like that of an alien as he lies pinioned to the platform that points into the circular tunnel of the MRI scanner. Four months before, prior to his infusion with the anti-aging gene inducer, the mask had held his head in precisely the same position.

Watching through the radio-frequency-screened window of the control room, Lucy slips her hand into Richard's when the platform moves forward and Tim disappears into the tunnel. Her grip tightens when the silence is shattered by a machine gun-like rat-a-tat-tat as the scanner makes magnetic resonance images of preprogramed cross sections of Tim's head and body. Comparison of these scans with the original scans will tell Lucy whether or not Tim is being cured. It will tell Richard whether or not he is leading science into a new era.

"You've been very brave, Tim," Lucy says as she helps him clamber from the platform after the scans have been completed.

Tim turns to Richard and winks. "It's not hard to be brave when the alternative is a coffin."

A momentary smile breaks through the tension in Richard's face.

"You will tell me, won't you Doc?" Tim asks. "Even if it's bad news?"

"Of course we will," Lucy says.

Richard places the MRI scans on the light box next to the corresponding ones taken before the infusion. With his heart pounding in his ribcage, Richard examines them for malignant side effects, but no black spots indicating tumors are visible on the X-ray-like films.

Anxiously he compares Tim's major organs. The brain shows little change from four months before. Tim's liver, lungs, and kidneys, however, have each increased in size by approximately ten per cent. Cross sections of his limbs show an average fifteen per cent increase in skeletal muscle. The degenerated vessel that had caused a heart attack now appears normal. The pounding in Richard's ribcage slows and a warm, euphoric flush spreads throughout his body. The combined results of the three tests expel forever the demons of doubt. He turns to Lucy with a grin of triumph. "I guess we did it."

Lucy hugs him. "Richard, I'm so proud of you for saving Tim's life. Let's go and tell him."

Richard looks at his watch. "He'll be asleep now. There'll be plenty of time tomorrow." Almost overcome by relief and exultation, he stretches his weary body. "I'm feeling bushed myself right now." There is, however, one person with whom he does want to share the good news before he sinks into bed.

As soon as she opens the door, the normally cool and restrained Maria flings her arms around Richard.

"How do you know?" he asks, taken aback.

She bursts out laughing. "Richard Trent, you don't come to my door at this time of the night grinning like a madman and expect me not to guess."

His grin widens. "You're right. All the tests show that Tim's aging degeneration is being reversed without any harmful side effects." The grin turns into a yawn. "I'm drained, but I wanted to tell you before I hit the sack."

"Which won't be for some time yet," Maria says. "Come."

She leads him through to her dining room that, like her study on the top floor of the Guardian's Tower, has been exquisitely renovated in Spanish colonial style, with black and white marble floor tiles, white walls, and dark mahogany furniture to complement the woodwork. After lighting candles on the dining room table and putting out two crystal flutes, she goes to the kitchen and returns with some antojitos and a bottle of vintage Bollinger.

Maria pays little heed to the food; her whole attention is fixed on Richard. She lifts up her flute and says, "To our partnership. May it continue to flourish and show just who is right."

"I'll drink to that," Richard says, deliberately echoing his response to the toast Maria had given after he'd signed the agreement with her.

He is still trying to come to terms with the enormity of what he has achieved since that foggy May day in San Francisco. With a single fifty-minute infusion he has activated a human body's own healing processes to repair the degenerative effects of aging. It is a feat that would have a far more profound impact on medical science than

Fleming's discovery of the antibiotic properties of penicillin. "Wait till Nathan Hill sees this."

"Why should he?" Maria asks.

"He's bound to after I've submitted my paper for publication. It'll be sent out for peer review."

She sips her champagne. "Are you sure it's wise to publish straight away?"

Richard frowns. "I've now got the evidence I need." God knows, he's waited long enough to show the whole world that he had been right from the very beginning.

"So you want to submit your work for peer review?"

"That's standard practice in science."

"Be honest with me, Richard. Who are your peers?"

Richard looks into his glass. He thinks of Nathan Hill's painstaking compilation of other people's work, of Don Straker identifying genes in order to patent possible commercial uses rather than seeking to understand their precise functions, of Larry Myers running his research on autopilot while he progressed his university career, of the older generation who once led their fields and who now served on committees far behind the rapidly advancing frontier of research, of the younger generation battling at that frontier but as yet no breakthroughs notched on their belts, and of his generation, not one of whom has achieved anything remotely as significant as his pioneering gene therapy.

"At UCLA you succeeded in rejuvenating skin cells and brain cells in laboratory culture," she says, "but that didn't stop them refusing you grants, attacking you on TV, and dismissing you from the university." She puts down her glass and gazes into his eyes. "Whenever has success been a protection against the jealousy of inferiors? Against powerful vested interests? Against small-minded bureaucrats? You're an outsider, Richard. You came to Mexico and broke the rules they invented. Will they welcome back the prodigal son with open arms or will they destroy your career, just as they destroyed Martin Cline's?"

48

"Richard, you must tell Tim and his parents." Lucy's shocked voice disturbs the morning calm in the garden at Paradise where Richard has asked her not to disclose the test results. Richard looks round uneasily from the white wrought-iron table where they sit next to the pool. Although the Lamberts are still in their suite in the visitors' lodgings, he wants to make absolutely sure that he and Lucy are not overheard. He rises and says, "Let's walk and talk this through."

He leads her away from the table, which is shaded by a large parasol, into the heat of the morning sun. Beyond the glinting blue pool stretches the lawn that gives way to scarlet hibiscus, white and pink bougainvillea, mariposa, and golden rain bushes. When they are part way across the lawn and Richard considers that they cannot possibly be overheard, he asks, "Why must I tell them?"

Lucy looks at him, unable to understand why he can't see the obvious. "Because Tim has the right to know."

"Don't I have the right to continue with my work?" Richard walks on towards the bottle-green hedge of limonaria that encloses the garden, separating it from the orchard, the vegetable garden, and the rest of the friary grounds. "If Tim and his parents know the results, they'll want to return to the US as soon as possible."

"Of course."

"But there's no way they'll be able to keep his cure secret."

She shakes her head in bewilderment. "Why should they? Tim's cure is sensational." She stares at him. "Why aren't you taking him on the first plane to Maryland and showing him to the FDA?"

"Because the FDA would come down on me like a ton of bricks. They'll get me barred from further research for conducting a clinical trial without their approval, just like they barred Martin Cline. And Cline's patients weren't even American citizens."

"You promised me that would never happen to us," she accuses.

"It won't if we keep Tim here just a few more months while Maria prepares the ground to get my work accepted."

She follows him through a gap in the hedge and into the orchard, on the farthest side of the grounds from the visitors' lodgings.

"Richard, for heaven's sake, you can't treat Tim like a laboratory monkey and keep him locked in a cage."

"Have a sense of perspective. Do you call the whole of the Yucatán a cage?"

"This is her idea, isn't it?"

"Don't be paranoid about Maria," he retorts. "Hasn't she enabled me to achieve this breakthrough when everyone else was opposing me?"

Lucy stops in the shade of a large cainito tree, from whose spreading foliage hang large purple-green plum-like fruit. "Did she remind you of the non-disclosure clause in our contracts?"

"This is my decision". He looks down on her young, innocent face. Innocent and naive. "You don't understand, Lucy. We're dealing with powerful vested interests here: the scientific establishment, the medical ethics lobby, and the pharmaceutical industry. Each has its own reasons for wanting to bar me. Something this big has got to be handled properly. Trust me. The time isn't yet right to announce the results."

"Tim and his parents trust us. You're asking me to deceive them?"

Why did she always have to see everything so simplistically? "Withholding information from the Lambert family does Tim no harm. It's a small price to pay if it gives Maria time to ensure that no one destroys my career."

Richard sees that his appeal to reason is getting nowhere: she is far too emotionally involved in the patient to appreciate the big picture. It leaves him no option but to remind her of her obligations. "I am instructing you, as my assistant," he says sternly, "not to disclose the results of tests carried out under my direction."

She looks up to him. Tears of anger well in her eyes and for a moment Richard thinks she will hit him. "I'm not going to lie to Tim," she says before turning her back on him and running through the orchard towards the friary.

Richard sips his beer thoughtfully at the plastic table in front of one of the hotels facing Hidalgo Park. It might once have been a park, but now it is a small square covered more by pale pink cobblestones than by grass, and closed on two adjacent sides by hotels converted from mansions whose belle époque designs reflect the wealth and French taste of late nineteenth century Yucatan plantation owners. Squatting Maya demurely offer beads and other handicraft for sale from colorful blankets spread on the cobblestones around the greened copper statue of yet another conquistador or else a later white fighter for independence, while seated mestizo couples demurely court on the white stone S-shaped benches called *confidenciales*, and families in their Sunday best promenade on wide pathways between islands of tamed trees. These people possess a dignified fatalism that Richard finds impossible to accept.

Maria has confirmed what, deep down, he already knew: if you want to succeed at anything in life you cannot rely on the good will of others, be they individuals, institutions, governments, or deities. You must take whatever action is necessary to forge your own destiny.

Bells peal from the twin towers of the Jesuit church, whose unadorned sun-bleached south face occupies the block on the other side of the street that forms the northern boundary of Hidalgo Park.

Richard looks at his watch. Surely the Lamberts had finished with mass by now?

Tim, Martha, and Vince at last emerge onto the street, which is closed to traffic for the regular Sunday entertainment. They pause in the square to watch a mariachi band set up their instruments on a temporary stand before they stroll through the growing crowd to join Richard.

"Hope we haven't kept you waiting," Martha says as Richard helps her ample frame into a chair shaded by a parasol from the midday heat.

Tim clambers unaided into a chair next to Richard. "How is Lucy?" he asks. His voice has lost its croakiness.

"She still has headaches and finds it difficult to sleep," Richard replies.

"Don't you think it'll cheer her up if we visit her?" Vince asks.

Richard is still angry with Lucy for refusing to cooperate. Better that she is ill in bed than blurting out what the tests show. "She isn't able to see visitors right now. Besides," he adds as a further disincentive, "she might be infectious and I can't put Tim at risk."

"We're worried," Martha says. "What's wrong with her?"

Richard shrugs. "I don't know. A physician's coming tomorrow."

"Poor thing," says Martha. "We wanted to talk with you both."

Richard holds out his palms in a gesture of helplessness.

"We hope you don't mind, Doctor," Vince says, "but we wanted to see you, like away from the clinic."

Away from Maria Snowe is what he really means. "Fine," said Richard, knowing full well what is on their minds. "Let's order lunch first."

"We're very grateful for all that Miss Snowe has done for us, believe me," says Vince after the waiter has departed. "We don't want to offend her. But the thing is, Doctor, Tim wants to go home."

"Right," Tim says.

"We felt it would be easier talking to you and Lucy first," says Vince, raising his voice above the brass trumpets of the mariachi band.

"Tim's health has improved enormously," says Martha. "He doesn't need a wheelchair."

"Just look at him," says Vince.

The change is unmistakable without the results of Richard's tests. Tim's thin, saggy translucent skin is now taut and flesh-cultured. His arms and legs are rounder and showing signs of muscle.

"I *feel* good, thanks to you, Doc," says Tim. "I'm strong enough to go to school and show them that I may be small and ugly but I'm no dumbo. Lucy said I'm an A student in science. I'm going to make it to college and major in molecular biology, just you watch me."

Richard sees the fire in Tim's button eyes. It is the same fire that had burned in him. His fire had been ignited by Father Lawrence showing him DNA. Now it is he who has ignited Tim's fire by showing him how it is possible to use DNA to correct nature's mistakes and cure the "incurable" disease of progeria. He has little doubt that Tim's body now possesses the strength to sustain the consuming passion that would enable him to achieve his goal. "I must strongly advise against going home," he says.

"Why, Doc?" Tim asks.

Richard avoids Tim's trusting eyes. "The new tests are inconclusive. There've been certain improvements, but we don't know if these are temporary or if they'll produce any adverse side effects. I need to monitor you carefully for some time yet."

"We've thought about that," says Vince. "An attending physician at the Boston Children's Hospital used to monitor Tim's health. I'm sure he'd be happy to do that again and keep you informed of any developments."

This is the last thing Richard wants. A pediatrician who had Tim's medical records would demand full details of the treatment that had brought about such a dramatic and unprecedented change in Tim's condition. "This is an experimental therapy. Until I'm convinced of its efficacy, it would be irresponsible of me to release you from my medical supervision."

"We understand your caution, Doctor," says Martha, "and we really appreciate how honest you are with us. But your treatment is like a miracle. Other progeric children should be able to benefit from it."

Richard swallows. "Maria and I explained the need for the non-disclosure clause in the agreement you signed. There are people, powerful people, who think that I've acted irresponsibly by giving Tim a therapy that the United States government hasn't approved."

"You've acted with total responsibility throughout," Vince declares. "Martha is right. What you've done for Tim is nothing less than a miracle. When we show them how much Tim has improved, the Sunshine Foundation's going to be behind you one hundred and ten per cent."

Richard puts himself at their mercy. "I'm asking you to delay your return for a few months until Maria has prepared the ground for disclosing details of Tim's treatment. If the federal health authorities find out now that I've ignored their rules, they'll bar me from working in this field."

"That's disgraceful," Vince says. He puts down his glass of beer. "Let me tell you, Doctor, I worked for the Democratic Party at the last election. I know our local congressman. When we get back, I'm personally going to tell him how brilliant you are and how badly you've been treated by the government. Don't you worry about a thing."

Richard stares into his beer. Is his life's work and the transformation that he offers medical science in the future to be put in jeopardy because this family can't wait to get back to the States and boast about him?

49

Richard grasps the door handle of Lucy's room. For what seems an eternity he hesitates in the sweltering heat of the upper cloister. Finally he turns the handle and enters.

The shutters are closed against the afternoon sun, leaving cracks of light that stripe the opposite wall. A ceiling fan whirs a cooling draft. She lies asleep, facing the wall, in the narrow bed. Compared to the luxuriously renovated Guardian's Tower that Maria occupies and the remodeled hacienda that Maria has bought for him, this room is little better than when it had been a Franciscan lay brother's cell. Instead of a crucifix and an idealized portrait of St Francis on the wall, however, there is one poster of the DNA double helix and another of an elk grazing in South Dakota's Sand Lake Wild Life Refuge.

The only other adornments stand on the table by the cloister window. A silver-framed photograph shows a happy Lucy in her graduation gown. She stands between a proud woman with gray hair pulled back in a bun from a weathered face and a gaunt man with an uncompromising expression who appears ill at ease in a suit. Next to it is a bunch of white roses languishing in a laboratory conical flask. The lonely blooms bring home to Richard just how isolated Lucy is here. At UCLA she had the company of Dorothy and the others in the house at Palms, and in San Francisco she lived with her uncle and aunt. But in Paradise the two Mexican nurses who speak English keep to themselves. Her only friends are Tim and his parents—apart from Richard.

Lucy doesn't stir when he closes the door behind him. Her breathing is shallow. Her right hand is curled in a tight little fist next to her face.

The physician that Maria had summoned found no infection or other physical cause for her fever, headaches, and sleeplessness. He prescribed paracetamol and sleeping tablets, and advised her to drink plenty of bottled mineral water and rest as much as possible. She was suffering from delusions, he told Richard afterwards, and in his opinion her symptoms were psychosomatic.

Lucy had told Richard that she had been drugged. Her behavior convinced Richard that the root of her illness was her paranoia about Maria.

That paranoia makes his task now even more difficult. After he had told her the Lamberts were determined to return to the States, despite all his attempts to change their minds, she asked if they would call and see her before they left. When Richard ushered them into the room, he worried that she would spill out the test results. As soon as she saw Tim her face lit up. Holding one hand awkwardly behind his back, Tim said, "I don't want to leave when you're not well, Lucy." His button eyes glanced up from her bed to Richard. "But if I'm going to become a genetic engineer like the Doc, I've got to go to high school."

"Yes," she said, sitting up in bed. "You go to school, Tim."

"Make sure you get better." He gave her one of his wicked grins. "I'm going to be big and strong when I next see you."

"Miss Snowe has generously offered her plane to fly us back from Boston whenever we want," Vince said.

"No, Tim, you stay in America," Lucy insisted.

"No way," said Tim. "I'm coming back to see you at Christmas." He winked at her. "I'll even let Doc Cannibal here take some more skin samples."

"No," she said ardently. "Stay in America."

The tiny figure removed his hand from behind his back and thrust a bunch of white roses at her. She leaned forward to take them. He bobbed his disproportionately large head to kiss her and then retreated in adolescent confusion.

On the stone staircase down to the lower cloister Martha turned to Richard. "What *is* wrong with Lucy, Doctor?"

"It's a fever," he said. "She'll soon be as right as rain."

Richard helped Alvaro carry their baggage from the visitors' lodgings to the clinic's Land Cruiser parked in the courtyard by the Guardian's Tower. Maria joined him to watch them climb into the Land Cruiser: first, the plump and pale Martha in floral sundress and straw hat, followed by the balding, suntanned Vince with a larger paunch than when he'd arrived, and finally the dwarf-like Tim wearing his Red Sox baseball cap, who clambered enthusiastically on board after telling Alvaro to leave his wheelchair for the next patients because he didn't need it any more. They bubbled with anticipation, like a family on their first trip to Disneyland.

As Alvaro drove the Land Cruiser slowly out of the dusty courtyard and through the opened black wrought-iron gates in the limestone wall, Richard was gripped with dread that premature disclosure of his unapproved gene therapy would provoke a bar on his work and leave him a scientific pariah. Instead of responding to the Lamberts' noisy waves, he silently cursed them for their selfishness in disregarding his entreaties to delay their return.

Later, when Maria relayed the news, it had taken him an age to recover from the shock. Maria offered to inform Lucy, but Richard knew that this was a task he must undertake himself. Now, standing in her room, he looks at Lucy's wan, sleeping figure and agonizes how best to tell her.

He sits on the narrow bed; beneath the single sheet her legs rest hotly against his thigh. "Lucy," he says gently.

Her eyes remain closed.

"Lucy," he repeats, louder.

Her eyes flicker into recognition. "Richard."

Slowly she sits up. Her hair falls unkempt to shoulders bared except for the narrow straps of a white cotton nightdress. He thinks how vulnerable she looks.

"Lucy, I have some terrible news." He takes hold of her hand. "There's been an accident." Her small, hot hand tightens her grip on his. "The plane came down over the Gulf. I'm afraid there were no survivors."

She turns her head to the white roses, her face contorts, and she lets out an hysterical scream, "No!"

He puts an arm round her shoulders and tries to calm her. She stares at him, her complexion ashen. "She's murdered them."

"It was an accident," he repeats gently.

"No!" she protests vehemently. "It wasn't an accident!"

"Lucy," he says, stroking her hand, "it's a great shock, I know."

Large luminous brown eyes burn into his. "She's destroyed all living proof. I told you she came back to Eden Therapy when you were on vacation and killed the monkeys. Now she's killed Tim."

"You don't know what you're saying," he soothes. "The pilot radioed air traffic control at Mérida. He reported an explosion. Then… then they lost contact."

"She planted a bomb," Lucy says as though stating the obvious.

"The wreckage indicates that the explosion was in the fuel tank. The officials believe an electrical spark ignited vapor in the tank."

"You can't believe that," she insists. "When Bew threatens to tell the FDA that we rejuvenated old monkeys, he dies. When Vince wants to tell everyone how we cured Tim, he dies."

"You know Bew was murdered by his pickup." Richard releases his hand and goes to the stand by the hand basin. "You're putting two and two together and making ten."

"Why can't you see it?" she says in frustration. "All living proof and all witnesses except you and me are dead."

He pours out a glass of bottled water. "Drink this." He holds out the glass in front of him.

Her slender arm reaches out and dashes the glass to the floor. "You can see the answer to science problems like no one I've ever known, but your greatest strength is your greatest weakness. You're so focused on proving that your discovery is the great genetic breakthrough that you can't see anything else." She stares angrily at him. "Or is it that you don't *want* to see anything that stops you achieving your goal?"

"Back at Eden Therapy you thought that Maria was taking me on vacation to murder me," he retorts.

Lucy stares straight ahead at the poster of the DNA double helix. "She doesn't want anyone to know the truth about the anti-aging gene."

He sits down on the edge of the narrow bed and tries again to reason with her. "It's one thing to ask the Lamberts to delay their return, it's quite another to blow up three passengers and two crew of a plane that cost millions of dollars."

"That's peanuts compared with the fortune she'll make by monopolizing your treatment."

"That doesn't make sense." He is losing patience with her paranoia about Maria. "If she wanted to do that she would have patented the treatment and sold a license to one of the big multinational pharmaceutical corporations."

Lucy puts both her hands around his left hand, which lies on his lap. "What do you really want, Richard? To cure diseases or make lots of money?"

He pulls his hand away, angry that she should even ask that. "You know the answer."

"I know that the best way to treat diseases isn't to stay in a private clinic in Mexico outside US health regulations," she insists.

"I'm not just treating diseases like everyone else," he retorts. "I've developed a gene therapy that will rewrite the medical textbooks."

"Then make the technique freely available," Lucy says animatedly, "so that others can use it to treat heart disease, Alzheimer's, and all the other aging diseases."

"I told you. I'll do that when the time is right."

She grasps his hand again and speaks with desperation. "Promise me you'll take our data to America, publish the results, and ask FDA approval for your treatment before she destroys any more evidence."

"I'll think about it," he says to calm her. He extricates himself and goes to the door. He turns. Her hair is disheveled, her face is white, and her pupils are dilated.

"Be careful, Richard," she implores. "Take away the lab books, the videos, and the MRI scans without telling her. She's ruthless: she kills anyone who threatens to disclose the truth."

50

Richard steps from the shuttered room into the glare and heat of the upper cloister. Below, in the center of the garth, Maria is seated with her back to him at the carved stone table beneath the overhanging branches of the large silver-trunked ceiba tree. With her black veil of hair falling to the shoulders of a black dress she might have been a nun studying scripture. Is it possible, he wonders, that there are grounds for Lucy's paranoia?

He makes his way round the cloister, past the Guardian's Tower, until he comes to an arched opening in the whitewashed wall. In the stillness of early afternoon the stairwell echoes to the slap of leather sandal against stone as he descends to the lower cloister. He steps from the terracotta tiling out onto the grass of the garth.

Maria looks up from her book at his approach. Cracks of sunlight pierce the shadowing foliage of the sacred Mayan tree of life and glint on the silver filigree bracelet she wears around her left wrist. "How did Lucy take the news?"

"Even worse than I'd feared." He sits down opposite her. "She was very close to Tim."

Maria nods understandingly. "I imagine she blames me for their deaths."

Richard studies the expression on her face. Surely no murderer would be so calm and collected? "She thinks you planted a bomb in the plane."

"Why?"

"Because you want to monopolize a secret anti-aging treatment in a private clinic outside US jurisdiction in order to make a fortune."

Maria sighs. "What did Dr. Hernandez say about Lucy's mental state?"

Richard recalls the sympathetic eyes of the mestizo physician with a drooping mustache who patiently answered his questions over coffee in Richard's office. "He said she appeared to be highly stressed and was suffering from delusions."

"Poor Lucy," Maria says. "She's very disturbed. She can't accept that another woman has your best interests at heart." Maria shakes her head sadly. "Deep down she'd rather you fail than succeed with my help."

"Whatever else you think about Lucy, she wants me to succeed."

Maria gives him a quizzical look. "Has she asked you to take your research data to the States and submit it to the FDA without telling me."

Richard hesitates and stares at the table. He doesn't want to betray Lucy, and yet…

"Surely Lucy knows Martin Cline's fate," Maria says. "Is that what she wants for you?"

Over her shoulder, framed by two square stone pillars and the arch of part of the upper cloister, Richard can see the closed wooden shutters of the room from which he'd come. "Are you prepared to set aside the non-disclosure clause in our agreement, let me publish the results, and make the therapy freely available when the time is right?"

"Haven't I always said that the purpose of our agreement is to enable you to do whatever you want?" Maria asks with hurt in her voice.

"I'm sorry," Richard says. "I didn't mean to doubt your word. But I have to be certain."

She reaches across and puts a hand on his. "I understand how distressing all this must be for you, Richard." She rises. "Come and have some lunch, keep up your strength."

"I'm not hungry."

"Just something light," she says before turning towards the cloister.

Richard follows Maria from the whitewashed cloister down a vaulted passage whose thick walls are built from masonry rubble bound by lime mortar. He wonders if the shock of Tim's death has tipped Lucy over the edge. Perhaps he ought to pursue Hernandez's suggestion that Lucy might benefit from psychiatric counseling if her condition doesn't improve.

They emerge into the brightness of the stone-flagged patio. Maria turns left and goes down two steps to the garden at the rear of the friary. Near the purple-flowering balce tree, the blue water of the swimming pool gleams in the sun.

Maria sits down at the poolside table shaded by a large parasol, where he'd asked Lucy not to reveal Tim's test results. Alvaro appears with a bottle of white wine in an ice bucket and two glasses. He opens the bottle and fills the glasses. "To eat, Madre?" he asks.

"Some antojitos for two."

"As you wish, Madre."

Richard sips from his glass and ponders. The wine is cool and soothing. The afternoon sun has transformed the calm water of the swimming pool into a mirror that reflects a blue sky wisped by traces of cirrus. A gentle breeze wafts from the bushes, bearing the sweet scent of the small, white, waxy tulip-shaped mariposas.

Alvaro returns with a tray and places a half dozen small dishes on the table. "Will that be all, Madre?"

"That's all, thanks, Alvaro." Maria picks up a tortilla topped with shredded turkey, pickled onion, and avocado slices.

"Will you begin preparing the ground right away so that I can publish as soon as possible?" Richard asks as he spears a small spicy sausage with his fork.

"There we have a problem. With Tim dead and his body—well, I understand it was barely identifiable—we no longer have any proof that the therapy works."

The fork stops half way to Richard's mouth. "That's nonsense! I've got lab notebooks, videos of the monkeys, and test results on Tim before and after gene therapy."

She finishes her salbute before asking, "Has any scientist ever faked results?"

"Faked results?" He puts down his fork and stares at her. "Why?"

"Has it ever happened?" Maria repeats.

He shrugs. "The literature is riddled with cases. Sumerlin's work on skin grafts—"

"Usually in support of extraordinary claims?"

"I suppose so."

"How easy would it be to fabricate lab books that demonstrate the efficacy and safety of the anti-aging gene inducer?"

He frowns. "Why should I?"

"That's not the question, Richard. How easy would it be if you did want to fake it."

"Pretty easy, I guess."

"And to doctor the videos, MRI scans, blood tests, and the rest so that the 'before' results become 'after', and vice versa?"

"If that's your intention, it wouldn't be difficult. But I don't see the point. I've got actual results. I don't need to fake anything."

She leans across and places a hand on his. "Poor, trusting Richard. I know that. But without living proof, the onus would be on us to prove to Hill and rest of the skeptics that your records aren't faked."

In the reflecting surface of the pool he sees Hill's swept-back steel hair, Abe Lincoln beard, and witch hunter eyes scorning the fibroblast rejuvenation results he'd just given to the Cold Spring Harbor meeting.

Her cool hand still rests on his. "And because it's against their rules, the FDA won't let you repeat the clinical trial you've carried out in Mexico in order to validate your claim." She releases his hand

and leans back. "OK, it's a worst-case scenario. But you must decide whether you want to risk it."

He pours himself another glass of wine.

"Take your time, there's no hurry. As your greatest admirer, I'm simply suggesting that you think it through. Do you have a responsibility to FDA bureaucrats in Maryland or to posterity?"

He drinks from his glass and stares at the swimming pool.

"Do you want to risk your research being stopped now, before we've shown that your discovery is a major scientific advance—"

He looks up angrily. "Of course I've shown it. Tim—"

"We've shown to our satisfaction," she intervenes, "if not the FDA's, that you've developed a treatment for progerics. There are less than thirty in the world. When the scientific history of this decade is written, your unproven claim might give you a footnote on one page. But what evidence do we have that your discovery is the great scientific breakthrough that prevents all aging diseases in normal people, instead of merely treating acute symptoms of a rare disease?"

"I know it will," Richard insists.

"So do I. But even if the scientific establishment underwent some collective Damascene conversion and welcomed you back with open arms, will they allow you to test your full gene therapy on healthy humans?"

"What's the alternative?"

She gazes at him and he answers his own question with another. "Continue my work here?"

"Produce the ultimate, irrefutable living proof that no one can deny."

He thinks of Lucy's reaction when he'd first asked her to join him in Mexico. "Some Indian we buy cheaply?"

She shakes her head sadly. "Oh Richard, when will you trust me as I trust you?"

"Meaning?"

Richard is reminded of the first time he saw her: Maria's large black eyes produce a gaze of formidable strength. "I volunteer to test your treatment."

51

Early the following morning Richard drives to Paradise Clinic with a renewed sense of purpose: what he plans is the logical conclusion to his discovery that Labor Day evening at UCLA, the final test of whether he really has found the holy grail of genetics. His tall, lean figure, dressed in T-shirt and shorts, lopes down the north cloister along which cowled friars had strolled to their workrooms. At the electronic lock next to the laboratory door he inserts his plastic card and punches six digits. The paneled mahogany door swings open and Richard freezes. A noise from inside the lab raises the hairs on the back of his neck.

He slips inside and carefully closes the door behind him so that it makes no noise. Soundlessly he passes the drinking fountain and the coffee machine in the lobby before pausing at the white swing door. The sound of a metal drawer sliding on its runners disturbs the quiet. He thrusts open the door.

"Richard!" Lucy turns round, startled. "You gave me a shock." In her hands are two large buff envelopes. She is standing next to the opened drawer of the filing cabinet near the low, embrasured window that looks out onto the garth. It is the cabinet in which he keeps the MRI films.

"What are you doing?" he demands. "I thought you were ill in bed."

"I came in to help you."

"Help me?" He stares at the neat pile of blue lab notebooks and a collection of videos on the white lab bench behind her.

"I'm collecting the evidence we'll need for the States before she can destroy it."

Dr. Hernandez was right. "Maria's not going to destroy anything and we're not going to the States," he says firmly.

She looks at him, barely able to believe the evidence of her own ears. "Richard, you promised."

"I promised to think about it." He picks up the videos and begins returning them to the wall cupboard near the filing cabinet.

Lucy grabs his arm. "You've no choice. You owe it to Tim."

He stares down at her hand on his arm and she releases it. "Owe what to Tim?"

"To cure others like him, of course. He idolized you. You can't let him down again."

"Again? What on earth are you talking about? How did I let him down?"

She stares at him. "We let Maria kill him."

He slams the cupboard door and turns round angrily. "Don't be paranoid! What was Tim's quality of life when Maria first met him?"

She recoils from his vehemence.

"I'll tell you what it was like," Richard says. "He'd been forced to quit school. He'd already had one heart attack. He couldn't walk far without getting short of breath. He'd never have survived another Boston winter."

"What are you saying?"

"Isn't it obvious? I restored his health and extended his lifespan. Maria provided luxury accommodation in a warm climate and anything he wanted. He wanted to go to the beach. He was chauffeured there inside half an hour. He wanted toys and a computer.

He got them. He wanted to swim. You taught him in the pool here. He wanted to learn biology and genetics. We taught him." His hands tremble in indignation as he picks up the lab books and puts them back on the shelf from which Lucy had removed them. "My treatment and Maria's generosity gave him the childhood that progeria had denied him."

"Then go back to the States," she challenges. "Tell the FDA and cure other progerics like Tim."

"I can't. Not yet. I've no proof."

"What do you think all this is?" She waves the MRI films at him.

He snatches them from her. "You think these will convince Hill and the rest?"

Lucy winces at the bitterness of his tone.

"You can't be so naive as to trust in the open-mindedness of my so-called peers after all they've done to me," he says as he thrusts the envelopes back in the filing cabinet.

"You prefer to trust that woman?"

"That woman, as you put it, has enabled me to take my discovery from a tissue culture dish and develop a gene therapy that will revolutionize medical science."

"And now you're repaying her by helping her make a fortune outside US health regulations," Lucy accuses.

"You really have lost contact with reality," he explodes. "Why can't you see that this is nothing to do with making money?"

"Then what is it about?"

He stares at her large reproachful brown eyes. It is difficult to believe that this is the same woman who had gazed in astonishment and admiration when he explained the implications of his discovery in the UCLA lab. "It's about obtaining the ultimate, irrefutable proof that I'm right about switching on this gene in a normal human."

Lucy sinks onto a swivel chair by the window and looks out to the garth, to the seat below the ceiba tree where Maria had been reading the previous day. All the newly restored brightness has gone from her eyes. She shakes her head sadly. "Richard. Oh Richard. You've changed. What has she done to you?"

"How dare you say that!" he erupts. "*She* has faith in my ability."

"And I don't?" Lucy flares.

"*She* is putting her own life on the line. That's how much she believes in me."

"Life on the line?"

"She's volunteered to test the gene inducer on herself."

"Richard!" Pain and bewilderment fill her eyes, like those of a foal rejected by its mother. "You promised to use your discovery to cure disease. That woman has no disease."

Richard strides up and down the lab, past the benches stacked with bottles and loaded with the very latest equipment paid for by Maria. "Pasteur discovered the technique of inoculation to prevent bacterial disease. Now he's called the father of medicine. *I* have discovered a way to inoculate people against the diseases that kill most people in the developed world. Can't you see that I must prove it?"

"Richard, stop and listen to me," she demands. "Chisako's mother was living in Hiroshima when the atomic bomb was dropped. She died of cancer four years later."

He comes to a halt in front of her. "I'm very sorry for Chisako's mother, but I fail to see what she has to do with my research."

"Because you've got tunnel vision, that's why. You're so obsessed with proving you're right that you can't see anything else." She makes one final appeal to him. "Richard, we went blindly into the nuclear age, we can't afford to go blindly into the age of human genetic engineering."

"Slogans, cheap slogans," Richard retorts. "Do you think I'm blind? Haven't I tested my discovery on animals and then on a progeric?"

Her pallid face looks at him and sees a stranger.

"Lucy, why can't you accept that if I can genetically engineer a healthy human so that her body continues to repair itself, it will be the most significant achievement in the history of medical science?"

"Because you've got a responsibility for the consequences of your work. You've got to obtain approval from the proper authorities before you take a step like this."

"My responsibility is to science," he declares, "not to a bunch of petty bureaucrats advised by Hill, Straker and the others who blocked my work in the past because they're incapable of appreciating a revolution in medicine."

She shakes her head in despair. "Richard, if you act like God then I won't help you."

"In that case you can quit," he says angrily.

52

The temperature continues to climb and so did does the humidity: the rainy season is upon them. Each morning a burning sun drives water vapor from the surface of the Gulf. Invisibly the vapor accumulates and heats in the lifeless air. It saps the energy, penetrates clothing, and condenses on the skin producing streams of warm, sticky sweat. Each midday the rapidly massing vapor is forced upward by the heat and condenses in the cold upper atmosphere as a white haze which obscures the sun that has created it. By early afternoon the heavens rumble as it wells into gray storm clouds that struggle to contain its mounting pressure, and then it bursts from the clouds and pours down in a savage tropical torrent.

On the afternoon of Maria Snowe's infusion the torrent beats a ferocious tattoo on the friary church windows, but the operating room is cocooned from the elements. A generator stands by to take over should the mains electricity supply fail, humming air conditioning units maintain an equable climate, and the canopy of halogen lamps bathe the operating table in a bright, almost natural, light. Next to the table, above a bank of instruments, rows of spiky waves colored yellow, green, red, and blue cross a computer monitor, alert to any changes in the patient's condition. Nothing and no one inside the operating room is affected, save for one of the Mexican nurses who crosses herself each time a flash of lightning illuminates the fresco of the Virgin Mary.

Richard is barely aware of the storm raging outside. The fear that gripped him prior to infusing Tim with the anti-aging gene inducer is replaced by an excitement that is almost sexual. Maria Snowe is young, and the medical checks and scans show that she is in good health. Dressed in a loose-fitting white hospital gown, she reclines on the pillows plumped against the raised backrest of the operating table.

"It's the first time I've seen you in bed," he says as he wields the needle of the intravenous catheter.

"There's a first time for everything, Richard."

He takes hold of her left arm, strokes it with a wad of cotton wool soaked in ethanol, pierces the skin with the tip of his needle, and slides it into her cephalic vein.

He glances again at the heart rate, oxygen level, and other readouts on the monitor, and checks the setting on the IVAC pump that interrupts the transparent plastic tube connecting the bottom of the pendulous vinyl bag of pink liquid to the vein in Maria's arm. His hand hesitates over the switch on the pump. She had scorned the ritual of the patient consent and signed without reading the form, but Richard feels obliged to give her a final opportunity to withdraw. "Maria, are you sure you're prepared to meet your Maker?"

Her black eyes fix his and her lips part in a smile. "I already have."

The tropical storm could not sustain its ferocity. By mid afternoon it exhausts itself. The only traces it leaves are pools of water on the cloister's terracotta tiles and these shrink in the hot glare of a sun that reclaims a cloudless blue sky.

Maria disdains the wheelchair and walks through the cloister's puddles to the Guardian's Tower. Richard insists that she goes to bed and stays there for twenty-four hours, with one of the nurses on immediate call in the Tower's living room.

The marble-floored bedroom is light and airy and dominated by a double bed with a carved mahogany headboard. Maria lies back against the pillows, beneath a single white sheet, and offers Richard one naked arm while holding the sheet over her breasts with the other arm. He feels her eyes on him while he checks her pulse and blood pressure. He would love to climb into that large comfortable bed with her, but he has several hours' work ahead.

After leaving the Guardian's Tower Richard heads back towards the former church. As he enters the cloister he catches a glimpse of Lucy watching from the upper level. In the operating room the other nurse hands him Maria's labeled blood samples, which he takes through to the lab. Lacking practice in many of the techniques he normally left to Lucy, his resentment of her disloyalty grows as weariness creeps up on him and his analyses becomes slower and slower. By the time he finishes the garth is silvered by a bright full moon.

The following morning Richard oversleeps. As soon as he arrives at Paradise he goes to the Guardian's Tower and dashes up the stairs to the living room. The duty nurse apologizes and says that Señorita Snowe insisted on getting up.

Richard finds Maria having coffee at her favorite spot, beneath the shade of the ceiba tree in the center of the garth. She invites him to join her and assuages his concern by saying that she's never felt better. "Besides, we have to deal with this." She hands him a letter.

Written in Lucy's meticulously neat handwriting, the letter states that she cannot work for a company that has ignored her pleas not to proceed with an unethical treatment. It is addressed to Maria, not to him: her rejection of him is total. Richard's pang of regret is overcome by a deeper feeling of betrayal. Since she confirmed her refusal to help take his work to a successful conclusion there is no point in her staying around like some accusing angel. "The sooner she leaves the better," he says.

Maria pours him coffee. "Do you know what she intends to do?"

"You don't think…?" Richard's mind races ahead. Could Lucy undermine the announcement of his pioneering treatment? He jumps to his feet. "I'd better talk to her before she does anything foolish."

Maria shakes her head. "Not a good idea, Richard."

"Why not?"

"Why do you think she wrote to me, not to you?" She sighs. "Hell hath no fury like a research assistant that's scorned."

"But we can't let her sabotage everything that we've achieved."

"Don't be angry with her. Dr. Hernandez thinks she's suffering from a psychiatric condition. Shall I handle the problem while you decide what we do next?"

"Do that." He sits down. The implications of Lucy's letter throw his plan into disarray. He intended to wait several months after Maria's infusion before disclosing the results of his work: that period would provide incontrovertible proof that aging damage to her body has been reversed with no harmful side effects; it would also allow Maria time to prepare the ground for his announcement. He thinks back to the NewsHour with Jim Lehrer and its consequences. He can't allow the reactionaries to win the propaganda war and prevent him from revolutionizing medical science. "Her defection could whip up a big publicity campaign. For all we know, she may have already told someone about my work. We need to take the initiative and hold a press conference now."

"What do you want to say?" Maria asks.

"Isn't it obvious? That I've developed a fifty-minute treatment that will banish aging diseases from the face of the earth."

"Who will benefit from the treatment?"

"I'm a scientist who's developed the treatment. It's not my responsibility to decide who receives it."

"You sound like the Los Alamos scientists."

He puts down his coffee cup. "Say again?"

"They thought their responsibility stopped at discovering how to make a nuclear explosion. It was someone else's responsibility to kill a few hundred thousand civilians with it."

"Come on. You're talking like Lucy. This is a *medical* breakthrough."

"Do you want your anti-aging treatment sold exclusively to those wealthy enough to pay the highest price?"

"Of course not," he says, aghast at the thought.

"You want to make it available to everybody, without limitation of wealth, gender, race, or creed?"

"Right."

She nods and then rises and walks towards the cloister. She stops to wait for him by the old rubber tree in the corner of the garth. The woody stem and branches of a strangler fig coil round its trunk and boughs like copper-cultured boa constrictors. So tightly do they squeeze, and so extensively do they pervade, that they deform the tree and pull it down towards the ground where some of the fig's stouter trailing branches have rooted. "What about those developing countries barely able to feed their people?" she asks when he reaches her. "How would they cope with the population explosion caused by the old generation not dying off but new generations still being born? Is it good to replace death from aging by death from starvation?"

Richard frowns.

"If you limit the anti-aging treatment to the developed world," she continues, twisting one of the fig's tendrils round her fingers, "what would happen when the pension funds go bankrupt, triggering a collapse of stock markets, major companies, and whole economies? When future generations can't get whatever jobs remain because the current generation doesn't age and won't relinquish its means of survival? Is it good to replace death from aging by an immortality of poverty and anarchy?"

"These are matters for governments, not researchers," he responds instinctively.

"Precisely who in government would decide how to use your treatment?"

He hesitates. "I suppose it would be referred it to the National Bioethics Advisory Commission, the National Institutes of Health, the Food and Drug Administration…" His voice tails off.

"So we're back to government bureaucrats advised by Nathan Hill, Don Straker, and the rest? Add self-serving politicians to the brew and what do we get?" She releases the tendril and strolls on into the cloister.

Either global disaster, he concludes, or else suppression of my work, with the rich and the powerful fighting to keep the treatment to themselves.

"Will history forgive you for handing over your creation to venal men without a fraction of your intellect or your vision?" she asks. "Is that what you really want, Richard?"

But if I do take responsibility for deciding how my treatment is used, he reflects, who *should* benefit from it?

Maria continues round the cloister, enters the Guardian's Tower, and climbs its marble-tiled steps. At the top of the staircase on the third floor, instead of going through the door to her study, she opens another door in the white stucco wall. Richard follows her up the worn stone steps of a circular staircase that snakes round the tower. They emerge onto a flat roof protected by a stone balustrade that gives a commanding view of the friary below and the countryside beyond. She rests her hands on the balustrade and looks towards the gateway in the perimeter wall where the signpost of the Clinica de Paraíso shows a serpent coiled round the staff of Asclepius.

"Imagine," she says, "if Asclepius were alive today. What would he have achieved by now?"

Richard leans on the balustrade next to her and ponders the question. In two and a half thousand years Asclepius would have learned of anatomy, blood circulation, the cellular structure of the body, and the existence of germs and viruses; of the use of sanitation and antiseptics to protect against hitherto devastating infections; of anesthetics to enable the surgical repair or removal of malfunctioning parts of the body; of vaccines and antibiotics to counter microbial diseases; of X-rays and other imaging techniques to revolutionize the diagnosis of diseases; and of the DNA double helix and the genetic information it encodes to enable genetic engineering to activate the body's own repair mechanisms. "I guess he would have moved on from incantations, herbs, and snake oil."

She turns to face him. "What could *you* achieve in another two and a half thousand years?"

"Me?"

"Remember what you told me at Keith Harris's house by Cold Spring Harbor?" "After three and a half billion years of evolution by nature, DNA technology now provides the tools to intervene in that process. It gives us the potential to cure the cause of all diseases, extend our lives, raise our intelligence, normalize the insane, and pacify the violent. Genetic engineering gives us the power to take control of human evolution." He realizes she is repeating his words exactly. She gazes at him. "Do you not possess that power?"

"I was talking about science in general. I'm just one scientist."

"Just like hundreds of thousands of others? Richard, why do you shrink from your greatness? Would a Darwin, a Mendel, or even a Watson stop now?"

He smiles ruefully. "It's a nice fantasy."

"Fantasy?" she queries. "Haven't I always provided everything you want to develop your research?"

He gazes down on what once had been a Mayan temple atop a pyramid next to a courtyard of priests' living quarters. It had been destroyed and rebuilt by the Franciscans as a friary to worship a more powerful god, and now it has been transformed by Maria Snowe into a shrine for genetic engineering. "This is crazy talk, Maria. I can't stay here out in the jungle and simply continue my research."

"Why not?"

He turns to look at her. "For starters, a few years down the line people are going to want to know why you haven't aged."

"When I said that I needed to prepare the ground to ensure your work isn't barred, how did you think I'd do it?"

"I left that to you. I had enough on my mind getting the science right."

"Think about it," she presses him.

"Lobby key decision-makers?"

"How?"

He shrugs, uncomfortable out of his own field. "I guess you'd show them the benefits of what I've discovered."

"You think that showing them would persuade them to support your work?"

"Then I don't see how—"

"Name me one leading politician or businessperson who would rather degenerate into diseased old age and death rather than stay vigorous and active."

He looks at her in astonishment. "You planned to bribe them with the treatment you've had?"

She shakes her head. "Of course not. How would we control them once they were immortalized?"

Understanding begins to appear on his face.

"My anti-aging genes continuously produce the protein that repairs aging damage, right?" she asks.

"So we give them a shot of the protein?"

"Can you do it in such a way that they wouldn't be able to find out what stops them from aging?"

"No problem. I could make an artificial plasma containing thousands of proteins and mask the immortalin."

"How long before they'd need a booster?"

He looks thoughtful. "If I add certain chemicals that delay the breakdown of proteins, give a depot injection instead of an intravenous one, we could be looking at a year before someone needs another shot."

"I know most of the people who matter in politics, business, and the media in Mexico. I target contacts whom I know are susceptible.

Very discreetly, and on condition of strict confidentiality, I offer them an infusion at this clinic that will delay their aging damage by a year."

"They become dependent on us for regular boosters?" he asks, intrigued by her stratagem.

"In the beginning we ask only small favors, like introductions to key people that I don't know."

"Then we increase our requests?"

"We want them to ensure that there's no media coverage and that no one bars your work." She smiles. "That wouldn't be in their interests either."

He follows her reasoning.

"Leaving you free to embark on the greatest endeavor in the history of science."

He gazes beyond the perimeter wall of the friary grounds. Henequen plantations, abandoned to the jungle when nylon replaced natural fiber for rope-making, stretch as far as he can see, broken only by palatial Spanish haciendas and the thatches and corrugated tin roofs of villages for their Maya peons. Humankind hasn't moved on much further since the days of the Conquistadors, he reflects. How long are we fated to remain in this evolutionary stage? We have developed the ability to reason, and yet we are still impelled by an aggressive instinct that causes individuals, tribes, and nation states to fight each other. We are still driven by a greed that achieves affluence for one third of the world by exploiting the two thirds who are abandoned to famine and disease; still fated by the brevity of our lifespan to destroy for immediate gain the biosphere on which humankind's long term survival depends; and still threatened by a technological evolution that has outstripped biological evolution so that the human race possesses the power to wipe out life on earth without the intelligence or the wisdom to harness that power for the benefit of all.

"Richard. You mustn't think short term, as though you have to accomplish your objectives in the next thirty years or so." She takes his face in her hands and kisses him full on the lips. "You don't have to grow old and die."

53

Richard Trent stirs restlessly in the large double bed. Through the window he watches the fainter stars fade as the black sky turns indigo. He switches on the bedside lamp, climbs out of bed, and puts on a cotton robe and sandals.

The bedroom door opens onto the terracotta-tiled veranda. This runs east-west, apart from two short south-facing wings, and overlooks the corral. Richard walks through the semi-darkness to the far wing. Its carved cedar door dates from the eighteenth century, but inside is a modern kitchen. He pours water into the reservoir of an electric coffee maker, spoons out from a bag enough beans for three strong cups, grinds them, tips the grind into the machine's filter, and switches on. He waits, savoring his favorite aroma, while the machine splutters and gurgles. By the time he takes the flask of coffee and a cup to the table on the veranda, all the twinkling stars have dissolved into a deep blue background, leaving only the silver disk of the moon.

This is the time of day in the Yucatán he likes best, the time of gentle coolness before the sun rises above the horizon and, in the words of the Maya, splits the stones with its heat. The only sound is the continuous chirping of cicadas, and that soon becomes one with the pregnant stillness which hangs over the soft purple hue beyond the corral wall. He understands why the Franciscans had valued this hour after vigils for their private meditation.

After abandoning the Catholic myth that he could gain everlasting life in heaven, Richard dreamed of achieving immortality by making a great discovery in medical science, one that would be marveled at for centuries to come. As the years flowed by and that prospect seemed to be slipping from his grasp, his thoughts strayed to the immortality option available to lesser men: passing on his immortal genes to his children who would pass them on to their children, and so on until the end of time. But he has no children. He is the last in the family to bear the Trent name. When he dies, the Trent genes will exist no more. He will exist no more. He will vanish as the dawn mist before the sun.

To the east the deep blue yields to a diffuse band of azure that highlights a dark flat horizon. The azure spreads upwards, leaving in its wake a hazy salmon-pink smear above the skyline. As the deep blue retreats before the azure, green jungle emerges from the soft purple hue. A cock crows. The crowing prompts trillings, intermittent flutings, chattering, and what sounds like a repeated single dash of Morse code. Above the treetops the east face of the Guardian's Tower flushes pink, and then glows golden in the first rays of the sun.

The greatest scientific endeavor in human history beckons him. Darwin had seen that all current species have evolved from very different ancestors. Mendel had seen how physical traits are inherited in discrete parts, or genes, with half the genes derived from each parent. Watson and Crick had seen how the DNA molecule normally takes the form of a double helix of complementary strands whose chemical composition explains what genes are, how the strands unwind to be copied, and how they code for a cell to make proteins. Later researchers had shown how sections of DNA in the majority of a genome cooperate to regulate how genes function, giving a better understanding than Darwin of how evolution works. He, however, has seen how to intervene and direct evolution.

Once he became ageless he would have the time to supersede nature's evolutionary process and replace it by a rational scheme of genetic engineering. He could accomplish in a few hundred years what nature would take hundreds of thousands of years, if ever, to achieve: the evolution of ultrahumans who would be born without defects, who would never age, who would be immune to radiation and to all diseases, who would be highly intelligent and non-aggressive, and who would possess whatever other genetic qualities he chooses to incorporate. Such ultrahumans would acquire the wisdom and perspective of countless normal human lifetimes, transcending instinctive short-term self-interest in favor of rational cooperation for the common good.

And what is the alternative to pursuing his vision as all the great pioneers before him had done, regardless of the incomprehension or hostility of their contemporaries? Hand over his results to the FDA, who would bar him from all human genetic research for undertaking an unauthorized clinical trial, while myopic and venal men fight over the spoils of his genius, either suppressing his work or else unleashing chaos and famine in the world.

It is with a sense of destiny that Richard drives through the jungle late that morning to the Paradise Clinic. Heavy clouds are massing as he brakes his air-conditioned jeep to a halt and points the invisible beam of his electronic controller at the black wrought-iron gate. Slowly the gate slides behind the golden limestone wall. Thunder rumbles. A presaging drop of rain falls on the clinic's signboard and trickles down the serpent coiled round the staff of Asclepius, who had been slain by a thunderbolt from Zeus because his healing powers spared men from death and usurped the function of the gods. A wry smile crosses Richard's face: another myth that science is about to usurp.

He drives through the opened gate, parks, and climbs out of the jeep. Clammy, oppressive heat dampens the back of his shirt when he emerges from the passageway into the deathly silence of the lower cloister. It is as if the sparrow-sized Talpacoti doves, which normally coo from the branches of the ceiba tree in the garth, await the storm with bated breath. Spots of rain spatter the terracotta-tiled floor like drops of blood.

Richard turns right and strides between the square stone pillars on one side and the whitewashed wall and mahogany doors of the library, meeting room, and vestry on the other side of the barrel-vaulted east cloister. He rounds the corner pillar into the north cloister in which there is only one, electronically locked, door.

His security card gives him access to the lobby of the converted church. Beyond the drinking fountain and coffee machine, a white swing door leads him into the voluminous general lab, whose white benches and shelves of bottles are dimmed by clouds that seemed to press against the high narrow windows of the former nave. He heads straight for another white door, which displays a fluorescent orange triangle formed from three contiguous circles superposed on the center of a fourth circle of identical diameter. Below the emblem black capital letters warn "BIOHAZARD", and beneath that "Admittance to Authorized Personnel Only". Richard opens this door into the changing room and puts on protective clothing. Only when the door through which he entered is shut does the interlock system allow him to open the final white door.

The inner sanctum, converted from the Lady Chapel, has no other door. Its focus is the airtight glass window of the Class III biological safety cabinet that stands on a white work surface below the arched window in the far wall. Here Richard sets about making enough targeted retroviral vector containing the anti-aging gene inducer to infect every cell in his body.

54

Richard removes the final cell culture flask from the Class III biological safety cabinet. The clear plastic flask with blue plastic screw top resembles an airline half-bottle of vodka, except that its sides are perfectly flat and it is partly filled with a pink culturing solution. He places it horizontally on the white bench. Invisible to the human eye, cells adhering to the bottom surface of the flask are producing retroviral particles that contain the anti-aging gene inducer. He opens the door of the incubator below the bench and, holding the flask in the same position, he places it carefully on the top shelf, next to two similar flasks maintained at body heat inside the incubator. All he needs to do now is wait while a hundred trillion vector particles are produced.

From the biohazard lab he goes into the clothing change room, where he disposes of his laboratory cap, smock, plastic shoe covers, and latex gloves like a snake shedding old skin. The trickiest stage of the operation, requiring concentration, keen eyesight and steady hands, is over. Release from the tension flows through his body with a strange, tingling excitement at the enormity of what he has committed himself to. No euphoric high of discovery, not even the discovery of the real function of the anti-aging gene, compares with this heady, almost surreal, anticipation of the transformation he is about to undergo and the limitless possibilities it opens up for him.

Once he is infused, his eyes will never lose their focus over the years, his hands will never become shaky and, most important of all, his mental faculties will never deteriorate. On the contrary, his activated anti-aging genes will restore him to his prime and maintain him at the peak of his capabilities for an indefinite time. And time is what he needs. Human genetic engineering is in its infancy, where chemistry was at the beginning of the nineteenth century and modern physics at the beginning of the twentieth century. He is about to give himself the time and faculties to develop this fledgling science so that he can engineer the next stage in the evolution of *Homo sapiens*.

So as not to let the prospect overwhelm him, he decides to concentrate on one step at a time. And the next step, he thinks to himself giddily, is to have a well-deserved cup of coffee. He presses the red button on the wall to open the interlock door that leads into the general lab.

A coffee beaker lies on its side on a white lab bench. A small pool of brown liquid has formed between the beaker and a pill bottle. Puzzled, he goes to investigate.

Then he sees her. Lucy is near the embrasured window overlooking the garth, next to the swivel chair on which she'd been sitting when he told her to quit. She wears her huipil, the Christmas present from the Lamberts. She is curled on the floor in a fetal position. Flaxen hair radiates from her head like a Byzantine halo and her eyes stare without seeing.

Richard grabs the empty pill bottle. The label says Lorazepam, the sleeping tablets that Dr. Hernandez had prescribed for her. Her brow is cold. Richard sticks his fingers down her throat, but she doesn't retch. Frantically he pumps the flat of his hands up and down on her stomach. Her body jerks like a doll's, but when he stops she lies still. In desperation he blows into her mouth while pinching her nostrils. After ten minutes of strenuous effort he kneels by her body and concedes defeat. All the signs indicate that she's been dead for some time.

Tenderly he straightens her legs and body, and crosses her arms over her breast, but when his trembling fingers try to close Lucy's eyelids they won't move. Memories flood him with an overpowering sense of loss. The infectious smile that began with her eyes and lit up her whole face. The stimulation of their scientific discussions. The almost telepathic understanding that developed between them. The reassuring touches on his arm when she knew things were going badly for him. The tangible thrill of her excitement when their experiments succeeded. The passion of her belief in him when the scientific establishment scorned and rejected him. The dignified way she sacrificed their growing personal relationship so that Maria would hire her to help him pursue the dream they shared. The dedication to seeking a cure for diseases. The compassion with which she looked into his eyes when he feared that Maria was about to hand over his project to Bew. The open-mouthed gasps of unrestrained ecstasy when they made love. The unfaltering instinct for what was right that he came to rely on until paranoia about Maria unbalanced her.

And how has he repaid her? With angry words of rejection, words that had driven her to take her own life while he assumed she was trying to sabotage his work. Right now he wishes he had a God to believe in. He bows his head and asks her to forgive him.

With tears in his eyes he looks up at the sound of the lab door opening. Cool and elegant, despite the storm raging outside, Maria comes in. She stops when she sees him.

"Lucy," he says helplessly. "She's… she's dead."

"Are you sure?"

He nods inconsolably.

"I'll call Hernandez," Maria says in the voice she assumes when taking control of a situation.

"I'm responsible."

"Hernandez has already reported on her mental state. He'll confirm she committed suicide while the balance of her mind was disturbed. Nobody will hold you responsible."

Does she always have to be so calm? Doesn't she understand how distraught he is? "I'm to blame," he insists.

Maria's voice mellows. "Richard, you really mustn't blame yourself for Lucy's jealousy of our relationship." She reaches out and takes his hand. With a heavy heart he climbs to his feet. "You were always so kind to her. But Lucy wanted to monopolize you, and when she saw that she couldn't, she turned against you, despite everything you'd done for her. How can that be your fault?"

"But—"

"I know what it's like to lose someone who's been close to you," Maria soothes. "At least Lucy died quickly, without pain. I had to watch Dad suffer from cancer for eighteen months, and then my mother degenerate into Alzheimer's." She shudders at the memory. "When I found out that I'd inherited the gene for early onset Alzheimer's, I nearly went out of my mind. I was determined I would never die like they did."

"Now you won't."

"Thanks to you." She reaches out a hand and strokes his hair.

He looks away, to Lucy's body.

"Come," Maria says, "let's go to my office."

"No. I can't… I can't leave her here on her own."

"It'll be some time before Hernandez can come to examine the body and release it for cremation. We should leave it as you found it until he arrives."

"I'll wait here."

"Richard, Lucy made her decision. Now you must let her go and look to the future."

"It's not something I feel like doing right now."

She links his arm and draws him away from Lucy's body. "Lucy tried to stop your great work while she was alive. Are you going to let her defeat you from the grave or are you going to use your unique talents to transform the human species while I transform the world."

He stares at her. "Transform the world?"

"Do you think we can live forever in the world as it is? For a start, look at how the planet's non-renewable resources are being destroyed. And for what? So people can make profits in their lifetimes. They won't be around to suffer the consequences of ecological disaster, but we will."

She sits on the swivel chair by the embrasured window. "We can have increased intelligence, be immune to all diseases and radiation, possess no aggressive instincts, and yet still be shot by a madman, bombed by self-styled freedom fighters, or plunged into a nuclear war."

"That's human nature."

"And your genetic engineering will change that."

"Yes, but that will take decades if not hundreds of years."

"Exactly. That's why I need to deal with the practical problems that face us in the short term."

"How?"

"The same way I'll ensure your scientific work isn't blocked. Lucy thought we wanted to monopolize your discovery in order to make a fortune." Maria shakes her head sadly. "It just shows how limited her mind was. What's money? It's nothing compared with the power to cheat aging and death."

"You've thought this all through?" he asks.

"Just as you've thought through the science. The number of people who pull the wires in this world is actually very small. I met most of them when the Trilateral Commission invited Snowe Software to advise how they could prevent the Internet from undermining their global financial and political interests." She gives a disparaging laugh. "They're mainly vain, egotistical men. Once they're dependent on us for their regular anti-aging infusions, they'll see the sense in protecting the biosphere, ensuring the destruction of nuclear and biological weapons, stopping exploitation of the Third World for short term gain, and providing economic and healthcare aid to the world's poor in order to achieve lasting global stability."

Her gaze is challenging. "Aren't these the practical measures we need if we're to live for ever without being threatened by man-made catastrophes?"

"Absolutely," he replies. Maria may have arrived there from a pragmatic assessment, but what she is proposing is a vision of the enlightened and equitable society he plans for a more highly evolved human species.

"Well worth the sacrifice of a few lives," she concludes.

"A few lives?" He isn't sure that he's heard correctly.

"Bew, the Lamberts and the plane crew," she says, as though stating the obvious.

All the suppressed suspicions creep out of the dark recesses of his subconscious to confront him with the truth he hadn't wanted to know. "You *did* have them killed?"

"Surely you realized that?"

Richard lowers his head and the sightless eyes of Lucy gaze up at him. He sees disheveled hair, a white face, and burning eyes insisting: *Why won't you see it? All living proof and all witnesses except you and me are dead.*

"She knew," Maria says.

Be careful, Richard, Lucy's voice in his head continues, *she's mad: she kills anyone who threatens to disclose the truth.* The allegations that he'd dismissed as paranoia return to haunt him with a greater horror yet. Maria had shown no surprise when she saw Lucy's lifeless body.

"So I did what was necessary." Maria's voice conveys not the slightest hint of remorse. "Don't worry," she adds. "Hernandez thinks it was a psychiatric condition, not the drug I put in her food, that caused her delusions and her fever."

Lucy had been right all the time. And she'd paid for it with her life. He backs away from Maria and turns towards the door.

"Where are you going?" Maria calls after him.

He looks over his shoulder and his eyes blaze with hatred. "To get the police."

"You can't do that," she says calmly.

"Just watch me."

"Who wanted that 'avaricious blackmailing piece of shit' wiped from the face of the earth?" she asks.

"I didn't want Tim and his family murdered," he protests.

"Who came to me in desperation? Who said that he'd tried everything but had failed to persuade the Lamberts not to return to the States? Who wanted me to stop them boasting about you to a government that would bar your work? Just like you wanted me to handle everything that got in the way of you doing your science."

Lucy's words return to accuse him. *Your greatest strength is your greatest weakness. You're so focused on proving that your discovery is the great genetic breakthrough of all time that you can't see anything else. Or is it that you don't want to see anything that stops you achieving your goal?* Slowly he retraces his steps to Lucy, whom he'd callously rejected.

"Who said that we couldn't let her sabotage everything we've achieved?" Maria asks.

And he had asked Maria to deal with the problem. He falls to his knees, cradles Lucy's cold young body in his arms, and buries his face in the white cotton of her huipil. She had understood him and she had loved him, despite his obsessive drive to prove that he was right. Remorse surges through him like a chemical released into his bloodstream: it tightens his throat muscles and convulses him with uncontrollable sobs. Hot tears spill over and wet the huipil.

"You've always known we must make sacrifices if we're to achieve our goal," Maria says.

It had begun so imperceptibly, he sees now, after he'd signed that accursed agreement. The first sacrifice had been the truth, when he lied to *Science* about the results of his brain cell experiment and then about the purpose of his research to the staff he recruited. He continued to sacrifice his principles by deciding that he alone should determine the ethics of his pioneering work. From there it was but a short step to rejoice that the blackmailing Bew had been murdered by a gay pickup and dismiss Lucy's suspicions. As for what followed, how could he have been so focused on his goal that he failed to see what had become of him? Everything and everyone—even Lucy—had been sacrificed on the altar of his ambition. Tenderly he lays her body back on the floor. "How many more humans must we sacrifice to create paradise on earth for the new race of immortals?" he asks bitterly.

"Only when it's necessary," Maria replies. "Their lives are so short anyway, it hardly matters if we end them a little early, provided we do it as humanely as possible."

She might have been talking of the monkeys he'd used to test his gene therapy. He rises from his knees and stares at her. What kind of monster has he created?

"Five hundred years ago North America had no great civilization to compare with the Maya in these lands," Maria says as she slides off the chair. "In that time it has become the superpower that dominates the globe. Imagine what you and I can achieve in a thousand years."

Lucy was right: she is mad. "Do you really believe Alvaro's prophecy that you're the reincarnation of a Mayan goddess who will give birth to a new world?"

"I believe we were destined for each other," she replies. "You were the only one who could save me from the curse of the Alzheimer's gene. But you needed my help to do it." She glances round the laboratory, gleaming with the latest instruments. "Once you'd achieved that, you didn't want to stop there, and neither did I."

He turns away, not wanting to hear any more, but her seductive voice continues. "We make a perfect team, Richard. You possess the vision and the scientific ability, while I possess the practical skills to help you turn that vision into reality."

He wants to escape, but where can he go?

"Look at me, Richard," she commands.

Her flawless complexion glows with the vitality of an eighteen-year-old. It will never be ravaged by time or disfigured by disease. She is the living, irrefutable proof of what he has achieved and what he could go on to achieve. He shakes his head despairingly; he can't put the genie back in the bottle.

"The greatest project in science is waiting to begin." Her unblinking gaze draws him like a rabbit to a snake. "History will record that it was Richard Trent who genetically engineered a more highly evolved race who know neither disease nor death, a race of immortals who will act as guardians of our planet and its people for eons to come."

This *is* madness. And yet what alternative is he left with now? If he confesses to the authorities what they've done, not only would he incur a lifetime bar from human genetic research, he would face certain conviction for complicity in murder and spend the rest of his life in prison.

The unwavering gaze that invests her beauty with an imperial quality are transformed by a softening of her eyes and a parting of her lips that make her even more desirable. Her husky voice caresses his willpower. "You and I have crossed the Rubicon. You know we can never go back." She opens her arms to embrace him. "You're the only man who is my equal."

Her heady scent is intoxicating. Her breasts press against his chest as her arms draw him to her. "Infuse yourself with the vector,

Richard," she breathes into his ear, "and then let's consummate our partnership."

Over her shoulder he sees the door to the biohazard lab, where the body heat of the incubator is helping to replicate vector particles containing the gene switch he has developed from his discovery that Labor Day evening so long ago. Then he had vowed that he and Lucy would develop the discovery into a treatment for aging diseases and never permit it to be monopolized for personal gain. His eyes are drawn down to Lucy's lifeless body. Overwhelmed by hatred for the demon who has seduced him from his vow, his hands encircle the inviting silky smoothness of Maria's neck.

She screams and grabs his wrists, and tries to pull them away as his thumbs seek her windpipe. "I only ever did what you wanted," she pleads hoarsely."

"No! No! No!" The more strenuously he denies it, the more he knows she is right. His hatred turns into self-hatred and his grip tightens.

Desperately she writhes and struggles to escape, kicking and fighting with all the strength in her body to hold onto life. Her breath comes in hoarse gasps, her eyes bulge, and her hands slip from his wrists. As though to hold him in a final embrace her arms reach out round his neck.

Fingertips press against his flesh, but there is little force in them as they probe his vertebrae. His thumbs find their target and she utters a choking sound. Then he feels a prick as the base of his neck. It sends a shiver like an electric shock down his spine. Numbness spreads out from the prick, across his shoulders, down his arms to his wrists and out to his fingers. From the base of his spine it spreads to his pelvis and then down his legs, which weaken and buckle. As the strength drains from him, his hands lose their grasp on her neck and slide down her body, vainly trying to grab hold of the material of her dress for support as he sinks to his knees and topples over.

Lying on his side, he feels nothing below his neck except numbness; he can move neither arms nor legs. Panic grips him as he fights to draw in breath and expand his lungs. Only when he discovers that he can breathe if he inhales and exhales slowly does his panic subside. Gingerly he twists his head to look upwards. Maria is leaning against a lab bench, wheezing. Between the thumb and index finger of her left hand she holds a small, silver serpent's head from which projects a short needle-like tongue.

When she regains her composure, Maria turns to gaze down at him. "Richard, Oh Richard, why did you try to kill me?" She kneels next to him.

His eyes focus on the sharp end of the serpent's head pin that Maria holds a few inches from his face. Beads of sweat form on his brow as he lies powerless, completely at her mercy.

"How could you give up living forever with me?" she says. "Never suffering pain or death? Doing what you've always dreamed of doing? You could have become the greatest scientist the world has ever known. Why did you throw it all away?" She shakes her head disconsolately. "I wanted you to be the father of my children."

Death will be a release from the horror of what he has done, he thinks as he stares at the pin.

"What is in the pin?"

"A drug used by the ancient Maya," Maria replies. "Priests gave it to the young women who were to be sacrificed to the gods so that they wouldn't feel the pain of the knife."

"And now you're going to sacrifice me."

Her black unblinking eyes stare at him. "You're the only one left alive who knows my secret." She sighs. "But how can I kill my savior?"

Carefully Maria slots the pin into the silver filigree bracelet round her right wrist and clips the serpent's head back in place.

She stands up and goes through to the biohazard lab, returning after a while with the three flasks of pink liquid containing the anti-aging gene inducer. Immobile from the shoulders down, he strains his neck to watch as she unscrews each flask and empties its contents into the sink in the lab bench. Then she pours in a bottle of hydrochloric acid before turning on the tap and flushing it all down the sink.

Methodically she sets about collecting the MRI films, the videos and the lab books that Lucy had wanted him to take to the FDA, and puts them into one of the black plastic bags used for lining the large trash bin in the lab. Satisfied that she has removed all the evidence, she comes and stands over him. "The paralysis will wear off in a day or so, by which time I'll be long gone." She turns and looks at Lucy's body. "I suggest you stick to the suicide story to explain her. If you tell them about me, nobody will believe you: they'll assume you killed her."

She picks up the black plastic bag. "Goodbye, Richard. The knowledge of what you spurned will haunt you the rest of your life."

But as he watches her go, Richard Trent knows that what will haunt him the rest of his life are the ghosts of those who have been murdered because of his ambition and the fear of what he has let loose into the world.

THE END

Also by John Hands

Fiction

Perestroika Christi

Darkness at Dawn

Brutal Fantasies

Nonfiction

Housing Co-operatives

COSMOSAPIENS Human Evolution from the Origin of the Universe

THE FUTURE OF HUMANKIND Why We Should Be Optimistic

9 781806 231263